CARDIGAN

CARDIGAN

By ROBERT W. CHAMBERS

Illustrations by HENRY C. PITZ

WILDSIDE PRESS

ILLUSTRATIONS

CARDIGAN

CARDIGAN

CHAPTER ONE

ON THE 1st of May, 1774, the anchor ice, which for so many months had silver-plated the river's bed with frosted crusts, was ripped off and dashed into a million gushing flakes by the amber outrush of the springtime flood.

On that day I had laid my plans for fishing the warm shallows where the small fry, swarming in early spring, attract the great lean fish which have lain benumbed all winter under their crystal roof of ice.

So certain was I of a holiday undisturbed by schoolroom tasks that I whistled boldly as I sat on my cot bed, sorting hooks according to their sizes. It was, therefore, with misgiving that I heard Peter and Esk stamp down to the schoolroom, dragging their hornbooks along the balustrade.

Now we had had no tasks set us for three weeks, for our schoolmaster, Mr. Yost, journeying to visit his mother in Pennsylvania, had been shot and scalped at Eastertide near Fort Pitt—probably by some drunken Delaware.

My kinsman and guardian, Sir William Johnson, who, as all know, was Commissioner of Indian Affairs for the Crown, had but recently returned from the upper castle with his secretary, Captain Walter Butler; and, preoccupied with the lamentable murder of Mr. Yost, had found no time to concern himself with us or our affairs.

However, we had discovered that, having dispatched a messenger with strings and belts to remonstrate with the sachems of the Lenni-Lenape—they being, as I have said, suspected of the murder—Sir William had also written to Albany for another schoolmaster to replace Mr. Yost; and it gave me, for one, no pleasure to learn it, though it did please Silver Heels, who wearied me with her devotion to her books.

So, hearing Esk and fat Peter on their way to the schoolroom, I took alarm, believing that our new schoolmaster had arrived; I seized my fish rod and started to slip out of the house. I was seen in the hallway, however, by Captain Butler, Sir William's secretary, and ordered to report to him at the schoolroom.

I, of course, paid no heed to Mr. Butler, but walked defiantly downstairs, although he called me twice in his cold, menacing voice. And I should have continued triumphantly out of the door and across the fields to the river had not I met Silver Heels dancing through the lower hallway, her slate and pencil under her arm, and loudly sucking a cone of maple sugar.

"Oh, Michael," she cried, "you don't know! Captain Butler has consented to instruct us until the new schoolmaster comes from Albany."

"Oh, has he?" I sneered. "What do I care for Mr. Butler? I'm going out! Let go my coat!"

"No, you're not! No, you're not!" singsonged Silver Heels. "Sir William says you are to take your ragged old book of gods and nymphs and be diligent lest he catch you tripping! So there, clumsy foot!"—for I had tried to trip her.

"Who told you that?" I answered, sulkily, snatching at her sugar.

"Aunt Molly. She set me to seek you. So now who's going fishing, my lord?"

The indescribable malice of her smile, her singsong mockery as she stood there swaying from her hips and licking her sugar-cone, roused all the sullen obstinacy in me.

"If I go," said I, "I won't study my books, anyway. I'm too old to study with you and Peter, and I won't! You will see!"

Sir William's favorite ferret, Vix, with muzzle on, came sneaking along the wall, and I grasped the lithe animal and thrust it at Silver Heels, whereupon she kicked my legs with her moccasins, which did not hurt, and ran upstairs like a wildcat.

There was nothing for me but to go to the schoolroom. I laid my rod in the corner, pocketed the ferret, and went slowly up the stairs.

At eighteen I was as willful a dunce as ever was held re-lucant in a schoolroom. Destined, against my will, for Dart-mouth College by my guardian, who very well understood that I desired to be a soldier, I had resolutely set myself against every schoolroom accomplishment, with the result that I pre-sented an ignorance that might well have shamed a lad of ten. Yet Sir William, undaunted and bent on making me a man of learning, continued to hold me on the school bench long after I deemed myself far too old to be set down there.

For three weeks I had been half hoping for continued re-lease from the books I detested, but now, to my dismay and rage, Sir William had set me once more in the schoolroom—and under Mr. Butler, too!

"Master Cardigan," said Mr. Butler when I entered the room, "Sir William desires you to prepare a recitation upon the story of Proserpine."

I muttered rebelliously, but jerked my mythology from a pile of books and began to thumb the leaves noisily. Presently, tiring of dingy print, I moved up to the bench where sat the children, Peter and Esk, a-conning their hornbooks.

Silver Heels pulled a face at me behind her French-grammar book, and I pinched her arm smartly for her impudence. Then, casting about for something to do, I remembered the ferret in my pocket, and dragged it out. Removing the silver bit, I permitted the ferret to bite Peter's tight breeches, not meaning to hurt him. But Peter screeched and Mr. Butler birched him well, knowing all the while it was no fault of Peter's; yet such was the nature of the man that, when he was angry, the innocent must suffer when the guilty were beyond his wrath.

I had remuzzled the ferret, and Peter was smearing the tears from his cheeks, when Sir William came in, very angry, saying that Mistress Molly could hear us in the nursery, and that the infant had fallen a-wailing with her new teeth.

"I did it, sir," said I, "and Mr. Butler punished Peter ——"

"Silence!" said Sir William, sharply. "Put that ferret out the window!"

"The ferret is your best one—Vix," I answered. "She will run to the warren and we shall have to dig her out ——"

"Pocket her, then," said Sir William, hastily. "Who gave you leave to pouch my ferrets? Eh? What has a ferret to do in school? Eh? Idle again? Captain Butler, is he idle?"

"He is a dunce," said Mr. Butler, with a shrug.

"Dunce!" echoed Sir William, quickly. "Why should he be a dunce when I have taught him? Granted his Latin would shame a French priest, and his mathematics sicken a Mohawk, have I not read the poets with him?"

Mr. Butler sharpened a quill in silence.

"Gad!" muttered Sir William. "Have I not read mythology with him till I dreamed of nymphs and satyrs and capered in my dreams? Micky!"

"Sir!" I replied, sulkily.

Then he began to question me concerning certain gods and demi-gods. He lounged by the window in his spurred boots and scarlet hunting-coat, and at every slap of the whip over his boots, he shot me through and through with a question which I had neither information nor inclination to answer before the grinning small fry.

These sat looking on—Esk with ink on his nose, Peter in tears, a-licking his lump of spruce, and that wildcat thing, Silver Heels ——

With every question of Sir William I felt I was losing caste among them. Besides, there was Mr. Butler with his silent, deathly laugh—a laugh that never reached his eyes.

Slap came the whip on the polished boot-tops, and Sir William was at it again with his gods and goddesses:

"Who carried off Proserpine? Eh?"

I looked sullenly at Esk, then at Peter, who put out his tongue at me.

"Who carried off Proserpine?" repeated Sir William. "Come now, you should know that. Come now—a likely lass, Proserpine, out in the bush pulling cowslips, bless her little

fingers—when—ho!—up pops—eh?—who, lad, who in Heav·
en's name?"

"Plato!" I muttered at hazard.

"What!" bawled Sir William.

I felt for my underlip and got it between my teeth, and for
a space not another word would I speak, although there began
to sound in Sir William's voice that hollow roar which always
meant a scene. His whip, too, went slap-slap! on his boots,
like the tail of a big dog rapping its ribs.

He was perhaps a violent man, Sir William; yet none outside of his own family ever suspected it, he having so perfect
a control over himself when he chose. And I often think that
his outbursts toward us were all pretense. At all events, none
of us ever was the worse for his roaring.

"Come, sir! Come, Mr. Cardigan!" said Sir William, grimly.
"Out with the gentleman's name—d'ye hear?"

It was the first time in my life that Sir William had spoken
to me as Mr. Cardigan. It might have pleased me had I not
seen Mr. Butler sneer.

I glared at Mr. Butler.

Slap! went Sir William's whip on his boots.

"Answer me, sirrah!" he shouted in a passion. "Who carried
off Proserpine?"

"The Six Nations, for aught I know!" I muttered, disrespectfully.

Sir William's face went redder than his coat, and he stood
up very straight and still.

"Turn the children free, Captain Butler," he said in a low
voice.

Mr. Butler flung back the door. The children followed him,

Esk bestowing a wink upon me, Peter grinning and toeing in like a Devon duck, and that wildcat thing, Silver Heels ——

"You need not wait, Captain Butler," said Sir William, politely.

Mr. Butler retired, leaving the door swinging. Out in the dark hallway I fancied I could still see his shallow eyes shining. But I may have been mistaken.

"Michael," said Sir William, "go to the slate."

I walked across the dusty schoolroom.

"Chalk!" shouted Sir William, irritated by my lagging steps.

I picked up a lump of chalk, balancing it carelessly in my palm.

Something in my eyes may have infuriated Sir William.

The next moment he had me by the arm, then by the collar, whip whistling like the chimney wind—and whistling quite as idly, for the blow never fell.

I freed myself; he made no effort to hold me.

"Keep your lash for your hounds!" I stammered.

He did not seem to hear me, but I planted myself in a corner and cried out that he dare not lay his whip on me. It was a shameful thing to taunt him with, for he had promised me never to lay rod to me; and I knew, as all the world knows, that Sir William Johnson had never broken his word to man or savage.

But still I faced him mutinously. I was conscious that, great boy though I was, I deserved the lash and yet I was angered that he should seem to threaten me with it. I faced him, now hurling safe defiance, now muttering revenge, until the scornful rebuke in his eyes began to shame me into silence.

Presently Sir William said, as though to himself: "If the boy's a coward, no man can lay the sin to me."

"I am not a coward!" I burst out, all aquiver again, "and I ask your pardon, sir, for daring you to lay whip on me—knowing your promise!"

Sir William scowled at me.

"To prove it," I went on, desperately, "I will give you leave to drive a fish-hook through my hand and cut it out with your knife; and I'll laugh at the pain—as did that Mohawk lad when you cut the pike hook out of his hand!"

"What have I to do with your fish-hook and your Mohawks?" shouted Sir William, with a hearty oath.

Mortified, I shrank back while he fumed and cracked his whip.

"You assume the airs of a man," he roared—"you with your eighteen unbirched years—you with your gross ignorance and grosser impudence! A vicious lad, a bad, undutiful, sullen lad, ever at odds with the others, never diligent save with the fishing-rod—a lazy, quarrelsome rustic, a swaggering, forest-running fellow, without the polish or the presence of a gentleman's son! Shame on you!"

I set my teeth and shut both eyes, opening one, however, when I heard him move.

"I'll polish you yet!" he said, with an oath. "I'll polish you, and I'll temper you like the edge of a Mohawk hatchet."

"One red belt," I answered, impudently, meaning that I defied him.

"Which you will cover with a white belt before the fires in this hearth are dead," he answered, gulping down the disrespect.

He laid his heavy hand on the door; then, turning, he bade me write with the chalk on the slate the history of Proserpine in verse, and await his further pleasure.

Sir William had shut the schoolroom door upon me. I listened. Had he locked it I should have kicked the paneling out into the hallway.

With a bit of buckskin I dusted Esk's sum and Peter's scrawls from the great slate, slowly, for I was not yet of a mind to begin my task.

I opened the window behind me. A sweet spring wind was blowing. Putting up my nose to scent it, I saw the sky bluer than a heron's egg, and a little white cloud a-sailing up there all alone.

That year the snow had gone out in April. Now, on this second day of May, robins were already running over the ground below the schoolroom window, a-tilting for worms like jacksnipes along the creek.

Leaning there in the breezy casement, I tried to forget that silly jade, Proserpine, in attentively observing the birds. Then the distant sparkle of the river caught my eye, and straightaway my thoughts slipped into their natural channel; and I laid my plans for the taking of that bull-trout who had so grossly deceived and flouted me the past year—aye, not only me, but also that master of the craft, Sir William himself.

Thinking of Sir William, my lagging thoughts drifted back again to my desk. It maddened me to pine here, making rhymes, while outside the sweet wind whispered: "Come out, Michael—come out into the green delight!"

Now Sir William had bidden me not only to write my verses, but also to bide here awaiting his good pleasure. That

meant he would return by and by. I had no stomach for
further quarrels. Besides, I was ashamed of my disrespect
and temper, and, indeed, selfish, idle beast that I was, I did
truly love Sir William because I knew he was the greatest
man of our times—and because he loved me.

Resolved at last to accomplish some verses as proof of a
contrite and diligent spirit, I set to work; and this is what I
made:

> Proserpine did roam the hills,
> Intent on culling daffydills;
>   Alas, in gleeful girlish sport,
>   She wandered too far from the fort,
> Forgetting that no belt of peace
> Bound the people of Pluto from war to cease;
>   Alas, old Pluto lay in wait,
>   To ambush all who stayed out late;
> And with a dreadful war whoop he
> Ran after the doomed Proserpine—

Absorbed in my task, and, moreover, considerably affected
by the piteous plight of the maid, I stepped back from the
slate and for a moment conceived a generous idea of introducing somebody to rescue Proserpine and leave Pluto dam-
aged—perhaps scalped. Reflection, however, dissuaded me.

I did not feel at liberty to rescue Proserpine in my verses
or plump a war arrow into Pluto. I knew it would enrage
Sir William.

As I stood there, breathing hard, resolved to finish the
wretched maiden quickly and let the meter go a-limping,
behind me I heard the door stealthily open, and I knew that
long-legged wildcat thing, Silver Heels, had crept in.

I pretended not to notice her, and she stood behind me, very still. Clearly, she was reading my verses, and I became angry. Not to show it, I made out to whistle and to draw a picture of a fish on the slate. Then she knew I had seen her and laughed hatefully.

"Oh," said I, "if there is somebody come a-prying, it must be Silver Heels!" And I turned around, pretending amazement at the justness of my hazard.

"You saw me," she answered, disdainfully.

"It is your hour for the stocks," I hinted.

"I won't go," she retorted.

To secure the grace of carriage necessary for a young lady of quality, and to straighten her back, which truly was as straight as a pine, Sir William and Mistress Molly were accustomed to strap her to a pine plank and lock her in the stocks for an hour at noon, forbidding Peter, Esk, and me to tickle the soles of her feet.

It was noon now; I could hear the guard changing at the north blockhouse—tramp! tramp! tramp! across the stony way.

"If you don't go to the stocks now," I said, "you'll be sorry when you do go."

"If you tickle my feet, you great booby, I'll tell Sir William," she retorted.

"Will you go, Silver Heels?" I insisted.

"My name isn't Silver Heels," she observed, coolly tilting back and forth on heels and toes. "Call me by my right name and perhaps I'll go—and perhaps I won't. So there, Mr. Micky Dunce!"

"If I call you Felicity Warren, will you go?" I inquired, cautiously.

"There! you have called me Felicity Warren!" she cried in triumph.

"I didn't!" said I, in a temper. "I only said that there was such a person. Anyway, you toe in like a Mohawk. Anyway, you're half wildcat, half Mohawk."

"It's a lie!" she flashed. "I'm all white to the bones of my body!"

It was true. She was kin to Sir William and niece to Sir Peter Warren, but, to torment her, we feigned to believe her one of Mistress Molly's brood, half Mohawk, as were Esk and Peter; and it madded her. Besides, had not the Mohawks dubbed her Silver Heels a year ago when, with naked flying feet, she had beaten us all in the foot race before Sir William and half the people of the Six Nations?

The prize had been a Barlow jackknife, which, before the race, I had looked upon as mine.

"You are a Mohawk," I said, resentfully. "Also, you are a catchild beneath notice. When you are hungry you cry, 'Miau! *Eso cautfore!*'—like Peter."

"I don't!" she said, stamping her moccasin.

"Anyway," said I, "the guard is changed these ten minutes, and Sir William will come to find you here a-prying. *Esogee cadagcariax*," I added, incautiously.

"Who is Mohawk now!" she cried, clapping her hands. "Bah, Mister Micky, it is spoon-meat *you* require to make you run the faster after jackknives!"

This outrageous taunt ruffled me. I attempted to hold my head in the air and look down at the presumptuous child, but her eyes were almost on a straight line with mine, though she was but fifteen and I eighteen.

"I'm nearly as high as you," she said.

"I can jump and touch the ceiling," said I, and did so.

She strove in vain, then called me dunce, and vowed what brains I had were in my feet. For that, and because she pushed me, I seized the chalk and wrote high on the slate.

"Silver Heels is Mohock she toes in like ducks."

She caught up the buckskin to wipe out the taunt, jostling me till the ferret in my pocket jumped out and ran round and round the room.

I jostled her; then she gave me a blow and a quick shove, whereupon I stumbled, pulling her to the floor to rub her face with chalk. She twisted and turned, kicking and striking, while I rubbed chalk into her skin, till of a sudden she coiled up and bit me clean through the hand.

I was on my feet with a bound; she also, all white in the face and her eyes aflame.

The blood began welling up, running into my palm and along the fingers to the floor. At that same instant I heard the door of the nursery open, and I knew that Sir William was coming through the hall to the schoolroom.

From instinct I thrust my wounded hand into my breeches pocket.

"Don't tell!" whispered Silver Heels, in a fright. "Don't tell—and here is the jackknife."

She thrust it into my right hand, then sped across the floor to the open window, and over the sill, dropping light as a cat on the grass below.

My first impulse was to follow her and give her such a spank as Mistress Molly administered the day she trounced her for pushing Peter into the creek. However, it was already too late; Sir William was coming quickly along the hall, and I had scarce time to step to the slate when he marched in, his fish-rod in his hand but his mind obviously on me.

He came straight toward me and stared at the slate whereupon my verses stared back, white and unfinished; and at first

SHE SPED ACROSS THE FLOOR AND OVER THE SILL

his brows knitted and he said, "Fudge, fudge, fudge!" Then of a sudden he sat down on the bench, clapping his hand to his brow.

"O Lord!" said he, and fell a-laughing, while I, hot,

ashamed, and a little dizzy, my breeches pocket being full of blood, gnawed my lips and glowered askance.

"The Lord's will be done," said he, taking breath. "Who am I to ordain when He who fashioned yon towhead designed it to hold neither Latin nor the classics?"

"It pleases you to laugh, sir," I muttered.

"Pleases me! Pleases me, quotha! Lad, it stabs me like a French dirk, nor can I guard the thrust in tierce! I have been wrong. If you are not born a scholar, 'twas the mint mark I could not read aright; and no blame to you, lad, no blame to you. Micky boy! Shall we leave Cæsar to go marching with his impedimenta and his Tenth Legion? Shall we consign the hypothenuse of all triangles to those who mend pens from the quills of wild geese which better men have brought down with a single ball?"

I was regarding him wildly, uncertain of his meaning.

"Shall we," cried Sir William, heartily, "bid the nymphs and dryads farewell forever, lad, and save our learning for Roderick Random and a bowl of cider and the bitter nights of December?"

His meaning was dawning upon me slowly, for what with the pain of my hand and the dizziness, I was perhaps more stupid than usual.

"No," said Sir William, with a thump of fist on his knee, "the college which my Lord Dartmouth has endowed is a haven for those who seek it, not a prison for men to be driven to."

He paused.

I gazed at him in silence while the blood, overrunning my leather pocket, ran down to my knee-buckles.

He sat in meditation, shaking his head.

The blood began stealing down my stocking towards my shoe. I turned the leg so he could not observe it.

"Come, lad," he said, finally, brightening up, "learning lies not always between thumbed leaves. I wish only that you bear yourself modestly and nobly through the world; that you keep faith with men, that your word once given shall never be withdrawn.

"This is the foundation. It includes courage. Further than that, I desire you, once a purpose formed and a course set, to steer fearlessly to the goal.

"I know you to be brave and honest; I know you to be a very Mohawk in the forest; I believe you to be merciful and tender underneath that boy's thoughtless and cruel hide.

"As for learning, I can do no more for you than I have done and have offered to do. If it pleases you, you may go to England and learn the arts, bearing, and deportment you can never acquire here with us. No? Well, then, stay with us. I want you, Micky. We Irish are fond of each other—and I am an old man now—I am nigh sixty years, Michael—sixty years of battle. I should be glad of rest—with those I love."

My heart was very soft now. I looked at Sir William with swelling affection.

"There is one last thing I wish to add," he said, gravely, almost sadly. "Perhaps I may again refer to it—but I pray that it may not be necessary."

I sat up and rubbed my eyes to clear them from the sickly faintness which stole upward from my throbbing hand.

"It is this," he continued, in a low voice. "If it ever comes to you to choose between His Majesty our King and—and your native land—which God forbid!—go to your closet and kneel down, and stay there on your knees, hours, days!—until you have learned your own heart. Then—then—God go with you, Michael Cardigan."

He rose, and his face was years older. Slowly the color came back into his cheeks; he fumbled with the brasswork on his fish-rod, then smiled.

"That is all," he said. "Let Pluto chase Proserpine wherever he likes, lad. Where is that ferret? What! Running about unmuzzled! Hey! Vix! Vix! Come here, little reptile!"

"I'll catch her, sir," said I, stumbling forward.

But as I laid my hand on Vix the floor rose and struck me, and there I lay sprawling and senseless, with the blood running over the floor; and Sir William, believing me bitten by the ferret, pouched the poor beast and lifted me to a bench.

He must have seen my hand, however, for when a cup of cold water set me spluttering and blinking, I found my hand tied up in Sir William's handkerchief and Sir William eyeing me strangely.

"How came that wound?" he asked, bluntly.

I could not reply—or would not.

He asked me again whether the ferret bit me, and I was tempted to say yes. I hated Silver Heels, but could not betray her, and it was easy to clap the blame on Vix.

"Sir?" I stammered.

"I asked what bit you," he said, icily.

I tried to say Vix, but the lie, too, stuck in my throat.

"I cannot tell you," I muttered.

"Then," said Sir William, with a strange smile of relief,

"I shall not force you, Michael. May I honorably ask you how you come by this jackknife?"

I shook my head. My face was on fire.

"Very well," he said. "Only, remember that you are a man, now—a man of eighteen—and that I have today treated you as a man, and shall continue. And remember that a man's first duty is to protect the weaker sex, and his second duty is to endure from them all taunts, caprice, and torments without revenge. It is a hard lesson to learn, Micky, and only the true and gallant gentleman can ever learn it."

He smiled, then said:

"Pray find our little Silver Heels and return to her the jackknife, which was her wampum belt of faith in the honor of a gentleman."

And so he walked away, smoothing the fur of the red-eyed ferret against his breast.

A MAN ON HORSEBACK RODE . . . AT A GALLOP AND CLATTERED
AWAY DOWN THE HILL

CHAPTER TWO

WHEN Sir William left me in the schoolroom, he left a lad of eighteen puffed up in a glow of pride. I was to be received at last as a man among men!

I had entered the schoolroom that morning a lazy, sullen, defiant lad. Now I was free to leave the accursed trap forever, a man of discretion, responsible before men.

What a change had come to me, all in one brief May morning! A great tide of benevolent condescension for the others swept over me, a ripple of pity and good will for the hapless children whose benches lay in a row before me.

I no longer detested Silver Heels. I walked on tiptoe to her bench. There lay her quill and inky horn and a foolscap book sewed neatly and marked:

FELICITY WARREN
1774
Her Booke

Poor child, doomed for years still to steep her little fingers in ink powder while, with the powder I should require hereafter, I expected to write fiercer tales on living hides with plummets cast in bullet molds!

Cramped with importance, I cast a contemptuous eye upon my poem which embellished the great slate, and scoured it partly out with the buckskin.

"My books," said I to myself, "I will bestow upon Silver Heels and Esk." And I carried out my philanthropic impulse, piling speller, reader, and arithmetic on Esk's bench. My Cæsar, my pair of globes, my compass, and my algebra I laid with Silver Heel's copy-book.

For fat Peter, because I had allowed Vix to bite his tight breeches, I left a pile of jacks beside his hornbook, namely, a slate-pen, three mended quills, a birchen box of ink powder, a screw to trade with, two tops and an alley, pumice, a rule, and some wax.

Having bestowed these gifts with a light heart, I walked slowly around the room, and I fear my walk was somewhat a strut.

I know my head was all swelled with vain imaginings: I saw myself in a flapped coat and lace, fingering the hilt of a sword at my hip, saluted by the sentries and the militia. I saw myself riding with Sir William as his deputy. I heard him say, "Mr. Cardigan, the enemy are upon us! We must fly!"—and I: "Sir William, fear nothing. The day is our own!" And I saw a lad of eighteen, with sword pointing upward and one

"SIR WILLIAM DINES EARLY," HE SAID IN HIS COLD, MENACING WAY
AS I FOLLOWED HIM DOWNSTAIRS

hand twisted into Pontiac's scalp lock, smile benignly upon Sir William, who had cast himself upon my breast, protesting that I had saved the army and that the King should hear of it.

Truly I painted life in cloying colors; and always, when I accomplished gallant deeds, there stood Silver Heels to marvel and to stamp her little moccasins in vexation that I, the pride and envy of all men—I, the playmate she had in her silly ignorance flouted—now stood so far beyond her.

In a sort of ecstasy I paraded the schoolroom, the splendor of my visions dulling eyes and ears, and it was not until he had called me thrice that I observed Mr. Butler standing within the doorway.

The unwelcome sight cleared my brains like a dash of spring water in the face.

"It is one o'clock," said Mr. Butler, "and time for your carving lesson. Did you not hear the bugles from the forts?"

"I heard nothing, sir," said I, giving him a surly look.

"Sir William dines early," he said in his cold, menacing way as I followed him downstairs. "If he has to wait your pleasure for his slice of roast, you will await his pleasure for the remainder of the day in the schoolroom."

"It is not true!" I said, stopping short in the lower hallway. "I am free of that ratty pit forever! And of the old ferret, too," I added, insolently, with a glance that left him in no doubt as to whom I meant.

"Be careful, sirrah. I could call you out for that," he said, staring at me.

"Then do it!" I retorted, angrily.

And suddenly all the hatred and contempt I had so long

choked back burst out in language I now blush for. I called him a coward and a Huron. I heaped abuse upon him; I dared him to meet me; nay, I challenged him to face with rifle or sword, when and where he chose. And all the time he stood staring at me with that deathly laugh of his.

"Measure me!" I said, venomously. "I am as tall as you, lacking an inch. I am a man! This day Sir William freed me from that spider web you tenant, and now in Heaven's name let us settle that score which every hour has added to since I first beheld you!"

"And my honor?" he asked, coldly.

"What?" I stammered. "I ask you to maintain it with rifle or rapier! Blood scours tarnished names!"

"Not your blood," he said, with a stealthy glance at the dining-room door. "Not the blood of an untried boy. That would rust my honor. Wait. Wait a bit, until you have had a year among men. A year runs like a spotted fawn in cherry time!"

"You will not meet me!" I blurted out, mortified.

"In a year, perhaps," he said, absently.

Then from within the dining-hall came Sir William's roar; "Body o' me! Am I to be kept here at twiddle-thumbs for lack of a carver?"

I stepped back, bowing to Mr. Butler.

"I will be patient for a year, sir," I said. And so opened the door while he passed me, and into the dining-hall.

"I am sorry, sir," said I, but Sir William cut me short with:

"Hold your tongue, sir! I am asking a blessing!"

So I buried my nose in my hollowed hand and stood up, very still.

Having given thanks in a temper, Sir William's frown relaxed and he sat down and tucked his finger-cloth under his neck with an injured glance at me.

"Zounds!" he said, mildly. "Hell hath no fury like a fisherman kept waiting. Captain Butler, bear me out."

"I am no angler," said Mr. Butler in his deadened voice.

"That is true," observed Sir William, as though condoling with Mr. Butler for a misfortune not his fault. "Perhaps some day the fever may scorch you—as it has our young kinsman, Micky—eh, lad?"

I said, "Perhaps, sir," with eyes on the smoking joint before me. It was Sir William's pleasure that I learn to carve; and, in truth, I found it easy, save for the carving of a goose or a wild duck.

We were but four to dine that day: Sir William, Mr. Butler, Silver Heels, and myself. Mistress Molly remained in the nursery, where were also Peter and Esk, inasmuch as they slobbered and fouled the cloth, and so fed in the play-room. Colonel Guy Johnson remained at Detroit, Captain John Johnson was on a mission to Albany, and Thayendanegea was in Quebec. Our small company seemed lost in the great dining-hall.

After I had carved the juicy joint, the gillie served Sir William, then Mr. Butler, then Silver Heels. As Saunders placed her serving, I gave her a look which meant, "I did not tell Sir William," whereupon she smiled at her plate.

"Good appetite and good health, sir," said I, raising my wine-glass to Sir William.

"Good health, my lad!" said Sir William, heartily.

Glasses were raised again and compliments said, though

my face was sufficient to sour the Madeira in Mr. Butler's glass.

"Your good health, Michael," said Silver Heels, sweetly.

I pledged her with a patronizing amiability that made her hazel-gray eyes open wide.

I sat there, somewhat dizzied by my new dignity, yet not deaf to the talk that went on.

Mr. Butler and Sir William spoke gravely of the discontent now rampant in the town of Boston, and of Captain John Johnson's mission to Albany. At first I listened greedily, sniffing for news of war, but presently, understanding little of their discourse save what pertained to the Indians, I lost interest.

I even forgot my new dignity, and secretly pinched a bread crumb into the shape of a little pig that I showed to Silver Heels. She thereupon pinched out a dog with hound's ears for me to admire.

I was roused by Sir William's voice in solemn tones: "Now, God forbid I should live to see that, Captain Butler!" and I pricked up my ears once more, but made nothing of what followed, save that there were certain disloyal men in Massachusetts and New York who might rise against our King and that our Governor Tryon meant to take some measures concerning tea.

"Well, well," burst out Sir William at length; "in evil days let us thank God that the fish still swim! Eh, Micky?"

With that, he rose and we all stood up. Sir William, brushing Silver Heels on his way to the door, passed his arm around her and tilted her chin up.

"Now do you go to Mistress Mary and beg her to place you in the stocks for an hour. Will you promise me, Felicity?"

Silver Heels began to pout, but the baronet packed her off, and went out to the portico, where one of his Scotch gillies attended with gaff, spear, and net-sack.

"Oho," thought I, "so it's salmon in the Sacondaga!" And I fell to teasing that he might take me, too.

"No, Micky," he said, soberly. "It's less for sport than for quiet reflection that I go. Don't sulk, lad. Tomorrow, perhaps."

"Is it a promise, sir?" I cried.

"Perhaps," he laughed. "If the cards turn up right."

That meant he had some Indian affair on hand, and I fell back, satisfied that his rod was a ruse and that he was really bound for one of the council fires at the upper castle.

So he went away, and I back into the hall, whistling, enchanted with my new liberty.

I had now been enfranchised nearly three hours, and had already rashly used these first moments of liberty in picking a mortal quarrel with Mr. Butler. But I had long felt that Mr. Butler and I would some time meet. Now that at last our tryst was in sight, it did not disturb me; nor, now that he was out of my sight, did I feel impatient to settle it, so accustomed had I become to waiting for the inevitable hour.

I strolled through the hallway, hands in pockets, still whistling, and so came to the south casement. Pressing my nose to the pane, I looked into the young orchard where the robins ran in the new grass; and I found it delicious to linger indoors, knowing I was free to go out when I chose, and none to cry, "Come back!"

So I mounted the stairway, seeking my own little chamber. Once inside, sitting down on my cot, I surveyed my domain proudly.

There were my books, not much thumbed. Still I cherished them because they were gifts of Sir William or relics of my honored father. I cherished, too, the decorations on my walls. There I had placed pictures of the best running-horses at Newmarket; also, four prints of a camp at Watteau. In addition, there hung above the door a fox's mask, my whip, my hunting-horn, my spurs, and two fish-rods made for me by Joseph Brant, who is called Thayendanegea, chief of the Mohawk, and of Six Nations, and brother to Aunt Molly.

In this room also I kept my black lead pencil made by Faber, a ream of paper from England, and a lump of red sealing-wax.

I had written, in my life, but two letters: one, three years since, I had written to Sir Peter Warren to thank him for a sum of money sent for my use; the other to a little girl named Marie Livingston, whom I knew in Albany when Sir William took me there for the probating of some papers.

She had written me a letter signed "your cozzen Marie," Mr. Livingston being kin to Sir William, and it had given me much pleasure. But I had not yet written again to her, though I meant to do so. She had yellow hair which was pleasing, and she did not resemble Silver Heels in complexion or manner, having never flouted me.

Thus, as I sat there on my cot, scenes of my life came jostling me like long-absent comrades, softening my mood until I fell to thinking of those honored parents I had never seen. For the day that brought life to me had robbed my mother of

Mr. Cayuga must have seen that he was fast in a trap; yet neither by word nor glance did he appear to observe it.

The sun had set. A chill from the west sent the shivers creeping up my legs as I called a soldier and bade him kindle a fire for us. Then on my own responsibility I went into the storeroom and rummaged about until I discovered a thick red blanket.

A noise at the guard door brought me running out of the storeroom to find my Cayuga making to force his way out, and the soldiers shoving him into the guest-room again.

"Fall back!" I cried, my wits working like shuttles; and quickly added in the Cayuga tongue: "Cayugas are free people; free to stay, free to go. Open the door for my brother who fears his brother's fireside!"

There was a silence; the soldiers stood back respectfully; a sergeant opened the outer door. But the Indian, turning his hot eyes on me, swung on his heel and reëntered the guest-room, drawing the flint from his rifle as he walked.

I followed and laid the thick red blanket on his dusty shoulders.

"Sergeant," I called, "send McCloud for meat and drink, and notify Sir William as soon as he arrives that his brothers of the Cayuga would speak to him with belts!"

I was not sure of the etiquette required of me after this, not knowing whether to leave the Cayuga alone or bear him company. Tribes differ; so do nations in their observance of these forms. One thing more puzzled me: here was a belt-bearer with messages from some distant branch of the Cayuga tribe; yet the etiquette of their allies, our Mohawks, decreed that belts should be delivered by sachems or chiefs, well escorted.

One thing I, of course, knew: that a guest, once admitted, should never be questioned until he had eaten and slept.

But whether or not I was committing a breach of etiquette by squatting there by the fire with my Cayuga, I did not know.

Considering the circumstances, however, I called out for a soldier to bring two pipes and tobacco; and when they were fetched to me, I filled one and passed it to the Cayuga, then filled the other, picked a splinter from the fire, lighted mine, and passed the blazing splinter to my guest.

If his ideas on etiquette were disturbed, he did not show it. He puffed at his pipe and drew his blanket close about his naked body, staring into the fire with the grave, absent air of a cat on a wintry night.

Now, stealing a glance at his scalp lock, I saw by the fire-light the stumps of two quills fastened in the knot of his crown. The next covert glance told me that they were the ragged stubs of the white-headed eagle's feathers and that my guest was a chief. This set me in a quandary. What was a strange Cayuga chief doing here without escort, without blanket, yet bearing belts? Etiquette absolutely forbade a single question. Was I treating him properly? Or would my ignorance of what was due him bring trouble and difficulty to Sir William when he returned?

Suddenly resolved to clear Sir William of any suspicion of awkwardness, I rose and said:

"My brother is a man and a chief; he will understand that in the absence of my honored kinsman, Sir William Johnson, and in the absence of officers in authority, the hospitality of Johnson Hall falls upon me.

"Ignorant of my brother's customs, I bid him welcome, because he is naked, tired, and hungry. I kindle his fire; I bring him pipe and food; and now I bid him sleep in peace behind doors that open at his will."

Then the Cayuga rose to his full noble height, bending his burning eyes on mine. There was a silence; and so, angry or grateful, I knew not which, he resumed his seat by the fire, and I went out through the guardroom.

Without delay, I sought Mistress Molly in the nursery, and told her what I had done. She listened gravely and without comment or word of blame or praise, being in this like all Indians. But she questioned me, and I described the strange belt-bearer from his scalp lock to the sole of his moccasin.

"Cayuga," she said, softly. "What make was his rifle?"

"Not English, not French," I said. "The barrel near the breech bore figures like those on Sir William's dueling pistols."

"Spanish," she said, dreamily. "In his language did he pronounce *agh* like *ahh?*"

"Yes, Aunt Molly."

She remained silent for a moment. Then she smiled and dismissed me, but I begged her to tell me from whence my Cayuga came.

"I will tell you this," she said. "He comes from very, very far away, and he follows some customs of the Tuscaroras, which they in turn borrow from a tribe which lives so far away that I should go to sleep in counting the miles for you."

With that she shut the nursery door, and I, no wiser than

before, sat down on the stairs to think and to wait for Sir William.

A moment later a man on horseback rode out of our stables at a gallop and clattered away down the hill. I listened for a moment, then thought of other things.

CHAPTER THREE

A T LATE candle-light, Sir William still tarrying, I went to the north blockhouse, where Mr. Duncan, the lieutenant commanding the guard, gave me somewhat surprising news.

"An express from Sir William has at this moment come in," said he. "Sir William is aware that a belt-bearer from Virginia awaits him."

"How could Sir William, who is at Castle Cumberland, know that?" I began; then was silent, as it flashed into my mind that Mistress Molly had sent an express to Sir William as soon as I had told her about the strange Cayuga. That was the galloping horseman I had heard.

Pondering and perplexed, I looked up to find Mr. Duncan smiling at me.

"I understand," said he, "that Sir William is pleased to approve your conduct touching the strange Cayuga."

"How do you know?" I asked, quickly, my heart warming with pleasure.

"I know this," said Mr. Duncan, laughing, "that Sir William has sent me something for you, a present, in fact, which I am to deliver to you on the morrow."

"What is it, Mr. Duncan?" I teased; but the laughing officer shook his head, retiring into the guardroom and pretending to be afraid of me.

The soldiers, lounging around the settles, pipes between their teeth, looked on with respectful grins. Clearly, even they appeared to know what Sir William had sent to me from Castle Cumberland.

As I stood in the guardroom, eager, yet partly vexed, away below in the village the bell in the new stone church began to ring.

"What is that?" I asked, in surprise.

The soldiers had all risen, taking their muskets from the racks. In the stir and banging of gunstocks, my question perhaps was not heard by Mr. Duncan, for he stood silent, untwisting his sword knots and eyeing the line that the sergeant was forming.

A drummer and a trumpeter took station; the sergeant, at a carry, advanced and saluted with, "Parade is formed, sir."

" 'Tention!" sang out Mr. Duncan. "Support arms! Carry arms! Trail arms! File by the left flank! March!" And with drawn claymore on his shoulder he passed out into the starlight.

I followed; and now, standing by the blockhouse gate, far away in the village I heard the rub-a-dub of a drum and a loud trumpet blowing.

Nearer and nearer came the drum; the trumpet ceased. And now I could hear the tramp, tramp, tramp of infantry on the hill's black crest.

"Present arms!" cried Mr. Duncan, sharply.

A dark mass suddenly loomed up close in front of us, taking

the shape of a long column, which passed us, tramp, tramp, tramp.

Then our drum rattled and the trumpet sang prettily, while Mr. Duncan rendered the officer's salute as a dark stand of colors passed, borne furled and high above the slanting muskets.

Baggage wains began to creak by, great shapeless hulks rolling in on the black ocean of the night, with soldiers half asleep on top, and teamsters afoot.

The last yoke of oxen passed, dragging a brass cannon.

" 'Tention!" said Mr. Duncan. "Support arms! Trail arms! 'Bout face! By the right flank, wheel! March!"

Back into the blockhouse filed the guard.

Mr. Duncan sent his claymore ringing into the scabbard, and strolled off toward the new barracks, east of the Hall.

"What troops were those, sir?" I asked, respectfully.

"Three companies of Royal Americans from Albany," said he. Then he added, "There is to be a big council fire held here. Did you not know it?"

"No," said I, slowly, reluctant to admit that I had not shared Sir William's confidence.

"Look yonder," said Mr. Duncan.

Far out in the pale starlight, south and west of the hall, I saw fires kindled, one by one, until the twinkle of their lights ran for a mile across the uplands. On a hill in the north a signal fire sent long streamers of flame straight up into the sky. Other beacons flashed out in the darkness, some far distant.

"It is the Six Nations gathering," said Mr. Duncan. "We expect important guests."

"What for?" I asked.

"I don't know," said Mr. Duncan, gravely. "Good night, Mr. Cardigan."

"Good night, sir," I said, thoughtfully, then cried after him, "And my present, Mr. Duncan?"

"To-morrow," he answered, and passed on his way a-laughing.

I walked quickly back to the Hall, where I encountered Esk and Peter, well bibbed, cleaning the last crumb from their bowls of porridge.

"Did you see the soldiers?" cried Esk.

"Look out of the back windows," added Peter. "The Onondaga fires are burning on the hills."

"Oneidas," corrected Esk.

"Onondagas," persisted Peter.

"Where is Silver Heels?" I asked.

Mistress Molly came into the hall from the pantry, keys jingling at her girdle, and took Peter by his sticky fingers, bidding Esk follow.

"Bedtime," she said, with her pretty smile. "Michael, Felicity is being dressed by Betty. If Sir William does not return, you will dine with Felicity alone; and I expect you to conduct exactly like Sir William."

"Yes, Aunt Molly," said I, with dignity.

Esk and Peter, being instantly hustled bedward, left lamenting and asserting that they too were old enough to imitate Sir William.

Silver Heels, with her hair done by Betty, and a blue sash over her fresh-flowered cambric, passed them on the stairs, coming down, pausing to wish Mistress Molly good night, and slyly to pinch fat Peter.

"Felicity," said Mistress Molly, "I trust you will conduct this evening as befits your station."

Silver Heels made Mistress Molly a deep reverence in reply, waited on the landing until she heard the nursery door close, then flung her legs astride the balustrade and slid down like a flash.

"Have you seen the soldiers, Micky?—and the fires on the hills?" she cried. "Tomorrow all the officers will be here, and I am to wear my hair curled, and my pink dress and tucker!"

We sat down on the stairs together as friendly and polite as though we never quarreled; and she chattered on, finally breaking off to exclaim:

"Micky, go and put on your silk breeches and lace cuffs and we will be gay and grand to dine!"

I ran to my chamber, and bathed, and dressed in all my finery. Then I descended the stairs, to find my lady Silver Heels parading before the pier glass, while a gillie threw open the doors of the dining-hall.

And that night Silver Heels and I grandly supped alone together in the great hall, Mr. Butler having hurriedly ridden to his home, and Sir William still being absent.

We conducted ourselves with vast dignity, save that I took occasion, when the gillie who served us was out of the room, to slip a handful of caraway cakes into my pouch to eat at my pleasure later.

After supper, when we sat somewhat sleepily together on the stairs, Silver Heels mocked at me for this greedy trick, reproaching me because I had taken to playing the high and mighty, whereas all could plainly see I was nothing but a boy like Esk or Peter.

"My legs," she said, drowsily, "can touch the floor from the third stair as well as yours," and she stretched them down to prove it, falling short an inch.

"If you are no longer a child," said I, "why do they harness you to the backboard and make you wear pack-thread stays?"

This madded her.

"You shall see," she said, in a temper—"you shall see me in flowered caushets, silk stockings, and shoes of Paddington's make, which befit my station and rank! You shall see me in paduasoy and ribbons and a hat of gauze! I shall wear pompadour gloves and shall take no notice of you, with your big hands and feet, *pardieu!*"

"Nor I of you," said I, "tricked out in your silk flummery." And I drew a caraway from my pocket and bit deep.

"Yes, you will," said Silver Heels. "Give me a caraway, piggy."

Sitting there in the dark, nibbling in silence, I could hear the distant stir of the convoy at the barracks, and wondered why the soldiers had come. Surely no one would dare threaten Sir William Johnson, the greatest man in the colonies, and very dearly esteemed by our King?

"They say," said Silver Heels, "that there are men in Boston who have defied even the King himself."

"Never fear," said I, "they'll all hang for it."

"Would you like to fight for the King?" she asked, civilly enough.

I said I should like to very much, and I might have said more if black Betty had not come downstairs, her double earrings ajingle, calling her "li'l' Miss Honeybee" to come to bed.

Silver Heels stood up, rubbing her eyes and stretching.

"Good-night, Micky," she said, with her mechanical curtsy, and took Betty's black hand.

I went myself to my chamber gladly; for, what with the excitement of the morning, the arrival of the Cayuga and, later, the soldiers, my head was tired and confused.

I slept soundly, and I waked late to hear the bugle playing at the barracks, and Sir William's hounds baying in their kennels.

Dub! dub! rub-a-dub-dub! Dub! dub! rub-a-dub-dub!

The guard was changing at the blockhouse, while I, all shivers, dashed cold water over me from head to foot and rubbed my limbs into a tingle.

As I did so, I recalled that that day I was to receive the present Sir William had send me from Castle Cumberland. I hurried into breeches and shirt; made of my hair a neat queue and tied it; put on my buckskin vest with flaps, and my short hunting-shirt over it.

Then I hastened down the stairs, impatient to find Mr. Duncan and have my present. Nay, so fast and blindly did I speed that, swinging around the balustrade, I plumped clean into Sir William, coming up.

"What's to do! What's to do!" he exclaimed, testily. "Is there no gout in the world, then, wooden feet!"

"Oh, Sir William! My present from Castle Cumberland!" I stammered. "Is it perhaps a salmon rod?"

"Now the wraith of old Isaac pinch ye!" said Sir William,

half laughing, half angry. "Fish-rod! Gad! It's a new algebra you need!"

"You promised not to," said I, stoutly.

"Did I?" said Sir William, with a twinkle. "So I did, lad; so I did! Well, perhaps it is not an algebra book, after all."

"Then let us go to Mr. Duncan and get it now," I replied, promptly.

"You may not want my present when you see it," argued Sir William, who did ever enjoy to plague those whom he loved best.

But I pulled him by the arm, and he pretended to go with reluctance and many misgivings.

At the door of the north blockhouse Mr. Duncan rendered Sir William the officer's salute, which Sir William returned.

"Mr. Duncan," said he, "have you knowledge hereabouts of a certain present sent for Mr. Cardigan, here?"

"Now that you mention it, sir," replied Mr. Duncan, gravely, "I do dimly recall something of the sort."

"Was it not a schoolbook?" inquired Sir William.

"It was a parcel," replied Mr. Duncan, dubiously. "Belike it hid a dozen good stout Latin books, sir."

I endured their plaguing with rising excitement. What could my present be?

"Take him in, Mr. Duncan," said Sir William at last. "And," to me, "remember, sir, that you forget not your manners when you return to me here.

Cramping with curiosity, I followed Mr. Duncan into his own private chamber, which connected with the guardroom, and saw an officer's valise at the foot of his bed.

"It is for you," he said. "Open it."

I perceived my own name painted on the leather side, and the next instant I had stripped the lid back. Buff and gold and scarlet swam the colors of the clothing before my amazed

MICKY IN HIS NEW UNIFORM

eyes; I put out a trembling hand and drew an officer's vest from the valise.

"Here are the boots, Mr. Cardigan," said the lieutenant, lifting a pair of dress boots from behind a curtain. "Here are the hat and sword, too, and a holster with pistols."

"Mine!" I gasped.

"By this commission of our governor," said Mr. Duncan, solemnly, drawing from his breast a parchment with seal and tape. "Mr. Cardigan, let me be the first to welcome you as a brother officer."

I had gone so blind with happy tears that I scarce could find his kind, warm hand outstretched, nor could I decipher the commission as cornet of horse in the Royal Border Regiment of irregulars.

He mercifully left me then, and I stood striving to realize what had arrived to me.

But I did not tarry long to devour my uniform with my eyes. One after another my hunting shirt, vest, leggings, shoon, flew from me. I pulled on the buff breeches and laced them tight, drew on the boots, set the vest close and buttoned it, then put on the coat and hat, and lastly tied my silver gorget.

I set my sword belt, hung the sword with one glove in the hilt, and so, walking on air, I passed the guardroom with all the soldiers at stiff attention, and came to Sir William.

Stopping short at three paces, heels together, I gave the officer's salute.

Sir William's lips twitched as he rendered the salute; then he stepped forward with arms outstretched, and I fell into them like a blubbering schoolboy.

Even to Sir William I could not have described my happiness and pride, my impetuous thirst for service, my solemn boyish prayers that I might conduct nobly in the eyes of all men, for God and King and country.

But Sir William presently laid both hands on my shoulders, and looked at me a long while with kindly, understanding eyes.

"My boy," he said, "the key to it all is faith. Keep faith with all men; keep faith with thyself. This wins all battles, even the greatest and last!"

Very soberly we returned to the Hall, where a small company were assembled for breakfast—Mistress Molly, Major Wilkes of the battalion that had arrived the night before, Captains Priestly, Borrow, and McNeil, of the same regiment, my friend Lieutenant Duncan of the militia, and Silver Heels.

When Sir William and I entered the Hall the officers came to pay their respects to the baronet, and I, red as a Dutch pippin, crossed the room to where Mistress Molly stood with Silver Heels.

I bent to salute her hand, cocked hat crushed under one arm; but Mistress Molly put her arms around me and kissed me on both cheeks.

"I knew all about it," she whispered. "We are very proud, Sir William and I. Be tender and faithful. It is all we ask."

Dear, dear Aunt Molly! While life lasts can I ever forget those sweet, grave words of love, spoken to a boy who stood alone on the threshold of life?

Slowly I turned to look at Silver Heels, all my vanity, conceit, and condescension vanished.

She had turned quite pale, and she wished me happiness in a low, lifeless voice.

Chilled by her greeting, I returned to Sir William, who presented me to the guests with unconcealed pride.

"My kinsman, Mr. Cardigan, gentlemen; Captain Cardigan's only son!"

The officers greeted me most kindly, some claiming acquaintance with my honored father, and all speaking of his noble death before Quebec.

Then we sat down to breakfast, a breakfast I scarcely tasted; but I listened with all my ears to the discourse touching the late troubles in New York and Massachusetts concerning the importation of tea by the East India Company. The discussion soon became a monologue, for the subject was one Sir William understood A to Zed.

"Look you," said Sir William—"look you, gentlemen; I yield to no man in loyalty and love to my King, but this I know and dare maintain: that his Majesty is misled by his ministers, and neither he nor they suspect the truth concerning these colonies!"

The officers listened, all attention.

"Gentlemen," said Sir William, blandly, "you all are aware that since last December the Atlantic Ocean is become but a vast pot of cold tea."

The laughter which followed sounded to me a trifle strained. But Sir William went calmly on.

"Very well," he said. "But whether we laugh or condemn, let us remember that those colonists who gathered at Griffin's wharf and made tea enough for the world to drink were fighting for a principle, not for a price.

"God forbid that I, a humble loyal subject of my King, should ever bear out the work of rebels or traitors. But I solemnly say to you that the rebels and traitors are not the counterfeit Indians of Griffin's wharf, not the men who fired the *Gaspee* aflame from spirit to topmast. But they are those who whisper evil to my King at St. James's—and may God have mercy on their souls!"

In the hush that followed, Sir William leaned forward, his heavy chin set on his fists, his eyes looking into the future which he alone saw so clearly.

None durst interrupt him. The officers watched him silently.

There he sat, this great Irishman, eyes on vacancy; a plain man, a baronet of the British realm, a member of the King's Council, a major-general of militia, and the superintendent of the Indian Department in North America.

A plain man, but a vast landowner, the one man in America trusted blindly by the Indians, a man whose influence was enormous; a man who was as simple as a maid, as truthful as a child, as kind as the Samaritan who passed not on the other side.

A plain man, but a prophet.

There was a step at the door; Mr. Duncan spoke in a low tone with the orderly, then returned to Sir William.

"The Indian belt-bearer is at the blockhouse, sir," he said.

Sir William rose. The officers made their adieux and left. Only Sir William, Mistress Molly, Silver Heels, and I remained in the dining-hall.

The baronet looked across at Mistress Molly, and a sad smile touched his eyes.

She took Silver Heels by the hand and quietly left the room.

"Michael," said Sir William, "listen closely, but remain silent concerning what this belt-bearer has to say. My honor is at stake, my son. Promise!"

"I promise, sir," said I, under my breath.

The next moment the door behind me opened and the Indian stole into the room.

CHAPTER FOUR

I NOW for the first time obtained a distinct view of the
stranger as he stepped forward, throwing the blanket from
him, and stood revealed, stark naked save for clout and pouch,
truly a superb figure.

For a space he and Sir William stood face to face in silence;
then the belt-bearer, looking warily around at the empty room,
asked why Chief Warragh received his brother alone.

"My brother comes alone," replied Sir William, with em-
phasis. "It is the custom of the Cayuga to send three with each
belt. Does my brother bear but a fragment of one belt? Or
does he think us of little consequence that he comes without
attestants?"

"I bear three belts," said the Indian, haughtily. "Nine of
my people started from the Ohio; I alone live."

Sir William bowed gravely, and, motioning me to be
seated, drew up an armchair of velvet and sat down, folding
his arms in silence.

Then, for the first time in my life, I sat at a figurative council fire and listened to an orator of those masters of oratory,
the peoples of the Six Nations.

Dignified, chary of gesture, the Cayuga, facing the baronet,
related briefly his name—Quider, which in Iroquois means

Peter; his tribe, which was the tribe of the Wolf, the totem being plain on his breast. He spoke of his journey from the Ohio, and of the loss of the eight who had started with him, all dying from the smallpox within a week. He spoke respectfully of Sir William as the one man who had protected the Six Nations from unjust laws, from incursions, from white men's violence and deception.

And then he began his brief speech, drawing from his pouch a black belt of wampum:

"*Brother*: With this belt we breathe upon the embers which are asleep, and we cause the council fire to burn in this place and on the Ohio, which are our proper fireplaces.

(A belt of seven rows)

"*Brother*: The unhappy oppression of our brethren by Colonel Cresap's men, near the Ohio carrying-place, is the occasion for our coming here. Our nation would not be at rest, nor easy, until they had spoken to you about it. They have now spoken—with this belt!"

(A black and white belt)

"*Brother*: What are we to do? Lord Dunmore will not hear us. Colonel Cresap and his men, to whom we have done no harm, are coming to clear the forest and cross our free path which lies from Saint Sacrement to the Ohio. What shall we do? Instead of polishing our knives we have come to our brother Warragh. Instead of seeking our kin the Mohawk and the Oneida with painted war belts to throw between us and them, we come to our brother and ask him, by this belt, what is left for us to do? Our brothers have taught us there is a God. Teach us He is a just God—by this belt!"

(A black belt of five rows)

During this speech Sir William sat as still as death, neither by glance nor by gesture betraying the surprise, indignation, and alarm which this exposure of Colonel Cresap's doings caused him.

As for me, I, of course, vaguely understood the breach of faith committed by Colonel Cresap in invading the land of our allies, and the danger we might run should this Cayuga chief go to our Mohawks and Oneidas with war belts and inflammatory appeals for vengeance on Cresap and his men. That he had instead come to us most splendidly attested to the power and influence of Sir William among these savages.

It is seldom the custom to reply to a speech before the following day. I was prepared, therefore, when Sir William, holding in his right hand the three belts of wampum, rose and thanked the Cayuga for his talk, praising him and his tribe for resorting to arbitration instead of the hatchet, and promising an answer on the morrow.

The Cayuga listened in silence; then, resuming his blanket, he turned on his heel and passed slowly and noiselessly from the room, leaving Sir William standing beside the armchair, and me erect in the embrasure of the casement.

Now, for the first time in my life, I saw a trace of physical decline in my guardian. His hand, holding the belts, had fallen a-trembling; he made a feeble gesture for me to be seated, and sank back into his armchair, absently running his fingers over the polished belts.

"At sixty," he said, as though to himself, "strong men should be in that mellow prime to which a sober life conducts."

After a moment he went on: "My life has been sober and without excess—but hard! very hard! I am an old man, a tired old man."

Looking up to meet my eyes, he smiled, watching the sympathy which twisted my face.

"All these wars! All these wars! Thirty years of war!" he murmured, caressing the belts. "War with the French, war with the Maquas, the Hurons, the Shawnees, the Ojibways! War in the Canadas, war in the Carolinas, war east and west and north and south! And—I am tired."

He let the belts slide to the floor.

"I have worked with my hands," he said. "This land has drunk the sweat of my body. I have not spared myself in sickness or in health. My arms are tired; I have hewn forests away. My limbs ache; I have journeyed far through snow, through heat, from the Canadas to the Gulf—all my life I have journeyed on business for other men—for men I have never seen and shall never see—men yet to be born!"

There came a flush of earnest color into his face. He leaned forward toward me, elbow resting on the table, hand outstretched.

"Why, look you, Michael," he said, with childlike eagerness, "I found a wilderness and I leave a garden! Look at the valley! Look at this fair and pretty village! One hundred and eighty families! Three churches, a free school, a courthouse, a jail, barracks—all built by me; stores with red and blue swinging signs, bravely painted; inns with the good green bush aswing! Might it not be a Devonshire town? Ah—I forgot; you have never seen old England."

Smiling still, kind eyes dreaming, his head sank a little, and he clasped his hands in his lap.

"Lad," he said, softly, "the English hay smells sweet, but not so sweet as the Mohawk Valley hay to me. This is my country. I am too old to change where in my youth I took root among these hills. To transplant me means my end."

The sunlight stole into the room through leaded diamond-panes and fell across his knees like a golden robe. The music from the robins in the orchard filled my ears; soft winds stirred the lace on Sir William's cuffs and collarette.

Presently he roused, shaking the dream from his eyes.

"Come!" he said, in a voice that held new vigor. "Life has but one meaning—to go on, ever on, lad! 'Tis a long doze awaits us at the journey's end."

I bent and picked up the three belts, placing them on the table near him.

"Thank you, Michael," he said, heartily. "And I must say that in this matter of Cayuga, you have conducted admirably. Had you received the Cayuga with less welcome or more suspicion, or had you met him haughtily, I do not doubt that he would have made mischief for me among my Mohawks."

"He had war sticks painted red, in his pouch, sir," I replied.

"No doubt! No doubt! And a red war belt, too, belike! They were meant for my Mohawks had he met with a rebuff here. Oh, I know them, Michael, I know them. A painted war belt flung between that Cayuga and the sachems of my Mohawks would have set the whole Six Nations—save, perhaps,

SIR WILLIAM JOHNSON

the Oneidas—a-shining up rifle and hatchet for Cresap and his men!"

Sir William struck the mahogany table with clinched fist.

"Curse Cresap!" he barked. "That fatuous fool to go a-meddling with the Cayugas in their own lands, held by them in solemn covenant forever inviolate! What does the sorry ass want? A border war, with all this trouble betwixt King and colonies hatching?"

Sir William slapped the table again with the flat of his hand.

"Look, Michael. Should war come betwixt King and colonies, neither King nor colonies should forget that our frontiers are crowded with thousands of savages who, if adroitly treated, will remain neutral and inoffensive. Yet here is this madman Cresap turning the savages against the colonies by his crazy pranks on the Ohio!"

"But," said I, "in his blindness and folly, Colonel Cresap is throwing into our arms these very savages as allies!"

Sir William stopped short and stared at me with cold, steady eyes.

"Michael," said he, presently, "when this war comes—as surely it will come—choose which cause you will embrace, and then stand by it to the end. As for me, I cannot believe that God would let me live to see such a war; that He would leave me to choose between the King who has honored me and mine own people in this dear land of mine!"

He raised his head and passed one hand over his eyes.

"But should He in His wisdom demand that I choose—and if the sorrow kills me not—then, when the time comes, I shall choose."

"Which way, sir?" I said, in a sort of gasp.

But he only answered, "Wait!"

Stupefied, I watched him. It had never entered my head that there could be any course save unquestioned loyalty to the King in all things.

Feeling as though the bottom had fallen out of something, I sat there, my fascinated eyes never leaving Sir William's somber face.

What, then, were these tea-hating rebels that Sir William should defend them at breakfast and in the faces of half a dozen of His Majesty's officers? I knew little of the troubles in Massachusetts save that they concerned taxes, and I had little sympathy for people who made such an ado about a shilling or two.

Something of these thoughts may have been easily read in my face, for Sir William said, with some abruptness:

"It is not money; it is principle that men fight for."

I was startled, although Sir William sometimes had a way of rounding out my groping thoughts with sudden spoken words which made me fear him.

"Well, well," he said, laughing and rising to stretch his cramped limbs; "this is enough for one day, Michael. Let the morrow fret for itself, lad. Come, smile a bit! Nay, do not look so sober, Micky. Who knows what will come? Who knows—who knows?"

"I shall stand by you, sir, whatever comes," said I.

But Sir William only smiled, drawing me to him, one arm about me. He held me there for an instant; then released me.

"Get you gone, lad," he said, "out into the sunshine of the

day. It might be well if you would take Warlock for a gallop and get the tickle out of his heels."

Kind Sir William! Well he knew that nothing could give me more pleasure than to mount his great horse and gallop off in my new uniform.

Flushing, I uttered fervent stumbling thanks and ten minutes later was mounted on Warlock, who plunged and danced at the slap of my sword scabbard on his flanks, and well-nigh shook me from my boots.

"Spare spur, lad! Let him sniff the pistols!" called Sir William, who had come out to watch my start. "He will quiet when he smells the priming, Michael."

I drew one of my pistols from the holster and allowed Warlock to sniff it, which he did, arching his neck and pricking forward two wise ears. He satisfied himself that it was a real officer he bore and no lout pranked out to shame him before other horses; then we were off. For a brief pace of time I forgot all perplexing problems.

Yet I was to be challenged by still another vexing question on that very day.

Upon my return from my ride, Silver Heels waved to me from the garden, and I strolled out to join her there. She was seated on the stone bench near the beehives, and moved over very modestly to make room for me. Presently she spoke of my new honors, and there was neither malice nor teasing in her voice.

"I had not thought that you were so nearly a man to be appointed cornet of horse," said she.

"And you," said I, magnanimously, "are almost a woman." But I said it from courtesy, not because I believed it.

"Yes," she replied, indifferently, "maids may wed at sixteen years."

"Wed!" I repeated, laughing outright.

"Aye. Mother was a bride at sixteen."

I was silent in my effort to digest the idea. Silver Heels marry in another year! Absurd!

Not to rebuff her with scorn, I said: "Indeed, you are quite a woman. Perhaps in a year you will be one! Who knows?—for a year is such a long, long time, Silver Heels."

"It is a very long time," she admitted.

"And to love, one must be quite old," said I.

"Yes, that is true," she conceded, reluctantly, "but not always." After a silence she said, "Michael, I have a secret."

"Yes?" I returned, indifferently.

"Will you promise never, never to tell?" she asked.

Her earnestness piqued my curiosity, but I promised with a tolerant smile.

"Well, then," she said, lowering her voice, "I am sure that Mr. Butler is in love with me."

"Mr. Butler!" I cried out. "Why, he's an old man! Why, he's nearly thirty!"

Angry incredulity choked me, and I sat scowling at Silver Heels and striving to reconcile her serious mien with such a tomfool speech.

"If you shout my secret aloud," she said, "I shall tell you no more, Micky."

Again, troubled and astonished at her sincerity, I expressed my disbelief in a growl.

"He keeps me after school hours," she said, "and he certainly does conduct in most romantic manners, vowing he will wait for me, declaring that I must love him one day, that I am no longer a child, that he has adored me since I was but twelve."

"How long has this gone on?" I demanded.

"These three months," said Silver Heels, without embarrassment.

"And—and you never told me?"

She shook her head frankly.

"No, you were but a lad, and you could not understand such things."

For a moment I felt so small that I could have yelled aloud my vexation. What! I too young to be told the secrets of this chit of a child with her ridiculous airs and pretensions!

"But now that you are become a man," she continued, serenely, "I thought to tell you of this because it tries my patience, yet pleases me, too, sometimes."

Boiling with fury and humiliation, I gave her a piece of my mind. I said that Mr. Butler was a sneak, a bully, and an old fool in his dotage to make love to a baby.

She listened, frowning a little.

"He is not old," she said, firmly; "thirty years is but a youth's prime, which you will one day comprehend."

Such condescension well-nigh finished me. I could find neither tongue nor words to speak my passion.

"He is a gentleman of rank and station," she said, primly. "If he chooses to protest his solicitous regard for me, I can but courteously discourage him."

"You little prig!" I exclaimed, grinding my teeth. "I will teach this fellow Butler to abuse Sir William's confidence!"

"I have your promise not to reveal this," said Silver Heels, coolly.

I groaned; then remembering that Mr. Butler had partly promised me a meeting, I caught Silver Heels by both hands and looked at her earnestly.

"I also have a secret," said I. "Promise me silence, and you shall share it."

"I promise," she whispered.

Then I told her of my defiance, of the meeting Mr. Butler had half pledged me, and I swore to her that I would kill him, eye to eye and hilt to hilt, not alone for his contempt and insults to me, but for Sir William's honor and for the honor of my kinswoman, Felicity Warren.

"The beast!" I snarled. "That he should come a-suing you without a word to Sir William! Do gentlemen conduct in such a manner toward gentlewomen? Now hear me! Do you swear to me never to stay again after school, never to listen to another word from this sneaking fellow until you are sixteen, never to receive his addresses until Sir William speaks to you of him? Swear it! Or I will go straight to Mr. Butler and strike him in the face!"

"Micky, what are you saying? Sir William knows all this."

Taken aback, I dropped her hands, but in a moment seized them again.

"Swear!" I repeated, crushing her hands. "I don't care what Sir William says! Swear it!"

"I swear," she said, faintly. "You are hurting my fingers!"

I scarcely heard her, being occupied with my anger against Mr. Butler. And to think that Sir William approved of his suit!

Little by little, however, the hot anger cooled in my veins, leaving a refreshing youthful confidence that all would come right. And sitting there with Silver Heels, I confided to her that I too had been in love, that the object of my respectful passion was one Marie Livingston, who would undoubtedly be mine at some distant date. I then revealed my desire to see Silver Heels suitably plighted, drawing a pleasing portrait of an imaginary suitor who should fill all requirements.

To this she replied that she found a striking likeness between that portrait and her secret ideal, and that she should be very glad to encounter the portrait in the flesh.

It hurt me a little that she had not recognized in me many of the traits I had painted for her so carefully, and presently I disclosed myself as the mysterious original of the portrait.

"You!" she exclaimed. Then, not to hurt me, she said it was quite true that I did resemble her ideal, and only lacked years and titles and wealth and reputation to make me desirable for her.

"I believe, also," she said, "that Aunt Molly means that we marry. Betty says so, and she is wiser than a black cat."

"Well," said I, "we can't marry, can we, Silver Heels?"

"Why, no," she said, simply. "There's all those things you lack."

"And all those things you lack," said I, sharply. "Now, Marie Livingston ——"

"She is older than I!" cried Silver Heels.

"And those things I lack come with years!" I retorted.

"That is true," she answered.

"Suppose you wait for me?" I proposed. "If I wed not Marie Livingston, I will wed you, Silver Heels."

I meant to be generous, but she grew very angry and vowed she would rather wed one of the gillies than me.

"I don't care a fig," said I. "I only meant you to be suitably wed one day, and was even willing to do so myself to save you from Captain Butler."

"A sorry match, *pardieu!*" she snapped, and fell a-laughing. "Michael, I will warn you now that I mean to wed a gentleman of rank and wealth, and wear jewels that will blind you! And I shall wed a gallant gentleman of years, Michael, and scarred with battles, and I shall be 'my lady!'—mark me! Michael, and shall be well patched and powdered as befits my rank! I shall strive to be very kind to you, Michael."

Her cheeks were aflame, her eyes daring and bright. She rose, picked up her skirt, and mocked me in a curtsy, then marched off, nose in the wind, to join Sir William, who was just entering the garden.

I sulkily watched her go. The absurd child! Giving herself such airs of maturity! I wished she could know how fully Sir William had taken me into his confidence—how completely he reckoned me a man among men.

CHAPTER FIVE

I T WAS not yet dawn as Sir William and I set off for the
Cayuga's lodge, which stood beyond the town on a rocky
knoll, partly cleared of trees.

The stars lighted us through the streets of Johnstown. Then
the town sank below us as we climbed toward Quider's lodge,
knee-deep in dewy thistles.

The spark of a tiny council fire guided us. Coming nearer,
we smelled black birch burning, and we saw the long thread
of aromatic smoke mounting steadily to the paling stars.

We passed a young basswood tree from which hung a flint,
symbol of the Mohawks. From another chestnut sapling dan-

gled the symbol of the Cayugas, a pipe. All at once we saw Quider, standing motionless before his lodge.

Sir William drew flint and tinder from his pouch, and sent a spark flying into the dry tobacco of his pipe. He drew it to a long glow, twice, and passed it to Quider.

I saw the Cayuga's face then. It was a strange red; yet it was not painted. He seemed ill; his eyes glittered like the eyes of a lynx.

And now, as the Indian sank down into his blanket before the fire, Sir William produced a belt from the folds of his cloak and held it out. The belt was black, with two figures woven in white on it. The hands of the figures were clasped together. It was a chain belt.

"*Brother*," he said, slowly: "The clouds which hang over us prevent us from seeing the sun. It is, therefore, our business, with this belt, to clear the sky.

(Gives the belt)

"*Brother*: We have heard what you have said about Colonel Cresap; we believe he has been misled, and we have rekindled the council fire at Johnstown with embers from Onondaga, with embers from the Ohio, with coals from our proper fireplace at Mountain Johnson.

"We uncover these fires to summon our wisest men so that they shall judge what word shall be sent to Colonel Cresap, to secure you in your treaty rights which I have sworn to protect by these strings!"

(A bunch of strings)

"*Brother*: By this third and last belt I send peace and love to my brethren of the Cayuga; and by this belt I bid them be

WE SAW QUIDER STANDING MOTIONLESS BEFORE HIS LODGE

patient, and remember that I have never broken my word to those within the Long House, nor yet to those who dwell without the doors."

(A large black belt of seven rows)

Then Sir William drew from his girdle a belt of wampum, so white that in the starlight it shimmered like virgin silver.

"Who mourns?" asked Sir William, gently, and the Indian rose and answered: "We mourn—we of the Cayuga—we of the three clans."

"What clans shall be raised up?" asked Sir William.

"Three clans lie stricken—the Wolf, the Plover, the Eel. Who shall raise them?"

"Brother," said Sir William, gravely: "With this belt I raise three clans; I cleanse their eyes, their ears, their mouths, their bodies with clean water. With this belt I clear their path so that no longer shall the dead stand in your way or in ours."

(The belt)

"Brother: With these strings I raise up your head and beg you will no longer sorrow."

(Three strings)

"Brother: With this belt I cover the graves."

(A great white belt)

In the dead stillness that followed the northern hilltops slowly turned to pink and ashes. The day had dawned.

When again we reached the village, cocks were crowing in

every yard; the painted weather-vanes glowed in the sun; legions of birds sang.

We passed through the cold shadowy street and out into the sun-warmed road again, and came at last to the Hall.

All that day Sir William sat in his library, writing, with Mr. Butler; so there was no school, and Peter, Esk, Silver Heels, and I went a-fishing in the river.

That day was the last of the old days for us. But how could we suspect that, as we waded in the shallows there, laughing, chattering, splashing one another, and then climbing out on the banks at times to lie deep in the daisies?

We played all our old games again. I whittled whistles for Peter and Esk; I skipped flat stones; I colored Silver Heels' toes yellow with dandelion juice so she should ever afterward wade in gold—this at her own desire.

The late sun settled in the blue ashes of the western forests as we pulled on our stockings and moccasins and gathered up our strings of silvery fish.

For a whole day I had carefully forgotten that I was anything but a comrade to these children; but I did not know how wise I had been to lay by, in my memory, one more perfect day ere the evil days came and the years drew nigh wherein, God wot! I found no pleasure.

As we came home through the orchard I saw Sir William sitting wearily on the stone seat near the beehives.

He heard us, and turned his head to smile a welcome. But there was that in his eyes which told me to stay there with him after the others had trooped in to be fed, and I waited.

Presently he said: "Quider is sick. Did you discover anything in his face that might betoken—a—fever?"

"His eyes," I said.

"Was he blotched? My sight is dim these years."

"His face was over-red," I answered, wondering.

Sir William said nothing more. After a little while he rose, leaning on his cane, and I passed heavily under the fruit trees toward the house.

That night came our doctor, Pierson, galloping from the village with an urgent message for Sir William. Later I saw soldiers set out with bayonets on their muskets, and with them the doctor, leading his horse.

In the morning we knew that the smallpox had seized the Cayuga, and that our soldiers patrolled Quider's lodge to warn all men of the black pest.

The days that followed were busy days for us all—days fraught with bustle and perplexity.

All Sir William's hopes of averting war were now centered in the stricken Cayuga. Rambling by starlight, he and I watched the candle burning in Quider's lodge door as though it were the flame of life, now flaring, now sinking in its socket.

On such rambles he seldom spoke, but sometimes he leaned on my shoulder, and his very hand seemed burdened with the weight of his cares.

Once, however, when from the sentinels we learned that Quider might live, Sir William appeared almost gay, and we walked to a little hill, all silvery in the light of the young moon, and rested on a rock.

"Black Care rides behind the horseman, but—I have dismounted," he said, lightly. "Quider will live, I warrant you, barring those arrows of outrageous fortune of which you have doubtless heard, Michael."

"What may those same arrows be marked with?" I asked, innocently.

"With the totem of Kismet, my boy."

I did not know that totem, and said so, whereupon he fell a-laughing and demanded, "Michael, what will the world outside think of one like you?"

"I shall say to the world I come from Ko-lan-e-ka, and that I am kin to you, sir," said I.

"The world will say, 'He comes from Da-o-sa-no-geh, the place without a name; let him return to The-ya-o-guin, the Gray-haired, who sent him out so ignorant.' "

"Do you say that, sir, because I am ignorant of the poets?" I asked.

"Even women know the poets in these days," he said, smiling. "You would not wish to know less than your own wife, would you?"

"My wife!" I exclaimed, scornfully.

"Why, yes!" said Sir William, much amused. "You will marry one day, I suppose."

After a moment I asked:

"Is Silver Heels going to marry Mr. Butler?"

"I hope so," replied Sir William, a little surprised. "Mr. Butler is a gentleman of culture and wealth. Felicity has no large dower, and I can leave but little if I provide for all my children. I deem it most fortunate that Captain Butler has spoken to me."

"If," said I, slowly, "Silver Heels and I are obliged to marry somebody, why can we not marry each other?"

Sir William stared at me.

"Are you in love with Felicity?" he asked.

"Oh no, sir!" I cried, resentfully.

"Is she—does she fancy she is in love with you?" insisted Sir William, in growing astonishment.

"No! no!" I said, hastily, for his question annoyed and irritated me. "But I only don't want hèr to marry Mr. Butler; I'd even be willing to marry her myself, though I once saw a maid in Albany ——"

"What the devil is all this nonsense?" cried Sir William, testily. "What d'ye mean by this idiot's babble? Eh?"

The expression of my face at this outburst first disconcerted, then sent him into a roar of laughter. Such startled and injured innocence softened his impatience; he carefully explained to me that, as Felicity had no fortune, and I barely sufficient to sustain me, such a match could but prove a sorry one for Silver Heels and for me.

"If you were older," he said, "and if you loved each other, I should, perhaps, be weak enough not to interfere. But it is best that Felicity should wed Mr. Butler, and that as soon as may be, for I am growing old very fast. This I say to you, Michael; but you must never hint to others that I complain of age or feebleness. Do you understand?"

"Yes, sir," I answered, soberly.

"Besides," said Sir William, with a forced smile, "I have much to do yet; I mean to accomplish a deal of labor before I—well, before many weeks. Come, lad, we must not grope out here seeking unhappiness under these pretty stars. We are much to each other; we shall be much more—eh? Come, then; Quider will live, spite of those same slings and arrows of which you know not the totem marks."

So we went home, comforted and hopeful; but the morrow

brought gravest tidings from Quider's lodge, for the Cayuga had fallen a-raving in his fever, and it was necessary to tie him down lest he break away.

Weighed down with anxiety concerning what Colonel Cresap might be doing on the Ohio, dreading an outbreak that must surely come if the Cayuga belts remained unanswered, Sir William, in his sore perplexity, turned once more to me and opened his brave heart.

"I know not what intrigues may be afoot. But I know this, that should Cresap's colonials in their blindness attack my Cayugas, a thousand hatchets will sparkle in these hills, and the people of the Long House will never sit idle when these colonies and England draw the sword!"

Again that cold, despairing amazement crept into my heart, for I could no longer misunderstand Sir William that his sympathies were not with our King, but with the provinces.

"I cannot understand, sir," I broke out, "why we should warn Colonel Cresap. Is it loyalty for us to do so?"

Sir William turned his sunken eyes on me.

"It is loyalty to God," he said.

The solemn peace in his eyes awed me; the ravage that care had left in his visage frightened me.

He spoke again:

"I may have to answer to Him soon, my boy. I have searched my heart; there is no dishonor in it."

And so it went on, Sir William and I walking sometimes alone together on the hillsides, speaking soberly of that future which concerned our land and kin, I listening in silence with apprehension ever growing.

Yet always his love and confidence made me proud. Was I

not the only person in the world who knew his sentiments and his desire to stop Colonel Cresap on the Ohio, lest, in ignorance, he should turn the entire Six Nations against the colonies?

Had he not told me, sadly, that he could not speak of this plan even to his own son, Sir John Johnson, lest his son, placing loyalty to the King before obedience to his father, should thwart Sir William, and even aid Colonel Cresap to anger the Cayugas?

He told me, too, that he could not confide in Mr. Butler or in his father, Colonel John Butler; neither dared he trust his sons-in-law, Colonel Claus or Colonel Guy Johnson, although they served as his deputies in Indian affairs.

All of these gentlemen were, first of all, loyal to our King, and none of them would raise a finger to prevent Colonel Cresap from driving the Six Nations as allies into the King's arms.

"What I am striving for," said Sir William to me, again and again, "is to so conduct that these Indians on our frontiers shall take neither one side nor the other, but remain passive while the storm rages. To work openly for this is not possible. If it were possible to work openly, and if Quider should die, I would send such a message to my Lord Dunmore of Virginia as would make his bloodless ears burn! And they may burn yet!"

At my expression of horrified surprise Sir William hesitated, then struck his fist into the open palm of his left hand.

"Why should you not know it?" he cried. "You are the only one of all I can trust!"

He paused, eyeing me intently.

"Can I not trust you, dear lad?" he said, gently.

"Yes, sir," I cried, in an overwhelming rush of pity and love. "You are first in my heart, sir—and then the King."

Sir William smiled and thought awhile. Then he continued: "You are to know, Michael, that Lord Dunmore, governor of Virginia, is, in my opinion, at the bottom of this. He it is who has sent the deluded Cresap to pick a quarrel with my Cayugas, knowing that he is making future allies for England. It is vile! It is a monstrous thing! It is not loyalty; it is treason!"

He struck his pinched forehead and strode up and down.

"Can Dunmore know what he is doing? God! The horror of it!—the horror of border war! Has Dunmore ever seen how savages fight? Has he seen raw scalps ripped from babies? Has he seen naked prisoners writhing at the stake, drenched in blood, eyeless sockets raised to the skies?"

He stood still in the middle of the room. There was a sweat on his cheekbones.

"If we must fight, let us fight like men," he muttered, "without fear or favor, without treachery! But, Michael, woe to the side that calls on these savages for aid! Woe to them! Woe! Woe!"

This outburst left me stunned. Save for Sir William, I knew not where now to anchor my faith.

LORD DUNMORE

CHAPTER SIX

NOW the dark pages turning in the book of fate were
flying fast. First to the Hall came Joseph Brant, called
Thayendanegea, brother to Mistress Molly, and embraced
us all. He was a frank, affectionate youth, though a blooded
Mohawk.

Clothed like an English gentleman, bearing himself like a
baronet, he conducted to the admiration and respect of all,
and this though he was the great war chief of the Mohawks,
and already an honored leader in the council of the Six
Nations.

I noticed, however, that though Sir William had hitherto

trusted Brant in all things, he spoke not to him of Quider's mission.

That week there were three council fires at the Lower Castle, which Brant and Mr. Butler attended in company with a certain thin little Seneca chief called Red Jacket, a filthy, sly, and sullen creature, who was, perhaps, a great orator, but all the world knew him for a glutton and a coward.

Our house had now been thronged with Indians for a week. Eleven hundred Mohawks, Cayugas, Senecas, Onondagas, and a few Tuscaroras lay encamped around us. Suddenly Sir John Johnson arrived at the Hall, and with him Colonel Daniel Claus and his lady from Albany. There, day by day, new guests arrived. Johnson Hall, Colonel Guy Johnson's house, and the house of Colonel John Butler were soon crowded to over-flowing. Sachems and chiefs of the Oneidas arrived, officers from the Royal Americans and from the three regiments of Militia which Tryon County maintained, officers from my own troop of irregular horse quartered at Albany, and finally, in prodigious state, came our Governor Tryon from New York, with a troop of horse.

The house rang with laughter and the tinkle of glasses from morning until night; on the stairs there swept a continuous rush and rustle of ladies' petticoats. There were maids and lackeys and footmen and chair-bearers and slaves thronging porch and hallway.

As by a magic touch the old homely life had vanished.

And now, piling confusion on confusion, comes from the south my Lord Dunmore from Virginia, satin-coated, foppish, all powder and frill, and scented like a French lady. But, oh, the gallant company he brought to Johnson Hall—those courtly Virginians with their low bows and noiseless movements, elegant as panthers, suave as Jesuits, and proud as heirs to kingdoms all.

For two days, however, I saw little of the company, for by Sir William's orders I lodged at the blockhouse with Mr. Duncan, keeping an eye on the pest-hut where lay the stricken Cayuga, barely alive.

As for Silver Heels, I saw her but twice, and then she disappeared entirely. I was sorry for her, believing she had been cooped within the limits of nursery and play-room; but I had my pity for my pains, as it turned out.

It came about in this way: I had been relieved of duties at the blockhouse and ordered to dress in my new uniform, to accompany Sir William to a review of our honest Tryon County militia, now assembling at Johnstown and Schenectady.

It was early morning, with the fields all dewy, when I left my chamber, booted, hair powdered in a club and tied with black, and my new silver gorget shining like the sun on my breast. I was in dress uniform, scarlet coat, buff smalls, sash and sword glittering, and I meant to cut a figure that day. But, Lord! Even on the staircase I found myself in a crowd of officers all laces and sashes and gold brocade, and buttons like yellow stars dancing on cuff and collar. My uniform was but a spark in the fire.

I made my way into the hall, but found it packed with ladies, all a-fanning and rustling, with maids tying on sunmasks and pinning plumes to rolls of hair that towered like the Adirondacks.

Hat under arm, hand on hilt, I did bow and smile and

thread my way through until I stood at last in the portico with the fresh wind in my face.

Then I perceived Sir William, attended by Sir John and Colonel Claus, inspecting the guard at the north blockhouse, and I made haste to join them, running fast, to the danger of my powdered hair, which scattered a small snowy cloud in the wind.

"Gad! The lad's powdered like a Virginian!" said Sir William, laughing. He dusted the powder from my shoulders and turned me around, muttering: "Gad! a proper officer! A well-groomed lad, eh, Jack?"

"Yes," said Sir John, indifferently. He gave me a damp finger to press; then his gaze wandered to the meadows below, where the brown-and-yellow uniforms of Colonel Butler's militia regiment spread out like furrows of autumn leaves.

I paid my respects to Colonel Claus, who honored me with a careless nod, and passed before me to greet Colonel John Butler and his son, Captain Walter Butler.

I stood behind Sir William, observing the officers as they came up to join the staff and stand and watch the two remaining regiments marching into the meadow below.

They had built a gayly painted wooden pavilion in the meadow for the ladies and Governor Tryon and my Lord Dunmore, and now came the coaches and calashes burdened with beauty, and the Virginians, all ahorse, caracoling beside the vehicles, a brave, bright company, by Heaven!

Behind us the grooms were bringing up our mounts, and I slyly looked for Warlock, doubting lest he be 'portioned to some horseless guest. But there the dear fellow stood, ears pointed straight at me, and snorting for the caress of my hand on his muzzle.

"Mount, gentlemen!" said Sir William, briskly, setting toe to the stirrup held by a gillie; and up into our saddles we popped.

As we entered the meadow at a trot I caught a quick picture of the pavilion with its flags, its rows of ladies unmasking, fluttering gay kerchiefs and fans and scarfs; and my Lord Dunmore, all over gold and blue, blinking like a cat in the sun. This I saw clearly, but as we broke into a gallop across the clover the colors there on the pavilion ran like tinted fires; yet it seemed, as I flew past, that I had seen a face up there which I knew well yet did not know. Surely it was not Silver Heels.

But there was no time for speculation now. Rub-a-dub-dub! Bang! Bang! Our brigade band was marching past, with our head groom playing a French horn very badly, and old Norman McLeod a-fifing it, wrong foot foremost. Sir William cursed under his breath and rubbed his nose in mortification.

"Hayfoot! Strawfoot!" simpered a cornet of dragoons behind me, and I turned on him and gave him a look.

"Did you say you were hungry?" I whispered, backing my horse gently against his.

"Hungry?" he stammered.

"You mentioned hay, sir," I said, fiercely.

He turned red as a pippin but did not reply.

Swallowing my anger and my shame for our militia yokels, I glared at the head of Colonel Butler's regiment, now passing, and was comforted, for the clodhoppers marched like regulars with a solid double rank of fifers shrilling out "Down, Derry, Down!" as smart as you please.

After them came a regiment of green-coated varlets. Then followed our three companies of Royal Americans. And after them marched a regiment in yellow and red.

There was a sham battle of the troops; and all in all, it was a fine pageant, and pleased everyone. I was sorry when the last cartridge was spent and the brigade band played, "God Save the King."

We followed Sir William to the pavilion, dismounting there to ascend the stairs and pay our respects to the Governor and to Lord Dunmore.

"Come with me, Michael," said Sir William, and I followed the baronet into the inclosure.

Lord Dunmore was tricked out like a painted actor, neither old nor young, but too white and pink and without any red blood in him, as far as I could see. His fingers were like white bird's claws loaded with jewels.

When he saw Sir William he fell a-tapping his snuff-box and bobbing and smiling.

"Lud! Lud!" he said, a-simpering. "Lud! Lud! Sir William! A gallant *fête*! A brave *defilé*! Militia, not regulars, you say! *Vive Dieu*, Sir William, a most creditable entraining!"

"My aide-de-camp, Lord Dunmore," said Sir William, bluntly. "Your Lordship will remember Captain Cardigan who died before Quebec? His son, my Lord!—and my dear kinsman, Michael Cardigan, cornet in the Borderers."

"Strike me!" simpered Lord Dunmore. "Strike me, now, Sir William! He has his father's eyes—*vrai Dieu*! Curse me if he has not his father's eyes, Sir William!"

At this remarkable discovery I bowed and said it was an honor to be considered like my father in any particular.

SHE WAS VERY DELICATE AND PRETTY IN
HER POWDER AND PATCHES

"Burn me!" murmured his Lordship. "Burn me, Sir William, what a wit he has, now!" And he peeped at me, squeezing his eyes into two weak slits.

Apparently surfeited with admiration, he invited Sir William to take snuff with him; then turning to Governor Tryon, who had just come into the stall, he fell to smirking and exclaiming and vaporing until I, weary and cloyed, turned my attention to the crowd.

But soon a deep, pleasant voice sounded close beside me, and looking around, I saw our Governor Tryon smiling at me.

"I knew your father," he said. "It is a privilege, Mr. Cardigan, to address the son of so gallant a gentleman."

I replied warmly and gratefully, yet with military deference, and I saw Sir William observing me, well pleased at my bearing.

"In these times," said the governor, "it is a pleasure to meet with modest loyalty in the younger generation. Loyal to parent, loyal to King! I predict we shall hear from you, Mr. Cardigan."

"Please God, sir," I replied, blushing scarlet, for into my mind crept that wavering doubt which, since Sir William had talked with me, haunted me like a shadow.

The governor passed by with his clanking dragoons, among them the young jackanapes who had presumed to sneer at our yeomanry, and we delivered a pair of scornful glances at each other.

And now my Lord Dunmore's boudoir on wheels drove up, and his purring lordship minced off in the midst of his flame-colored Virginians.

The ladies were rising, tying on sunmasks, and one lady there was, in a mask and silvery cloak, who looked at me so long through the eye-holes that I felt my heart begin a-beating. Another, in mask and rose mantle, lifted the linen a trifle, displaying a fresh, sweet, smiling mouth. This one in rose turned twice to look at me, and it amused me to feel my heart go a-bumping at my ribs so loud, for she did truly resemble Marie Livingston.

Sir William and Colonel Claus had joined Lord Dunmore in his coach. I rode back to the Hall with a company of Virginians and dragoons.

Coming to the Hall, I met Sir William, whose smiling face grew haggard at sight of me, and he drew me apart, asking of news from Quider.

"He still lives, sir," I replied, my heart aching for Sir William.

For a moment he stood staring at the ground; then, bidding me report to Mr. Duncan at the blockhouse, he walked away to disguise his anxious visage again with the oldest mask in the world—a smile.

That night Sir William provided two great banquets for our guests, one at the courthouse in Johnstown, the other at Johnston Hall.

The splendid banquet at the courthouse was given to all the visiting officers except Lord Dunmore, Governor Tryon, and their particular aides.

Colonel Claus and his lady presided as host and hostess, representing Sir William and Mistress Molly.

The other banquet was given at the same hour in our house, to honor Lord Dunmore and Governor Tryon.

There were gathered in the hallway and on the stairs a vast company of ladies and gentlemen when I came down from my little chamber to wait on Sir William. Here was the great Earl of Dunmore in a ring of fluttering ladies, and there was our Governor Tryon in purple silk from head to foot. There also was my kinsman, Sir John Johnson, with his ungracious carriage, and old Colonel Butler with his eyes of a hawk. I caught sight, too, of my impudent dragoon lad who had offended at the pavilion, and I will not deny he appeared to be an elegant and handsome officer.

Making my way carefully amid rustling petticoats and a forest of waving fans, I passed Mistress Molly on the arm of Sir William, touching my lips to her pretty fingers, which she held out to me behind her back.

People passed me and repassed with laughter and whisper, and the scented wind from their fans swept my cheek.

Suddenly it seemed as though the voice of Silver Heels sounded in my ears. Turning, I saw that the voice came from a young girl standing behind me. She was very delicate and pretty in her powder and patches, with a pair of great hazel eyes like Silver Heels'. Certainly she had Silver Heels' voice, and her trick of widening her eyes, too, for now she perceived me, and ——

"Why, Micky!" she cried.

"Silver Heels!" I stammered, striving to believe my eyes.

I stared almost piteously at her, trying to find my own familiar comrade in this delicate stranger, smiling breathlessly at me with sparkling teeth set on the edge of her painted fan.

In her triumph she laughed that laugh of silver which sounded ever of woodlands and birds.

"Silly!" she whispered. "I told you so. And it has come true; my gown is silk, my stockings silk, my shoes are Paddington's make and silken to the soles!"

"How did you grow?" I gasped.

"Have I grown? Oh, my gown and shoes help. And see my egrets! Are they straight, Micky?"

Ere I could attempt to compose my thoughts, comes mincing my impudent dragoon, who seemed to know her, for he brought her a ribbon to tie above her elbow, explaining it was a new conceit from New York.

"It's this way," he explained, utterly ignoring my presence; "I tie this bow of blue above your elbow, so—with your gracious consent. Now for a partner to lead you to the table I seek some gentleman and tie a blue bow to his swordhilt."

"Pray tie it to Mr. Cardigan's," said Silver Heels, mischievously. "I have much to say to him for his peace of mind."

The dragoon and I regarded each other with menacing composure.

"To deprive you of such an honor, sir," said he, coolly, "I protest reduces me to despair; but the light blue bows have already been awarded, Mr. Cardigan."

Instinctively I glanced at his own swordhilt, and there fluttered a light-blue ribbon. At the same moment I perceived that Silver Heels had been perfectly aware of this.

Mortified as I was, and stinging under the dragoon's impudence, I controlled myself sufficiently to congratulate him and courteously deplore my own ill fortune.

"Let not your lady hear that!" said Silver Heels, with her fan hiding her lips. "How do you know, sir, which partner fate and Mr. Bevan may allot you?"

Mr. Bevan and I regarded each other in solemn hostility.

"May I have the honor of attaching this ribbon to your hilt, sir?" he asked, stiffly.

"You may, sir," said I, still more stiffly, "if it is necessary."

He tied a red bowknot to my hilt; we bowed to each other; then, with a smile for Silver Heels, he saluted us again and strolled off with his nose in the air and his hands full of ribbons of every hue—the fop!

"Who is that pitiful ass?" I said, turning to Silver Heels.

"Why, Michael!" she protested.

"Oh, if he's one of your friends, I ask indulgence," said I, mad enough to pluck the blue knot from her arm.

"Truly, Michael," she sniffed, "you are still very young."

She seated herself by the big clock; I sat beside her, sullenly, and glanced at her sideways. Her self-possession and obvious indifference to me completed my growing discomfort. I looked at her small, silk-covered toes pushing out under her petticoat.

"Is the dandelion juice on them yet?" I asked, with piteous playfulness.

"Don't talk like that!" she said, sharply, drawing her feet in. And with that petulant movement the playmate I had so often bullied slipped away from me forever, leaving in her place a dainty thing of airs and laces to flout me. At moments, as I sat there, I could have yelled aloud in my vexation.

Lord! how they all ogled her, gentlemen and ladies, old and young, and I heard whispers around me that she was a beauty and would be rich one day. My Lord Dunmore, too, came a-dancing pit-pat! till I thought to hear his bones creak inside his white silk.

I might have taken a pride in her had not all these bobbing pigeons come crowding about to share openly my unconfessed admiration. But they bowed and strutted and posed and flattered, pressing closer until she was shut from my sight by a circle of coat-skirts, tilted swords, and muscular calves in silken stockings.

Presently our fiddlers and bassoons started the "Huron";

there was a flutter to find ribbons that matched, and a world of bustle and laughter.

I had now been crowded up against our tall clock in the hall, and stood there striving to get a glimpse of Silver Heels, forgetting that somewhere in the crush a lady with a scarlet ribbon on her arm might be waiting for me. And doubtless I should have remained there, gnawing my lip, till doomsday, had not Silver Heels espied me and come fluttering through the crowd with:

"Oh, Micky! Have you seen your lady? Your old friend Marie Livingston! But she is wedded now; she is that pretty Mrs. Hamilton from Saint Sacrement. Oh, you lucky boy! All the officers are raving over her! But I asked her if she remembered you, and she said she didn't, so there!"

"Silver Heels," I began, with the first appealing glance I had ever bestowed on a woman—"Silver Heels, I want to tell you something."

But she cried: "You must not detain me, Michael. Mr. Bevan is waiting for me."

And with that she was gone into the whirl, leaving me high and dry against my clock, and furious over I knew not what. For truly I myself did not know what it was I had been about to say to Silver Heels. As for this Mrs. Hamilton, it madded me to hear of her. If Marie Livingston had wedded another, what cared I about her?

Mrs. Hamilton, forsooth! With that ape of a New-Yorker setting himself in my rightful place beside Silver Heels! And what stabbed deepest was that Silver Heels plainly preferred him to me—the ungrateful minx!

Sulking there under the tall clock, I happened to lift my

eyes and perceived on the stairs that same lady who had half raised her sunmask at the review—I mean the one in the rose mantle, not the other in the silvery cloak, whom I now knew had been Silver Heels.

Down the stairs rustled my lady of the rose mantle, and something in my memory stirred at sight of her smiling face.

Now she was looking straight at me, and I perceived that she wore my colors. Marie Livingston! I should never have known her; so we were quits, the affected minx! And this was Mrs. Hamilton!—this bright-eyed girl with her smooth rose-petal skin and her snowy hand on the balustrade. Could I be mistaken? Surely she wore my colors! I pressed through the throng to the stairway. Now at last I could pay Silver Heels in her own wampum, and I meant to do it under her very nose.

I met Mrs. Hamilton at the foot of the stairs, and made her a bow that I knew must be impressive. But she insisted on matching ribbons very carefully, thus hurting my pride somewhat. When she could no longer doubt that our ribbons matched, she made me a whimsical reverence, and took my arm with a smile, and a cool: "Oh, I faintly recall you now, Mr. Cardigan. How you have grown!"

Out into the wilderness of silver and candlelight we passed, stood behind our chairs while my Lord Dunmore chattered a blessing, and then seated ourselves amid a gale of whispers.

Through the flare of the candles I saw Brant and Sir John Johnson near us, and also that filthy Indian, Red Jacket, both hands already in a dish of jelly, a-gobbling and grunting to himself. Presently I perceived Silver Heels and Mr. Bevan, nearly opposite to us, and strove to catch her eye. But Silver Heels took small notice of me; she sat there smiling and silent, head a little lowered, while that insufferable coxcomb whispered into her ear and smirked, till the very sight of the man sickened me.

Stung to the quick by her indifference to my presence, I resolved to show her that I cared not a whit for her or her dragoon. So I loosened my tongue and set it wagging so smartly that I think I astonished Mrs. Hamilton, who had been observing Mr. Bevan with her fixed smile. At any rate, she gave me a long, pleasant stare, and presently her fixed smile became very sweet and pretty, although I thought a trifle mocking.

"Is it not amusing?" she said, coolly. "Here you sit with me, when you would give your towhead to be prattling into Mistress Warren's ears; and here sit I at twiddle-thumbs, devising vengeance on Mr. Bevan, who belongs to me!"

Amazed, perplexed, and disconcerted, I blurted out, "I thought you had a husband."

She colored up like fire for a moment, but the next instant she was laughing at me as though I were a ninny.

"Please tell me your Christian name," she said, sweetly. "I really do desire to recall it."

"My name is Michael," said I, suspiciously.

"Was it not Saint Michael who so soundly spanked the devil?" she asked, with her innocent smile. "Truly, Mr. Cardigan, you were well named to chastise the wicked with such sturdy innocence!"

I fumed inwardly, for I had no mind to be considered a gaby among women.

"I am perfectly aware, madam, that it is the fashion for

charming women to turn boys' heads," said I, "and I wish you might turn Mr. Bevan's head till you twisted it off his neck!"

"I'd rather twist yours," she said.

"Twist it off?" I asked, curiously.

"I—I don't know. Look at me, Mr. Cardigan."

I met her pretty eyes.

"No, not quite off," she said, thoughtfully. "You are a nice boy, but not very bright. If you were you would pay me compliments instead of admonition. You might even make love to me."

"That would be a privilege," said I. "You are certainly the prettiest woman in Johnson Hall tonight, and if you've a mind for vengeance on your faithless dragoon yonder, pray take me for the instrument, Mrs. Hamilton."

"Hush!" she said, with a startled smile. "I may take you at your word."

"I am taking you at yours," said I, recklessly.

In the dull din of voices around us I heard Silver Heels' laugh, but the laugh was strained, and I knew she was looking at me and listening.

"I don't know what you mean," said Mrs. Hamilton, reddening, "but I know you to be a somewhat indiscreet young man who handles a woman as he would a club to beat his rival to the earth withal."

"I mean," said I, in a low voice, "to make love to you and so serve us both. Look at me, Mrs. Hamilton."

"I will not," she said, between her teeth.

"Tell me," I pleaded, "what is your Christian name? I do really wish to know, Mrs. Hamilton."

Spite of the angry red in her cheeks she laughed outright, glanced sideways at me, and laughed again.

"My name is Marie Hamilton, of Saint Sacrement, please you, kind sir," she lisped, with an affected simper that set us a-laughing together.

"If you ever had your heart stormed you had best prepare for no quarter now!" I said, coolly.

"Insolent!" she murmured, covering her bright cheeks with her hands and giving me a glance in which amusement, contempt, curiosity, and invitation were not inharmoniously blended.

So amid the low tumult, the laughter, and the crystal tinkle of silver and glass, I made reckless love to Mistress Marie Hamilton, charging the citadel of her heart with insincere and gay abandon.

"In what school have you been taught to make love, sir?" she said, at last, breathless, amused, yet exasperated.

"In the school of necessity, madam," I replied.

"I pray you teach something of your art to Mr. Bevan," said she, spitefully.

"I am teaching him now," said I.

It was true. The dragoon was staring at Mrs. Hamilton in undisguised displeasure. As for Silver Heels, she observed us with a scornful amazement that roused all the cruelty in me, though I knew I was losing her innocent belief in me and tearing my respectability to shreds under her clear gray eyes.

For a bud from Mrs. Hamilton's caushet I threw away the pure faith of my little comrade; for a touch of her hand I blighted her trust; and laughed as I did it.

Now the healths flew thick and fast from Sir William and

Lord Dunmore, the titled toastmasters, and we drank His Majesty George the Third in bumpers that set the Indians a-howling like timber wolves at Candlemas.

Toast followed toast in a tempest of cheers, through which the yelps of the Indians sounded faintly.

Mistress Molly we pledged with a shout, and she returned our courtesy with gentle gravity, but her eyes were for Sir William alone.

Then Lord Dunmore gave:

"Our lovely heiress, Mistress Warren!" ending in a drunken hiccough, and poor Silver Heels half rose from her seat as though to fly to Mistress Molly.

Red Jacket was on his feet now, very drunk, slavering and mouthing, and Brant and I dragged him out into the garden, where his squaw took charge, leading him lurching and howling down the hill. Before I returned, the ladies were in the hallway and the card-room, the gentlemen following in groups from the table.

But Sir William had disappeared, and I hunted vainly for him until I encountered Mrs. Hamilton, who directed me to the library, whither, she averred, Sir William, Governor Tryon, and Lord Dunmore had retired.

"State secrets, Master Michael," she added, saucily. "You had best find Mr. Bevan and start those same lessons we have discussed."

"Let me instruct him by proxy," said I, drawing her under the stairs, and ere she could protest or escape, I kissed her lips three separate times.

She was in tears in an instant, something I had not counted

on, and it needed my most earnest acting to subdue her indignation.

I had my arm around her, and my coat was all powder and rouge, when something made me look around. There was Silver Heels going toward the pantry with Betty, doubtless to pouch some sweets for her black nurse. Her head was steadily lowered, but face and neck were glowing, and I knew she had perceived us, and that she despised us with all the strength of her innocent soul.

Stunned with the conviction that I had gone too far, I made out to play my miserable farce to an end and led Mrs. Hamilton out where Mr. Bevan could pounce upon her—as he did with an insolence that I had little spirit to resent.

Then I hastened to the pantry where Silver Heels stood before the rifled dishes, hands to her face, and black Betty a-petting her. But at sight of me she turned scarlet and shrank back, nor would she listen to one word.

"What yoh done to mah li'l' Miss Honeybee?" exclaimed Betty, wrathfully. "I done 'spec' yoh, Mars Ca'digan, suh! Yaas, I 'spec' yoh is lak all de young gemmen!"

Then the old witch began a-crooning: "Doan yoh cyah, li'l' Miss Honeybee, doan yoh mind nuff'n! Huh! Had mah s'picions 'bout dat young Mars Ca'digan. Doan yoh mind him no moh'n a blue-tail fly!"

"Very well," said I, angrily, "you may do as you choose and think what you like. As for your fool of a dragoon, Mrs. Hamilton will settle him, and if she doesn't I will."

My foolish outburst seemed to rouse a panther in Silver Heels, and for a moment I believed she meant to strike me. But the storm swept over, leaving her with eyes wet.

"You have spoiled my first pleasure," she said, in a low, trembling voice. "You have conducted like a clown and all beheld you making shameful love to Mrs. Hamilton! Oh, Betty, Betty, send him away!" she sobbed.

"Silver Heels," I said, choking, "can you not understand that it is I who wish to wed you?"

Again the panther blazed in her gray eyes, but her lips were bloodless as she gasped: "Oh, the insult! Betty—do you hear? He would marry me out of pity! That is twice he has said it!"

"I said it before because I would not have you marry Mr. Butler," said I, wincing. "But I say it now because—because— I love you, Silver Heels."

All her hot scorn of me was in her eyes. I saw it and set my teeth hard, hopeless now forever, even of her careless affection.

And so I left her there, with Betty's arms around her. But as I went away, chilled with self-contempt and mortification, heedless, utterly careless what I did to degrade myself further in her eyes, came black Betty a-waddling to pluck me by the sleeve and whisper:

"Doan yoh go to wed wif nobody, Mars Ca'digan, suh! Doan yoh go foh to co't nobody. Mah li'l' Miss Honeybee ain't done growed up yet, suh. Bime-by she'll know moh'n she 'spec's 'bout gemmens, suh."

But my evil nature was uppermost, and I laughed and bade Betty mind her own affairs, leaving her there grumbling and mumbling about "fool boys" and "li'l' fool Honeybees," till the clatter from the card-room shut her voice from my ear.

I TURNED AND RAN TOWARD THE MISTY WILDERNESS

CHAPTER SEVEN

WHEN I came to the library the door stood partly open, and I could see a party of gentlemen lounging within over their wine and filberts; so thinking no harm to enter, I walked in and sat down on the arm of a leather chair by the window.

Nobody had observed me, however, and I was on the point of respectfully making known my presence to Sir William, when I saw Walter Butler rise and shut the door. Turning to rejoin the company around the table, he saw me, and stood still.

"Well?" inquired Sir William, testily, looking up at Mr. Butler. "When you are seated, sir, I will continue."

"If Mr. Cardigan has been here all this time, I, for one, was not aware of it," observed Mr. Butler, coldly.

I began to explain to Sir William that I had but that moment come in, when he interrupted, querulously.

"Tush! tush! Let be, let be, Captain Butler! My young kinsman has my confidence, and it is time he should know something of what passes in his own country."

"At eighteen," observed my Lord Dunmore, with a maudlin chuckle, "I knew a thing or two, I'll warrant you—curse me, if I didn't, Sir William!"

"Doubtless, my lord," said Sir William, dryly. "And now, gentlemen, concerning our show of force here, I have only to say—with all respect to Governor Tryon—that I do not believe it will produce that salutary effect on the discontented in New York and Boston which Governor Tryon expects."

"Gad! I do expect it!" said Tryon, briskly. "Look you, Sir William, you and your militia dominate the country, and these rascals must be brought to understand it. Trust me, the Yankees will know of this militia display before the post rides into Boston!"

"Add our Mohawks to the militia," observed Walter Butler, in a colorless voice.

Sir William's jaw was set hard, but he said nothing.

"Add the whole Six Nations," hiccoughed Lord Dunmore, leering at Sir William. "Come, now! curse me blind! but we shall have the whole Six Nations." And he winked his weak eyes at Walter Butler, a proceeding observed by me and by Sir William.

Not for a moment now did I doubt that Lord Dunmore had set Colonel Cresap to drive the Cayugas into a hatred for the colonies, nor did I doubt that Walter Butler knew all about this plan.

There came a brief silence, broken by the clear, sarcastic tones of Sir William.

"I beg permission to submit to Governor Tryon the opinion of a country baronet—for what that opinion may be worth."

"With pleasure," said Governor Tryon, cordially.

"And this is my opinion," continued Sir William, "that, firstly, the disaffected classes in Boston and New York will not care a fig for our show of militia; that, secondly, if they should once entertain a suspicion that England, in the event of war, proposes to employ savages as allies to subdue rebellion, we should have tomorrow the thirteen colonies swarming like thirteen hives to sting us all to death."

As he paused, Walter Butler spoke in his passionless voice:

"It is come to the point where either the rebels are to win over the Indians, or where we must take measures to secure their services. I beg Sir William to make it clear to us what chances we have to win the support of the Six Nations—in the event of a rebel rising against the King's authority."

The tangled knot was cut; the cat had sprung from the bag. Yet nobody by glance or word or gesture appeared to be aware of it.

Sir William's manner was perfectly composed as he spoke, eyes fixed on his wineglass.

"Captain Butler believes that it has come to this: that either those in authority or the disaffected must seek allies among these savage hordes along our frontiers. Gentlemen, I am not of that opinion. If war must come between England and these colonies, let it be a white man's war; in mercy, let it be a war between two civilized peoples, and not a butchery of demons!

"I do solemnly believe that it is possible to so conduct that these savages will remain neutral if war must come."

He lifted his eyes and looked straight at Lord Dunmore, raising his voice slightly but betraying no passion.

"And, gentlemen, as I am His Majesty's Intendant of Indian Affairs in North America, I shall now do all that I can to pacify my wards, to keep them calm and orderly in the event of war. Were I to do otherwise, I must account to my King for a trust betrayed, and I must answer also to Him whom King and subject alike account to."

On Walter Butler's lips a sneer twitched; my Lord Dunmore wiped his bleared eyes with a rag of lace and stared at everybody with drunken gravity.

"I know not," said Sir William, slowly, "what true loyalty may be if it be not to save the honor of our King. And if there are now those among his counselors who urge him to seek these savages as allies, I say it is a monstrous thing and an inspiration from hell itself."

He swung on his elbow and fixed his eyes on Walter Butler.

"You, sir, know something of border war. How, then, can you propose to let loose these Indians on the people of our colonies?"

"Lest they let loose these same savages on us," replied Mr. Butler, calmly.

Sir William frowned.

"You do not know the colonists, Mr. Butler," he said. "What marvel, then, that my Lord North should misunder-

stand them and think to buy their loyalty with tuppence worth
o' tea?"

"Come, come, Sir William!" cried Governor Tryon, laughing, and plainly anxious to break the tension. "Did I not know
you to the bone, sir, I should deem it my duty to catechize you
concerning the six articles of loyalty!"

"I, too, i' faith!" squeaked Lord Dunmore. "Skewer me!
Sir William, but you talk like a Boston preacher—aye—that
you do, and ——"

"Have done, sir!" cut in Sir William, with such bitter contempt that the faces of all present sobered quickly. But Lord
Dunmore only blinked stupidly and sucked his thin lips, too
drunk to understand how like a lackey he had been silenced.

Sir John Johnson and Colonel Claus exchanged puzzled
glances. But I noticed that Mr. Butler never took his eyes from
Sir William's darkening visage.

"There is one more matter," said the baronet, "that I may
be pardoned for introducing here; it is a matter touching on
my own stewardship, and as that concerns my King, I deem it
necessary to broach it."

He turned again deliberately on Lord Dunmore.

"It has come to my knowledge that certain unauthorized
people are tampering with a distant tribe of my Cayuga Indians. I know not what the motives of these men may be, but
I protest against it, and I shall do all in my power to protect
my Cayugas from unlawful aggression!"

"Damme!" gurgled Lord Dunmore. "Damme, Sir William,
d'ye mean to accuse me? Curse me! Skewer me! Claw me raw!
but it is not fair," he sniveled. "No, it is not fair! Take your
hands off my sleeve and be done a-twitching it, Captain But-

ler! Damme! I never set Cresap on. Will ye have done a-pinching my arm, Captain Butler?"

The ghastly humor of the exposure, the ludicrous self-conviction of his tipsy lordship—for nobody had mentioned Cresap—the startling disclosure, too, of Walter Butler's interest in the plot—for that it was a plot no longer could anybody doubt—cast a gloom over the company.

Then Sir William's sarcastic voice pierced the silence.

"I trust your lordship would not believe that any gentleman present could harbor suspicions of a foul conspiracy between your lordship and Captain Butler, to incite my Cayugas to attack white men!"

Walter Butler's slow eye rested on Lord Dunmore, on Sir William, and then on me. But his bloodless visage never changed.

"Gentlemen, gentlemen, let us have harmony here," protested Governor Tryon, half in jest, half in earnest. "Nobody believes that my Lord Dunmore is seeking trouble with your tame Indians, Sir William. If this fellow Cresap be imposing on the Cayugas, I doubt not that my Lord Dunmore will recall him and deal with him severely.

"No, I won't! Claw my vitals if I do!" snapped his lordship, in the drunken sulks, and straightway fell a-squabbling with Walter Butler, who had again laid a hand on his arm.

For Captain Butler knew his treachery had been discovered, and his shameless impudence in openly attempting to muzzle his noble partner in conspiracy passed all bounds of decency.

I saw the angry light glimmer in Sir William's eyes, and I knew it boded no good to Walter Butler as far as his hope of Silver Heels was concerned. A fierce happiness filled me. So now, at last, Sir William was discovering the fangs in his pet snake!

Lord Dunmore had succeeded in reversing a decanter of port over himself and Colonel Claus, and the latter, mad as a wet cat, left the room swearing audibly, while his playful lordship threw a few glasses after him and then collapsed in a soiled heap of silk and jewels.

Sir William was steadily staring at Walter Butler; I, too, had my eye on him. When he left the table to saunter toward the door, Sir William rose immediately to follow him, and I after Sir William.

He saw us coming as he opened the door, and surveyed us with cool effrontery as we joined him in the hallway.

"I shall not require your services hereafter as my secretary, Captain Butler," said Sir William. "Will you kindly hand your keys to me?"

"At your command, Sir William," replied Mr. Butler, drawing the keys from his pocket and presenting them with an ironical inclination.

"Mr. Butler," continued Sir William, with reddening face, "I consider myself released from my consent to your union with my kinswoman, Miss Warren!"

"As to that, sir," observed Captain Butler, cynically, "I shall take my chances."

I heard what he said, but Sir William misunderstood him.

"It is your mischance, sir, to put no harsher interpretation on it. But my decision is irrevocable, Mr. Butler, for I have destined Miss Warren to a loyal man, my kinsman, Michael Cardigan!"

"I'll take that chance, too," said Mr. Butler, bowing.

"What do you mean, sir?" demanded Sir William.

But Walter Butler only replied with such glare at me that Sir William involuntarily turned to find me, rigid, behind him. The next moment Captain Butler passed noiselessly out into the starlight, wrapping his black cloak around him.

Sir William followed him mechanically to the door, and I at his heels, burning for a quarrel with Walter Butler, and waiting only until Sir William should return to the library and leave me free to follow the treacherous villain.

But Sir William, seeing me slinking out, laid a hand on my shoulder and spun me sharply round on my heels to look into my eyes.

"Now what the devil are you up to?" he broke out, half divining the truth. "Michael! Michael! Don't be a fool! Are there not fools enough here tonight?"

"No, sir," I answered, sheepishly.

"That is not the way to serve me, lad," said Sir William, roughly. "Have I not sorrow enough without seeing you carried in here with a hole in your breast, you meddlesome ass?"

"I have a certain score to clean off," I muttered.

"Oh," observed Sir William, coldly, "a selfish quarrel—eh? I was a fond old fool to think I might count on you."

Tears started to my eyes; I could have bitten my tongue off.

"You can count on me, sir," I choked out. "I meant no harm. I am not selfish, sir; I care only for you."

"I know it, lad," he said, kindly. "And mind, I do not rebuke your spirit; I only ask you to learn discretion. This is no time to settle private matters. No man in America has that right now, because every man's life belongs to the country!"

"On which side, sir?" I faltered.

Sir William was silent for a while. Presently he took my arm and we walked out under the stars.

"My boy," he said, sadly, "I cannot decide for you. The decision must remain with yourself. But consider it well. Suppose, from a high motive of duty, you should suddenly resolve to embrace the cause of the plain people. Could you renounce your commission in the King's army to shoulder a firelock, perhaps a stable fork, in the ranks of your countrymen? Could you give up ease, hopes, position? Could you give up your friends and kinsmen? Could you give up what sum I shall leave you in my will? For Sir John would never let a penny of my money go to a rebel. Could you give up, if need be, the woman you loved? Think, and be not in haste to answer."

"Am I to decide tonight, sir?" I asked.

"God forbid!" he said, solemnly.

"I will say this," said I, "that where my heart is I would follow, in rags. And my heart is with you, sir."

He stood still, drawing me closer, but said nothing more, for there came running out of the darkness an officer with naked claymore shining in the starlight, and when he drew near we saw it was Mr. Duncan.

"The Indian is gone!" he panted. "Gone away crazed with fever! The doctor lies in the hut with a broken shoulder; Quider crushed it in his madness!"

Sir William swayed as though struck.

"The sentries chased him to the woods," continued poor Duncan, out of breath, "but he ran like a panther and—we had your orders not to fire. He will die, anyhow; the doctor says he will seek some creek or pond and die in the water like a poisoned rat. They are bringing the doctor now."

Up out of the shadow loomed two soldiers, forming a litter with their muskets, on which sat our doctor, Pierson, head hanging. And when Sir William came to him he looked up with a sick grimace and shook his head feebly.

"He broke those ropes as though they had been worsted," he said. "I tried to hold him down, but he had the strength of delirium, Sir William. I want that fat surgeon of the Royal Americans to set this bone," he added, weakly, and fell a-groaning.

Mr. Duncan started on a run for the barracks; the soldiers and the injured man passed on toward the guardhouse, and Sir William stood staring after them.

Presently he said, aloud, "God's will be done on my poor country!"

We walked back to the house together. Some of the guests were leaving, but the card-room was still crowded.

Sir William entered the hallway and looked around. In a corner of one window sat Mrs. Hamilton and Mr. Bevan, somewhat close together; in another window were gathered Colonel Claus and his lady and Sir John Johnson, whispering. Brant, surrounded by a bevy of fine ladies, was turning over the pages of a book and answering questions in polite monosyllables.

"And out of all my house," murmured Sir William, in a bitter voice, "not one whom I can trust—not one!—not one!"

After a moment I plucked at his sleeve reproachfully.

"Yes—I know—I know, my boy. But I need a man now—a man of experience, a man in bodily vigor, a man in devotion."

"You need a man to go to Colonel Cresap," I whispered.

For the first and only time in my life I saw that I had startled Sir William.

"Let me go, sir?" I entreated, eagerly. "If I am keen enough to read your purpose, I am not too stupid to carry it out. I know what you wish. I know you cannot trust your message to paper, nor to a living soul except me. I know what to say to Colonel Cresap. Let me serve you, sir, for I do long so to help you."

We had fallen back to the porch again while I was speaking, Sir William holding me so tightly by the elbow that his clutch numbed my arm.

"I cannot," he muttered. "Tomorrow Dunmore will set his spies to see that Cresap remains undisturbed. The Ohio trails will be watched for a messenger from me. Who knows what Dunmore's and Butler's men might do?"

"Dare they attack an officer in uniform?" I asked, astonished.

"What is there to prevent a shot in ambush? And are there no renegades in Johnstown to hire?" replied Sir William, bitterly. "Why, the town's full of them, lad; men as desperate as Jack Mount himself."

"But I know the woods! You, yourself, sir, say I am a very Mohawk in the woods!" I pleaded. "I fear no ambush though the highwayman Jack Mount himself were after me. Have I not been twice to the Virginia line with Brant? And remember I carry no papers to be stolen. I could first go with belts to the Cayugas, and tell the truth about Quider and his party. Then I would deliver the belts as you delivered them to Quider. Then I would find Cresap and show him what a fool he is."

"And so serve the enemies of the King?" said Sir William, looking keenly at me.

"And so serve you, sir," I retorted, in a flash. "Are you an enemy to the King?"

"But, my boy," said Sir William, huskily, "do you understand that you must go alone on this mission?"

I sprang forward and threw my arms around him with a hug like a young bear's.

"Then I'm going! I'm going!" I whispered, enchanted, while he murmured brokenly that he could not spare me and that I was all he had on earth.

But I would not be denied. I coaxed him to my little bedroom, lighted the candle, and made him sit down on my cot. Then I explained excitedly my purpose, and to prove that I knew the trails, I made a drawing for him, noting every ford and carrying-place, and I finally hazarded a guess as to the exact spot where Colonel Cresap might be found.

Also, in pantomime and whispers, I rehearsed the part I meant to play before the Cayugas, making the speeches that Sir William had made to Quider, as nearly as I could remember.

Together, then, we went over the trail, mile by mile, computing the circles I should be obliged to take to avoid the carrying-places, where spies were most to be feared.

"Dunmore rides south in a week," said Sir William. "But he will not wait till he reaches Virginia before he sends out his emissaries to urge Cresap on. You must beat them, lad, and go afoot at that."

"I can go the faster," said I. "Horses are useless in the Pennsylvania bush until you reach Crown Gap."

And so we sat there together on the bed, planning and suggesting precautions, till my candle sank into a lake of wax, trailing a long, flaring flame.

"There is one thing I have thought of," said I, soberly. "It is this: if I am going out as an enemy to the King, I cannot, for shame, aid me by wearing the King's uniform. Therefore, with your approval, sir, I will go in my buckskins, unless you believe that by this journey of mine I will benefit our King."

"Then," said Sir William, slowly, "you must go in your buckskins, lad."

The moment had come; I was face to face with it now.

"Am—am I to resign my commission in the Border Horse, sir?" I faltered.

Sir William considered me in silence, then broke out: "No, no! Not yet. Who knows but what this war may never break over us! No, no, my boy! Your errand is an errand of justice and mercy. I send you as my own messenger. It is my duty to protect my Cayugas, and it is yours to obey me. You may, for the present at least, retain your commission and your sword with honor. It is Dunmore and Butler we are fighting now, not our King."

"I shall go in my buckskins, anyhow," I said, cheerfully, and thankful that the evil moment had been put off—that evil moment which I now understood was surely coming for us both. He knew it, too; his face was gray and haggard.

As we sat there, my hand in his, staring at the phantoms of that ominous future, I heard Silver Heels come running up the stairs and stop at my door, calling out to Sir William.

When I opened the door she drew back scornfully, but,

catching a glimpse of Sir William within, she marched past me and perched herself on Sir William's knees, both arms around his neck.

What she whispered to him I could not hear, but he promptly shook his head in refusal, and presently it came out that she was teasing to be allowed to go with a certain fat dame, Lady Shelton, and make a month's stay with her at Pittsburg.

"I do so long to go," pleaded Silver Heels. "I have never been anywhere, you know. And we are to have such rare pleasures at the June running-races, with dancing every evening and a dinner given for me! Oh dear! I want to go so much! I truly do, sir, and I should be so happy and so thankful to you ——"

"In Heaven's name, stop your chatter, Felicity!" cried Sir William, striving to undo her arms from his neck, but she only kissed him and clung so tightly and reproachfully that he gave up in sheer fatigue.

"Oh, go, then! Go, you little witch! And mind you take Betty with you! And mind that Aunt Mary provides for you ere you go!"

Silver Heels embraced him rapturously with a little shout of delight, and sped away to the nursery without a glance at me. What did I care? I had begun to dislike her cordially; I could afford to, now that she in turn disliked Mr. Bevan.

I had also the savage satisfaction of remembering that she was free of Walter Butler forever, and I observed her departure grimly.

Presently Sir William rose and walked out into the hallway,

saying, with affected carelessness: "Then you will start before dawn, Michael?"

"Yes, sir," said I, cheerfully.

"I shall be in the library when you go. Stop there a moment."

His voice was quivering, but he did not flinch.

Back in my room, I lighted another candle and began making feverish preparations for departure. I gave little thought to Silver Heels. Excitement proved a lively antidote for sorrow.

Silver Heels? Silver Heels? What did I care now? Let her live to regret it all—after I had gone! I was off for glory and the green delight of the woodlands that I loved.

I made up my pack on the bed—a blanket, four pairs of Mohawk moccasins, a change of flannels, a spare shirt, and three pairs of knitted socks. Down in the storeroom I found cornmeal, salt, and pork, and tied each in its sack. Powder and ball were to be had in the guardhouse; so I ran across to the blockhouse for a supply. While I was there, I found Wraxall, our sottish Johnstown barber, still up, and had him shear off my queue and cut my hair *à la coureur-de-bois.*

Then I gathered up my ammunition and provisions and hastened back to the house. The place was dark save for a light in the library. I felt my way up the stairs and into my chamber, where I rolled my spare ammunition and provisions into my pack and buckled the load tightly.

Now, rapidly undressing, I donned a new hunting-shirt and leggings. Over my shoulders I slung powder-horn and bullet-pouch, slipped hatchet and hunting-knife into the clout pockets, and took my rifle from the corner. I lingered only to buckle my money-belt under my shirt, then hoisted my pack to my shoulders, blew out the candle, and stole into the hallway, trailing my rifle.

I crept down the stairs, went softly through the lower hall, through the card-room, and tapped at the library door. It was opened without a sound.

Sir William and I gazed silently at each other for a long time. I, for one, could not trust myself to speak. All the joy and exhilaration of adventure had suddenly left me; I felt the straps of my pack straining my shoulders, but the burden on my back was not so heavy as my heart's full load.

He seemed so old, so tired, so gray. Where was that ruddy glow, that full swell of muscle as he moved, that clear-eyed, full-fronted presence I knew so well? How old his hands appeared under the cuffs' limp lace! How old his careworn face, all in ashy seams! How old his slow eyes—how old, old, old!

Together, without a word, we passed through the dark house and out to the porch. Dawn silvered the east, but the moon in its first quarter lay afloat in the western clouds, and a few stars looked down through a sky caked with frosted fleece.

He embraced me in silence, holding me a long time to his breast; yet never a word was said, and never a sound fell on the night air save my desperate gulps to crush back the sob that strained in my throat.

Presently I was conscious that I left him and was running fast through the darkness, blind as a bat for the tears. When I finally halted and looked back, far away against the dawn I saw our house as a black mass, with a single candle twinkling in the basement. So I knew Sir William still kept his vigil in the library.

Dashing my sleeve across my eyes, I turned and ran on toward the misty wilderness. It was well that I could not know then how dark the days before me, or how bitter the conditions of my return to Johnson Hall.

A HUMAN HAND SHOT ABOVE THE RIVER BANK AND SEIZED
MY ANKLE

CHAPTER EIGHT

MY FIRST three weeks in the woods were weeks of
heaven. Never had I seen the forest so beautiful. Along
the stony beds of lost ravines I passed and saw the frosty
bowlders lie like silver mounds in the dawn, glimmering
through the steaming waters. I passed at eventide when the
sunset turned the cliffs to crumbling crags of gold, and I saw
massed mountain peaks reflected in pools where the shadows
of great fish moved like clouds.

I ate and drank and slept in the dim wood stillness undisturbed. And I lived well on that swift trail where the gray
grouse scuttled through the saplings, and in every mossy

streamlet the cold, dusky troutlings fought for the knot of scarlet yarn on my short hand line.

I had not met a soul on the trail, nor had I found any fresh signs save one, and that was the print of a white man's moccasin on the edge of a sandy strip near the headwaters of the Ohio, which is called the Alleghany, north of Fort Pitt.

This footmark disturbed me, although it was three days old and pointing north. But that signified nothing, for the man who made it had come in a canoe; yet I could find no sign that a canoe had been beached there, and it was clear that the man who left that mark was wading the river because he wished to leave no trail.

As I stole away from that footmark in the sand willows, I found myself priming my rifle and looking ever and anon behind me.

Early that morning I had approached, somewhat nearer than I meant to, the carrying-place on the Alleghany which lies directly in the Fort Pitt trail. Now, at midday, I found my pack very heavy and my shirt wet with exertion, but dared not halt until I had circled around that carrying-place. So I toiled on.

It was only when at last above the trees in the east I perceived the blue peak of a mountain that I knew I was safe enough; for the peak belonged to the Alleghany range, and I had steered a fine circle without losing a mile.

Nevertheless, I jogged on until I came to a thread of water curving through the moss. Here I knelt, let go my pack, and rolled over on the moss, dog tired.

But soon I roused myself to eat. For the first time since I had entered the wilderness I made no fire, but munched a cold breast of partridge and drove it into my stomach with bits of ash cake, drinking a mouthful between bites to moisten the dry cheer.

Now, as I sat there, a sudden instinct arose in me that I had been followed; nay, not so sudden, either, for the vague idea had been slowly taking shape since I had seen that sign in the river bed among the willows.

To be sure, the footprint had been three days old and it had pointed north. Yet, unconsciously, I rose, priming my rifle, and for a moment I stood there, ankle deep in moss. Then I lifted my pack and passed swiftly along the little brook towards the main trail. Presently I caught a glimpse of a shallow stream rushing noiselessly over a sand bottom, and on the other side of the stream I saw a notched tree, marking the Fort Pitt trail!

Now I deliberately made a string of plain foottracks along the sandy stream, pointing toward the shallowest spot. Here I forded and made more tracks; entering the Fort Pitt trail, I ran down this trail till I came to a brier, and on its thorns I left a few strings from my fringed hunting-shirt. Then I began to walk backward till I reached the spot where I had entered the trail from the sandy stream. I backed down this bank, forded the shallows, then waded upstream to my little thread of a brook, and up that brook till I found a great log choking it. And behind this log I squatted, panting, and astonished at my own performance.

But that feeling of being followed still haunted me. Rabbit-like, I huddled there. Nothing stirred as the long minutes passed while my eyes searched through a long vista where, across a sunny streak of water, the Fort Pitt trail ran southwest.

MY FIRST THREE WEEKS IN THE WOODS WERE WEEKS OF HEAVEN

The sun had spanned an hour's length on the blue dial of the sky; still nothing moved in the woods. Yet I sat on with my cheek on the cool moist log, my rifle in my lap, watching the trees along the Fort Pitt trail.

And as I watched, I saw a man come out on the sandy bank of the stream and kneel down where my tracks crossed to the water's edge.

Without a sound I sank down behind my log into a soft ball of buckskin.

The man was Walter Butler. I knew him, though he wore the shirt of a Mohawk and beaded leggings to the hips, and at that distance might easily have been taken for an Indian. He crouched there, examining my tracks for full a minute, then rose gracefully and followed, tracing them up to the Fort Pitt trail.

Here I saw two other men come swiftly through the trees to meet him. Then a canoe shot across my line of sight and stopped, held by the setting pole in midstream. It contained a white man, who leaned on the setting-pole, silently waiting.

The conference on the bank ended abruptly; I saw two of the men start south towards Fort Pitt, while Butler came hastily down to the water's edge and waded out to the canoe.

He took his place, the two setting-poles flashed in the sunshine, and the canoe shot out of sight.

My mind was working rapidly now. What did Captain Butler mean by following me? The answer came ere the question had been fully formed, and I knew he hated me and meant to kill me.

How he had learned of my mission, whether he had actually learned of it, or only suspected it from my disappearance, concerned me little. These things were certain; he was Lord Dunmore's emissary as I was the emissary of Sir William; he

HERE I SAW TWO OTHER MEN COME SWIFTLY THROUGH THE TREES

was bound for Cresap's camp as was I; and he intended to intercept me and kill me if that meant the winning of the race.

I must give up my visit to the Cayugas for the present. It was to be a race now to Cresap's camp.

For me, it would be a race under difficulties. Two of my enemies had gone by water and two by the Fort Pitt trail, and this threw me hopelessly into the wilderness without the ease of a trodden way.

Slowly I resumed my pack, reprimed my rifle, and turned my nose southward, bearing far enough west to keep out of earshot from the river and the trail.

At first I had looked upon Fort Pitt as a hospitable wayside refuge, marking nine-tenths of my journey toward Cresap's camp. But now I dared not present myself there, with Walter Butler hot on my trail, armed, doubtless, with some order of Lord Dunmore which might compel the officers at Fort Pitt to hand me over to Butler on his mere demand. For, although Fort Pitt was rightfully on Pennsylvania soil, it had long been claimed by Virginia, and it was a Virginia garrison that now held it.

I saw nothing for it but to push on through the gateway of the west, avoiding Butler's men as best I could, and seeking the silly, deluded Cresap under the very nose of my Lord Dunmore.

My progress was slow; at times I sank between tree roots, up to the thighs in moss; at times the flowering briers bade me tarry in their sharp, perfumed embrace. Now and then a wiry moose-bush snare enlaced my ankles and sent me sprawling, pack and all. Tired out before sunset, I knelt again, dropped my pack under a hemlock thicket, and crawled out on a heap of rocks that overhung a ravine.

A hundred feet below me the Alleghany flowed, a glassy stream tinted with gold, reflecting forest and cliff and a tiny triangle of cobalt sky.

How still it was below; how quiet the whole late afternoon world was.

Sprawling there on the warm rocks like a young panther in the sun, ears attuned to the faintest whisper of danger, I gnawed a strip of dried squirrel's flesh and sucked up the water from a dripping mossy cleft, sweet cheer to an empty belly.

What largely occupied my thoughts was how to obtain food when a single shot might bring Butler and his trackers hot on the scent. I looked down at the darkening river, where a wild mallard circled, and my mouth watered, for he was passing plump.

"If he be there in the morning," thought I, "perhaps I may risk a shot and take to my heels." For had I not thrown Butler and his crew from my trail as easily as I brush a bunch of deer flies from my hunting-shirt? Still, I knew he was no forest blunderer, this Butler man; and I did not mean to be over-confident.

And, Lord! how I hated him and wished him evil and black mischance. So, with thoughts of hatred and revenge, I saw the web of night settling over the world. Wrapped in my blanket, curled up in a bed of blueberry, I folded my hands over my body like a chipmunk and said a prayer. After that I reprimed my rifle, settled the stock in a crevice near my head, and lay down again. And all night long I lay on that borderland of sleep which men in danger dare not traverse lest a sound find them unready. Yet I rested and renewed my vigor.

Very early next morning, I brushed the dew from cap and blanket, primed my rifle afresh, and cautiously crawled to the cliff's brink.

Mist covered the river; I could not have seen a canoe had it been floating under my own crag; neither could I see my wild duck, though at times I heard his drowsy quack somewhere below, and the answering quack of his mate. Perhaps a whole flock had come in by night.

I had no mind to risk a shot, but I was fiercely hungry, and I meant to have a duck. So, shivering, I undressed and, stark naked, I picked my way down the cliff and slipped into the water like a mink. I swam without a splash, straight toward the quacking sound, seeing only blank fog, but meaning to seize the first duck by the legs if he were asleep or by his neck if he dived.

Soon all around me I felt the presence of live creatures stirring, and there began a peevish sound of half-awakened water-fowl, so that I knew I was near to a flock of them.

Suddenly, right in my face, a duck squawked and flapped; I grasped at the bird, but held only a fistful o' feathers. In an instant the mist around me rang with strong wings beating the water, and with a whistling roar the flock drove past, dashing me with spray till I, smothered and choked, flung up my arm toward a floating tree trunk. To my horror the log rolled completely over, and out of it two men fell, shrieking, on top of me, for the log I had grasped was a bark canoe, and I had spilled out my enemies on my own head.

We all went down, but I sank clear of the unseen men and rose again to swim for my life. They came to the surface behind me, and began shouting, evidently to others on the opposite bank. I swam swiftly for the foot of my cliff, emerged, and ran panting and dripping up the cleft.

The shouting below came clearly to my ears, also the splashing. I judged that the two men had thrown their arms over the capsized canoe, and thus, hands clasped, were making out to keep afloat.

Drying my bruised feet and dripping skin in my blanket, I hastened to dress and strap on my pack. When I was prepared, the sun was already scattering the mist and I made out the canoe floating bottom up, close inshore, and I heard the wrecked men paddling with their hands.

Presently Walter Butler's voice sounded from the bank, asking the swimming men the cause of their upsetting.

They replied that a deer, swimming the river, had planted one foot in their bow while they slept, and so overturned the canoe. But I knew that Walter Butler would not be long in discovering the tracks of my naked feet in the shore sands where I had landed; so I prepared to leave without further ado.

With a stomach stayed with a mouthful of corn and water, I started silently westward, meaning to make a circle and recross the river to take advantage of their sure pursuit by traveling on the Fort Pitt trail until again hunted into the forest.

It was useless to attempt to cover my tracks, for I could neither avoid breaking branches in the tangle, nor keep from leaving footprints on the soft moss. But I could trot along the tops of fallen logs like a partridge, and use every watercourse that wound my way. And this I did to check the pursuit which I knew must begin sooner or later.

It began even sooner than I expected. Resting a moment to scrutinize a broad stretch of barren ground around which I had just circled, I saw a man creeping among the rocks and berry-scrub, doubtless nosing about for my trail. A moment later another man moved on the eastern edge of the mountain flank, and at the same time, far up the river, I saw the canoe floating.

That was enough for me, and I started on a dog trot down the slope and along the river bed till I came to a bend from which the naked shoulder of the mountain could not be seen.

Thayendanegea had taught me to do what people thought I should be likely to do, but to accomplish it so craftily that they would presently think I had done something else.

When at length those who pursued me should find my trail, they would have no difficulty in following me down the long incline to the river where I now stood, ankle-deep in icy water. I had halted exactly opposite to the mouth of a rocky stream, and it was natural that I should ford the rapids here and continue, on the other bank, up that stream to hide my trail. They would expect me to do it; so this I did, and ran up the bed of the stream for a few rods, carelessly leaving a tiny dust line of cornmeal on the rocks, as though in my headlong fight my sack had started a seam.

Then I turned around and waded down the brook again to the river, out to the shallow rapids, and so, knee-deep, hastening southward again.

But scarcely half an hour had passed ere that accursed canoe appeared bobbing down the rapids, paddles flashing in the sun; and I took to the forest once more at a lively gait.

But I now changed moccasins for a brand-new pair of larger size, and reversed them, toe pointing to the rear. Every twenty paces, then, I stooped to brush up the pile of the velvet moss and so obliterate my tracks for the next twenty paces.

In this manner I traveled for three hours without sign of pursuit. Then my galled shoulders creaked for mercy, under my pack, and I struggled out once more into the Fort Pitt trail and stood panting and alert, drenched with sweat.

The trail had been trodden within the hour; I saw fresh signs of two different moccasins, and of a coarse boot of foreign style, all pointing southward. The mocassins were like one pair I had in my pack, of Albany make. Instinctively I changed my moccasins for the third time, and ran on, stepping carefully in the tracks of him who wore the Albany moccasins.

I had run nearly half a mile when a turn in the trail brought me out along the river. I scanned the stream thoroughly, but I could not see the opposite bank plainly because the forest rose from the water's edge, and low-arched branches screened the shore. Under these a canoe might lie, or might not.

It was clear I could not remain in the Fort Pitt trail with at least two of the Butler crew behind me. Should I take to the tangled forest again? My shoulders begged me not to. Of course, I knew full well the risk of traversing that open bit of trail, but it was such a few feet to safety—such a little risk. I trotted out on the open trail.

Instantly a shot echoed in the gorge, and the pack on my back jerked. With a mighty jump, I cleared the open and stood glued to a tree, peering across at the opposite shore.

There it was!—there came their accursed canoe like a live creature poking its painted snout out of the leafy screen, and I cocked and primed my rifle and waited.

There were two men in the canoe; one paddled gingerly, the other had reloaded his rifle and was now squatting in the bow. They were Wraxall, the barber, and Toby Tice!—tenants of Sir William, with homes and families in Johnstown. Their murderous treachery horrified me.

In a choked voice I hailed them.

"Go back, you clowns!" I called. "Shame on you, Toby Tice! Shame on you, Wraxall! What devil's work is this? Swing that canoe, I say! *Au large! Au large!*—or I'll drill you both with one ball!"

Suddenly Wraxall fired. Through the blue cloud I saw Tice sweep *au large*, and I stepped out and shot a ripping hole through their canoe as it heeled.

Wraxall was reloading desperately; Tice dropped on his knees and tried to draw the ripped flaps together.

Behind my tree I tore a cartridge open, rammed in a palmful of buckshot, primed, and fired, tearing the whole bow out of their flimsy bark craft. The canoe stood up like a post, stern in the air, and Wraxall lay floundering, while Tice shrieked and fell sprawling into the river, head first.

They were swimming my way now, but I shouted to them to sheer off, and at rifle point warned them across the river to land where they might.

I was still watching them to see they landed safely, and had half turned to take the trail again, when a human hand shot up above the river bank and seized my ankle, tripping me flat. The next moment a man leaped up from the shore where he had been crouching, but as I lay on my back I gave him a violent kick in the face and rolled over out of reach. Before I could grasp my rifle, his hatchet flew, pinning one flap of my hunting-shirt to the ground; and I wrenched the hatchet free and hurled it back at him, so that the flat of the blade smacked his face, and he dropped into the water with a scream.

Shaking all over, I rose and lifted my rifle, instinctively repriming. But the sight of the man in the mud, crawling about, gasping and blowing bloody bubbles, made me sick, and the next moment I turned tail and ran.

As I sped down the trail, over my shoulder I saw Walter Butler, planted out in the shoals of the river, taking steady aim at me, and I seized a tree and checked my course as his bullet sang past my face. Then I ran on, setting my teeth and vowing to repay that shot when my life was my own to risk again.

It was late in the afternoon when I turned once more from the trail and limped into the forest; and I was now close to exhaustion.

I had not been able to shake off pursuit, double and twist as I might. Again and again I saw those four, heads down to the trail, jogging along with horrid patience.

Once I doubled on them so close that I could see one of the band with his face tied up in a rag, doubtless the fellow who had tasted of his own hatchet. Walter Butler I could also distinguish, ever in the lead, rifle trailing. I began to repent me that I had not shot my enemies in the water when I had the chance; for truly I was in a sorry condition to proceed farther.

I fired my first long shot at them as they were entering a ravine below me, and I missed, for my hands were unsteady from my laboring breath.

This shot, however, delayed them and they now advanced more cautiously. An hour later I gave them a second shot. My aim was wavering; my bullet only made one man duck his head.

I was fighting for time now. If I could keep on until dark I had no fear for the morrow. I crept once more into the forest and staggered on.

Up and up I crawled. But now, when a vine tripped me, I could scarce make out to rise again. I sadly needed rest. If only the night would come quickly! But there were two long hours of daylight yet.

I caught a distant glimpse of them far below me, searching the ravine and river bank. I had a brief chance for breath; I rested my face on my rifle stock and closed my eyes.

I had been kneeling behind a granite rock in a bare waste of blueberry scrub, and presently, as I attempted to rise, I fell down, and began to claw around like a blind kitten. Stand up I could not. All over me a sweet numbness tingled. I heard a singsong drowsing in my ears: "They will kill you! They will kill you!" but it stirred no terror in me. What would it be, I wondered—a hatchet?—a knife at the throat? Maybe a blow with a rifle stock. What did I care? Sleep was sweet.

Then a quiver swept through me like an icy wind; with a pang I remembered my mission, my vow to Sir William. Darkness crowded me down; my head reeled. Yet I rose again to

I CAUGHT A DISTANT GLIMPSE OF THEM FAR BELOW ME

my knees. All around a thick night seemed to hem me in; I groped for my rifle; it was gone. Panic-stricken, I staggered up, drenched with dew, and saw the moon staring down at me.

Slowly I realized that I had slept; that death had passed me while I lay unconscious. But how far had death gone?—and would he not return by moonlight, stealthily? Aye, what was that under the tree there, that shape watching me?—moving, too—a man!

As I shrank back my heel struck my rifle. In an instant I was down behind the rock to prime with dry powder, but to my horror I found flint missing, charge drawn, pan raised. The shock stunned me for a moment; then I snatched at knife and hatchet, only to find an empty belt.

In fury and despair, I crouched flat with clinched fists, trembling for a spring; and at the same instant a tall figure rose from the bushes at my elbow, laughing coolly.

"Greeting, friend," he said. "God save our country!"

Speechless and dazed, I turned to face him, but he only leaned quietly on a long rifle and chuckled.

"There are some gentlemen yonder looking for you, young man," he said. "I sent them south, for somehow I thought you might not be looking for them."

Weakness had dulled my wits, but I found speech presently to ask for my knife and hatchet.

"Now! Now! Let us go slow, friend," he said, mockingly. "Let us converse on several subjects before you begin bawling for your playthings. In the first place, your manners need polish. I said to you, 'Greeting, friend. God save our country!' but you make me no polite reply."

And the big fellow continued to stand there, in his stringy buckskins and his coonskin cap, grinning down at me with careless good humor, waiting for me to speak.

"If you please," I said, weakly, "give me my hatchet and

knife and receive my thanks. Come, my good fellow, you detain me, and I have far to travel."

"Well, of all impudence!" he sneered. "Wait a bit, my young cock o' the woods. I don't know you yet, but I mean to ere you go out strutting o' moonlight nights."

"Will you give me my hatchet?" I asked, sharply, edging toward him.

For answer he snatched my rifle from me.

"Now," he said, grimly, "you come into camp and take supper with me, or I'll knock your head off and drag you in by the heels!"

Aching with fatigue and mortification, I stood there so perfectly helpless that the great oaf fell a-laughing again and, with a shrug of good-humored contempt, handed me back my rifle as though I were an infant.

"Don't grind your teeth at me," he chuckled. "Come to the camp, lad. I mean no harm to you."

He took a step up the slope, looked around in the moon-light encouragingly, then abruptly returned to my side and passed his great arm around me.

"I'm dog tired," I said, weakly, making an effort to walk; but my knees had no strength in them, and I must have fallen except for his support.

Up, up, up we passed through the foggy moonlight, he almost dragging me. We finally reached a plateau, and after a minute or two I smelled the camp fire. Presently I saw a single tree in the darkness, all gleaming red, and in a moment we entered a ruddy ring of light, in the center of which great logs burned and crackled.

Beside the fire was another *coureur-de-bois*, a meager little man, weasel-eyed and dingy as a summer fox. He looked up sharply as we approached, but beyond a grunt, he paid me no attention, and presently fell to stirring something in a camp pot.

There was a third figure there, too, seated at the base of a gigantic pine tree; a little Hebrew man, gathering his knees in his arms. Saul Shemuel!—who came every spring to Sir William for his peddling license, and sometimes sold us children gaffs and ferret muzzles.

He bade me good evening in an uncertain voice, and did not appear to know me; yet, although I doubted that even Sir William could have recognized me now, I feared this Jew.

The big man brought me a bowl of broth and spread a blanket for me close to the blaze. Shortly a delicious warmth enveloped me within and without, and that is the last I remembered that night.

CHAPTER NINE

IT WAS still dark when I awoke; the fire had become a pyramid of coals. By the dull glow I saw two figures moving; the big one presently crossed the dim crimson circle and sat down beside me, rifle balanced on his knees.

"I am awake," I whispered. "Is there any trouble?"

Without moving a muscle of his huge frame, the forest runner said: "Don't come into the fire ring. There's a man been prowling yonder, a-sniffing our fire, for the last four hours."

I drew myself farther into the darkness, shivering and rubbing my stiffened limbs.

"How do you feel?" he asked.

I told him I felt rested, and thanked him so earnestly for his great kindness to me that he began to chuckle to himself.

"Consider yourself fortunate, eh?" he repeated, rising to come and squat on his haunches beside me.

"Yes," said I, wondering what he found so droll in the situation.

"Ever hear of Catamount Jack?" he inquired, after a moment.

"Yes, if you mean Jack Mount, the highwayman. But you are mistaken; the man who follows me is not Jack Mount," I replied, smiling.

"Sure?"

"Oh yes," I said, bitterly. "I should know."

"What do you know about Jack Mount?" he asked.

"I? Nothing—that is, nothing except what everybody knows."

"Well, what does Mister Everybody know?" he inquired, sneeringly.

"They say he takes the King's highway," I replied. "There's a book about him, printed in Boston."

"With a gibbet on the cover," interrupted the big fellow, impatiently. "Oh, I know all that. But don't they say he's a rebel?"

"Why, yes!" I replied. "Everybody knows he set fire to the King's ship, *Gaspee* and started the rebels a-pitching tea overboard from Griffin's wharf."

Suddenly I stopped short and looked at him in amazement. *He* was Jack Mount! I did not doubt it for one moment.

And there was the famous Weasel, too—that little, shriveled comrade of his!—both corresponding exactly to their descriptions which I had read in the Boston book.

"Well," chuckled the forest runner, "do you still think yourself lucky?"

I managed to say that I thought I was, but my lack of

enthusiasm sent the big fellow into spasms of smothered laughter.

"Now, now, be sensible," he said. "You know you've a belt full of gold, a string of good wampum in your sack, and as pretty a rifle as ever I saw. And you still think yourself in luck? And you're supping with Jack Mount? And the Weasel's watching everything from yonder hazel bunch. And Saul Shemuel's pretending to be asleep under that pine tree? Why, Mr. Cardigan, you amaze me!" he lisped, mockingly.

So the little Hebrew had recognized me, after all. I swallowed a lump in my throat and rose to my elbow. With Jack Mount beside me, Walter Butler prowling outside the fire ring, and I alone, stripped of every weapon, what in Heaven's sight was left for me to do?

"So they say I take the King's highway, eh?" observed Mount.

"They say so," I replied, sullenly.

He burst out petulantly. "The gossipy fools! I never take a *rebel* purse!" And he fell a-muttering to himself: "King's highway, eh? Not mine, not his, not yours—oh no!—but the King's. By the mighty! I'd like to meet his Majesty of a moonlight on this same highway of his!"

He turned roughly on me, demanding what brought me into the forest; but I shook my head, lips obstinately compressed.

"Won't tell, eh?" he growled. "Well, I'll be cursed if you go free without a better accounting than a wag o' your head!"

Cade Renard, the Weasel, had come up while Mount was speaking, and his bright little eyes scanned me warily.

"What's his business?" he inquired of Mount. "I've

searched his pack again, and I can't find anything except the wampum belts."

I jumped up angrily, forgetting fear, demanding to know by what right he dared search my pack; but the impassive Weasel only blinked at Mount and chewed a birch leaf reflectively.

"What is he, Jack?" he asked again, with a jerk of his head toward me.

"Don't know," replied Mount. "Not worth the plucking, anyhow. Take his wampum belts, all the same," he added, with a terrific yawn.

"If you are a patriot," I said, desperately, "you will leave me my belts and meddle only with your own affairs."

Both men turned and looked at me curiously.

"*You* are no patriot," said Mount, after a silence.

"Why not?" I persisted.

"Aye—aye—why and why not?" yawned Mount. "I don't know if you won't tell. The devil take you, for aught I care! But you won't get your belts," he added, slyly.

"Why not?" I repeated, choking down my despair.

"Because you'll talk with your belts to some of these blasted Indians hereabouts," he grinned, "and I want to know what you've got to say to them first."

"I tell you that my belts mean no harm to patriots!" I repeated, firmly. "You say I am no patriot. But I am a better patriot than you, or I should not be in this forest today!"

"You are not a patriot," broke in Cade Renard. "You have proved it already!"

"You say that," I retorted, "because Jack Mount, the high-wayman, gives me the Boston greeting—'God save our country!'—and I do not reply. What of it? I'm at least patriot enough not to rob my own countrymen. I can say 'God save our country!' with better grace than either of you!"

The men exchanged sullen glances.

"That password is not fit for spies," said Mount, grimly.

"Spy? You take me for a spy?" I cried, in astonishment. "Well, if you are the famous Jack Mount, you've duller wits than people believe."

"I've wit enough left to keep an eye on you," he roared, starting toward me; but the Weasel laid his little, rough claw on the giant's arm, and at the same moment I saw a dark figure step just within the outer fire ring, holding up one arm as a sign of peace.

The man was Walter Butler. I dropped back softly into the shadows.

Slowly Jack Mount strolled around the rim of the fire circle, rifle lying in the hollow of his left arm.

"Well, Captain Butler," he drawled, "what can I do for you?"

"You know me, sir?" replied Butler in his colorless voice.

"Aye, we all know you," replied Mount, quickly, "even in your redskin dress."

"May I inquire your name, sir?" asked Butler.

"You may inquire, certainly you may inquire," said Mount, cordially. "You may inquire of my old friend, the moon. Gad! she knows me well, Captain Butler!"

After a silence Butler said: "You unintentionally misled me last evening, friend. The man I follow did not cross the river as you supposed."

"Really?" cried Mount, smiling.

There came another silence; then Butler spoke again:

"I am here on business of my Lord Dunmore; I am here to arrest a young man who is supposed to lie hidden in your camp. I call on you, sir, whoever you are, to aid me in execution of the law."

"The law! Gad! she's another acquaintance o' mine, the jade!" said Mount, laughing. "I suppose you bring that pretty valentine of hers—what some people call a warrant—do you not, Captain Butler?"

"I do," said Butler, moving forward and holding out a paper.

Mount took it and, while he read it, he deliberately shoved Butler back with his elbow to where he had been standing. And Butler could not avoid the giant save by retreating, step by step, out against the sky line, where a bullet could scarcely miss him.

Mount was now contemplating the warrant in deep admiration. He held it out at arm's-length, cocking his head on one side.

"Oh, Cade," he called out, cheerily, " 'Tis the same old valentine! Gad! Captain Butler, we have seen them in every one o' the thirteen colonies—my friend yonder and I!"

"You are doubtless a sheriff, sir," observed Butler, patiently.

"No," said Mount. "No, but I have had much business with sheriffs."

"Then you will understand, sir, the necessity of aiding the law," suggested Butler, holding out his hand for the warrant.

But Mount quietly pocketed the paper and began to whistle and reprime his rifle.

"May I trouble you for that paper?" asked Butler, with sinister politeness.

There was a pause. Butler's eyes stole around the camp fire, but only the little Hebrew was now visible, for I lay in the shadow and the Weasel had ominously vanished.

"You do not mean to retain this warrant, sir?" demanded Butler, his eyes searching the thickets for some sign of the ambushed Weasel.

"Oh, Captain Butler," said Mount, with a gigantic simper, "how can I resist you? Pray tell me who this bad young Michael Cardigan may be, and what he has done to get his name on this valentine?"

"It is a matter of treason," retorted Butler, sharply. "Come, my good man, have done with silly chatter and aid me to my duty in the King's name!"

Mount burst into a shout of laughter. "That's it! In the King's name! I've heard that, too—oh yes, I've heard that o' moonlight nights!"

Butler observed him in astonishment, but Mount held his sides and roared in his mirth: "Comes friend Butler with his warrant, tripping it through the woods, and singing of the King like a titmouse on a stump. Aye, singing to me to help him take a stout fellow in the King's name! Ha! Ha! Ha! This funny Mr. Sheriff Butler!" Then, in a flash, he wheeled on Butler, snarling, every tooth bared: "Blast you, sir! do you take me for your lackey or the King's hangman? To hell with you, sir! To hell with your King, sir! Did you hear me? I said, to hell with your King!"

Butler's face paled in the waning firelight. Presently he said, evenly: "I shall take care that your good wishes reach the King's ears. Pray, sir, honor me with your name and qual- ity, though I may perhaps guess both."

"No need to guess," cut in the big fellow, cheerfully. "I'm Jack Mount. I burned the *Gaspee*, I helped dump His Majesty's tea into Boston harbor, and I should be pleased to do as much for the King himself. Tell him so, Captain But- ler; tell my Lord Dunmore he can have a ducking, too, at his lordship's polite convenience."

Butler glared at him, but Mount only raised his coonskin cap and bowed mockingly.

"Will you deliver me my warrant and my prisoner?" de- manded Butler.

"No!" said Mount, abruptly changing his manner. "Make a new trail, you Tory hangman! March!" And he gave him a prod with his rifle.

Never had I seen such ferocity on a human face as I saw then on Mr. Butler's.

He backed out into the brush, at the point of Mount's long rifle; then the red fire-glow left him and he was gone into the darkness of early morning.

Mount came swaggering back, pausing to drop the warrant on the hot coals as he passed. The Weasel reappeared in a few minutes, took his rifle, and squatted down just beyond the firelight.

As Mount came up to me I rose and thanked him for the protection he had given so generously, and he laughed and laid one padded fist on my shoulder.

"Hark ye, friend," he said, "take your Indian belts and your pack and go in peace, for if Dunmore is after you, the sooner you start north the better. Go, lad. I'm not your enemy!"

"I go south," I replied, cautiously.

"Oh, you do, eh?" said Mount. "Are you bound for Cresap's camp, too?"

"Are you?" I asked, reddening.

He rubbed his chin, watching me with sulky eyes.

"You answer ever with a question!" he complained, fretfully. "I ask you this and you ask me that—tom tiddle! tiddle tom!—and I be no wiser now for all I have heard your name."

"I know Michael Cardigan," observed the Weasel, quietly coming up, buckling on his pack. "He's one of Sir William Johnson's household. That accounts for those peace belts of wampum. Shemuel, yonder, knows the lad."

"Oho!" exclaimed Mount, staring at me. "So you come on Sir William's business to the Cayugas? Ha! Now I begin to grasp this pretty game. Sir William wishes his Cayugas to sit tight while Cresap builds forth ——"

"Hush, for heaven's sake!" I pleaded, seeing that he had guessed all.

"Oh, I'll hush," he replied, eyeing me with frank curiosity. "I am no enemy to Sir William. A fairer and more honest gentleman lives not in these colonies, be he Tory or patriot! Oh, I'll hush, but everyone knows Sir William will not have the Indians take sides in this same war that's coming so fast upon us. It's no secret; every tavern taproom is full o' gossip that Butler means to rouse the Indians against us, and that Sir William will not have it!"

Astonished, I said nothing.

With a shrug, Mount hoisted his pack to his shoulders and stood watching Shemuel, the Hebrew peddler, strapping up his dingy boxes.

"Come on, Shemmy, you pigeon-toed woodchuck!" growled Mount.

The little Jew looked up at me slyly, his grimy fists buried in his geegaws.

"Perhaps the gendleman cares to look at some goots?" he observed, interrogatively. "I haff chains, buckles, pins, needles, buttons, laces ——"

Mount, with the toe of his moccasin, gently reversed Shemuel into one of his own boxes, then warning him to pack up if he valued his scalp, took my arm in friendly fashion and moved out into the gray woods.

"Touching this mission of yours to the Cayugas," he said, frankly, "I see no good to come of it, and I say this with all respect to Sir William. By the bye, Sir William has much to trouble him these days."

"I know that," said I, sadly.

"Oh no, you don't," smiled Mount. "There have been strange doings in Johnstown since you left. A change has come in a single week, lad. Neighbors no longer speak; the town is three parts Tory to one part patriot; even brothers hate each other. Two taverns known to be the meeting places of patriots have been set afire and shot into. Oh, the sands begin to run faster now, and men must soon take one side or t'other, for there's more troops going to Boston, and that means the end of King George!"

I did not perhaps realize fully the importance of all he said. But here was an opportunity to sound Mount on the Cresap affair, and I began earnestly.

"Can you not see that Colonel Cresap is driving the Cayugas into the King's ranks?"

"What do we care for the Cayugas?" replied Mount, contemptuously; and I could not make him see the foolish uselessness of angering the Six Nations. He was one of that kind who detested all Indians.

"What are we to do?" he demanded, sarcastically. "Give up the frontier and go back to Virginia with tails between our legs?"

"Better that than serve as silly tools for Dunmore!" I retorted, hotly.

"Dunmore!" sneered Mount. "We his tools, when the silly ass hasn't wits to twiddle his own thumbs?"

"He had the wit to send Butler to stop me!" I answered, bitterly.

Mount began to grin again slyly.

"Butler came for something else, too," he said. "Dunmore's suite traveled south the day you left, and ought to be in Fortress Pitt tomorrow."

"What of it?" I asked.

"Aye, that's it, you see. Since you left Johnstown, all are talking of the new beauty who threw over Walter Butler—what's her name—a certain Miss Warren, ward of Sir William; and it is commonly reported that the dispute over the Indians and the quarrel betwixt Butler and Sir William stopped the match."

"What of it!" I broke out hoarsely.

"Only that this beautiful Miss Warren came with Lord Dunmore's suite to Pittsburg, and Walter Butler has openly boasted he will marry her spite of Sir William or the devil himself. And here is the lady—and here comes her rash gallant tumbling after his jill!"

WE FILED AWAY INTO THE WEST IN PERFECT SILENCE

To hear her name in the southern wilderness, to hear these things in this place, told with a wink and a leer, raised a black fury in me. But with the greatest effort I controlled myself.

"Are you certain that Miss Warren is already in Pittsburg?" I managed to ask.

"We saw the ladies and the escort a week since," said Mount. "Was it not a splendid sight, Cade?"

"Gay and godless," replied the Weasel, buckling the straps on his pack more tightly. "Are you ready, Jack?"

Mount looked at me.

"Join us and welcome," he said, briefly. "It's safer than going alone."

We moved off due west, Mount leading, then Shemuel the peddler, then I, the Weasel trotting furtively in the rear.

After a while, with a glance at the sun, which was still shining directly in my face, strode up beside Mount.

"The Fort Pitt trail lies west by south," I suggested.

Mount grinned at me and rubbed his nose.

"Butler will be sitting up like a bereaved catamount in the Pitt trail for us," he said. "I've no powder to waste on him and his crew."

My answering grin acknowledged the wisdom of his leadership and I fell back into my place.

We filed away into the west in perfect silence until the sun stood in mid-heaven and the heat drove us to the nearest water.

Resting there to drink, I looked curiously at my three companions. Such a company I had never beheld. There was the notorious Mount, a giant in buckskins, with his paw like a bear's and his smooth, boyish face cut by the heavy crease of a scar below the right eye.

Beside him squatted the little Jew, dirty thumbs joined pensively, musing in his red beard. His boots had left the foreign mark I had seen the day before in the trail; the Weasel's moccasins were those of Albany make.

I examined the Weasel. Such a shrunken, serene, placid little creature, all hunting-shirt and cap.

But the mouths of all three men were curiously well made, bespeaking a certain honesty which I began to believe they perhaps possessed, after all.

"Well," cried Mount, suddenly, "what do you think of us?"

Somewhat embarrassed, I replied politely, but Mount shook his head.

"You were thinking, what a row of gallows birds for an honest man to flock with! Eh? Oh, don't deny it. You can't hurt my feelings, but you might hurt the Weasel's. Eh, Cade?"

"I have sensitive feelings," said the Weasel, dryly.

"I think you all stood by me when I was in distress," said I. "I ask no more of my friends than that."

"Well, you're a good lad," said Mount, getting to his feet and patting my shoulder as he passed me.

"Give him something to wreck his life and he'd make a rare ranger," observed the Weasel.

"Cade was in love," explained Mount, soberly. "Weren't you, Cade?"

The wizened little man nodded his head and looked up at me sentimentally.

"Yes," went on Mount, "Cade was in love and got married. His wife ran away somewheres. Didn't she, Cade?"

Again the little man nodded.

"And then," continued Mount, "he just hunted around till he found me, and we hit the down road together. Didn't we, Cade, old friend?"

Two large tears stole down the Weasel's seamy cheeks.

"She took our baby, too," he sniffed. "You forgot that, Jack."

"So I did, so I did," said Mount, pityingly. "Well, come on, friends, the sun's sliding galley west."

We marched on heavily, bearing down southwest toward the slow Ohio, now curving out below us, red as blood in the kindling coals of sunset. We journeyed on, hour after hour, until the big yellow moon floated above the hills and the river faded into the blue shadows of a splendid night.

Suddenly a light twinkled on the edge of a clearing, then another broke out, and soon all about us cabin windows gleamed brightly.

"Shoulder arms! Right wheel!" cried Mount; and we fled between two blockhouses and across a short bridge, and halted, grounding arms under the shadow of a squatty log fort.

The sentry had called out the guard, and the corporal in charge came up to us, lifting his lanthorn. He greeted Mount cheerfully, nodding and smiling at Renard also.

"Who is this he-goat with red whiskers?" he demanded, illuminating Shemuel's cheerful features.

"Friend of liberty," said Mount in a low voice. "Is Colonel Cresap in the fort, corporal?"

"No," said the corporal, looking hard at me. "He's off somewhere. Who is this gentleman, Jack?"

Mount did not hesitate; he laid his great paw on my shoulder and said: "He's a good lad, corporal. Give him a bed and a bowl o' porridge, and it's a kindness to Jack Mount you will do."

Then he held out his hand to me, and I took it.

"Good night, lad," he said, heartily. "We'll meet again tomorrow. I've a few friends to see tonight."

"Pray follow me, sir," said the corporal, and conducted me to the western barracks, where he lighted me to a tiny casemate and pointed to a door.

"We have messed, but there's some cold meat and a jug of cider for you," he said, affably. "Good night, sir."

"Good night," I said, "and pardon my importunity, but I have a message for Colonel Cresap."

"He returns to the fort tomorrow," said the soldier and retired, whistling "The White Cockade."

As for me, I sat down on the bed, and slipping my sack from my shoulders, rolled over on the blanket. Dawn was shining in through the loopholes of the casemate ere I unclosed my eyes to the world again.

Bang! went the sunrise cannon, and I sprang out of bed, dressed hurriedly, and ran out across the parade to the postern.

"How far is the Cayuga castle?" I asked the sentinel.

"About a mile up the river," he replied, adding: "It's not very safe to go there just now. The Indians have been restless these three weeks, and I guess there's deviltry hatching yonder."

"Don't they come in to the village at all?" I inquired.

"There's a Cayuga, now," said the sentry, pointing to a blanketed figure squatting outside the drawbridge.

I walked across the bridge and approached the Indian, who immediately rose when he saw me, as though he expected ill treatment—a kick, perhaps. The movement was full of sad significance to me, like the cowering of a mistreated hound.

So this was the result of Cresap's coming! With his bullying, overbearing pioneers!

The Indian was watching me sullenly. I held out my hand and said: "Peace, brother. I am a belt-bearer."

There was a silence. After a moment he took my hand.

"Peace, bearer of belts," he said.

"Our council fire is at Onondaga," I said.

"It burns on the Ohio, too," he replied, gravely.

"It burns at both doors of the Long House," I said. "Go to your sachems and wise men. Say to them that Quider is dead; that the three clans who mourn shall be raised up; that Sir William has sent six belts to the Cayuga. I bear them."

He stared at me for a full minute, then gravely turned north, across the cleared land, drawing his scarlet blanket over his face.

All that morning I waited patiently for Mount to come, believing that he could find me a lodging where I might lie hid until Colonel Cresap returned. I certainly could not remain at the fort without risk of arrest if Butler arrived in Cresap's camp with a new warrant.

And though bitterly disappointed at the news that Cresap was in Pittsburg, I durst not journey thither in search of him, for he might have started to return, and I should risk passing him on another trail. Then, too, on the morrow must I needs deliver my belts to the Cayugas at their castle. This without fail.

However, spite of my dangerous predicament, I was ravenously hungry, and cleaned my platter and bowl. Then I thanked my host, the corporal, and we shook hands, he evidently believing I was about to join my friend Mount.

The corporal aided me to strap on my pack, and finally, when I was prepared, he accompanied me to the parade-ground.

"My duties take me to the south stockade," he said, once more offering his hand. And again I thanked him for his hospitality so warmly that he seemed a trifle surprised.

"What friend of liberty could expect less?" he protested, smiling.

"Are you, too, of that fellowship?" I exclaimed, amazed to find rebels in uniform.

"You'll scarce find a Tory in the regiment," he said, beginning to be amused at my ignorance. "As for Colonel Cresap's colonists yonder, I'll warrant them all save some two score malignants like Greathouse, the storekeeper, and his friends.

His unsuspicious assumption that I was a rebel placed me in a most delicate and unhappy position.

"I am afraid I do not merit your confidence in matters touching the fellowship to which you and my friend Mount adhere," I said, stiffly. "I am not a patriot, corporal, and Jack Mount meant only a kindness to a brother man in distress."

Cloud cut me short with a hearty laugh.

"I guess Jack Mount knows what he is about," he said, clapping me on the shoulder. "Half our men are somewhat backward and distrustful, like you; but I'll warrant them when the time comes! Oh, I know them! It's your fawning, favor-currying Tory that I shy at! None o' that kind for me. I know them."

He stood there, serene, smiling, kindly; and I thought to myself that such a man must needs have at least an honest grievance to oppose his King withal.

"Well," he said, abruptly, "time is on the wing, friend. So fare you pleasantly, and—God save our country!"

UNCONSCIOUSLY I BEGAN TO WALK
TOWARD THE FOREST

"Amen," I replied, before I realized that I had acknowledged the famous patriots' greeting. He looked back to laugh significantly as he walked away.

Ill-pleased with my bungling in such a delicate situation, I stood on the parade, biting my lips in vexation and wondering where in the world to go.

I had no business to linger here; I felt that every minute

redoubled my danger. Yet again I asked myself where under heaven I could go, and I thought bitterly of Mount for leaving me here neglected.

Plainly the first thing to be done was to get out of the fort. This I accomplished without the slightest trouble, and I shortly found myself in the road which appeared to be the main street of Cresap's village.

The road encircled the fort, then ran west through a roughly cultivated country, dotted with log cabins. The hamlet itself seemed crowded in by the dark circle of the forest.

Unconsciously I began to walk toward the forest, yet with no idea what I should do there. Presently I passed a double log house, on the door of which was a curious signboard representing a large house with arms and legs like a man.

I needed salt; so I entered the tavern and made known my needs to a thickset fellow who lay in a chair smoking a clay pipe.

He rose instanter, all bows and smiles, begging me to be seated until he could find the salt-sack in the cellar; and I sat down, after saluting the company, which consisted of a half dozen men playing cards by the window.

They all returned my salute, but as they resumed their game I noticed that they began talking in whispers.

Presently the landlord came in with my small bag of salt, and set it on the scales with many a bow and smirk to beg indulgence for his delay.

"You have traveled far, sir," he said, pointedly; "there is northern mud on your hunting-shirt and southern burrs on your legging fringe. I have run the forests myself, sir, and I read as I run—I read as I run."

He was tying up my sack, and I could not courteously make an end to his chatter. Then, ere I could prevent it, he had brought a pewter of home-brew and set it before me.

I could do no less than taste the ale, and he picked up his pipe and begged the honor of sitting in my presence.

"Perchance, sir, you have news from Boston?" he asked, with a jolly laugh.

I shook my head as I raised my tankard, after tossing him a shilling for my reckoning. The men by the window had paused to listen.

"Well, well," he said, puffing his long clay into a glow, "these be parlous times, sir, the world over! And, between ourselves, sir, begging your pardon for the familiarity, sir, I have been wondering myself whether the King is wholly right."

The stillness in the room was intense.

"Doubt," said I, carelessly, "is no friend to loyalty."

"But," he suggested, "cannot even the King be deceived by unscrupulous counselors?"

"The King should know better than you whether his ministers be what you accuse them of being," I said, seriously.

"I meant no accusation," he said, hastily, "but I voiced the sentiments of many honest neighbors of mine."

"Sentiments that smack somewhat of treason," I interrupted, coldly.

I saw he was still far from satisfied concerning my real sentiments. I listened as I drank; the card players behind me were not playing.

"Landlord," I asked, carelessly, cutting short another argument, "what may your tavern sign mean with its house running loose on a pair o' legs?"

"It is my own name, sir," he laughed. "Greathouse! I flatter me there is some small wit in the conceit, sir, though I painted yon sign myself!"

So this was Greathouse, a notorious loyalist—this bloated lout who had been prying at me to learn my sentiments? The slyness of the fellow disgusted me, but I succeeded in leaving him with his suspicions lulled, and got out of the house without administering to him the kick for which my leg was itching.

From the corner of my eye I could see the card-players watching me from the window; it incensed me to be so spied upon, and I was glad when a turn in the road shut me out of their vision.

There were several houses just beyond me to the left; and at one, evidently a tavern, I perceived Jack Mount loafing in the doorway, and Shemuel seated on the horse block, eating a dish of fish with his fingers.

Still disgruntled with Mount, I would have returned his cheery salute with a sullen nod and not paused at the house.

But he came out into the road, asking what had gone amiss; whereupon I told him he had left me without advice or counsel, and that I had quitted the fort, not caring to be caught there by Butler and his warrant.

"Shame on you, lad, for the thought!" said Mount, angrily. "Do you think we do things by halves, Cade and I? The Weasel has been in touch with Butler's men all night, ready to warn you the moment they started for this camp! He's asleep in there, now," jerking his huge thumb towards the inn, "and I've just returned from seeing Butler well on the trail towards Pittsburg."

Ashamed of my complaint and deeply touched by the quiet kindness of these two men who had watched while I slept, I silently offered my hand to Mount. He took it fretfully, complaining that all the world had always misunderstood him, and vowing he would never more do kindness to man or beast or good red herring!

"Small blame if the world requites your generosity as stupidly as I do," said I; whereat he fell a-laughing and drew me into the tavern, vowing we should wash out all bitterness in a draught of ale.

Inside the tavern he presented me to a young man in homespun who had been sitting by the chimney, reading a letter—a quiet, modest gentleman of thirty, perhaps, somewhat travel-stained and spotted with reddish mud, evidently an arrival from the south.

He gave me a firm clasp of the hand and a curiously sharp yet not unkindly smile, promising to join us when he had finished his letter.

I had meant to tell Mount of my conversations with Corporal Cloud and with Greathouse, but hesitated because of the stranger by the chimney.

Mount, perhaps divining my intentions, assured me, "You may say what you please here, Mr. Cardigan, and trust this gentleman from Maryland as you trust me, I hope."

I had not caught the name of the young man from Maryland, and was diffident about asking. He looked up from his letter with a brief smile and nod at us, and we sat down beside a table and called for home-brew.

I began by telling Mount frankly that he had put me in a false position as a rebel. I retailed my conversation with Corporal Cloud, how I had felt it dishonorable to accept hospitality under a misunderstanding, and how I had deemed it necessary to confess me. But Mount only laughed at me over his brown tankard.

"Tiddle—diddle—diddle! Who the devil cares?" he said. "I wish half of our patriots possessed your tender conscience, friend Michael."

I swallowed a draught in displeased silence.

"I'm loyal to the King," I then said, bluntly, "and when I am ready to renounce him, I shall do so, not before."

"Certainly," observed Mount, complacently.

"Not that I care for Tory company, either," I added, in disgust, thinking of my encounter with Greathouse. And I related the affair to Mount.

The big fellow's eyes narrowed.

"A sneak!" he said. "A sly, mealy-mouthed sneak! Look out for this fellow Greathouse, my friend. By Heaven! I'm sorry he saw you! You can depend upon it the news of your arrival here will be carried to Butler. Why, this fellow, Greathouse, is a notorious creature of Lord Dunmore's, set here to spy on Colonel Cresap."

He set down his tankard with a bang.

"How long do you stay here?" he asked.

"Until I deliver my belts; that will be tomorrow."

"I thought you wished to see Colonel Cresap, too?" he said.

"I do; he will return today, they tell me."

Mount leaned over the table, folding his arms.

"Hark ye, friend Michael," he said. "Colonel Cresap, three-quarters of the militia, and all save a score or so of these villagers here are patriots. The Maryland pioneers mean to make a home here for themselves, Indians or no Indians, and it will be little use for you to plead with Colonel Cresap, who could not call off his people if he would."

"If he is a true patriot," I said, "how can he deliberately drive the Six Nations to take up arms against the colonies? I tell you, Dunmore means to have a war started here that will forever turn the Six Nations against us."

"Against *us?*" said Mount, meaningly.

"Yes—*us!*" I exclaimed. "If it be treason to oppose such a monstrous crime as that which Lord Dunmore contemplates, then I am guilty! If to be a patriot means to resist such men as Dunmore and Butler—if to defend the land of one's birth against the plots of these men makes me an enemy to the King, why—why, then," I ended, violently, "I am the King's enemy to the last blood-drop in my body!"

There was a silence. I sat there with clinched fist on the table, teeth set, realizing what I had said, glad that I had said it.

"Lord Dunmore represents the King," said Mount, smiling.

"Prove it to me and I am a rebel from this moment!" I cried.

"But Lord Dunmore is only doing his duty," urged Mount. "His Majesty needs allies."

"Do you mean to say that Lord Dunmore is provoking war here at the King's command?" I asked, in horror.

The young man by the chimney stood up and bent his pleasant eyes on me.

"I have here," he said, tapping the letter in his hand, "my Lord Dunmore's commission as major-general of militia, and His Majesty's permission to enlist a thousand savages to serve under me in the event of rebellion in these colonies!"

I had risen to my feet at the sound of the stranger's voice. Mount, too, had risen, tankard in hand.

"I am further authorized," said the young stranger, coolly, "by command of my Lord Dunmore, to offer twelve pounds sterling for every rebel scalp taken by these Indian allies of His Most Christian Majesty."

At that I went cold and fell a-trembling.

"By the mighty!" I stammered. "By the blood of man!—this is too much—this is too ——"

Crash! went Mount's tankard on the table, and, turning to the young stranger with a bow, "I bring you a new recruit, Colonel Cresap," he said, quietly. "Will you administer the oath, sir?"

Thunderstruck, I stared at the silent young man who stood there, grave eyes bent on me, tearing at the edge of his paper with his white teeth.

"Pray be seated, Mr. Cardigan," he said, smiling. "I know you have a message for me from Sir William Johnson. I hold it an honor to receive commands from such an honorable and upright gentleman."

He drew up a chair, motioned Mount and me to be seated, and leaned back, waiting for me to speak.

If my speech was halting or ill-considered, my astonishment at the identity of the stranger was to blame; but I spoke earnestly and without reserve, and my very inexperience must have pleaded with him, for he listened patiently and kindly, even when I told him, with some heat, that the whole land would hold him responsible for an outbreak on the frontier.

When I had finished, he thanked me for coming and begged me to convey his cordial gratitude to Sir William. Then he began his defense, very modestly and with frankest confession that he had been trapped by Dunmore into a pitfall the existence of which he had never suspected.

"I am today," he said, "the Moses of these people, inasmuch as I have, at Lord Dunmore's command, led them into this promised land. God knows it was the blind who led the blind. And now, for months, I have been aware that Dunmore wishes a clash with the Cayugas yonder; but until Sir William Johnson opened my eyes, I have never understood why Lord Dunmore desired war."

He looked at Mount as though to ask whether he had suspected Dunmore; and Mount shook his head.

"He is a witless ass," he muttered. "I see nothing in Mr. Cardigan's fears that Dunmore means trouble here."

"*I* do," said Cresap, calmly. "Why, Jack, it's perfectly plain to me now! We've been tricked. This very commission in my hands, here, is made out for the purpose of buying my loyalty to Dunmore. Can't you see?"

Mount shook his head.

Cresap flushed faintly and turned to me.

"What can I do, Mr. Cardigan? I have led these people here, but I cannot lead them back. I could not induce a single man to abandon the cabin he has built or the ground he has planted. And where should I lead them? Virginia is overpopulated. I have no land to give them except this, granted by the King—granted in spite of his royal oath, now broken to the Cayugas.

"You say the whole country will hold me responsible. I cannot help that, though God must know how unjust it would be.

"Were I to counsel the abandonment of this fort and village, Lord Dunmore would arrest me and clap me into Fort Pitt. Is it not better that I remain here and labor among my people in the cause of liberty?

"I can do nothing while a royal governor governs Virginia. But if the time ever comes when our Boston brothers sound the call to arms, I can lead out of this forest six hundred riflemen whose watchword will be, 'Liberty or Death!' "

He had grown pale while speaking; two bright scarlet patches flamed under his cheek bones; he coughed painfully and rested his head on his hand.

"Go to your Cayugas," he said, catching his breath. "Tell them the truth, or as much of the truth as Sir William's wisdom permits. I am here to watch, to watch such crafty agents as Greathouse and young Walter Butler, whom I met on the Pitt trail three hours since. Oh, I understand the situation now, Mr. Cardigan."

He frowned thoughtfully.

"Keep Sir William's Cayugas quiet if you can," he said. "I will watch Dunmore's agents that they do nothing to bring on war. I may fail, but I will do what I can. When do you speak to the Cayugas with belts?"

"At dawn," I replied, soberly.

"Poor devils," said Cresap, sadly, "poor, tricked, cheated

devils! This is their land. I should never have come had not Dunmore assured me the Cayugas had been paid for the country. And there is their great sachem, Logan, called 'The Friend of the White Man.' Greathouse has made a drunken sot of Logan and all his family. Aye, sir, I have seen Logan's children lying drunk in the road there by Greathouse's tavern—stark naked, drunk in the rain!"

After a moment I asked why he had not expelled this fiend, Greathouse, and he replied that he had, but that Dunmore had sent him back under his special protection.

"What on earth can I do?" he repeated. "The Cayuga camp is rotten with whisky. Their chiefs and sachems come to me and beg me to forbid the sale. I am powerless, for Lord Dunmore stands back of Greathouse. That mealy-mouthed spy is a nightmare to me!"

As we sat there, silent, I heard the rain drumming against the window. The room had grown very dark.

Cresap rose, holding out his hand to me.

"Shall I administer the oath of fellowship, my friend?" he asked.

"Not yet," I replied, taking his hand.

"When you are ready, Mr. Cardigan," he said, simply. "Will you lodge here? That is well; the fort is not safe. And, if I mistake not, young Butler will be here tomorrow to search for you. He begged me to have you arrested should you be in my camp."

"I shall be at the Cayuga castle by dawn," I said.

"And after that?" inquired Mount. "You are not going to leave us, are you, lad?"

"I have my message to deliver to Sir William," I answered, earnestly. "And," I added, "truly, I do not believe there is anything on earth that can prevent my delivering my message, nor retard my returning and slaying this frightful enemy of mankind, Walter Butler."

THE CAYUGA ENCAMPMENT

CHAPTER TEN

THE rain fell thickly until midnight, keeping me awake. I lay in my blanket under the roof, and slept when it ceased, but awoke before dawn.

By lanthorn-light, I dressed me, placing my belts in the bosom of my shirt. I left my pack with my landlord, Timothy Boyd, and the rugged old man nodded placidly, bidding me rest assured of its safety.

"There is foul company at the 'Greathouse Inn,'" he told me. "Greathouse received four guests an hour ago. Mount bade me warn you, sir."

I understood at once. Butler, Wraxall, Toby Tice, and the fourth member of the band had arrived in Cresap's camp.

But I cared not; I was about to accomplish my mission under their four noses.

"Is Mount sleeping?" I asked.

The old man laughed.

"I have never seen him sleep," he said. "He is out yonder somewhere, prowling."

"And Shemuel?—and Cade Renard?" I inquired.

"Shemuel is on his way to Pittsburg; Renard mouses with Mount. Is your rifle loaded, sir? There be foul company at the other inn. This night, too, did Greathouse make nine savages drunk with spirits. Have a care that they cross not your path, young man!"

"I wish you knew the Indians as well as I do," said I, smiling. "I fear them not. I think the whole world can be tamed with kindness."

Boyd shook his gray head, watching me in silence.

A brisk southwest wind was singing through the pines as I stepped out of doors and peered cautiously about. There was nothing stirring save the wind and the unseen leaves in the forest. I primed my rifle and stole forth into the starlit road.

To gain the river, whence the trail ran northward to the Cayuga camp, I was obliged to pass the fort, and consequently the Greathouse Inn. But I had no fear at this hour o' morning, and I trotted on along the stump fence until the first curve brought me to Greathouse's inn.

Shutters were drawn and bolted over every window, but candle-light streamed through loopholes in the taproom, and I caught odors of cooking, of rum toddy, and of tobacco smoke. Clearly Butler's company were supping after their long jog.

Satisfied that all was safe, I had silently begun skirting the road ditch shadowed by the fence, when a dark heap that I had taken for a stump in the road moved and moaned.

I stopped, frozen motionless. After a moment's wary reconnoitering I crept forward again, eyes fastened on that dim shape ahead.

When I came closer I understood. At my feet, in a drunken stupor, sprawled a young Cayuga girl, limbs plastered with mud, body reeking with the stench of spirits. Her black hair floated in a pool of rain.

I lifted the little thing and bore her to the shadow of the fence; but here, to my amazement, lay a drunken squaw, doubtless her mother, still clinging to an empty bottle; and along the ditch and fence I counted seven more young barbarians, all apparently of the same family and all lying in a sodden swoon.

This was the work, then, done by a single agent of my Lord Dunmore!

They lay there, glistening in the grass, the children naked, the mother in rags, breathing out poison under the stars.

There was nothing I could do for these victims of Greathouse. Heartsick, I turned away and passed swiftly down the muddy trail, hastening to mend my pace ere dawn should find me missing at the councilfires burning for me on the dark Ohio.

Ere I reached the river the eastern sky had turned saffron, but the drifted mist-banks lay heaped far out, so I could not see the water.

The Cayuga trail was broad and plain, however, and I took it at a wolftrot. On, on, north upon the trail, while through

TO GAIN THE RIVER I WAS OBLIGED TO PASS THE FORT

the brightening woods sleep fled with the mist and the world awoke around me.

And now a thread of blue smoke, drawn far down the trail,

set my nostrils wide and quivering; a flare of blinding yellow turned the world into gold. I had met the sun at the Cayuga camp; the tryst had been kept, thanks to the Lord!

Dark forms loomed up in the eye of the sun as I drew nigh; men who stood motionless as the pines where the council fire smoked.

"Peace!" I said, halting with upraised hand. "Peace, you wise men and sachems!"

"Peace!" repeated a low voice. "Peace, bearer of belts!"

I moved nearer, head high. And when I came to the edge of the fire I drew a white belt of wampum from my bosom and, passing it through the smoke, held it aloft, flashing in the sun, until every chief and sachem had sunk down into their blankets, forming a half-circle before me.

A miracle of speech came to me. I spoke as I had never dared hope I might speak. Forgotten phrases, caressing idioms, words long lost flew to aid me.

Belt after belt I passed through the fragrant birchsmoke; I spoke to them as Sir William had spoken to Quider with three belts, and my words were earnest and pitiful, for my heart was full of tenderness for Sir William and for these patient children of his.

The ceremony of condolence was more than a ceremony for me. With eager sympathy I raised up the three stricken tribes; I sweetened the ashes of the eternal fires; I cleared evil from the Cayuga trail, and laid the ghastly ghosts of those who stood in forest highways to confront the fifth nation of the great confederacy.

"Oonah! Oonah!" whimpered the wind in the pines, but I

stilled the winds and purified them, and I cleansed the million
needles of the pines with a belt and an enchanted word.

The last belt was passed, flashing through the smoke; the
chief sachem of the Cayugas rose to receive it, a tall, withered
man of the Wolf tribe, painted and draped in scarlet. His dim,
wrinkled eyes peered at me through the smoke.

For a long time the silence was broken only by the rustling
flames between us; then the old man placed the belt at his feet,
straightened up, and spoke feebly:

"*Brother*: It is to be known that the Six Nations never meet
in council when mourning, until some brother speaks as you
have spoken.

"*Brother*: We mourn great men dead. Our Father, through
you, our Elder Brother, has purified our fires, our throats, our
eyes. Where the dead sat among us, three tribes have you
raised up.

"*Brother*: Listen attentively!"

Behind him from the great painted lodge nine Indian boys
entered the fire circle and stood proudly with folded arms
and heads erect. And the old sachem laid his shaking hand
on each youth as he passed, always turning to peer at me as he
repeated in his feeble, cracked voice:

"We acquaint you that one of our sachems, called Quider,
is dead; we raise up this boy in his place and give him the
same name."

And after each boy had been named from one of the dead
Cayugas, he gave me a string of wampum to confirm it, while
the solemn chant of condolence rose from the seated chiefs
and sachems.

Hour after hour I stood with bent head and folded arms.

Sometimes I prayed as I stood, that evil be averted from these wards of our King; sometimes I grew hot with anger at the men who could so vilely misuse them.

So I dreamed there amid the scented birch smoke, the chant intoning with the mourning pines, somber visions took shape within my brain. I saw awful spectres of ruin and death crowding around a flabby creature of silks and laces, my Lord Dunmore, smirking at Terror wearing the merciless mask of Butler.

I swayed where I stood, then stumbled back out of the scented smoke. I opened my eyes dizzily. My ears were ringing with the interminable chant:

"*Sah-e-ho-na,*
Sah-e-ho-na."

I crossed my arms and waited, careful to keep out of the sweet smoke that had stolen away my senses and set me dreaming of horrors.

The sun hung above the pines, belted by a slender purple cloud, the forerunner of a gathering storm.

I watched the cloud growing until it smothered out the sun. And as I watched, the chant ended and, in silence, three chiefs arose and moved toward me through the smoke. One by one they spoke to me, naming themselves: Yellow Hand, Tamarack, the ancient sachem robed in scarlet, and lastly the war chief, Sowanowane.

It was Tamarack who continued:

"*Brother*: We have heard. The Three Ensigns of our nation have heard."

(A belt)

"*Brother*: We all bear patiently this great wrong done us by Colonel Cresap. We are patient because Sir William asks it of us. But under these tall pines around us lie hatchets, buried deep among the pine trees' roots. See, brother! Our hands are clean. We have not dug in the earth for hatchets."

(*A belt of seven*)

"*Brother*: We pray that our elder cousin, Lord Dunmore, will remove from us his agent Greathouse. We pray that no more spirits be sold to the Cayugas. We pray this because we cannot resist an offered cup. We pray this because we drink— and die. It is death to us, death to our children, death to our nation."

(*A black belt*)

"*Brother*: Bear our belts to our Father, Sir William Johnson, and to our elder cousin, Lord Dunmore. Intercede with them that they may heed our prayers."

(*A bunch of three*)

"*Brother*: Depart in health and honor, bearing these sacred belts of peace ——"

A frightful scream cut him short; scream after scream arose from the hidden lodges.

The assembly rose in a body, blankets falling to the ground, and stood paralyzed, silent, while the horrid screaming rose to an awful, long-drawn shriek.

Somebody was coming—somebody plodding heavily, shrieking at every step, nearer, nearer—an old woman who staggered out into the circle of the council, dragging the limp body of a young girl.

"Nine!" she gasped. "Nine slain at dawn by Greathouse! Nine of the family of Logan! Look, you wise men and sachems! Look at Logan's child! Dead! Slain by Greathouse! Nine! Mother and children lie by the road, slain as they slept; slain, sleeping the poisoned sleep of Greathouse! Dead! Dead! Dead!"

Stupidly the sachems stared at the naked corpse, flung on the blankets at their feet. The scented smoke curled over the murdered child, blowing east and south.

Sick with horror, I moved forward, and the stir seemed to arouse the sachems. One by one they looked down at the dead, then turned their flashing eyes on me. I strove to speak; I could not utter a sound.

The old sachem bent slowly and took a handful of ashes from the cold embers. Then, rubbing them on his face, he flung down every belt I had given him and signed to me to do the same with the belts delivered to me.

When I had dropped the last belt, Yellow Hand made me a sign, and every chief, save Sowanowane, the war chief, covered his head with his blanket. I fixed my eyes on the war chief, dreading lest he hurl a red belt at my feet. But he only bent his head, with a gesture bidding me depart. And I went, stunned by the calamity that had come as lightning to blast the work I had done.

As I dragged myself back, leaden-footed, behind me I heard the death wail rising, the horrid screaming of women, the fierce yelps of the young men, the thump! thump! thump! of the drum.

Overwhelmed, I wandered aimlessly into the forest and sat down. Long I sat there, and my shocked senses strove only to find some way to avert the consequences of the deed wrought by Greathouse. But the awful work had been done; the Gordian knot cut; my Lord Dunmore's war had begun at last. Now Cresap must fight; now the Six Nations would rise to avenge the Cayugas on the colonies; now the King would have the savage allies he desired so ardently, and the foul pact would be sealed with the blood of Logan's children!

"Never, by God's grace!" I cried out in agony, and stumbled to my feet, my head burning and throbbing. The woods had grown dim; the day was already near to its end—this bloody day! this sad day which had dawned so hopefully for all! Suddenly I began running through the forest, cursing as I ran.

"Faster, oh, faster," I muttered; "faster to slay this devil, Butler, who has counseled Greathouse to this deed!"

But truly, vengeance is the Lord's, and He alone may repay, nor was I the instrument He chose for His wrath. For, behold! a man rose up in my path and held me fast, a soldier, who shook me and shouted at me until my senses halted and returned. Presently I began to understand his words.

"Are you mad?" he repeated. "Can't ye see the savages across the river following? The Cayugas are loose on the Ohio! It is war!"

Other men crept up and dropped into cover behind the trees around me; some were colonial soldiers, some farmers, some hunters. All at once I saw Colonel Cresap come out into the trail close by, and when he perceived me he cried:

"Logan's children have been murdered by Greathouse! The Cayugas are swarming on the Ohio!"

I begged him to let me carry his promise to the Cayugas

that Greathouse should be punished and that his colonists would retire. He shook his head.

"Greathouse has fled to Pittsburg," he said. "I cannot retire with my people because they would not follow me. It is too late, Mr. Cardigan, Dunmore has sprung his trap. Ha! Look at that!" And he turned and shouted out an order to the soldiers around.

A dozen savages were fording the Ohio between us and the settlement. Already the soldiers were running through the woods along the river to head them off, and Cresap started after them, calling back for those who remained to guard the trail in the rear. Then a rifle went bang! among the trees; another report rang out, followed instantly by twenty more in a volley.

Down a low oak ridge, close by, I saw an Indian tumbling like a stone till he fell into a mossy holly. After him bounded a hunter in buckskins, long knife flashing.

"Cresap!" I panted. "Don't let him take that scalp! Have your men gone mad? You can stop this war! It is not too late yet, but a scalp taken means war! God in heaven! a scalp means war to the death!"

"Don't touch that scalp!" roared Cresap, hurrying toward the ranger, who was kneeling on one knee beside the dead Cayuga. "Nathan Giles! Do you hear me? Let that scalp alone, you bloody fool!"

It was too late; the ranger squatted, wrenching the scalp free with a ripping sound just as Cresap ran up in a towering rage.

"They take ours," remonstrated the ranger, tying the ghastly trophy to his belt by its braided lock of hair. "I guess I have a right to scalp my own game!" he added, sullenly.

Cresap turned to me with a gesture of despair.

"You see," he said, and walked slowly toward the river, where the rifles were ringing out below the shallow camp ford.

So now, at last, Lord Dunmore's war had begun without hope of mediation. There is nothing on earth to compensate for a scalp taken save a scalp taken in return. I had failed— failed totally.

All around me firelocks and rifles were banging; the woods swam in smoke; the war yelp sounded nearer and nearer.

But too miserable to shun danger, I sat down on a stone in the trail, my head in my hands, rifle across my knees. And I was sitting there in stupefied despair when a swift, dusky shape came creeping out of the brush.

The Indian was on me ere I could fire, one sinewy fist twisted in my hair, but his knife snapped off short on my rifle stock, and together, over and over we rolled, down a ravine among the willows, clawing, clutching, strangling each other, till of a sudden my head struck a tree, crack! And I knew nothing after that until the cool rain beating in my face awoke me. I lay very still, listening.

Somebody near by was trying to light a fire; I smelled the flint and the glowing tinder. My head was aching heavily; I could scarce stir it. But at length I raised myself on my hands and saw the spark from a flint fly into a ball of dry moss and hang there like a firefly until the tiny circle of light spread slowly into a glow.

A tufted head bobbed down beside the glow; unseen lips

CLAWING, CLUTCHING, STRANGLING EACH OTHER

blew the fire into a sudden blaze that brightened and flashed up, throwing ruddy shadows over bush and earth.

Then I saw that I lay on a hilltop in the rain, with dark, shaggy bushes hedging me. And under every bush crouched an Indian, whose dusky, half-naked body glistened with paint over which raindrops stood in brilliant beads.

I saw brilliant eyes watching me as I dragged myself nearer the fire. The red embers' glow fell on steel blades of hatchets, bathing them with blood color to the hilts.

Once when I attempted to sit up, an arm shot out of the shadow, making the sign for silence; and mechanically I repeated the signal and laid my head down again on the cool, wet ground.

All night I lay, perfectly conscious, beside the Cayuga fire, yet not alarmed, although a prisoner.

The Cayugas knew me as a belt-bearer from Sir William; they could not ill-treat me. Tamarack, Yellow Hand, and Sowanowane would vouch for me to this party of young men who had taken me.

As I lay there on the windy hilltop, through the rain across the dim valley I could see the battle lanthorns hanging on Cresap's fort, and I could hear the preparations for a siege, the hammering and chopping and cries of teamsters, the rumble of wagons over the drawbridge, the distant challenge of guards.

Beside me crouched my captors, alert and curious, dressing their ears to the distant noises. There were eleven of them; eleven lithe, muscular young savages, stripped to the belt, well oiled, and freshly painted for war. All wore the Wolf.

I spoke to them calmly, but they would reply to none of

my questions and finally they silenced me with sullen threats. This, however, did not disturb me, as I knew their sachems must set me free.

My head ached a great deal from the blow I had suffered; I was willing enough to lie quietly and watch the lights in the fort through the slow veil of falling rain; and presently I fell asleep.

The hot glare of a torch awoke me. All around me crowded masses of savages, young and old, women and youths and children. The woods vomited barbarians; they came in packs, hastening as though on some pressing affair.

Women near me were digging a hole, and presently came a strong young girl, bearing a post of buckeye, and set it heavily in the hole, fitting it while the others stamped in the mud around it.

The main crowd, however, had surged down into a hollow to the left, and of a sudden came three Indians driving before them a white man, arms tied, bloodless face stamped with horror.

As he passed the fire where I lay, I thought his starting eyes met mine, but he staggered on without speaking, down into the darkness of the hollow. I knew him. He was Nathan Giles, who had taken the first scalp in Lord Dunmore's war.

Shuddering, I sat up, turning my head toward the gloom below. There was not a sound. I waited, straining eyes and ears. My heart drummed on my ribs.

Suddenly the black pit below burst out in a sheet of light, shining on a thousand motionless savages; and in the center of a glare I saw a naked figure, bound to a tree, twisting through smoke-shot flames.

For a second only the scene wavered before me; then I gripped my temples and pressed my face down into the cool, wet grass. Awful cries rang in my ears; the garrison at the fort heard them, too, for they fired a cannon, and I heard distant drums beating to arms.

"Thus you are to die," repeated the Indians beside me. "Thus you will die here on this hill at dawn. Thus you will suffer in plain view of the fort! This for the death of Logan's children!"

And one to another they said: "He is weeping. He is a woman. He will weep thus when he burns."

I heard them, but for me there was no meaning in their words; none at all. My ears shrank from these awful cries, now piercing the very clouds above me.

Into my nostrils crept the stench of burnt flesh; it grew stronger and stronger. Silence fell, soothed by the whispering rain. Then out of the night came the dull noise of many people stirring. They were coming!

As I rose, a Cayuga youth seized me and threw me heavily against the post imbedded in the mud. I fought and strained and writhed, but they tied me, bracing me up stiff against the wet stake, trussed like a fowl for basting.

Around me the crowd was thickening; hundreds of tongues loaded me with insults; thrice a young girl reached out and struck me in the face.

They began piling wood around my feet and stuffing the spaces full of dry moss.

Through the falling rain I saw morning lurking behind the

eastern hills, and I cursed it, for the shock and terror had driven me out of my senses. I remember hearing a voice calling on God, but for a long time I did not know the voice was mine.

It was only when the same young girl who had struck me lighted a splinter of yellow pine and thrust it through my arm that my senses returned. I opened my eyes as from a swoon, seeing clearly the faces around me, red under the torches. And foremost among those in front stood Tamarack in his scarlet robes. Now my voice came back, seeking my lips; my parched tongue moved, and I called on Tamarack to hear me, but he shook his head, though I adjured him by the belts I had borne and received.

"Lies," he said. "You come not from Johnstown! Your belts are lies; your words lie! You come from Cresap! Cresap shall see how you can die for him!"

"I speak the truth!" I cried out in my agony. "I am a belt-bearer! I have laid the ghosts of your slain ones! Who dares send my spirit to teach your dead that you betray their ashes?"

There was silence. Presently somebody in the throng said, distinctly: "If he speaks the truth, let him go. We honor our dead." And other voices repeated:

"We honor our dead."

"He lies," said Tamarack.

"I speak truth!" I groaned. "If you honor your dead, free me, brothers of the Cayugas!"

"Free him!" cried many.

For a space the throng was quiet; then a distant movement to my left made me turn hopefully. The throng wavered, parted, opened, and a white man came elbowing his way to the stake.

He whispered to Tamarack; the aged sachem stretched out his arm, making a mystic sign.

Eagerly the white man turned and looked at me, and I cried out with rage and horror, for I was face to face with Walter Butler.

He spoke, but I scarcely heard him urging my death.

Terror, which had gripped me, gave place to fury, and that in turn left me faint but calm.

I heard the merciless words in which he delivered me to the savages; I heard him denounce me as a spy of Cresap. Then I lost his voice.

I was very still for a while, trying to understand that I must die. The effort tired me; lassitude weighed on me like chains. To my stunned mind death was but a word. Thought was suspended; sight and hearing failed; there was a void about me.

Presently, however, I became conscious that things were changing. Lights moved, voices struggled into my ears; forms took shape, pressing closer to me. An undertone, which I had heard at moments through my stupor, grew, swelling into a steady whisper. It was the ceaseless rustle of the rain.

A torch blazed up crackling close in front. My eyes opened; a thrill of purest fear set every sense aquiver. Amid the dull roar of voices, I heard women laughing and little children prattling. Faces became painfully distinct. I saw Sowanowane, the war chief, thumb his hatchet; I saw Butler, beside him, catch an old woman by the arm. He told her to bring dry moss. It rained, rained, rained.

They were calling to me from the crowd now; everywhere

voices were calling to me, "Show us how Cresap's men die!" Others repeated: "He is a woman; he will scream out! Logan's children died more bravely. Oonah! The children of Logan!"

Butler watched me coolly, leaning on his rifle.

"So this ends it," he said, with his deathly grimace. "Well, it was to be done in one way or another. I had meant to do it myself, but this will do."

I was too sick with fear, too close to death, to curse him. Pain often makes me weak; the fear of pain sickens me. It was that I dreaded, not death. Where my father had gone I dared follow, but the flames—the thought of the fire ——

I said, faintly: "Turn your back to me when I die. I have much pain to face, Mr. Butler; I may not bear it well."

"I will not!" he burst out with an oath. "I'm here to see you suffer!"

I turned my head from him, but he struck me in the face so that my mouth was bathed in blood. And planting himself before the stake, he cursed me.

"Know this before they roast you," he snarled. "I shall wed your pretty baggage, Mistress Warren, spite of Sir William! I shall bend her to my pleasure; I shall whip her to my feet. Ah! Ah! Now you rage, eh?"

I had hurled my trussed body forward on the cords, struggling, convulsed with fury.

Indians struck me and thrust me back with clubs, but I did not feel the blows. I fixed my maddened eyes on Butler and struggled.

But now the sachems were calling him sharply, and he backed away from me as the circle surged forward. Again the girl came out, bearing a flaming fagot. She looked up at me, laughed, and thrust the burning sticks into the moss and tinder stacked around me. A billow of black smoke rolled into my face, choking and blinding me, and the breath of the flames passed over me.

Twice the rain quenched the fire. They brought fresh heaps of moss, laughing and jeering. Through the smoke I saw the fort across the valley, its parapets crowded with people. Jets of flame and distant reports showed they were firing rifles, hoping perhaps to kill me ere the torture began. It was too far. The last glimpse of the fort faded through the downpour; a new pile of moss and birch bark was heaped at my feet.

This time the girl was thrust aside and a young Indian advanced, waving a crackling branch of pitch pine, roaring with flames. As he knelt to push it between my feet, a terrific shout burst from the throng—a yell of terror and amazement. Through the tumult I heard women screaming; in front of me the crowd shrank away, huddling in groups. Some backed into me, stumbling among the fagots; the young Indian let his blazing pine branch fall hissing on the wet ground and stood trembling.

And now into the circle stalked a tall figure, coming straight toward me through the sheeted rain—a specter so hideous that the cries of terror drowned his voice, for he was speaking as he came on, moving what had once been a mouth, this dreadful thing, all raw and festering to the bone.

Two blazing eyes met mine, then rolled around on the cringing throng; and a voice like the voice of the dead broke out:

"I am come to the judgment of this man whom you burn!"

"Quider!" moaned the throng. "He returns from the grave! Oonah! He returns!"

But the unearthly voice went on through the whimper of the crowd:

"From the dead I return. I return from the north. Madness drove me. I come without belts, though belts were given.

"Peace, you wise men and sachems! Set free this man, my brother!"

"Quider!" I gasped. "Bear witness."

And the dead voice echoed, hollow:

"Brother, I witness."

Trembling fingers picked and plucked and tugged at my cords; the bonds loosened; the sky spun round; down I fell, face splashing in the mud.

LOGAN

CHAPTER ELEVEN

I KNEW nothing more until, hours later, I came to my senses in the fort.

How I had managed to reach it I never knew. I did not remember that the savages had carried me; I had no recollection of walking. I was told that when the gate lanthorn had been set that night, a sentry had discovered me creeping in the weeds at the moat's edge.

All that evening I had lain in a hot sickness on a cot in the casemates. I had babbled and whimpered till the doctor had finished cupping me, but after that I had rambled little and, toward sunrise, had fallen asleep.

My own memories begin with an explosion that brought me stumbling blindly out of bed, to find Jack Mount firing through a loophole and watching me, while he reloaded, with curious satisfaction.

He guided me back to my cot, fed me and got my shirt and leggings on me. Then he helped me up to the parapet, where the Virginia militia were firing by platoons into the pines along the river.

Bands of shadow and sunlight lay across the quiet forests; the calm hills sparkled. But the blackened clearing around the fort was alive with crawling forms, moving toward the woods. They were Cresap's Maryland riflemen, reconnoitering the riverside pines.

Volley after volley swept the still pines until a thundering report from the brass cannon ended the fusillade, and we leaned out on the epaulement, watching the riflemen, who were now close to the lead-sprayed woods.

The banked cannon smoke came driving back into our faces. But presently, through the whirling rifts, we caught sight of men running toward us. Behind them, dusky figures were pouring out of the woods.

"Good Lord!" shouted an officer. "See the savages!"

"See the riflemen," mimicked Mount at my elbow. "I told Cresap to wait till dark."

Along the parapets the soldiers were firing frenziedly. On back came the riflemen pell-mell, into the fort. The pulleys clanked; the drawbridge rose, groaning on its hinges.

Below us, the pursuing savages had taken cover like quail. Every charred tree root sheltered an Indian; the young oats were alive with them; they lay among the wheat, the bean poles; they crouched behind manure piles.

"Are all the settlers in the fort?" I asked Mount.

"Every man, woman, and child came in last night," he said. "They'll never go back. Look, lad!"

All around us, house after house was bursting into black smoke and spouts of flame. Fire leaped like lightning along those pine walls.

Soldiers and farmers came hastening up to the parapets, carrying buckets of water, for Cresap feared the sparks from the burning village. But there was worse danger than that: an arrow, tipped with blazing birch-bark, fell on the parapet and ere anyone could pick it up, another whizzed into the epaulement, setting fire to the logs. Faster and faster fell the flaming arrows. I forgot my weakness and fatigue, and found myself nimbly speeding after the fiery arrows and knocking out the sparks with an empty bucket.

All at once the fiery shower ceased. Presently we saw that the savages were falling back to the forest. Then our cannon began to thunder, and the militia fell in for volley firing again while, below, the drawbridge dropped and our riflemen stole out into the haze.

I was resting on the parapet when Mount and Cade Renard came up, carrying a sheaf of charred arrows.

"I just want you to look at these," began Mount, dumping the arrows into my lap. "The Weasel he says you know more about Indians than we do. To what tribes do these arrows belong?"

"Cayuga," I replied, wondering. "Cayuga, of course! . . . Wait! . . . Why, this one is a Seneca war arrow!"

"I told you!" observed the Weasel, grimly nudging Mount.

Mount stood silent and serious, watching me picking up arrow after arrow.

"Here is a Shawnee hunting-shaft," I said, startled, "and— and this—this is a strange arrow to me!"

I held up a slender, delicate arrow, tipped with steel.

"That," said Mount, gravely, "is a Delaware arrow."

"The Lenape!" I cried, astonished. Suddenly the terrible significance of these blackened arrows came to me. The Lenni-Lenape had risen, the Senecas and Shawnees had joined the Cayugas. The Long House was in revolt!

"Mount," I said, quietly, "does Colonel Cresap know this?"

The Weasel nodded. "We abandon the fort tonight," he said. "We can't face the Six Nations—here."

"We make for Pittsburg," added Mount. "It will be a job to get the women and children through. Cresap wishes to see you, Mr. Cardigan."

They piloted me to the point where a stockade barred the passage to the magazine. Corporal Cloud heard us and opened the stockade gate, where we saw Cresap heaping up loose powder into a long train that led into the magazine. He glanced up at us quietly.

"Am I right about those arrows?" he asked Mount.

"Mr. Cardigan says there's a Seneca war arrow among 'em, too," replied Mount.

Cresap's keen eyes questioned me.

"It's true," I said. "The Senecas guard the western door of the Long House, and they have made the Cayugas' cause their own."

"Dunmore will be well pleased," said Cresap, bitterly, rising and turning the key of the magazine. "Throw that key into the moat, corporal," he directed.

"You know," he observed, turning to me, "that we abandon the fort tonight. It means the end of all for me. I shall receive all the blame for this war. But let Dunmore beware if he thinks to deprive me of command over my riflemen! I've made them what they are—not for my Lord Dunmore, but for my country, when the call to arms peals out of every steeple from Maine to Virginia."

Then his eyes gravely questioned mine.

"You will be with us, will you not, sir?" he asked.

"I have not made up my mind to fight our King," I answered, slowly. "But I have determined to fight his deputy, Lord Dunmore—and all others who interfere with my people!"

"Oh, I think you will be with us when the time comes," said Cresap, with one of his rare smiles; and he led the way out of the stockade.

"Cut a time fuse for the powder train and bring it to me at the barracks," he said to Cloud; and saluting us thoughtfully, he entered the casemates, where the women and children were gathered in tearful silence.

The day wore away in preparation for the march.

At nine o'clock that evening the postern was opened quietly; and after scouts had reported the coast clear, the column started in perfect silence.

When the rear guard had disappeared into the darkness, Cresap, Mount, Cade Renard, and I bolted the gates, drew up the drawbridge, locked it, and dropped the keys into the moat. Then Cresap and Mount ran across the parade toward the magazine, while Cade and I tied a knotted rope to the southern parapet and shook it free, ready for our descent. Soon the other two came hurrying back, bidding us hasten, for the fuse was afire and the fort would soon be blown up.

Down the rope, hand over hand, we tumbled, one after

another, and then ran as though the Six Nations were at our heels. After ten minutes at top speed we joined the rear guard and fell in with the major, panting.

As we did so, a roar shook the solid forest; a crimson flame shot up to the stars; then thunderous darkness buried us.

Half-smothered cries and shrieks came from the women and children in the long convoy ahead, but these were quickly silenced and the column hastened on into the night.

I tramped along beside Mount and Renard, and presently Mount asked me what I meant to do in Pittsburg.

"I mean to see Lord Dunmore," I replied, quietly.

"What are you going to do to old Dunmore?" asked the big fellow, grinning.

"See here, my good man," said I, "you are impertinent. I am an accredited deputy of Sir William Johnson, and my business is his."

"You need not be so surly," grumbled Mount.

"You've hurt his feelings," observed the Weasel, trotting at my heels.

"Whose? Mount's?" I asked. "Well, I am sorry. I did not mean to hurt you, Mount."

"That's all very well, but you did," said Mount. "I've got feelings, too, just as much as the Weasel has."

"No, you haven't," said the Weasel, hastily. "I'm a ruined man, and you know it. Haven't I been through enough to give me sensitive feelings?"

Mount nudged me. "He's thinking of his wife and baby," he said. "Talk to him about them. He likes it. It harrows him. Doesn't it, Cade?"

"It hurts fearful," replied the Weasel, looking up at me hopefully.

"You had a lovely wife, didn't you, Cade?" inquired Mount, sympathetically.

"Yes—oh yes. And a baby girl, Jack—don't forget the baby girl," sniffed the Weasel.

"The baby must be nigh fifteen years old now, eh, Cade?" suggested Mount.

"Sixteen, nigh sixteen, Jack. The cunning little thing."

"What became of her?" I asked, gently.

"Nobody knows, nobody knows," murmured the Weasel. "My wife left me and took my baby girl, and since that I've been a little queer in my head."

"The Weasel was once a gentleman," said Mount, in my ear. "He had a fine mansion near Boston."

"I hear you!" piped the Weasel. "I hear you, Jack. You are quite right, too. I was a gentleman. I have ridden to hounds, Mr. Cardigan. I was master of foxhounds, Mr. Cardigan. None rode harder than I."

"And then you came home one day and found your dear wife had run away with an officer from Sir Peter Warren's ships—eh, Cade, old friend?" said Mount, affectionately.

"And she took our baby—don't forget the baby, Jack," murmured the Weasel.

I had been looking ahead along the line of wagons, where a lanthorn was glimmering. The convoy had halted, and presently we walked on until we came to a group of militia officers and riflemen. Cresap was there and called to me.

As I approached, I was surprised to see a tall Indian standing beside Cresap, muffled to the chin in a dark blanket.

"Cardigan," said Cresap, "my scouts found this Indian walking ahead in the trail all alone. He seems to be simple-minded. I can't make him out. You see he is unarmed. What is he?"

I glanced at the tall, silent Indian.

"This man is a Cayuga and a chief," I said in a low voice.

"Speak to him," said Cresap. "He appears not to understand me. I speak only Tuscarora, and that badly."

I looked at the silent Cayuga and made the sign of brotherhood. His dull eyes regarded me steadily.

"Brother," I said, "by the cinders on your brow you mourn for the dead."

"I mourn," he replied, simply.

"A son?"

"A family. I am Logan."

Shocked, I gazed in pity on the stern, noble visage. Then I turned quietly to Cresap.

"This is the great Cayuga chief, Logan, whose children were murdered by Greathouse," I said.

Cresap turned a troubled face on the mute savage.

"Ask him where he journeys."

"Where do you journey, brother?" I asked, gently.

"I go to Fort Pitt," he answered, without emotion.

"To ask justice?"

"To ask it."

"God grant you justice," I said, gravely.

To Cresap I said, "He seeks justice at Fort Pitt from Lord Dunmore."

"Bid him come with us," replied Cresap, soberly. "He

may not get justice at Fort Pitt, but there is a higher Judge than the Earl of Dunmore."

I led Logan into a space behind the wagons. Here we waited in silence until the slow convoy moved, and then we followed as mourners follow a casket to the grave of all their hopes.

Hour after hour we journeyed unmolested; the stars faded, but it was not yet dawn when a far voice cried in the darkness and a light moved, and we knew that the warders of the fortress were hailing our vanguard at the gates of Pittsburg.

JACK MOUNT

CHAPTER TWELVE

I AWOKE in a flood of bright sunshine that was pouring over the sweet lavender-scented sheets on my bed. Leaping lightly onto the rag carpet in my bare feet, I stood looking out of the window.

This lodging, whither Mount and Renard had piloted me when our convoy passed the ramparts of Fortress Pitt, was a most clean inn called the "Virginia Arms." James Rolfe, our host, was a shrewd-eyed fellow whose nasal voice sounded continually through the house. I could hear him now, but I was more interested in watching the many passers-by I could see from my window.

Then the winding of a brass horn directed my attention down the street, where people were flocking around a public crier.

"Attention! Attention!" he cried, unfolding a paper, and began to read:

"By permission of the Right Honorable Earl of Dunmore, Governor of Virginia! Four days' sport on Roanoke Plain. The Colonial Club offering prizes of one hundred pounds and fifty pounds; the Richmond Club offering two purses of fifty pounds. Attention! Sport on the Roanoke, an even and delightsome plain, most sweet and pleasant. . . ."

And he read on and on about the coming horse races.

I turned back into the room and began my toilet. How strange to find this town, undisturbed in its rural pleasures, while scarce a night's journey to the north the dead lay in the charred embers of their own doorsills!

Other somber thoughts oppressed me; I had a hard rôle to play before Lord Dunmore; I had a harder rôle to act before Silver Heels, if she were still in Pittsburg.

It gave me no pleasure to find myself so near her. Of course, I had never loved her as men love sweethearts. Her sudden and amazing appearance as a woman had aroused my curiosity; her popularity and beauty my jealousy. That was all.

She was only my playfellow; she had never been anything else. I meant to see her and tell her so; I meant to ask her forgiveness for offending her; I meant to seek her friendly confidence once more, to warn her that she should not tarry here in these troublous times, but return at once to Johnson Hall, where Sir William could protect her.

Doubtless Silver Heels would go with me. Dunmore would be obliged to provide our escort.

I had laid my hand on the door-knob, intent on seeking breakfast below, when somebody knocked. It was Saul Shemuel.

"Goot day and greeding, sir," said the peddler, bowing and rubbing himself against the door like a cat. "Gott save our country, Mr. Cardigan. Mr. Mount begs you will join the gendlemens in room 13, sir."

"Who are you, anyway, Shemuel?" I asked, curiously.

"A peddler, Mr. Cardigan—only a poor peddler," he protested. "Pray, do not look as if you knew me, sir, should you see me abroad in the streeds, sir. But if you wish to speag to me, please to buy a buckle; one buckle if I shall seek you here, two buckles if I am to follow you in the streed, sir, three buckles if you would seek me in my lodgings, Mr. Cardigan. I live at the 'Bear and Cubs Tavern,' sir, on the King's Road."

"Very well," I said, somewhat amused. "Here's sixpence for you, Shemmy. Cut away now!"

"If I might speak von vort, sir," he began, however.

"Well?" I said.

"I haf often seen you, sir, at Johnson Hall."

"Well?"

"And I haf also sold gilt chains to Miss Warren."

"Well?" I demanded, sharply.

"Miss Warren iss here in Pittsburg, sir," he ventured.

"I supposed so," I said, coldly, "but that does not interest me."

"Maybe," he said, spitefully, "you don'd know somedings?"

"What things?"

"Miss Warren weds mit Lord Dunmore in July."

He was gone ere I could rally from the shock. My thoughts were awhirl. That child thrown into the arms of a thing like Dunmore! What possessed all these witless gallants to go mad over my play fellow? Why should this bloodless Dunmore seek to make her Countess of Dunmore and the first lady in Virginia?

And Silver Heels, had she sold her beauty for the rank that this toothless assassin could give her? How could she endure him? How could she look at him without scorn and loathing?

Agitated and furious, I paced the hallway, resolving to seek out my lady Silver Heels without loss of time, and conduct her back to the nursery where the little fool belonged.

Countess, indeed! I'd bring her to her sense! And wait— only wait until Sir William should learn of this!

Somewhat comforted at the thought of the baronet's anger, I pocketed my excitement and began to search for room 13, where, according to Shemuel, I was expected.

In a few moments I found the room and knocked. Corporal Paul Cloud admitted me.

Around a table in the center of the large room were gathered Jack Mount, Cade Renard, Jimmy Rolfe, our landlord, Timothy Boyd, and another man whom I had never before seen. Cresap was not there, but in a corner, wrapped in his blanket, sat the bereaved Cayuga chief, Logan, staring at the floor.

The company were at breakfast, but Mount jumped to

his feet and gave me a warm handclasp, leading me to a chair beside the stranger.

I saluted him, and he bowed silently in return. He appeared to be a man of forty, elegantly yet soberly dressed, wearing his own dark hair, unpowdered, in a queue—a gentleman in bearing, in voice, in every movement.

Mount in a subdued voice asked permission to present me, and the gentleman bowed, saying he knew my name from hearing of my father.

As for his name, I think anybody in the colonies—aye, in London, too—would know it. For the gentleman beside whom I had been placed was the famous Virginian, Patrick Henry.

There was little conversation at breakfast. Presently Mr. Henry left the table and sat down by Logan; their blended voices came to us like the murmur of the deep thrilling chords of a harp.

Mount came over beside me and spoke low: "Cresap was arrested last night by Doctor Connolly, Dunmore's deputy, and is to be relieved of his command."

"Why did they arrest Cresap?" I asked.

"Why? O Lord! the town is full o' people blaming Dunmore for this new war. So yesterday Dunmore called in Connolly and his fawning agent Murdy, and they went about town swearing that Dunmore was innocent and that the wicked Cresap did it all. Now Connolly has had Cresap arrested, and he swears that Dunmore will make an example of Cresap for oppressing the poor Indians!"

Horrified at such hypocrisy, I could only gasp while Mount went on:

"But this rattlesnake, Dunmore, has bitten off more than

he can poison. Logan's here to demand justice on Greathouse. And now you are here to protest in Sir William's name. Oh, it's a fine pickle Dunmore will find himself swimming in."

"When is Logan to have an audience with Dunmore?" I asked.

"Tonight, in the fortress. And, Mr. Cardigan, I took the liberty of announcing to the Governor's secretary, Gibson, that an envoy from Sir William Johnson had arrived with a message for Lord Dunmore. So you also are to deliver your message to the Governor of Virginia in the hall tonight."

"But," said I, puzzled, "does Dunmore expect a messenger from Sir William?"

"Haven't you heard from Shemuel?" asked Mount. "I told him to tell you that Dunmore wants to marry the beautiful Miss Warren, who's cutting such a swath here. He sent his offer by runner to Sir William, and he's expecting Sir William to throw the poor girl at his head!"

I gripped Mount's arm.

"Mark you, Mount," I said, choking back my passion, "this night my Lord Dunmore will learn some things of which he is ignorant. One of them is that my kinswoman, Miss Warren, is betrothed to me!"

The big fellow stared at me; then he seized my hand and wrung it.

"I must get her back to Johnstown at once," I said. "You must stick by me now, Jack Mount, for Heaven knows what trouble lies before me ere I shake the Pittsburg dust off my moccasins!"

After a moment Mount said, "I suppose you don't know where Butler is?"

"Is he back in Pittsburg?" I asked, faintly.

"He's in attendance on Dunmore, lad. Shemmy told me last night."

"Very well," said I, smacking my suddenly parched lips. "I will kill him before I leave Pittsburg."

Mr. Henry rose from his seat beside Logan and came over to us.

"Mr. Cardigan," he said, "I know from Mount something concerning your mission here. I know you to be a patriot, and I believe that your honorable guardian, Sir William Johnson, will aid us with all his heart in whatever touches the good of our country. Am I not right?"

"Sir William's deeds are never secret, sir," I replied, cautiously. "All men may read his heart by that rule."

"Sir William has chosen in you a discreet deputy, to whom I beg to pay my sincerest compliments," said Mr. Henry, smiling.

"I can say this, sir," I replied, with a bow, "that I have heard him many times commend your speeches and the public course which you pursue." ·

"Sir William is too good," he replied, bowing.

"Aye, sir," I said eagerly, "he is good! I do believe him to be the greatest and best of men, Mr. Henry. I am here as his deputy, though without orders, now that my mission to Colonel Cresap has failed. But, sir, I shall use my discretion, knowing Sir William's mind, and this night I shall present to my Lord Dunmore a reckoning which shall not be easily canceled!"

"In the face of all his people?" asked Mr. Henry, curiously.

"In the face of the whole world, sir," I said, setting my teeth with a snap.

He held out his finely formed hand. I took it respectfully.

When he had gone away I drew Mount and Renard aside and asked them where Miss Warren was staying. They did not know.

"We'll find Shemuel; he knows," suggested Mount.

I assented, and we three, clad in our soiled buckskins, descended the stairway and sallied forth into the sunlit streets of Pittsburg.

It was on Pitt Street that we found Shemuel, trudging toward the King's Road. He saw us immediately, but made no sign as we approached until I asked the price of gilt buckles, and purchased three. Then he whined and protested he could not make change, and ended by begging us to follow to the "Bear and Cubs," just opposite, where change might be had in the taproom.

The "Bear and Cubs" was a squalid tavern, but into it I followed. Curiously enough, Shemuel appeared to suspect in advance what I wanted.

"If you hatt dold me this morning—ach!—bud I pelieved you care noddings, Mister Cardigan. She wass waiting to see you, sir, at Lady Shelton's in the Boundary ——"

"Did you tell her I was here?" I asked, angrily.

"Och yes! I wass so sure you would see her ——"

Exasperated, I shook my fist at the peddler.

"You miserable, tattling fool!" I said, fiercely. "Will you mind your own business hereafter?"

"It wass to hellup you, sir," he protested. "I dold you she wass to marry Lord Dunmore; if you hatt asked me I could haff dold you somedings more ——"

"What?"

"The banns will be published tomorrow from efery church in Pittsburg, Richmond, and Williamsburg!"

I glared at him, catching my breath.

"Sir," he whined, "I ask your pardon, but I haff so often see you in Johnstown, and Miss Warren, too, and—and I pelieved you—you lofed her ——"

I looked at him savagely.

"Ach! I will mix me no more mit kindness to nobody!" he muttered. "Shemmy, you mint your peezeness and sell dem goots in dot pasket-box!"

"Shemuel," I said, "what did she say when you told her I was in Fort Pitt?"

"Miss Warren went white like you did, sir, and then she sat down under the drees, and she cry mit herselluf."

"And you came to get me? And my manner made you believe I did not care to see Miss Warren?"

"Miss Warren she knew I hatt come to fetch you. I dold her so. When I passed py dot Boundary again, she wass waiting under the drees ——"

"How long since?"

"It is an hour, sir."

I fumbled in my belt and pulled out a gold piece.

"Thank you, Shemmy," I muttered, dropping it into his greasy cap. "Tell Mount and Renard where I have gone. Where is Lady Shelton's house?"

He led me to a back window and pointed out the Boundary road. Then he told me to keep on toward the north until I came to a large, white-pillared house on a terrace, surrounded by an orchard.

As I walked swiftly toward the Boundary my irritation increased with every stride; it appeared to me that the world was most impudently concerning itself with my private affairs. First, Mount had coolly arranged for my reception by Dunmore; and now the peddler, Shemuel, had calmly made a rendezvous for me with Silver Heels. The free direction of my own affairs appeared to be slipping away from me. I meant to put an end to that.

As for Silver Heels, no wonder the announcement to her of my presence here had frightened her into tears. She knew well enough, the little hussy, that Sir William would not endure her to wed such a man as Dunmore.

I found no difficulty in discovering the great, white-pillared house, set in an orchard.

There was a lady in the orchard, with her back turned toward me, leaning on a stone wall and apparently contemplating the town below. At the craunch of my moccasins on the gravel path she looked around, and then came hastily toward me.

"Are you a runner from Johnstown?" she asked, sharply.

I stood still. The lady was Silver Heels. She did not know me.

She did not know me, nor had I recognized her at first. And this change had come to us both within four weeks' time!

That she did not recognize me was less to be wondered at. The dark mask of the sun, which I now wore, had changed me to an Indian; anxiety, fatigue, and my awful peril in the Cayuga camp had made haggard a youthful face. In these weeks I had grown tall; I was thin as a kestrel, too.

But that I had not recognized her till she spoke distressed

me. She, too, had grown tall; she looked shockingly frail; and with her painted cheeks and powdered hair, and her laces and her frills, she might have been a French noblewoman from Quebec. It were idle to deny her beauty, but it was the beauty of death itself.

"Silver Heels," I said.

Her hand flew to her bosom. Good cause for fear had she, the graceless witch!

After a moment she turned and walked back to the wall. She leaned on it, looking out over the town again, and I followed her.

"Silver Heels," I asked, "are you afraid to see me?"

"No!" she said.

"Do you know why I am here?" I demanded.

She shrugged her shoulders. "Why you are here? Yes, I know why."

"Why, then?" I snapped.

"Because you believed that Marie Hamilton was here," she said, and laughed. "But you come too late, Micky," she added, spitefully. "Your bonnie Marie Hamilton is a widow now, and already back in Albany to mourn poor Captain Hamilton."

My ears were growing hot.

"Do you believe —— " I began,

But she turned her back, saying, "Oh, Micky, don't lie."

"Lie!" I cried, exasperated.

"Fib, then. But you should have arrived in time, my poor friend. Last week came the news that Captain Hamilton had been shot on the Kentucky. If you had only been here! But pray follow Mrs. Hamilton to Albany. She talked of nobody but you! she treated Mr. Bevan to one of her best silk mittens ——"

"What nonsense is this?" I cried, alarmed. "Does Mrs. Hamilton believe I am in love with her?"

"Believe it? What could anybody believe after you had so coolly compromised her ——"

"What?" I stammered.

"You kissed her, didn't you?"

"Silver Heels," said I, angrily, "do you suppose I am in love with Mrs. Hamilton?"

"Why did you court her?" demanded Silver Heels.

"Why? Oh, I—I fancied I was in love with you—and—and so I meant to make you jealous, Silver Heels. Upon my honor, that was all!"

The set smile on Silver Heels's lips did not relax.

"So you fancied you loved me?" she asked.

"I—oh—yes. Silver Heels, I was such a fool ——"

"Indeed you were!" she told me.

"There's one thing certain," I said. "I don't feel bound in honor to wed Mrs. Hamilton. I like her; she's pretty and sweet. But I don't want to wed anybody. I could wed you, if I chose, now, for Sir William wishes it, and he promised me means to maintain you."

"I thank Sir William—and you!" said Silver Heels, turning pale under her rouge.

"Oh, don't be frightened," I muttered. "I can't have you and—and my country, too. Silver Heels, I'm a rebel!"

She did not answer.

"Or at least I'm close to it," I went on. "I'm here to seek Lord Dunmore."

As I pronounced his name I suddenly remembered what I had come for, and stopped short, scowling at Silver Heels.

"Well, Micky?" she said, serenely. "What of Lord Dunmore?"

In a shamed voice I told her what I had heard. She did not deny it. When I drew for her a revealing portrait of the Earl of Dunmore, she only smiled and set her lips tight.

"What of it?" she asked. "I am to marry him; you and Sir William will not have him to endure."

"It's a disgraceful thing," I said, hotly. "If you cannot perceive the infamy of such a marriage, then I'll do your thinking for you and stop this shameful betrothal now!"

"I shall wed Dunmore in July."

"No, you won't!" I retorted, stung to fury. "Sir William has betrothed you to me. And, by Heaven! if it comes to that, I will wed you myself, you little fool!"

"You!" she blazed, clinching her slender hands. "Wed you! Not if I loved you dearer than hope of Heaven, Michael Cardigan!"

"I do not ask you to love me," I retorted, sullenly. "I do not ask you to wed me, save as a last resort. Renounce Dunmore and return with me to Johnstown, and I promise you I will not press my suit. But if you do not, by Heaven! I shall claim my prior right under our betrothal, and I shall take you with me to Johnstown. Will you come?"

"Lord Dunmore will give you your answer," she said, looking wicked and shaking in every limb.

"And I will give him his!" I cried. "Pray you attend tonight's ceremony in the fortress, and you will learn such truths as you never dreamed!"

I wiped my hot forehead with my sleeve, glaring at her.

"I think," said she, coldly, "you had best go."

"I think so, too," I sneered. "I ask your indulgence if I have detained you from the races, for which I perceive you are attired."

"It is true; I remained here for you, when I might have gone with the others."

Suddenly she broke down and laid her head in her arms.

Much disturbed, I watched her. Anger died out; I leaned on the wall beside her, speaking gently and striving to draw her fingers from her face. I begged for her confidence again; I recalled our old comradeship and asked pardon for all wherein I had hurt her.

Presently she answered a question; other questions and other answers followed; she raised her tear-marred eyes and dried them with a rag of tightly fisted lace.

To soothe and gain her I told her bits of what I had been through. But when I related the story of my great peril at the stake, she turned so sick and pallid that I ceased, and took her frail hands anxiously.

"What is the matter, Silver Heels," I said. "Never have I seen you like this. Have you been ill long? What is it, little comrade?"

"Oh, I don't know—I don't know, truly," she sobbed. "But I am so tired, so strangely ill of I know not what."

"You *do* know," I said. "Tell me, Silver Heels."

She raised her eyes to me, then closed them. Neck and brow were reddening.

"You are not in love?" I demanded, aghast.

"Aye, sick with it," she said, slowly, with closed lids.

It was horrible, incredible! And all I could say was: "Oh, Silver Heels! Silver Heels! That man! It is madness!"

"What man?" she asked, opening her eyes.

"What man?" I repeated. "Do you not mean that you love Dunmore?"

She laughed a laugh that frightened me, so wickedly bitter it rang in the summer air.

"Oh yes—Dunmore, if you wish—or any man—any man. I care not; I am sick, sick, sick! They have flattered and followed and sought me—great and humble, young and old—and never a true man among them—all wicked save one."

"And he?"

"Oh, he is a true man—a true man, for he is stupid and vain and tyrannical and violent—and a fool to boot, Michael —a fool to boot. But I love him."

"Who is this man?" I asked, cautiously.

"Not Dunmore, Michael."

"Not Dunmore? And yet you wed Dunmore?"

"Because I love the other, Michael, who coolly plans to mate me with a blooded mate to his taste. Because I am dying of the humiliation, Michael, and would wish to die so high in rank that even death cannot level me to him. Now, tell me whom I love."

"Heaven knows!" I said, in my amazement.

"True," she said. "Heaven knows I love a fool."

"Who is this fellow?" I insisted.

But she only laughed at me. And now her laughter cut, with its undertone ringing with tears.

"Very well," said I, "you shall not have Dunmore for spite

of a fool unworthy of you; and you shall not have the fool, either."

"I am not likely to get him," she said, wearily. "I pray you, dear friend," she added, "bid me good-by now. I am tired, Michael—tired to the soul of me."

She held out her slim hand. I took it; then I bent to touch it with my lips.

"You will not wed Dunmore?" I asked.

She did not reply.

"And you will come with me to Johnstown on the morrow, Silver Heels?"

There was no answer.

"Silver Heels?"

"If you are strong enough to take me from Dunmore, take me," she said, in a dull, tired voice.

"And—and from the other—the one you love—the fool?"

"He will leave me—when you leave me," she answered.

"You mean to say this pitiful ass will follow you and me to Johnstown!" I cried.

"Truly, he will!" she said, hysterically, and covered her face with her hands. But whether she was laughing or crying I could not determine; and I stalked wrathfully away, deter-mined to teach this same fool that his folly was not to my taste.

GIBSON

CHAPTER THIRTEEN

THE so-called "Governor's Hall," which stood within the limits of the fortifications, served sometimes as a court-house, sometimes as a temporary jail, often as a ballroom, occasionally as the Governor's residence when he came to Fort Pitt from Williamsburg. The Governor lived then on the second floor, and under his white-and-gold apartments stretched a long, blank, stone hall, around the walls of which ran a wooden balcony.

It was in this gloomy hall that my Lord Dunmore consented to receive the old Cayuga chief, Logan.

Towards dusk, that day of my talk with Silver Heels, a company of red-coated British infantry, with drummers leading, left the barracks opposite our inn, and marched away toward "Governor's Hall." A crowd of men and boys trailed behind, drawn by curiosity to catch a glimpse of Logan, "The

214

White Man's Friend," who was to ask justice this night of the most noble Governor of Virginia.

When the distant batter of the drums had died away, I left my window and descended the stairway into the street below, where Jack Mount and the Weasel swaggered to and fro, awaiting my coming.

We soon found ourselves in a crowd, the current of which swept down the King's Road toward the fortress. Presently the people ahead of us stopped and, looking over their heads, I saw the dark shape of the "Governor's Hall." As we stood there, coach after coach came rolling up to deposit its burden of bejeweled beauty. And all these people, all these dainty dames and gallants, had come curious to see the famous Logan —to hear the great Cayuga orator ask why his little children had been murdered by the white men!

The Weasel and I followed Mount through the crowd, elbowing our way to the portal, where Mr. Patrick Henry awaited us and passed us through the sentries and guards.

Candle-light softened the bare walls and benches; candle-light set silks and jewels in a blaze where the ladies, banked up like beds of rustling roses, choked the wooden balcony above our heads. Here and there were the scarlet coats of colonial and British officers.

At the end of the hall was a stone platform. The gilded chair in the center was for the Governor; the tables that flanked it for his secretaries.

For envoys, deputies, and for all plaintiffs, red benches faced the platform; behind these stretched rank on rank of plain, unpainted seats for the public.

We took seats on the last of the red benches, and in one

corner of it I perceived Logan sitting bolt upright, eyes fixed on space, brooding. Mr. Henry took his seat beside the stricken chief; next followed Jack Mount and the Weasel. I sat down beside the Weasel, and turned around to watch the people filling up the hall. They were serious, sober-eyed people, and, unlike the gay world in the galleries, had apparently not come to seek amusement in the dumb grief of a savage.

"They are mostly patriots," whispered the Weasel, "but peppered with Tories and sprinkled with Dunmore's spies."

"I see Paul Cloud and Timothy Boyd sitting there together," I observed. Then I caught a glimpse of the scarred, patched-up visage of the man whom I had made to taste his own hatchet. Startled, and realizing now the proximity of Walter Butler, I hunted the hall for him with hot, eager eyes. I could not find him, but in a corner I discovered his two creatures, Wraxall and Toby Tice. Where the cubs were, the old wolf was not far away, that was certain.

The Weasel nudged me, and I turned to see the platform before me alive with gentlemen, chatting and seating themselves.

The commotion on the platform was stilled as a gorgeous tipstaff advanced, banging his great stave on the stones and announcing the coming of his Lordship the Earl of Dunmore, Royal Governor of His Majesty's colony of Virginia. God save the King!

Swish! swish! went the silken petticoats as the gallery arose; the people on the floor rose, too, with clatter and scrape of benches.

Ah! There he was!—painted cheeks, pale eyes, smirk, laces, bird-claws and all—mincing toward the gilded chair.

Before he was pleased to seat himself, he peered up into the balcony and kissed his finger tips; and I, following his eyes, saw Silver Heels sitting with her sad eyes fixed, not on my Lord Dunmore, but on me.

Before I met her eyes I had been sullenly frightened, dreading to speak aloud in such a company. Now, with her deep, steady eyes meeting mine, fear fell from me. I smiled gayly up at her, and she smiled back at me.

Again the Weasel began twitching at my sleeve, and I bent beside him, listening and watching the gentlemen on the platform.

"That's John Gibson, Dunmore's secretary—the man in black on the Governor's left! That loud, bustling fellow on his right is Doctor Connolly, Dunmore's deputy for Indian affairs. He arrested Cresap to clear his own skirts of blame for the war. Behind him sits Connolly's agent, Captain Murdy. Murdy's agent was Greathouse. You see the links in the chain?"

"Perfectly," I replied, calmly, "and I mean to shatter them."

We were near enough to the platform to hear the Governor chattering with Gibson and Doctor Connolly.

"*Que dieu me damne!*" he said, spitefully. "But you have a *mauvais quart d'heure* ahead, Connolly!—curse me if you have not! Faith, I wash my hands of you, and you had best make your sulky savage yonder some good excuse for the war."

Connolly's deep voice replied evasively, but Dunmore clipped him short:

"Oh no! Oh no! The people won't have that, Connolly! Body o' Judas, Connolly, you can't make them believe Cresap started this war!"

Connolly whispered something.

"Eh? What? I say I wash my hands o' ye! And mind you clear me when you answer your filthy savage. I'll none of it, d'ye hear?"

Doctor Connolly flushed darkly and leaned back.

"And, Connolly," continued Dunmore, "you had best announce the restoration of Cresap to rank and command. Ged! —that ought to put the clodhoppers yonder in good humor, to keep them from sniveling while your dirty savage speaks."

Presently Connolly arose, and briefly announced the restoration of Cresap to command. There was no sound, no demonstration. Those in the balconies cared nothing for Cresap; those on the floor cared too much to compromise him with applause.

I heard Dunmore complaining to Gibson that the first part of Connolly's program had fallen flat, and that he, Dunmore, wanted to know what Gibson thought of refusing Logan the right of speech.

Gibson nervously shook his head and signaled to the interpreter to take his station; and when the interpreter advanced, announcing that the Governor of Virginia welcomed his brother, Logan, chief of the Cayugas and "The White Man's Friend," I saw Patrick Henry touch Logan on the shoulder.

Slowly the Indian looked up, then rose like a specter and fixed his sad eyes on Dunmore.

There was a rustle from the throng, then dead silence, as

from the old warrior's throat burst the first hollow, heartsick word:

"Brother!"

Oh, the grim sadness of that word!—the mockery of its bitterness!

Logan slowly raised his arm:

"Through that thick night which darkens the history of our subjugation, through all the degradation and reproach which has been heaped upon us, there runs one thread of light revealing our former greatness, pleading the causes of our decay, illuminating the pit of our downfall, promising that our dead shall live again! Not in the endless darkness whither priests and men consign us is that thread of light to be lost; but from the shadowy past it shall break out in brilliancy, redeeming a people's downfall, and wringing from you, our subjugators, the greeting—*Brothers!*

"*Fathers*: For Logan, that light comes too late. Death darkens my lodge. All within lie dead. Logan is alone. He, too, is blind and sightless; like the quiet dead, he hears not; nor can he see darkness or light.

. "For Logan, light or darkness comes too late."

The old man paused; the silence was dreadful.

Suddenly he turned and looked straight at Dunmore.

"I appeal to any white man if he ever entered Logan's lodge hungry and he gave him not meat; if he ever came cold and naked and he clothed him not!"

The visage of the Earl of Dunmore seemed to grow small and corpse-like.

Logan's voice grew gentler.

"Such was my love," he said, slowly. "Such was my great love for the white men! My brothers pointed at me as they passed, and said, 'He is the friend of white men.' And I had even thought to live with you, but for the injuries of my brothers, the white men.

"Unprovoked, in cold blood, they have slain my kin—all! —all! not sparing woman or child. There runs not a drop of my blood in the veins of any living creature!

"Hearken, *Brothers!* I have withstood the storms of many winters. Leaves and branches have been stripped from me. My eyes are dim, my limbs totter, I must soon fall. I, who could make the dry leaf turn green again; I, who could take the rattlesnake in my palm; I, who had communion with the dead, dreaming and waking; I am powerless. The wind blows hard! The old tree trembles! Its branches are gone! Its sap is frozen! It bends! It falls! Peace! Peace!

"Who is there to mourn for Logan? Not one!"

The old man bent his head and covered his face with his blanket. Through the stillness the painful breathing of the people swept like a smothered cry; women in the balcony were sobbing; somewhere a child wept uncomforted.

Patrick Henry leaned across to me; his eyes were dim, his voice choked in his throat.

"The great orator!" he whispered. "Oh, the great man!— greatest of all! The last word had been said for Logan! I shall not speak, Mr. Cardigan—it were sacrilege—now."

He rose and laid one arm about the motionless chief; then very gently he drew him out into the aisle. There was not a sound as they passed slowly out together, those great men who had both struck to the hilt for the honor of their kindred and of their native land.

Now, when at last Logan had disappeared, a living specter of reproach, those gathered there to listen breathed again, and hastened to forget that glimpse which they had caught of the raw heart of all tragedy—man's inhumanity to man.

Dunmore came slowly from his trance, mechanically preening his silken plumage and ruffling like a meager bird.

People breathed deeply, shifted in their seats, and turned around. Some stood up to go; chairs and benches grated on the stones.

I had already determined to defer my interview with Lord Dunmore because, after the great chief's speech, my poor words must fall stale. So I rose and touched Mount. But before he could find his feet, I heard Doctor Connolly speaking again and caught the name of Sir William Johnson.

"If the messenger from Johnstown be present," continued Doctor Connolly, "let him be assured of a warm welcome from his Lordship, the Earl of Dunmore, Governor of Virginia."

So the infatuated Dunmore, grasping at a straw to dam the current of public sentiment, thought to win sentimental favor with the news of his betrothal.

His purpose was plain to me and loathsome as I stood there, watching him simper. I would not speak now.

But presently, looking around, I found that all those who had risen had again seated themselves and that I stood there all alone. It was too late to seek cover, and Connolly was smiling encouragingly at me.

"Are you not a messenger from Sir William Johnson?" he prompted, with his domineering smile of patronage.

"Yes, Doctor Connolly," I replied, slowly.

There was a pause. Dunmore tapped on his box and fell a-smirking and bridling, with sly, rheumy glances at the gallery.

"Lord Dunmore," I said, steadily, "ere I inform you why I am here, you shall know me better than you think you do.

"I am not here to tell you of that chain which links the Governor of Virginia with the corpse of Logan's youngest child—nor to count the links of that chain backward, from Greathouse to Murdy, to Gibson, to Connolly, to ——"

"Stop!" burst out Connolly, springing to his feet. "Who are you? What are you? How dare you address such language to the Earl of Dunmore?"

Astonished, furious, he stood shaking his fist at me. Dunmore sat in a heap, horrified, with the simper on his face stamped into a grin of terror. The interruption stirred up my blood to the boiling.

"I do not reply to servants," I said. "My business here is not with Lord Dunmore's lackeys. If the Earl of Dunmore knows not my name and title, he shall know it now! I am Michael Cardigan, cornet in the Border Horse, and deputy of Sir William Johnson, Baronet, His Majesty's Superintendent of Indian Affairs for North America!

"Who dares deny me right of speech?"

Dunmore lay in his chair, a shrunken mess of lace and ribbon; Connolly appeared paralyzed; Gibson stared at me over his table.

"I am not here," I said, coolly, "to ask your lordship why this war, falsely called Cresap's war, should be known to honest men as 'Dunmore's war.' Nor do I come to ask you why England should seek the savage allies of the Six Nations, which this war, so cunningly devised, has given her ——"

"Treason! Treason!" bawled a voice behind me. It was Wraxall; I recognized his whine.

"But," I resumed, pointing my finger straight at the staring Governor, "I am here to demand an account of your stewardship! Where are those Cayugas whom you have sworn to protect from the greed of white men? Where are they? Answer, sir! Where are Sir William Johnson's wards of the Long House? Where are the Shawnees, the Wyandottes, the Lenape, the Senecas, who keep the western portals of the Long House? Answer, sir! for this is my mission from Sir William Johnson. Answer! lest the King say to him, 'O thou unfaithful steward!'"

Hubbub and outcry and tumult rose around me. Dunmore was getting on his feet; Connolly flew to his aid, but the Governor snarled at him and went shambling out of the door behind the platform, while in the hall the uproar swelled into an angry shout: "Shame on Dunmore! God save Virginia!"

An officer in the gallery leaned over the edge, waving his gold-laced hat.

"God save the King!" he roared, and many answered, "God save the King!" but that shout was drowned by a thundering outburst of cheers: "God save our country! Hurrah! Hurrah! Hurrah!"

"Three cheers for Boston!" bawled Jack Mount, jumping

up on his bench; and the rolling cheers echoed till the throng went wild.

Mount caught me up in his arms and shouldered his way toward the door; others crowded around, patting my legs and cheering. Out we went past the sentinels, where for a moment I thought soldiers and people would come to blows.

But Mount waved his cap and shouted: "The ladies! Honor the ladies!" and the crowd fell back as the excited dames and maidens from the balcony entered coaches and chairs and disappeared into the depths of the starlight.

I could not find Silver Heels, and presently I gave up that hope, for the throng, hustled by the soldiers, began shoving and pressing until the breath was near squeezed from my body and I made out to slip back with Mount and Renard to the open air.

"Look sharp!" Mount said, eagerly. "There will be heads to break anon. Ha! See them running yonder! Hark! Do you not hear that, Cade? Clink—whack! Bayonet against cudgel! They're at it, lad! Come on! Come on! Give it to the Tories!"

The next instant we were enveloped in the mob that hurled itself against the soldiers. The fight was desperate and silent, save for the whipping swish of ramrods whistling, the dull shocks of blows, or the ringing crack of a cudgel on some luckless pate.

Before long it began to go hard with the King's soldiers, but they stuck to the mob like bulldogs, giving blow for blow so stanchly that I called out to Jack Mount: "Look at them, Jack! What very gluttons for punishment! Nobody but British could stand up to us like that!"

A crack on the sconce from a ramrod transformed my admiration into fury, and I drove my right fist into the eye of one of these same British soldiers, receiving at the same moment such a jolt in the body that I went sprawling and gasping about until Mount pulled me out of the crush.

When I had found my breath again, I prepared to return to the fray, which had now taken on a more sinister aspect.

THE NEXT MOMENT WE WERE LOCKED IN A STRUGGLE

Bayonets had already been used; a man was leaning against a tree near me, bleeding from a wound in the neck, and another reeled past, tugging at a bayonet that had transfixed his shoulder.

But the end came suddenly now; horsemen were galloping up behind the jaded soldiers; I saw Shemuel dart out of the swaying throng and take to his heels. Then the Weasel came scurrying past and called out to me. Mount followed, lumbering on at full speed. The throng scattered in every direction, and I with them.

Mount, Renard, Shemuel, and I crossed the Boundary and headed for the dirty alley that conducted to the rear door of Shemuel's inn. We were about to enter this lane when, without warning, five men rushed at us. The next moment we were locked in a struggle. At first, there was not a sound but strained gasps and heavy breathing; but presently a piercing yell echoed through the alley, and Shemuel ran squattering into the inn. He had stuck a handful of needles into his assailant's leg, and the man bounded madly about, howling with dismay.

As for me, I found myself clutched by that villain, Wraxall, while Toby Tice tried to tie my wrists. But the Weasel fell upon them both and kicked them so heartily that they left me and took to their heels.

And now came the host of Shemuel's inn, lanthorn in one hand, a meat knife in the other, and after him a tapboy, an hostler, and Shemuel. But reinforcements had arrived too late —too late to help us take the impudent band, which had fled— too late to bring to life that dark mass lying quiet in the filth of the alley.

Mount seized the lanthorn and lowered it beside the shape on the ground.

"His neck is broken," he said, briefly.

One by one we took the lanthorn and looked in turn on the dead.

"Greathouse," whispered Mount, moving the body with his foot.

"Greathouse, eh?" grumbled the host of the inn. "Well, he can't lie here behind *my* house." And he caught him by the heels and dragged him to a black spot under a rotten shed. There was a cistern there. I moved away, feeling strangely faint. Mount linked his arm in mine.

Presently there sounded a dull noise under the ground, a shock and thick splashing.

Mount shrugged his shoulders and turned away indifferently. The Weasel and I followed, and together we traversed the market square unmolested, and headed for the "Virginia Arms," discussing the utterly unprovoked attack on us by Butler's band.

"One thing is clear—they were after you," observed Mount, turning on me.

"Acting on Butler's orders," I agreed, grimly.

We came finally to our inn, weary and ready for rest. But before I mounted to my chamber I bade a servant fetch me writing materials. Then, ere I sought my bed, I wrote three letters.

One, to Sir William, told him simply that I had failed in my mission; that I was setting out for Johnson Hall on the morrow with Felicity, and that I would explain all upon my arrival.

The next, to Silver Heels, told her I was leaving on the following morning for Johnson Hall and bade her be prepared to accompany me with Black Betty.

And the third letter, addressed to the Earl of Dunmore, Royal Governor of Virginia, informed his lordship that my kinswoman, Mistress Felicity Warren, was my betrothed; that she was leaving Pitt with me on the morrow; and that I claimed the escort it was my right to demand and his lordship's duty to furnish.

With great labor I wrote these letters, and then with weary satisfaction I sought my bed.

CHAPTER FOURTEEN

I WAS awakened shortly after daylight by a hubbub outside, and I lay in bed, listening, half asleep. About six o'clock the Weasel opened my chamber door, saying that Pittsburg was filling with refugees from the frontier.

I asked him whether messengers had brought me answers to my letters from Lord Dunmore and Miss Warren, and he replied in the negative and shut the door.

About seven I arose. I found that exhausted fugitives from the smoking, blood-soaked frontier were still streaming in, to be taken care of by the people of the town.

To and fro the good people of Pitt hastened on their errands of pity; others, having done their part, gathered in groups discussing openly the riot of the previous evening.

People and soldiers had at last come to blows; blood had flowed, although nobody exactly understood for what reason it had been shed. Patched pates and plastered cheeks were plentiful about the streets, but there appeared to be no effort to arrest any citizen whose body or apparel bore marks of the conflict. Citizens and soldiers eyed one another askance, but apparently without rancor or malice.

That morning I settled my reckoning with my host of the "Virginia Arms." As he appeared uneasy about the reckoning of Jack Mount and the Weasel, I settled that, too. I paid Rolfe somewhat scornfully, however, for I felt that the friends of liberty ought to trust each other implicitly.

I was curt with the fellow as he left my room; but when Cade Renard strolled in a few moments later, I was astonished to learn that this same James Rolfe had aided Mount to throw the tea-chests into the sea, and had beggared himself in contributing to every secret patriotic society in Boston.

"He'll lend me what he has," said the Weasel, "but he would be unpleasant if I attempted to escape from here without a reckoning. I am glad you paid; we have no money. We were speaking of tapping a certain fat Tory magistrate again ——"

"Taking the road?" I exclaimed.

"No, just the judge's purse," the Weasel returned, blandly.

I looked at the little man in horror. He met my gaze with an innocent look.

"If," said I, stiffly, "you or Mount require money, I beg you will borrow it from me as long as we travel together."

There was little profit in continuing the subject; if Renard and Mount chose to justify their reputations, I could not prevent them.

It was now past eight o'clock and still no reply had come to me from either Dunmore or Silver Heels. I was fairly atwitch with restless anxiety. Nor was the Weasel's continued conversation soothing.

"If you were not a deputy of Sir William Johnson's, Dunmore would have jailed you for what you said," he remarked. "You have cast the last grain into the scales and they have tipped him out, repudiated and dishonored. But Walter But-ler lives, friend Michael. Beware, sir!"

"There are other things that disturb me far more at the moment," I returned, unable to conceal my restlessness.

Just then Mount came in noisily.

"Mr. Cardigan is in some pressing trouble," the Weasel promptly told him.

"It is only that I have no letter from Dunmore or from Miss Warren," I muttered.

Mount and the Weasel were sympathetically silent. We sat there, gnawing our knuckles.

"Do you think the runner I hired to carry my letter to Sir William will be scalped?" I presently asked, turning to look at Mount.

"He *has* been scalped," said Mount, quietly.

Thunderstruck, I sprang to my feet, and finally found tongue to ask how he knew.

"Why, lad," he said, modestly, "I followed your runner last night, and he had not gone ten paces from this inn ere a man left the shadow of the trees yonder to dog us both. I caught the fellow by the market yonder, and trounced him soundly. Then I followed your runner, but they delayed me at the fortress gate. When I cleared the sentries I started to run; but my journey was short!"

He paused, then added, abruptly, "Your messenger lay dead by the wood's edge."

"I had not dreamed the savages were so near," said I, horrified.

"*Some* savages are," he observed.

"What do you mean?" I asked, huskily.

"I mean that Walter Butler's men did this and that your letter is now in Dunmore's hands."

Rage tore at me. But Mount and Renard reasoned with me sternly.

"The sooner you leave Pitt the safer for you," said Mount. "The town talks of little but your accusation of Dunmore last night. Dunmore and Butler will treat you as they did your messenger if you give them half a chance. Tush, lad! This is no time for boyish fury. Get your kinswoman, Miss Warren, out of this town. Get her out tonight. Why, lad, the Governor is crazed with the disgrace you have brought upon him! Trust me, he will stop at nothing where he can strike unseen."

"You mean he will not answer my letter or accord me escort?" I asked, astonished.

"If he furnished you escort, it would be an escort of murderers who would take care you never saw Johnstown," said the Weasel.

At that moment Rolfe came up from below, bearing a letter for me, and saying that it had been brought hither by a servant in Lady Shelton's livery.

I took the letter; the seal had already been broken.

Rolfe pointed to it, shaking his head. "I so received it, Mr. Cardigan. That seal may have been broken by accident, but you best know, sir, what your foes might gain by a knowledge of your letters."

"The sooner we leave here the happier we shall be," said the Weasel, cheerfully. "Jimmy Rolfe, that stout post chaise, well provisioned, and four strong horses might help us tonight, eh, friend?"

"I cannot pay for that," I said, blankly, looking up from my letter.

"The chaise is yours," said Rolfe, resentfully. "Pay when you can, sir; I trade not with friends in need." And he went out, disrespectfully slamming the door.

"A rare man," said Mount, "but touchy, lad, touchy."

"He is a loyal friend," I said, reddening. "I have much to learn of men."

"And men have much to learn of you, lad!" said Mount, heartily. "Come, sir, read your nosegay, and may it bring you happiness! Weasel, turn thy back and make pretence to catch flies."

I went over to the window and, leaning against the bars, read:

DEAR COZZEN MICHAEL,—I am not permitted to accompany you today to Johnstown, it being a racing day and I pledged to attend with Lady Shelton.

And oh, Micky, why did you say such things to Lord Dunmore last night? I have been ill of it all night and in a fever for fear they may harm you. Moreover, Lord Dunmore came here in a white fury and showed me the letter you had written to him. He says that you are not the messenger he expected, though you may be a deputy, and he vows he will not give me up but will publish the banns today in Pitt, come what may. Which has frightened me so I write to you that I do not wish to be a countess any more and would be glad to go to Aunt Molly and Sir William.

I will rise from bed at eleven o'clock tonight and go out into the orchard with Black Betty. Pray you, cozzen, greet me with a post chaise and take me away from these dreadful, dreadful people.

Your cozzen,
FELICITY.

Postscriptum

To witt, even though we be affianced as you have told Lord Dunmore, I will not wed you. Let this be understood.

Having read the letter, I stood reflecting. I had a mind to follow Silver Heels to the races, trusting that I might find a moment to warn her most solemnly not to fail us. Mount thought the idea wise and offered to bear me company. The Weasel agreed to remain and assist Rolfe to equip and furnish our post chaise for a long journey.

It was arranged that Silver Heels and Black Betty were to ride in the chaise, and I with them; that Mount and the Weasel would sit the horses as postilions, and that Shemuel should ride atop. It was further decided that as the northern and western frontiers were impassable in view of the border war, we should take the post road to the Virginia border, make for Williamsburg, and from there turn north.

I gave the Weasel money for his purchases, and Mount and I started off for the races.

We were striding along in silence when Mount suddenly stopped in the middle of the King's Road and looked back.

"What's amiss?" I asked.

"Nothing except that we are followed," said Mount, warily.

I stared about, but could see nobody who appeared to be observing us, though there were numbers of people on the King's Road, doubtless also bound for the races.

"Are you sure we are followed?" I asked.

"Not quite," said Mount. "I shall know anon. Trust me in this, lad, and take pains to do instantly what I do. Perhaps my life may pay for this day's pleasure."

"I will take great care to imitate you," I answered, anx-iously.

Unquestioned by any sentry, we passed on out into the country.

Suddenly Mount jerked his head over his shoulder.

"I think I am right; I think I know the jade," he said.

"Is it a woman who follows us?" I asked, amazed.

"Aye, a bit of a lass, maybe eighteen or thereabouts."

"You know her?"

"And she me," said Mount, grimly. "Harkee, friend Mi-chael, her father is—gad! I can scarce say it to you, but—well—her father is what they call a thief-taker."

"What has that to do with us?" I asked.

Mount spoke with an effort: "Because I have stopped some few purse-proud magistrates upon the highway, they say evil things o' me. That lass behind us means to follow me and tell her lout of a father where I may be found."

I was horrified, and he saw it and stopped short.

"You are right," he said, simply. "A gentleman cannot be found in such company. Go on alone, lad!"

"Jack!" I said, hotly. "Do you believe I would cry quits now? A plague on you! Come on, sir!"

His firm mouth relaxed and quivered a little; he hesitated, then strode on beside me, muttering something about gentle blood and what's bred in the bone.

We were now in sight of the flag-covered pavilion on Roanoke Plain, and on either side of us the road was lined with drinking-booths and peddler stands and show tents. Around them the townspeople clustered; but, depressed by the sickening knowledge of Mount's peril, I had no stomach for such tawdry pleasures. Nor had he, for he scarcely glanced at the booths as we passed.

Suddenly he said, "This will not do; I have been hunted long enough!"

"What are you going to do?" I asked.

"Hunt in my turn," he said grimly.

"Hunt—what?"

"The lass who hunts me. Follow, lad. On your life, do as I do. Now, then! Gay! Gay! Ruffle it, lad! Cut a swagger, cock your cap, and woe to the maid who is beguiled by us!"

The change in him was amazing; his airs, his patronage, his chaff, his lightning wit!—it was the old Mount again, quaffing a great cup of ale, pledging every pretty face that passed, glorious in his self-esteem, amusing in his folly, a dandy, a ruffler, a careless *coureur-de-bois*, and king of them all without an effort.

Peddler and gypsy were no match for him; his banter silenced the most garrulous; his teasing pleased the wenches.

"Which is the maid?" I asked, under my breath.

"Yonder, stopping to stare at gingerbread. Now she turns; mark! It is she with the pink print and the chip hat."

"I see her," said I.

She was a healthy, red-cheeked, blue-eyed girl, with lips a trifle over-full. She appeared uneasy and uncertain, watching Mount when he raised a laugh, and laughing herself as excuse, though her mirth appeared to me strained.

She had been edging nearer, and now stood close to us, at the entrance to an arbor wherein were set benches in little corners.

"Will no maid pity me!" exclaimed Mount. "I shall be lonely sitting by myself in yonder arbor!"

With that, he turned to find her who had followed him close to his elbow.

He smiled in her face and made her a very low bow, drawing a furrow through the dust with the fluffy tail on his coonskin cap.

"If I knew your name," he said, "I might die contented."

She seemed startled and abashed, but Mount bent beside her to whisper and smile and entreat her to taste a glass of currant wine with us.

I do not know to this day why she consented. Perhaps she thought to confirm her suspicions and entrap some admission from Mount. At any rate, we three soon sat in the arbor, and Mount did set such a pace for us that ere I was aware our cakes and wine had disappeared and he had his arm around the silly maid.

Intensely embarrassed and ill at ease with this pothouse gallantry, I regarded them sideways in silence, impatient for Mount to end it all.

The end had already begun; Mount rose lightly to his feet and drew the girl with him, turning her quietly by the shoulders and looking straight into her eyes.

"Why do you follow me?" he asked, coolly.

The color left her face; her eyes flew wide open with fright.

"I shall not hurt you, little fool!" he said. "I had rather your father, the thief-taker, took me, than harm you. Yes, I am that same Jack Mount. You are poor; they will pay you for compassing my arrest. Come, shall we seek your father, Billy Bishop, the taker of thieves?"

He drew her toward the gate, but she fell a-whimpering and caught his arm, hiding her face in his buckskin sleeve.

Disgusted, I waited a moment, then turned my back and walked out into the sunshine, where I paced to and fro until at last Mount joined me, wearing a scowl.

As we turned away together I glanced into the arbor and saw our lass still sitting at the table with her head buried in her arms and her pink shell-hat on the grass.

As for Mount, he said nothing except that, though he no longer feared the girl, he meant hereafter to trust to his heels in similar situations.

SIR TIMERSON CHANK

CHAPTER FIFTEEN

A S WE came to the high stockade that surrounded the Roanoke Racing Plain, a bell struck somewhere inside; there was a moment's silence, then a roar, "They're off!" and the confused shouting and cheering of the crowd.

I paid the gate-keepers the fee they demanded, and we entered.

Bowered in trees the lovely pale green meadow lay, cut by the bronzed oval of the course. Pavilion and field glowed in the colors of fluttering gowns; white and scarlet and green marked the line where half a dozen mounted jockeys walked their lean horses under the starter's tower.

I fixed my eyes on the pavilion to search it through and through for Silver Heels, but the task seemed hopeless. So I sought to discover Lady Shelton, a large, sluggish lady whom I had noticed at Johnstown. I could not find her, either.

With my arm on Mount's, I paced the sward, my eyes again

searching the pavilion. Where was Silver Heels? Where had the little baggage hid herself?

The fox-hunting gentry in pink were coming across the field in a body. As they passed us, a strangely familiar eye met mine and held it—the puzzled eye of one of the red-coated young men. Where had I seen him before? Suddenly I knew him, and at the same moment he left the company and came hastily up to me, offering his hand. The fox-hunter was my old acquaintance, Mr. Bevan, the dragoon, and he had actually recognized me under my sunburn and buckskins. Rivals never forget.

There was no mistaking his cordiality, however, and I should have been a churl not to have met him fairly by the hand he offered.

"I heard you speak in 'Governor's Hall,' " he said. "You have become famous, Mr. Cardigan, since we last met."

"You would say 'notorious,' " I rejoined, smiling.

He protested vigorously:

"No! No! I understand you are not of our party, but, believe me, were I a—a—patriot, as they say, I should be proud to hear a comrade utter the words you uttered in 'Governor's Hall'!"

"Did I say I was a rebel?" I asked, laughing.

"Well," he rejoined, "if that speech did not commit you, we are but a dull company here in Pittsburg."

He glanced after his comrades, who were now entering the canopied space where refreshments lay piled; and he straightway invited me, turning with a bow to include Jack Mount.

I made our excuses, which Mr. Bevan accepted regretfully. Then again he offered me his hand, so frankly that I drew him aside and begged his indulgence for my boorish behavior at Johnson Hall.

"The fault was mine," he said, instantly. "I sneered at your militia and deserved your rebuke. Had I not deserved it, I should have called you out, Mr. Cardigan."

Then his friendly eyes grew grave and he began bending his hunting-whip into a bow, absently regarding Mount, who was resignedly seating himself under a near-by tree.

After a moment he looked back at me, saying, "Do you know that this morning the banns were published for the wedding of Lord Dunmore and your kinswoman, Miss Warren?"

So in spite of my letter, Dunmore had done this shameful thing! I think my scowling face gave Bevan his answer, for he laid his hand on my arm.

"It is no shame," he said, "for me to tell you that Miss Warren has refused me. How can a heart be humbled that has loved such a woman?"

"She is not a woman yet," I said, harshly. "She is a child, and a willful one at that! Sir, it maddens me to see men after her, and she but fifteen!"

"Miss Warren celebrated her sixteenth birthday with a dinner at Lady Shelton's a week since," said Bevan, coloring up.

I thought a moment. Yes, that was true; Silver Heels was sixteen now. And the barriers of childhood no longer barred the men who hunted her!

"I have told you this," said Bevan, stiffly, "because I believed you were in love with Miss Warren and must suffer great pain to learn of her betrothal to Lord Dunmore."

"And—what then, sir?" I asked, angry and perplexed.

"This, Mr. Cardigan! That this marriage is a monstrous thing, and that I do most earnestly believe that Miss Warren loves a man more worthy of her."

"What man?" I demanded, sharply.

"You should not ask me that!" he retorted, more sharply still.

"But I do! You know him, I take it."

"Yes." He said no more, and his smile puzzled me.

After a moment's silence I asked, "Is he worthy of her?"

"What man is?" he answered, quietly.

"Oh, many men. Pardon, but you are in love, and so are blinded. I see clearly. I know my cousin, and I know that she is a willful maid who has raised the devil out o' bounds, and is ready to run to cover now."

Bevan was red in the face.

"It is a kinsman's privilege to criticize," he said.

"A kinsman's duty!" I added. "And it is also my duty to think now of my cousin's honor and happiness. God help the man who bars our way northward!"

"If you mean to take her," said Bevan, in a low voice, "I wish you Godspeed. But how can you pass the fort, Mr. Cardigan?"

"Do you believe Dunmore would detain us?" I asked, blankly.

"I know he would if he heard of it in time."

I thought a moment and then, on the impulse, told Bevan what our plans were.

When I had told him all, he said, very quietly: "I am glad you told me this. I will be at the King's Road gate tonight. If there is trouble with the sentries I will vouch for you."

His generosity touched me deeply, and I told him so.

"Could a gentleman do less?" he asked, gravely. Then he offered me his hand in farewell, pressing mine firmly.

"You know Miss Warren is here?" he asked, cautiously.

"I am seeking her," said I.

"She walked to the hill, yonder, with Lady Shelton, after the last race," he said, pointing with his whip to a far wooded knoll behind the paddocks.

"Dunmore is searching everywhere for her," he added, significantly.

So we parted, I warm with gratitude, he quietly cordial.

Mount rejoined me somewhat fretfully. Together we crossed the paddock and started up the wooded knoll. We were perhaps halfway up the slope when I heard a footstep behind us and glanced back. What was my astonishment to behold the Weasel trotting along at our heels.

"Where on earth did you come from?" I asked.

"From the 'Virginia Arms'," he replied, seriously. "I like to be near Jack."

Mount smiled at the little careworn man with wonderful tenderness.

"Come, Cade, old friend," he said, "let us sit here in the grass while our young gentleman lightly goes a-courting!"

So I left the pair sitting on the sod and climbed the remaining half of the slope alone.

Now, no sooner had I reached the top of the knoll than I perceived Silver Heels, sitting upon a rock, reading a letter; and when I drew near, my moccasins making no sound, I could not help but see that it was my letter she perused so diligently.

It gratified me to observe that she apparently valued the instructions in it.

"Silver Heels," I began kindly.

She started, then thrust the letter into her bosom.

"Oh, Michael, you are insufferable!" she cried.

"What!" I exclaimed, astonished.

Her eyes filled and she sprang up.

"I know not whether to laugh or cry, so vexed am I!" she stammered, and called me booby and Paul Pry.

"I am not spying," said I, hotly. "Don't pretend that scrawl was a love letter, for I know it to be my own!"

"Ah, you *did* come spying!" she flashed out, stamping her foot furiously.

"Lord! was there ever such a spiteful maid!" I cried. "I came here to have a word with you concerning our journey this night. I care not a penny whistle for your love letters. Can you not understand that?"

She turned somewhat pale and stood still. "Yes," she said, slowly, "I understand."

I had not meant to speak harshly, and I told her so. She nodded, scarcely listening. Then I spoke of our coming journey, and explained our plans.

She acquiesced, saying she was ready, and she even thanked me for my interest in her welfare.

"How came you to find me out, here in my retreat?" she then asked, slowly.

"Mr. Bevan told me," I replied.

"Poor Mr. Bevan!" she murmured. "How jealous you were of him."

"He is a splendid fellow," I declared, much ashamed.

"SILVER HEELS," I BEGAN KINDLY

She nodded, but said no more. I sat down on the grass beside her, and for a while no word was spoken. But presently she said, with an effort: "Michael, I—I never told you, but I was very glad when you came to explain to me that night in the pantry."

"Well," said I, stiffly, "you certainly concealed your pleasure. Lord, child, how you scored me!"

"I know it," she muttered. "I was a perfect fool. You see, I —I was hurt so deeply that it frightened me ——"

"You ought to have known that I meant nothing," said I. "Mrs. Hamilton tormented me till I—I—well, whatever I did was harmless. Anyway, it was done because I thought I loved you—I mean like a lover, you know ——"

"I know," said Silver Heels.

"But now I know the difference between hurt vanity and love," I added, complacently.

"I, too," said Silver Heels. "But there is little use in our discussing these things. Sir William does not wish—he told me to tell you, if I saw you in Pittsburg—he does not wish ——"

"Go on," I said.

"Sir William has changed his mind."

"Well?" I urged.

"I—I am not to wed you," she stammered.

"Of course not," I said, rather blankly. "But I thought Sir William desired it. He said that he did. He said it to me!"

"He no longer wishes it," said Silver Heels.

"Why?"

"I don't know," she answered, faintly. "Do—do you care?"

"Care? Why—why, I don't know. It is not very pleasant to

be forced to conclude that you are too poor and humble to wed your own kin if you wish to. See here, Silver Heels, why should Sir William drive me away from you?"

"You have never needed driving," said Silver Heels.

"Yes, I have!" I retorted. "Didn't you drive me away for Bevan?"

After a silence she stole a glance at me.

"Would you come back—now?"

Something in her voice startled me.

"Why—yes," I stammered, not knowing exactly what she meant. "I cannot see that there is such difference in rank between us that Sir William should forbid me to wed you."

"I was afraid," she ventured, "that perhaps—perhaps Sir William thought you had become too fine for me."

This was a new idea, but it did not gratify me.

"I'll tell you this," said I, "that if I loved you in that way—you know what I mean—I'd wed you, anyhow!"

"But I would not wed you!" she said, haughtily.

"You would not refuse me?" I asked, in amazement.

"I should hate you—if you were above me—in rank!"

"Even if you loved me before?"

"Ah yes—even if I loved you—as I love—him whom I love."

Her clear eyes were looking straight into mine now, and suddenly my heart began to beat heavily.

Silver Heels dropped her eyes; her fingers, twisting a daisy stem, were all atremble.

Presently I said, "Who is this fool whom you love?"

I had not thought to fright or hurt her, but she flushed and burned until all her face was surging scarlet to her hair.

"Silver Heels," I stammered, catching her fingers.

At the touch a strange thrill struck through my body and I choked, unable to utter a word; I caught her fingers and drew them, interlocked, from her eyes. Her eyes! Their beauty amazed me; their frightened, perilous sweetness drew my head down to them. Breathless, her mouth touched mine. Then suddenly she had gone, and I sprang to my feet to find her standing tearful, quivering, with her hands on her throbbing throat. I leaned against a sapling, dazed, my thoughts whirling rapturously.

With a sort of curious terror she watched me leaning there. Then of a sudden she dropped on the rock and fell a-weeping without a sound; and I knelt beside her, now crushing her shoulders close to me, now kissing her little hands.

Why she wept I knew not, nor did she—nor did I ask her why.

I heard the wind blowing somewhere in the world, but where I cared not. I heard blossoms discreetly stirring, and dusky branches interlacing. My ears were filled with voiceless whisperings: "I love you, I love you." Then, when my sweetheart had also heard, she turned and put both arms around my neck, linking her fingers, and her gray eyes looked down at me, beside her knees.

"Now you must go," she was repeating, touching her little French hat to straighten it, but with eyes and lips tenderly smiling at me. "My Lady Shelton and Sir Timerson Chank will surely return to catch you here if you hasten not—dear heart."

"But will you not tell me when you first loved me, Silver Heels?" I persisted.

"Well, then—if you must be told—it was on the day when you first wore your uniform and I saw you were truly a man!"

"That day! When you scarcely spoke to me?"

"Aye, that was the reason. Yet now I think of it, I know I— I have always loved you dearly."

"But," I insisted, "you grew cool enough to wed Lord Dunmore ——"

"Horror! Why must you ever hark back to him when I tell you it was not I who did that, but a cruelly used and foolish child, stung with the pain of your indifference ——"

"Oh, Silver Heels!" I murmured, all self-reproachful.

But she was already smiling again, with her slender hands laid on my shoulders.

It was at that very instant that Lady Shelton came wheezing up over the hill, and her eyes instantly fixed themselves on us. After her puffed Sir Timerson Chank, and behind him came mincing Lord Dunmore in a rare temper.

Lady Shelton paddled up to Silver Heels, halted, and panted at her. Then she turned and panted at me, and began scolding in a sort of babyish fury, while Sir Timerson Chank bore down on my left, ranting till I savagely bade him hold his tongue. In sheer astonishment he obeyed me, but Dunmore danced and vapored and fingered his smallsword till my hands itched to throw him into the blackberry thicket.

"If," said I to Lady Shelton, "you are pleased to forbid me your door, pray remember, madam, that your authority extends no farther! I shall not ask your permission to address my cousin, Miss Warren—nor yours!" I added, wheeling on Sir Timerson Chank.

"Sir Timerson! Sir Timerson! Arrest him! You are a magistrate. Arrest him! Oh, I'm all of a twitter!" panted Lady Shelton.

But Sir Timerson Chank made no sign of compliance.

"Lord Dunmore," I said, "by what privilege do you assume to vapor and handle the hilt of your smallsword in Miss Warren's presence?"

"Sink me!" cried Lord Dunmore. "Sink me now, Mr. Cardigan! I will have you to know that I have privileges, sir! Crib me! but I will assert my rights!"

"Your—what?" I replied, contemptuously.

"My rights, sir!" He raised his quizzing glass to peer at me. "Crib me, if I don't believe that the lad's moon-mad. A guinea to a China horse that the lad's moon-mad. Sink me if he isn't!"

How I controlled myself I scarcely know, but I strove to remember that a hand raised to Lord Dunmore, Governor of Virginia, meant the ruin of my plans for the night. As I stood staring at the wizened macaroni, aching to take his sword, break it, and spank him with the fragments, I saw Jack Mount and the Weasel cautiously reconnoitering the situation from the hill's edge.

Ere I could motion them away they had made up their minds that I was in distress, and now they came swaggering into our circle.

"Trouble with this old scratch-wig?" inquired Mount, nodding his head sideways toward Lord Dunmore.

"Damme!" gasped Dunmore. "Do you know who I am, you beast?"

"I know you're a ruddled old hunks," said Mount, carelessly. "Who may the other guinea wig-stand be, Mr. Cardigan?"

As he spoke he looked across at Sir Timerson Chanks; then suddenly a low whistle escaped his lips.

"Gad!" he exclaimed. "It's our fat Tory magistrate or I'm a codfish!"

"Fellow!" roared Sir Timerson, his face purpling. "Fellow! Thunder and Mars! Lord Dunmore, this is Jack Mount, the highwayman!"

For an instant Dunmore stood transfixed; then he screamed out: "Close the gates! Close the gates, Sir Timerson! He shall not escape! Call the constables, Sir Timerson. Call the constables!"

Mount had paled a little, but now, as Sir Timerson began to bellow for a constable, his color came back and he stepped forward, laying a heavy hand on the horrified magistrate's shoulder.

"Come now, come now," he said. "Stop that bawling! You Tory hangman, if I ever took a penny from you it was to help drive you and your thieving crew out of the land! Do you hear that? Now go and howl for your thief-takers, and take his lordship here with you!" And he gave Sir Timerson a shove.

Lady Shelton shrieked as Sir Timerson went wabbling down the hill, but Mount turned fiercely on Dunmore, shaking his huge fist.

"Hunt me down if you dare!" he growled. "Move a finger to molest me and the people shall know how you stop public runners, and scalp them, too! Oho! Now you scare, eh? Out o' my way, you toothless toad!"

Dunmore shrank back appalled, and then made off after Sir Timerson down the hill and toward the pavilion.

"Come," said I, "that will do for the present, Jack. Look yonder! Your friend, the magistrate, is toddling fast to trap you. You should be starting if you mean to get out of this scrape a free man."

"Pooh!" replied Mount, swaggering. "I've time to dine if I chose, but I'm not hungry. Come, Cade, we'll be strolling on."

But the Weasel did not appear to hear him. He stood staring at Silver Heels with an expression so strange that for a moment I feared he had gone stark mad.

"Cade!" repeated Mount. "What is the matter, Cade? What do you see? What on earth troubles you, old friend?" And he stepped quickly to the Weasel's side, I following.

"Cade!" Mount cried again, shaking his comrade's arm.

The Weasel turned a ghastly face.

"Who is she?" he motioned with his lips.

"Do you mean Miss Warren?" I asked, astonished.

"A ghost," he muttered, shivering in every limb.

Presently he began to move toward Silver Heels, but Mount and I drew him back.

"Cade! Cade!" cried Mount, anxiously. "Don't look like that, for Heaven's sake!"

"For Heaven's sake," repeated Renard, trembling.

His eyes were dim with tears. Mount leaned over to me and whispered, "He is mad!" But the Weasel heard him and looked up slowly.

"No, no," he said. "A little wrong in the head, Jack, only a little wrong. I thought I saw my wife, Jack, or her ghost—aye, her ghost—the ghost of her youth and mine ——"

A spasm shook him; he hid his face in his hands a moment, then scoured out the tears with his withered fingers.

"Ask the young lady's pardon for me," he muttered. "I have frightened her."

I walked over to Silver Heels, who stood there beside Lady Shelton, and drew her aside.

"He is a little mad," I said. "He thought he saw in you the ghost of his lost wife. Sorrow has touched his brain, I think, but he means no harm. Speak to him, Silver Heels. I owe my life to those two men."

She stood looking at them a moment, then, laying her hand on my arm, she went slowly across to Mount and Renard.

They uncovered as she came up; the Weasel's face grew dead and fixed, but the pathos in his eyes was indescribable.

"If you are Mr. Cardigan's friends, you must be mine, too," said Silver Heels, sweetly. "All you have done for him you have done for me."

Fascinated, Mount gaped at her, tongue-tied. But Renard stepped forward and took her small hand in his with a peculiar dignity and grace. Then he bent and touched her fingers with his lips. He did not speak, and presently I took Silver Heels by the hand and led her back to Lady Shelton.

"Madam," I said, "if aught of harm comes to these two men through Lord Dunmore betwixt this hour and the same hour tomorrow, there is not a hole on earth into which he can creep for mercy. Pray you, madam, so inform the gentleman."

Then I turned to Silver Heels, who impulsively stretched out both hands. The next moment I rejoined Mount and Renard, and we passed rapidly through the grove and down the hill to the stockade, where Mount drove out a plank with his huge shoulder, and we were free of Roanoke Plain.

At ten o'clock that night I sat in the coffee-room of the "Virginia Arms," waiting until it was time for us to take Silver Heels away from Lady Shelton's. I was outwardly cool enough, I trust, but terribly excited, nevertheless, and scarce able to touch the food on my plate.

One by one I counted and discounted the dangers I ran: first, arrest at any moment as an accomplice of the notorious Jack Mount; second, assassination by Dunmore's agents; third, assassination by Butler's company; fourth, arrest and imprisonment as a suspected rebel and open advocate of sedition; fifth, danger from the Cayugas after our escape from Fort Pitt.

Should any of these things befall me, as well they might, what in the world would become of Silver Heels?

The post chaise, loaded and ready, stood in the mews with the four strong horses harnessed, and Jack Mount at their heads. It lacked an hour yet of the time appointed, and it was the suspense of that hour's waiting which set every nerve in my body aching. Again and again I went out into the mews, only to find Mount standing quietly at the horses' heads and the Weasel pacing up and down, plunged in reverie.

At last Shemuel appeared, slinking past the lighted inn windows and into the mews, where we waited in the starlight.

"I hear that the Monongahela is in flood," Mount said. "Is the wooden bridge all right, Shemmy?"

Shemuel did not know and went away to inquire, returning presently with the information that the Monongahela was over its banks, but the dam below the bridge had gone out, leaving the wooden structure safe.

"Then there won't be a ford for twenty miles," muttered Mount, "and I'm glad of it. Shemmy, just borrow four new axes of Rolfe, will you?"

Again Shemuel disappeared, and after a short absence came trotting back with a bundle of brand-new axes that he shoved into the boot.

The slow minutes dragged on. Hands clasped behind me, I walked up and down the muddy alley, heart beating heavily, watching the mouth of the alley for a lurking spy or a file of soldiers.

CHAPTER SIXTEEN

SUDDENLY we were all startled by a rattle of hoofs. Every man there reached for his rifle. Then the alley itself resounded with the clattering hoof-strokes of a hard-ridden horse. There was a rush, a shadow, and a breathless shout from the horseman: "Express—ho! Stand back! I pass! I pass."

"It's an express," muttered Mount, lowering his long rifle and leaning on it to watch the dark rider pull his frantic horse to its haunches and search in his wallet by the glow of the opening kitchen door.

Rolfe came out, holding his hands up for the packets.

"Three for you, Jimmy," said the bareheaded express-rider, passing the letters over. "Draw me a pot o' beer, for Heaven's sake."

"Where is your mate?" asked Rolfe, anxiously.

"Hiram? Full of war arrows t'other side o' Crown Gap. Here's his pouch."

"Scalped?" asked Rolfe, in a low voice.

"I reckon he is. He never knowed nothing after the third arrow. Them Wyandottes done it. Pass up that beer, boy."

He drained the pot and tossed it down dripping to the tapboy.

"News o' Boston?" asked Rolfe, meaningly.

"Plenty! Plenty! Port Bill in force. More redcoats landed, more on the way, more to come. Rich poorer; poor starving. That's all!"

He gathered his bridle and winked at a coy kitchenmaid among the hostlers and wenches who had gathered.

"Your beau has went to Johnstown, Sairy," he said. "I see him a-training, hay foot, straw foot, with old Sir Billy's Tryon County milish. That reminds me, Jim"—turning to Rolfe—"I've a packet for a certain Michael Cardigan, somewhere to be hunted up south o' Crown Gap ——"

"Right here!" said Rolfe, promptly, and the express-rider passed the letter to him. Then, with a careless, "See you later!" he wheeled his horse short and galloped back along the alley.

The crowd on the steps flocked back into the kitchen; the door closed, then opened to let out Rolfe, who advanced toward me, letter in one hand, flaring candle in the other.

"Light the coach lamps," I whispered and, taking the candle and letter, sat down on a pile of pine timber to read what Sir William had sent me:

DEAR LAD—By runners from the Cayuga I know how gallantly you have conducted. Dearer than son you are to me; prouder am I than any parent. If what we had hoped and prayed for has failed—as I can no longer doubt—it is so ordained.

I am holding the Mohawks back by their very throats, but mischief brews at the Upper Castle, whither Joseph (Thayendanegea) has gone with the belts from me.

A most deadly and bitter feeling runs flood in Johnstown; nightly outrages are reported to me, and I fear that the so-called patriots are quite as blameworthy as are the loyalists. Whig and Tory hate and wait.

Dear lad, the sands of my life are running very swiftly. I am so tired, so tired! Come when you can; I have much to talk over ere these same sands run out. If you, by hazard, pass through Fort Pitt, you will accompany Felicity on her return hither, which return I have instantly commanded her by this express. I have received a singular letter from my Lord Dunmore, which has astonished me. My answer to him I delay until Felicity returns.

Your Aunt Molly is well and sweetly anxious to see you safe home. Esk and Peter do flourish—yet I like not Peter's haunting the public houses where things are uttered to poison young minds. I have trounced him soundly seven times, and mean to continue.

The news from Boston is ominous. More ships are about to sail, bearing more troops and cannon. I know not how it will end! Aye—but I *do* know, and so must every thinking man. *Praemonitus, praemunitus!*

Michael, I have had a most strange and unpleasant letter from Sir Peter Warren, who incloses with it certain amazing documents. These papers were lately sent to him from Chatham dockyard, having been discovered under the cabin flooring of the warship *Leda*, which his brother lately commanded and which is now repairing at Chatham.

The documents concern Felicity—and us all—and I wish you to know that I no longer approve of your union with her, at least not until both she and you are fully acquainted with the contents of these documents.

And now, dear son, I can but wait for you to come. The house is dull without you. I have sometimes sought to drown care in the river, whither I go with gillie Bareshanks to fly-fish for trouts. But I am growing sad and old, and nothing pleases, though I do throw my flies as I did at thirty, looping each cast without a splash.

Always yr affectionate

WM. JOHNSON, Bart.

My eyes were swimming when I lifted them from the sheets of paper. For a moment I rested my head on my hands, feeling the rising tide of homesickness choking me. Then that subtle courage that a word from Sir William ever infused warmed my blood and calmed my beating heart.

I rose serenely, and burned the letter in the candle's flame. Then I looked at my watch, and was amazed to find that it lacked but a few moments to the time set for our departure from the "Virginia Arms."

Rolfe had already lighted the chaise lamps; Shemuel had crawled inside with our weapons, and Renard sat his post saddle, adjusting the stirrups; while Mount was climbing into the saddle of the nigh leader.

I stood holding my ticking timepiece under the coach lamp, eyes following the slow pointers traveling toward the hour.

And as I stood there, a woman came slipping swiftly into the alley, cloaked and bareheaded. She ran to the horse on which Mount was sitting and caught the forest runner by the fringe on his sleeve. I saw then that she was the thief-taker's child.

"Hoity-toity! what's tew pay?" fumed Rolfe. "Darn these bold wenches who ——"

"Keep quiet!" I said, sharply. "There's trouble abroad some where!"

"Oh, Mr. Cardigan," called Mount, softly, "Sir Timerson and a gang o' cudgels is coming up Pitt Street, and Bully Bishop's with them!"

The girl turned her frightened face to me:

"They came for father to take Jack Mount; I ran out the

back door, sir. Oh, hasten! hasten!" she wailed, looking at Mount and wringing her hands.

The big fellow stooped from his saddle and deliberately kissed her.

"Thank you, my dear," he said. "I'll come back for another before I die. *Au large*, Jimmy! Up with you, Mr. Cardigan!"

"Turn those horses! Take the back way!" whispered Rolfe.

The next moment I had wheeled the chaise and four back into the darkness and around a rambling row of sheds and stables. Following Rolfe, we came to a creaking gate swinging loosely, and then bumped out into a field, hub-deep in buttercups.

"I'll keep the scratch-wigs amused," whispered Rolfe, as I climbed to the forward seat and picked up my rifle; and away we jolted across the starlit pasture and out into a narrow, unlighted cattle lane, which we followed to the bars. These Shemuel let down, and Mount rode our horses out into the dark Boundary Road.

On we went at a slapping trot. Presently I saw the lighted windows of Lady Shelton's house glimmering among the trees. A lane led around the house to the right; up this dim path I directed the chaise and four until I found room to turn them back, facing the Boundary Road again. Here our chaise might lie concealed, and here I quietly bade Mount and the other two await me. Through the dim trees I stole up near the house. Then, as I leaned breathless against a tree, the fortress bell struck slowly, eleven times.

Second after second passed, minute followed minute, and my eyes never left the closed door under the pillared porch.

Presently I looked at my watch; a quarter of an hour had passed. Still I waited, waited.

Far away in the fortress the bell struck the half-hour. Suddenly the dark door opened; a heavy figure appeared in silhouette against the light. My heart stood still; it was Black Betty.

The negress peered out into the darkness, and looked up at the stars. Then, as though summoned from within, she turned quickly and entered the house, leaving the door wide open behind her.

Impatience was racking me now. Alarm, too. I waited until I could wait no longer; then I stole up to the porch. The hallway was empty; I stepped to the sill, crossed it, and surveyed the empty stairway and the gallery above. There was not a soul in sight. A door on my right stood open; I looked in, then entered the smaller of two rooms that were partly separated from each other by two folding doors.

Treading on the velvet carpet, I passed into the farther room. Not a soul to be seen anywhere. I strove to crush out the fear that was laying icy fingers on my breast, and turned to reënter the smaller room. But just at that instant I heard the front door close and voices sounding along the outer hallway. I stepped behind a gilt cabinet and drew my heavy knife, perfectly aware that I was trapped.

Through the carved foliage of the cabinet I saw three people enter the smaller room. They stood there in low-voiced consultation—Lady Shelton, my Lord Dunmore, and my mortal enemy, Walter Butler, tricked out in lace and velvet. Butler stood so near me that my hot hand could have fastened on his throat strings. He turned toward Dunmore with a gesture.

"Sir Timerson should find them tonight," he said. "Your thief-taker, Billy Bishop, is with them, I understand."

"They are to search every rebel rat-hole in town," cried Dunmore, eagerly. "They should claw them ere dawn, Captain Butler."

With that, he leered triumphantly at Lady Shelton.

"If I am to conduct Miss Warren," said Butler, gloomily, "you had best see her without delay, my lord."

"Come now," said Dunmore, slyly. "I am half minded to conduct her myself, Captain Butler, curse me if I am not. I hear you once vowed to wed her in spite of Sir William, and me, too! Damme! I've a notion you mean me ill, you rogue!"

"Your lordship is merry," sneered Butler.

"Faith, I am not over-merry," said Dunmore, plaintively. "I like not this night journey to Williamsburg, that's flat!—and I care not if you know it, Captain Butler."

"Then I pray you to release me from this duty," Butler returned.

Dunmore eyed him askance.

"If I merit your suspicions," added Butler, icily, "I beg to wish you good fortune and good night!" And he bowed very low and turned curtly toward the door.

"No! Damme if I suspect you!" cried Dunmore hastily. "Come back, Captain Butler! You shall conduct Miss Warren to Williamsburg. I say it! I mean it! Body o' Judas! am I not to follow as soon as I hang this fellow Mount and his rabble o' ragged pottle-pots?"

Butler came back, and—oh, the evil in his fixed stare as his kindling eyes fastened on Dunmore again!

"Will you be pleased—to—to receive Miss Warren immediately?" asked Lady Shelton in a flutter. "I have her closely watched wherever she takes a step. Lud! she would have been gone these two hours had not Captain Butler's man caught my footman with a guinea!"

"I have a copy of her letter," squeaked Dunmore, angrily. "Faith, I could scratch her raw for what she wrote to that dirty forest-running fellow, Cardigan!"

"Fie! Fie!" tittered Lady Shelton, hysterically.

But his lordship paid her small attention.

"The little baggage!" he muttered, and turned to Butler: "You had best attend in the room beyond, Captain Butler. Gad! I can soon persuade Miss Warren to go with you. Lady Shelton, send her to me. And then stay away until you're wanted," he added, brutally.

Lady Shelton stared at him with frightened eyes; then she pattered hastily out of the room.

Butler, with a shrug, swung on his heel and walked noiselessly past my hiding-place on into the big room beyond.

Dunmore stood listening and shaking out the long, delicate lace on his cuffs. Nobody came. He tiptoed over to a mirror and stood there, primping and preening, smirking, and ogling himself.

At any other time I should have been contemptuously amused, but my anxious thoughts had flown upstairs to seek the dear maid who had given herself to me.

Suddenly she appeared at the door. She stood there hesitating, smiling, her hands busy with the buckle of a silvery gray traveling coat adorned with row on row of dainty capes. Never, never had I seen her so lovely, and I could scarce restrain myself from greeting her. For a moment I thought she had perceived me through the cabinet's gilded foliage; but my presence was still all unsuspected.

At first sight of her hood and traveling coat, Lord Dunmore had scowled. But he recovered himself quickly and leered at her.

"Cruel one," he piped out, in ecstasy, mincing toward her—"cruel one, what do you ask that I may adore?"

"Your lordship's pardon," she said, gravely. "I am here to ask forgiveness."

"Granted! You have it," protested Dunmore, bowing and leading her to a chair. "You have grieved me, but man was made to grieve. I forgive, and give my love as guerdon."

"You are too generous," said Silver Heels, sorrowfully. "I may keep only your forgiveness, my lord."

She would have spoken again, but Dunmore dropped on both knees, ogling her with watery eyes. She half rose and drew back, but the infatuated fool drowned her protests with his shrill prattle, and pleaded his suit so passionately that my gorge rose and I could scarce contain myself.

Silver Heels shrank deep into her chair, begging him to rise. And at last he did, scowling his displeasure. Then, very gravely and pitifully, she told him that she did not love him, that she had given her love to another, and that she could now only ask his forgiveness.

He stood listening in silence at first; then his faded eyes narrowed with fury.

"D'ye mean to throw me over for that wood-running whelp, Cardigan?" he burst out. "Oh no, my lady, that cock won't fight. D'ye hear?"

The startling coarseness of the outbreak brought Silver Heels to her feet in frightened astonishment.

Dunmore was pacing the carpet like one demented.

"I will not be so used! Curse me if I will!" he snarled, biting his polished nails. "Hell's fury, madam! Will you throw me over for a buckskin lout? Fine sport, madam! Fine sport! So you think to make me the laughing-stock o' Virginia? So you plan to run off with this dirty forest runner in a post chaise—eh? Choke me if you shall!"

"Pray—pray let me pass," gasped Silver Heels, white with fright.

He caught the door in his hand, closing it, and planted himself with his back against it. Then he fumbled behind him for the key, but it was in the other side of the door.

"Oh no, not yet," he said.

"I must pass that door," repeated Silver Heels, breathlessly.

"Damme, you shall not!" he cried. "Curse me if I let you go to that buckskin lout of yours. You shall not go! You shall not!"

His voice ended in a shriek; the door behind him burst open, flinging him forward, and Black Betty appeared, eyes ablaze and teeth bared. The next instant Silver Heels sprang through the portal, the door banged, and I heard the key turn on the other side with a click.

Dumfounded, I looked stupidly through the window behind me; then my heart leaped up, for there, at the foot of the garden, stood a post chaise and four. There, too, were Silver Heels and Betty, setting foot to the chaise step. Dark figures aided them; the chaise door shut. I thanked God silently and turned to deal with these wicked men whom He had given into my hands.

Dunmore, insane with fury, was clawing at a window to raise it; Butler had come swiftly from the inner room and was trying the door. Finding it locked, he looked at Dunmore with a ghastly laugh.

"She's gone!" shrieked Dunmore. "Gone in a chaise! That black wench of hers did it! Let me out! Let me out! I'll claw them raw! I *won't* stay here! D'ye hear?"

"Give place there!" said Butler, brutally elbowing the frantic man aside. "Let me through that window, you doddering fool! You're done for; it's my turn now."

"What!" gasped Dunmore. Then terror blanched his face and he began to scream: "That was *your* chaise! You mean to cheat me! You mean to steal her! That was your chaise, and it's gone! No! No! Damme! you shall not catch them at the gates!" And he flung himself on Butler to drag him from the open window.

"Drive on!" shouted Butler to the people in the chaise.

Startled, I turned and stared through the window behind me. To my horror the horses started and the chaise began to move off. Even yet I did not comprehend that the chaise was not my own, but to see it slowly rolling away in the night terrified me, and I bounded out into the room—barely in time, for Butler had already forced Dunmore from the open window and had laid his hand on the wall to hoist himself out.

Quick as the thought, I balanced my heavy knife and let it fly like lightning. The blade whistled true and struck, pinning Butler's arm to the wall. He shrieked madly, twisting and turning to tear the blade loose. Dunmore ran around like a crazed rat, but I knocked him senseless with a chair, and sprang at Butler, who, writhing and ghastly pale, had just freed his left hand of the knife.

He ran at me with his sword, but I shattered my chair across his face, and seized him. A wave of fury blazed in my brain; I lifted the struggling wretch high and brought him down on the floor, where he crashed as though every bone in him were shattered.

As I reeled, panting, towards the window, the key turned in the locked door and Lady Shelton's frightened face appeared. When she saw me she rushed at me and screamed, but I thrust her out of my path, vaulted through the open window, and ran down the orchard slope. Then, as I sprang into the lane, I almost dropped, for there, where I had left it, stood my post chaise, awaiting me.

"Mount!" I shouted in terror. "Is she here?"

"Here?" he cried. "You are mad! Have you lost her?"

Through my whirling senses broke the awful truth.

"Out o' the saddle!" I shouted. "She has taken another chaise. It's Butler's men! Ride for her! Ride!"

"Gone?" thundered Mount, leaping to the seat, while I sprang to his vacant saddle. But I only lashed at the horses, and set my teeth while the pebbles showered through the flying wheels.

It seemed hours, yet it was scarcely five minutes, ere the gatehouse lights broke out ahead. Now we were galloping straight into the eye of the great brass lanthorn set above the guardhouse. There came a far call in the darkness; a shadow crossed the lamplit glare. I turned in my saddle and shouted: "Draw bridle!" and our four horses came clashing in a huddle.

HE RAN AT ME WITH HIS SWORD BUT I SHATTERED MY CHAIR
ACROSS HIS FACE

"Road closed for the night!" said a sentinel, walking toward us out of the darkness ahead.

"A post chaise passed five minutes ahead of us," began Mount, angrily.

"Tut! tut! my good fellow," said the sentry, "that's none o' your business. Back up there!"

"I wish to see Mr. Bevan," said I, scarce able to speak.

"Mr. Bevan's gone home to bed," said the soldier, impatiently. "He passed that other post chaise at a gallop, or it would have been here yet, I warrant you. Come, come, now! You know the law. Clear the road, now!—Turn your leaders, postboy.—Back up. D'ye hear?"

"I tell you I've got to pass!" I roared. "Stand clear!"

"If you move I'll shoot!" he retorted. Then he bawled out: "Ho, sergeant o' the quarter guard! Post number seven! ——"

"Drive over him!" I shouted, lashing at the horses. There was a jolt, an uproar, a rush of frantic horses, a shot that went wild—and we were safely by!

"Look out!' called Mount. "The tollgate's right ahead! There's a camp guard due there at midnight! Out with your coach lamps!"

Shemuel swiftly blew out the lights; darkness hid even the horses from our sight.

"Cut the pike!" cried Mount, suddenly. "We save six miles by the old Williamsburg post road! Turn out! Turn out!"

Far ahead the tollgate lamp twinkled.

"By Heaven! the guard is gone; there's only a sentry there!" exclaimed Mount.

"Pst!" muttered Renard. "We are the grand rounds, mind you. Answer, Jack!"

"Halt!" cried a distant sentry. "Who goes there?"

"Grand rounds!" sang out Mount.

"Stand, grand rounds! Advance, sergeant, with the counter-sign!" came the distant challenge again.

"Now," muttered Mount, leaping softly to the turf, "when I call, ride up to me. Hark for a whippoorwill!"

He vanished in the darkness. I waited, scarcely breathing.

"He won't kill him," whispered the Weasel. "You will see, Mr. Cardigan, how it's done. He'll get behind him—patience, patience—pst!—there!"

A stifled cry, suddenly choked, came out of the night; a lanthorn at the tollgate went out and the tollhouse door slammed.

"It's the keeper barricading himself," whispered Renard. "He thinks the sentry has been surprised and scalped. Hush! Mount is calling."

"Whippoorwill! Whippoorwill!" throbbed the whimper-ing, breathless call across the meadow; the Weasel answered it, and we trotted on until a dark shape rose up in the road and caught at the leaders, drawing them to a standstill. It was Mount.

"Here's the post road," he muttered. "I'll guide you into it." And he started east through a wall of shadow.

"Where's the sentry?" whispered Renard.

"In the ditch with his coat tied over his head and my new hanker in his mouth."

Soon Mount halted the horses. Shemuel lit the coach lamps, and under their kindling radiance a dusty road spread away in front of us. Mount unlocked a lighted coach lamp and went forward, holding the light close to the road surface. Several times he squatted to look close into the dust.

Presently he turned and ran back to us, returned the lamp to its socket, and sprang into his seat.

"They've taken the turnpike!" he cried, cheerily. "Now, lads! Whip and spur and axle grease! We've got them by half an hour, or I'll eat my coonskin cap!"

I sent my whip whistling among the horses, and away we bolted, chaise swaying. The gallop increased to a dead run as we whirled down an incline and out along a marshy road beside a swift stream.

"We catch them where the pike swings south into this road," called Mount.

Louder and louder blew the wind across the flats; wetter and wetter grew the road, until the splash of the horses grew to a churning, trampling roar. Like a flash the stream turned across the road; the shallow water boiled under our rush— a moment only—then into the wet road again, with the stream scurrying on our right.

"Get my ax loose from the boot, Shemmy!" cried Mount. "Draw rein, Cade! Now, Mr. Cardigan!" And he leaped to the ground and ran splashing through the road, calling out for us to follow at a walk.

Suddenly our horses' hoofs sounded hollow on a wooden bridge. We walked the horses over. Then came the echoing cracks of Mount's ax, biting the supports of the bridge, and presently Shemuel joined him, chopping like a demon.

"We lose time!" I groaned, turning to the Weasel. "Tell Mount to let the bridge go."

"We'll lose time if the bridge stands," said Renard, coolly.

"Dunmore's horse will take our trail sooner or later, and we may have to wait an hour for the chaise we are chasing."

Minute after minute dragged, timed by the interminable ax strokes. But at last, above the sharp ax strokes and the deep roar of the torrent, I caught the sound of creaking timbers. Crack! Crack! Then a long-drawn crackle of settling beams, a crash—and the choppers came running back.

"No need to gallop now," observed Mount, shoving the axes into the boot and climbing into his seat. "Walk the horses. We are an hour ahead yet. The roads cross just below here. Cheer up, Mr. Cardigan; we'll sight them over our rifles yet. And when Dunmore's horsemen come to the bridge yonder, they'll have some twenty miles to wander ere they can cross the Monongahela tonight. Lord! Won't Dunmore rage!"

Almost distracted with anxiety, I strove to regain self-command in discussing the course we should pursue. Mount was of my own opinion that our best plan was to take a forest road over the mountains and make straight for Philadelphia.

"There's a wood road over the mountains," he said. "Cade knows it. He came that way hunting his wife at Annapolis when the British fleet put in.

The Weasel turned in his saddle.

"Jack," he said, gently, "I know my wife is dead. We will never speak of her any more."

Mount was silent. Presently he jumped to the ground and came walking along beside my horse.

"I don't know," he muttered under his breath—"I don't know whether that's a healthy sign or not. Ever since Cade saw your lady—Miss Warren—he keeps telling me that his wife is dead. And somehow he has changed. Do you note it? His voice, now, is different—like a gentleman's. Somehow he makes me feel lonely."

I was scarcely listening, for just ahead I could see a signpost that must mark crossroads. I excitedly pointed it out to Mount.

"Aye," he said, coolly, "that's our runway. The game will cross here in an hour or so. Sit tight, Mr. Cardigan."

But I was out of my saddle and priming my rifle afresh before he could finish.

"Poor lad!" he said, pityingly. "Lord! but you're white as a crossroads ghost. Shemmy, take the chaise south till you come to a spring brook that crosses the road; it's a hundred yards or so. Cover the coach lamps with blankets. Cade, I guess you had better take this side of the road with me. We want to be sure o' the postboys. Mr. Cardigan, try to shoot the driver through the head. There's too much risk in a low shot."

"For Heaven's sake, be careful!" I groaned. "Remember the lady is in the chaise."

"There, there!" said Mount, affectionately clapping me on the shoulder. "You will have your dear lady safe in half an hour, lad. No fear that we will fail—eh, Cade?"

Then he bade the Weasel take his stand to the left, and posted me to the right; he himself sat down cross-legged under the signpost.

The silence weighed me down; awful fear shot through and through me. Suppose that, after all, they had gone north, risking the war belt for a dash through to Crown Gap?

I thought of Silver Heels, while straining my ears for the sound of the chaise that bore her. Strange, but in my fevered excitement I found myself utterly unable to bring her face to mind. And perhaps I should never see that dear face again.

Suddenly a faint, far sound in the night stilled every pulse. I saw Mount slowly rise to his feet and step into the shadow of the signpost. I myself stood up, icy cold now but calm, eyes fixed on the darkness that engulfed the road ahead.

Again the distant sound broke out in the stillness. Soon the noise of rapidly galloping horses sounded plainly; wheels striking stones rang out sharp and clear; two lights sparkled in the distance, growing yellower and bigger.

On, on they came, horses at a gallop, chaise lurching, right into the crossroads. Then a blinding flash and crash split the gloom, echoed by another, and then a third. I leaped from my cover into a frantic mass of struggling horses which Renard was dragging violently into the road ditch, while Mount, swinging his rifle, knocked down a man who fired at him and beat him till he lay still.

A shadowy form leaped from the seat in front and ran across my path, doubling and disappearing into the darkness; another slid from his horse, sinking to the ground without a sound.

As I sprang toward the chaise, the driver pitched off heavily, landing in a heap at my feet, face downward in the grass. Now the horses swung in front of me, plunging furiously in the smashed harness. Crash! went a wheel; the chaise sank forward; a horse fell.

"Look out! Look out!" shouted Mount behind me as I ran to the swaying vehicle.

"Silver Heels!" I cried, tearing at the door of the chaise. For a second I saw her terrified face at the window; her cry rang in my ears; then the door burst open and Wraxall sprang out, burying his knife in my neck.

Down we went together, down, down into a smothering darkness that had no end. Yet I remember, after a long, long time, looking up at the stars—or perhaps into her eyes.

Then my body seemed to sink again, silently as a feather, and my soul dropped out, falling like a lost star into an endless night.

WALTER BUTLER

CHAPTER SEVENTEEN

I KNEW afterward—long, long afterward—that I had been stabbed repeatedly. They had thought me already ended when they tore my assailant from my body and grimly dispatched him.

I appeared to be quite dead, and whether to bury me there or in some kinder spot, none could determine, while the dear maid I loved lay senseless in Black Betty's arms.

As it was afterward told to me in the saddest days of my life, so I tell what now befell the rescued, the rescuers, and that scarcely palpitating body o' mine, the soul of which floated on the dark borderland of Death. For it came to happen that dawn, lurking behind the eastern hills, warned Mount and Renard that day was on their trail to betray it.

My senseless sweetheart they bore to the waiting chaise and, my body still retaining some warmth, they bore that, too, because they dared not bury me before she had seen me dead with her own eyes.

All that day they rode west by north, climbing the vast divide. Then, when the western sun sank beyond the Ohio into the sea of trees, the winds of the east filled their nostrils and the long divide had been passed at last.

That night my dear love opened her eyes, and the darkness that enchained her fell, so that she crept to my feet as I lay in a corner of the chaise and laid her head on my knees.

Whether she thought me alive or dead none knew. Betty had bared my body to the waist and washed it. For a corpse they do as much. Later, without hope, Mount brought a pannikinful of blue-balsam gum, pricked from the globules on the trunk, and when Betty had once more washed me, they filled the long gashes with the balsam and closed them decently, strip on strip, with the fine cambric shift which my sweetheart tore from her own body.

Later, when the moon was coming up, they carried me, lying in a blanket, my sweetheart ever walking beside me. That night they thought me surely dead and watched without sleep lest the rigidity of dissolution surprise me ere my limbs had been laid straight. But the morning found me as I was, nor was I dead on the next morning, nor on the next, nor yet the next.

A still Sabbath in the forest gave them hope; for I had

opened my eyes, though I saw nothing. But that night Death sat at my right hand, and the next night Death cradled my head; and my dear love lay at my feet and looked Death steadily in the eyes.

The fever which loosened every muscle burned fiercely all night long, and my voice broke out from my body like a demon mocking within me. A few of the Lenape, roaming near, followed and shot at us toward dawn, driving us north into the forest, where the chaise was abandoned, the traces cut, and the horses loaded with corn.

North and south the runways of the Long House pierced the wilderness, and these were the trails they followed, the men on foot, bearing me on their litter of blankets and balsam boughs, the women crouching on the sack-laden horses.

As for me, I lived on through cold and heat, storm and stress, seeing nothing, hearing nothing, dumb, save when the demon hidden in my body mocked and laughed between my blackened lips. Hours came when there was no water, and the demon knew it and mouthed and cursed. Then he would turn on me and tear at my throat and gnaw me and thrust his claws into my brain.

At night he often stole my body and carried it where the darkness burned and charred. There he would take out my bones, one by one, and break them for the marrow to dry hard.

These things no one has told me. I remember them in sleep sometimes, sometimes waking.

What I have heard from others is vague, and to me unreal as a painted scene in a picture. I hear that I breathed through days that I never saw, that I opened my eyes on lands that are strange to me, that my babble broke primeval silences that God himself had sealed.

But there came a day when, sleeping, I smelled lavender in the forest, and I thought the wood had windows where a sweet wind blew. Truly, there was a window somewhere near me, for I found my eyes had opened and could see it where the curtains swayed in the sun.

Hours later I looked again; the window was still there, and the moon beyond, low among pines whose shapes I knew.

Hours came and faded into sunshine; days brought bright spots on the curtains; night brought the moon and the tall pines. Sweet fern, too, I smelled sometimes, and I heard a soothing monotone of familiar sound below me.

One night a new sound woke me, and I felt the presence of another person. Moonlight silvered the windows of a room that I knew; but I was very quiet and waited for the sun, lest the phantoms I divined should trick me.

Then came a morning when I knew I was in a bed and very tired; and knew, too, that I had made no mistake about the room.

When I first surely recognized it, my memory served me a trick, and I thought of the schoolroom below where the others were imprisoned—Silver Heels, Peter, and Esk. Slyly content to doze abed here in Sir William's room, I understood that I must have been lying sick a long, long time, but could not remember when I had fallen ill. One thing sure: I did not mean they should know that I was better; I closed my eyes when I felt a presence near, lying still as a mouse until alone again.

Sometimes my thoughts wandered to the others in the schoolroom with Mr. Yost, for I did not remember he had been scalped by the Lenape, and I pitied Silver Heels and Esk and fat Peter a-thumbing their copy-books and breathing chalk dust. Faith, I was well off in the great white bed, here in Sir William's room.

I could see his fish-rods on the wall, looped with silk lines and scarlet feather flies. There, too, hung his fowling-pieces above the mantel, pouch and horn dangling from crossed ramrods.

Soft! They are coming to watch me now. So I slyly close my eyes till they go away or give me the drinks they brew to make me sleep.

Our Doctor Pierson was here today and caught me watching him. They'll soon have me in the schoolroom now, though I do still play 'possum all I can.

Later that day I saw Colonel Guy Johnson come into the room and look at me, but I closed my eyes and lay quiet. When Sir William should come, however, I would open my eyes, for I had been desiring to see him since I saw his rods and guns. It fretted me at times that he neglected me, knowing my love for him.

The next day I saw Doctor Pierson beside me, and asked for Sir William. He said that Sir William was away and that I was doing well. We often spoke after that, and he was ever busy with my head, which no longer ached save when he fingered it.

Then one night I awoke with a cry of terror and found myself sitting upright, bathed in chilly sweat, shouting that the Cayugas were abroad and that I must hold them back by the throat till Sir William could arrive and restrain them.

Lights soon moved into the room; I saw Doctor Pierson and Guy Johnson, but the dammed-up floods of memory had broken loose like an old wound, and the past came crowding upon me so that I fell back on the pillows, convulsed and gasping, till the doctor gave me a draught and I drowsed *perdu.*

Day broke—the bitterest day of life I was to know. I felt it, listening to the rain; I felt it, in the footsteps that passed my door—footsteps I did not know. Why was the house so silent? Why did all go about so quietly, dressed in black? Was there some one dead in the house? Where was Silver Heels? Why had she never come to me? How came I here? Where were Jack Mount and Cade Renard? And Sir William, where was he that he came not near me—me who had lain sick unto death in his service and for his sake?

Dread numbed me; I strove to call, but my dumb lips froze; I strove to rise, and found my body wrecked in bed without power, without sense, a helpless, inert thing between two sheets.

Why was I here? Why was I alive if aught had harmed Silver Heels? God! And I safe here in bed? Where was she? Dead? Why do they not tell me? Why do they not kill me as I lie here if I have returned without her?

I must have cried aloud in my agony, for the doctor came running and leaned over me.

"Tell me! Tell me!" I stammered. "Why don't you tell me?" and strove to strike him, but could not use my arms.

"Quiet, quiet," he said, watching me. "I will tell you what you wish to know. What is it, then, my poor boy?"

"I—want—Felicity," I blurted out.

"Felicity?" he repeated, blankly. "Oh—Miss—ahem!—Miss Warren?"

I glared at him.

"Miss Warren has gone with Sir John Johnson to Boston," he said, dryly.

My eyes never left him.

"Is that why you cried out?" he asked, curiously. "Miss Warren left us a week ago. Had you only known her she would have been happy, for she has slept for weeks on the couch yonder."

"Why—why did she go?"

"I cannot tell you the reasons," he said, gravely.

"When will she return?"

"I do not know."

With a strength that came from Heaven knows where, I dragged myself upright and caught him by the hand.

"She is dead!" I whispered. "She is dead, and all in this house know it save I who love her!"

A strange light passed over the doctor's face; he took both my hands and looked at me carefully. Then he smiled and gently forced me back to the pillows.

"She is alive and well," he said. "On my honor as a man, lad, I set your heart at rest. She is in Boston, and I do know why, but I may not meddle with what concerns this family, save in sickness—or death."

I watched his lips. They were solemn as the solemn word

he uttered. I knew death had been in the house; I had felt that for days. I waited, watching him.

"Poor lad!" he said, holding my hands.

My eyes never left his.

"Aye," he said, softly, "his last word was your name. He loved you dearly, lad."

And so I knew that Sir William was dead.

CHAPTER EIGHTEEN

D AY after day I lay in my bed, staring at the ceiling till night blotted it out. Then, stunned and exhausted, I would lie in the dark, crying in my weakness, whimpering for those I loved who had left me here alone. Yet my thinned blood gradually grew warmer, and day by day its currents flowed with slightly increasing vigor through my emaciated body.

The dreadful anguish of my bereavement came only at intervals, succeeded by an apathy that served as a merciful relief. But most I thought of Silver Heels, and why she had left me here, and when she might return.

One late afternoon the doctor came with a dish of China oranges, which I found relief in sucking, my gums being as yet somewhat hot and painful. He made a hole in an orange and I sucked it awhile, watching him meditatively.

"Why does not my aunt Molly come to see me?" I asked.

"Dear lad," said the doctor, raising his eyebrows, "did you not know she had gone to Montreal?"

"How should I know it," I asked, "when you tell me nothing?"

"I will tell you what I am permitted," he answered, gently.

"Then tell me when my cousin Felicity is coming back! Have you not heard from Sir John Johnson?"

"Yes—I have heard," replied the doctor, cautiously.

I waited, my eyes searching his face.

"Sir John returns tomorrow," he said.

A thrill set my blood leaping.

"Tomorrow!" I repeated.

The doctor regarded me very gravely.

"Miss Warren will remain in Boston," he said.

The light died out before my eyes; presently I closed them.

"How long?" I asked.

"I do not know."

The orange, scarcely tasted, rolled over the bed and fell on the floor. I heard him rise to pick it up.

I opened my eyes and looked at the distant pines through the window.

"Doctor," I muttered, "I am heartsick for a familiar face. Where are the people who have lived in this house? It is scarce four months that I have been away; yet all is strange— new servants everywhere, no old, friendly faces. Is there not one soul unchanged?"

"Have I changed?" he asked.

"Yes—you are gray! gray!—and smaller; and you stoop when you sit."

After a moment he said: "These are times to age all men. Have you yourself not aged in these five months? You went away a fresh-faced lad! You return a man, singed already by the first breath of a fire which will scorch this land to the bedded rock!"

Presently I asked, "Is war certain?"

He nodded, looking at the floor.

"And—and the Six Nations?" I asked again.

"On our side, surely," he said in a low voice.

"On our side?" I repeated.

He looked at me suddenly, his mouth tightening.

"When I say 'our side' I assume you to be loyal, Mr. Cardigan," he said, curtly, and the hardening of his shrewd, kindly face amazed me.

"If you have become tainted with rebel heresy since you left us, thank God you have returned in time to purge your mind," he continued, sternly. "Sir William has gone—Heaven rest his brave soul!—but Sir John is alive to take no uncertain stand in the face of this wicked rebellion."

I looked at him serenely. Who but I should know what Sir William had thought about the coming strife? Those sacred confidences of the past had cleared my mind and made it up long since. But I only lay and looked at the doctor. I was too tired to argue.

"There is one man I should like to see," I said, "and that is Mr. Duncan. Will you send to the guardhouse and beg him to come to me, Doctor?"

"Aye, that I will, lad," he said, cheerily, picking up his hat and case of drugs.

After he left I must have fallen into a light sleep, for when I unclosed my eyes I saw Mr. Duncan beside me, looking down into my face. I smiled and raised one hand, and he took it gently in both of his strong, sun-browned ones.

"Well, well, well!" he muttered, smiling, while the tears stood in his pleasant eyes. "Here is our soldier home again —eh?"

I motioned feebly for him to find a chair beside my bed, and he sat down, still holding my hand in his.

"Now," I said, "explain to me all that has happened. Tell me everything."

"You mean—about Sir William?" he asked, gently.

"Yes—but that last of all," I muttered, choking.

After a silence he settled back and looked at me.

"You must know," he said, "that Colonel Guy Johnson is now superintendent of Indian affairs in North America for His Majesty. He has appointed as deputies Colonel Claus and Colonel John Butler ——"

"Who?" I exclaimed.

"Colonel Butler," repeated Mr. Duncan. "He and Joseph Brant are organizing the loyalists and Indians north of us. This border war in Virginia has set the Six Nations afire. There was but one man in the world who could have controlled them ——"

He paused.

"I know it," said I. "You mean Sir William."

"Aye, Mr. Cardigan, I mean Sir William. Well, well, there is no help now. It is Sir John Johnson's policy to win over the savages to our side; but I often think Sir William knew best how to manage them. It will be dreadful, dreadful! I would give all I possess to see the savages remain neutral in this coming strife."

"Do you also believe war is coming?"

"Surely, surely," he said, lifting his hand solemnly. Then he wiped his face with a laced hanker and pressed his temples, frowning.

After a silence I asked him what month of the year it now was.

"October," he said, pityingly. "Did you not know it?"

I tried to realize the space of time that had been wiped out from my memory.

"When did Sir William—die?" I muttered, painfully.

Mr. Duncan looked at me with tears in his eyes.

"On Monday, the eleventh of July."

"Tell me—all," I motioned with quivering lips.

"It is history," he said, simply. "I will tell you what I heard and what I witnessed.

"On the first of July we received news of the murder of Bald Eagle, a friendly Delaware chief. Rumor had it that one of my Lord Dunmore's agents had slain the old man, but that, of course, is preposterous. It is hard to sift truth out of rumors. Why, some said even that young Walter Butler had murdered the old man!"

"Go on," I said, grimly.

"Well, then, this murder was committed while the poor old man was sitting in his canoe on one of the streams near Fort Pitt. After tearing the scalp from the old man the murderer set him afloat in his canoe. The ghastly progress of the dead was seen by Indians and whites, and the news roused the Six Nations to fury.

"You know that even after the Logan outrage Sir William had held back the warriors of the Long House; but this fresh crime drove them frantic. They might still have held off had not Bald Eagle been scalped, but you know, Mr. Cardigan, that the Six Nations *always* regard the scalping of a murdered person as a *national* act, not an individual one, and *always* accept it as a declaration of war."

"I know," I said.

"The sachems of the Long House," continued Mr. Duncan, "immediately notified Sir William that they desired to see him without delay. Mr. Cardigan, nothing could prove more clearly the marvelous influence of Sir William over the savages than the fact that their first impulse was not to seize hatchet and knife, but to solicit a conference with Sir William, so that they might state their wrongs calmly and ask his advice. Lord! Lord! A great man died in last July; and who can take his place?"

Again he wiped his brow.

"The Indians came here in hordes," he resumed. "From morning till night Sir William was engaged in talking with them, persuading and promising and exerting himself tirelessly to hold the gathering tempest in check. He was even then far from well; his old trouble had returned; he could scarcely drag himself up here to this room when night came.

"By the seventh of July we had a thousand Indians assembled here. The sachems and chiefs were earnestly pleading for the congress. Sir William was sick abed and suffering pitifully, but he refused to listen to Doctor Pierson and rose, saying that the congress should never be delayed by anything but his own death.

"The weather was frightfully hot. The whole of the first day was occupied by the speeches of the war chiefs.

"The next day was the Sabbath. Sir William lay abed all day, unable to see for the frightful pains in his head. Yet the following day, at half-past nine in the morning, Sir William was at the fire, belts in hand."

"Yes?" I muttered, to urge him on as he paused. Lying there with my eyes half closed, I could see plainly the beloved face and figure of Sir William standing by that fire, with his belts.

His voice husky, Mr. Duncan continued:

"Never, never, Mr. Cardigan, had any one heard Sir William speak with such eloquence. Sick unto death as he was, he stood there in the burning July sun, hour after hour, in the cause of peace. He spoke with all the fire of youth; his words held the savages' grave and strained attention until the end."

Mr. Duncan paused again, staring at space as though to fix that last scene in his mind forever.

"I was commanding the escort," he said. "My men saluted as the Indians left the congress. When the last chief had disappeared, I saw that Sir William was in distress, and ran to him. He lurched forward into my arms. I held him a moment. He tried to speak, but all he could say was, 'Tell Michael I am proud—of—him,' and then fell back full weight. We got him to the Hall and laid him on the library couch. A gillie rode breakneck for Sir John, who was at the old fort nine miles away. Mistress Molly had gone to Schenectady; there remained no one of his own kin here."

Mr. Duncan leaned forward, with his face in his hands.

"Sir John came too late," he said, "Sir William died utterly alone."

As I lay there I could hear the robins chirping outside, just as I had so often heard them from the schoolroom. Could this still be the same summer? Years and years seemed to have slipped away in these brief months between May and October.

"Where is he buried?" I asked.

"In the vault under the stone church he built in the village. When you can walk—we will go."

"I shall walk very soon now," said I.

After a moment I asked who had succeeded Sir William.

"In title and estate Sir John succeeds him," said Mr. Duncan, "but the King has conferred the Intendancy of Indian Affairs on Colonel Guy Johnson."

"Is he as close a friend as ever of Colonel Butler and Joseph?"

"Quite. Joseph Brant is a special deputy, too."

"Then God save our country," I replied, and closed my eyes.

"When Sir John returns from Boston you will hear the will read," said Mr. Duncan, presently.

"When does he return?" I asked, opening my eyes.

"Tomorrow, we hope."

"Why did he go?"

"I do not know," said Mr. Duncan, frankly.

"Why did he take Miss Warren?"

"I'm sure I do not know," he answered.

"Will she return with him?"

"I cannot say—but I suppose she will," replied Mr. Duncan, looking curiously at me.

"The doctor says she will not return with Sir John."

"Ah!"

"Why?"

"Lord, lad, I don't know!" he exclaimed, amused.

"Did Miss Warren see me while I was ill?"

"Aye, that she did," he cried. "She never left you; they could not drag her away to eat enough to keep a bird alive. And all the time Sir John was fuming and impatient to be off to Boston, but Miss Warren would not go until the doctor was able to promise on his sacred honor that you would recover completely in mind and body."

"And then?" I muttered.

"Why, then Sir John would no longer be denied, and she must needs journey with him to Boston."

"And she left no word for me?"

"None with me. But I heard her ask Sir John how soon you would be able to read if she wrote you."

Presently—for I was becoming very tired—I asked about the two forest runners who had brought me hither, not mentioning their names for prudence's sake.

"I don't know where they are," said Mr. Duncan, rising to go. "The little, mild-spoken man disappeared the day that Sir John and Miss Warren left for Boston. The other, the big, swaggering fellow, abandoned by his running mate, hunted about the village for a week, swearing that there was foul play somewhere, and that his comrade would never willingly have deserted him. Then our magistrate, Squire Bullock, was robbed on the King's highway—aye, and roundly cursed for a Tory thief—by this same graceless giant who brought you here. They sought for him, but you know how those fellows travel. He may be in Quebec now, for aught I know—the impudent rascal."

After a moment I said, "Miss Warren, you say, cared for me while I lay ill?"

"Like a mother—or fond sister."
I closed my eyes partly.
He looked down at me and pressed my hand.
"I have tired you," he said, gently.
"No, you have given me life," I answered, smiling.

CHAPTER NINETEEN

LONG before Sir John returned I was dressed and making hourly essays at walking, first in the house, then through the dooryard to the guardhouse, where I would sit in the hot sun and breathe the full-throated October winds. My eyes grew clear and strong, my lean cheeks filled, my wasted limbs once more began to bear me with the old-time lightness and delight.

On warm, spicy days Mr. Duncan and I would seek the stone church, sitting silent for hours in the purple and crimson rays of the stained window, watching the golden dust bands slanting on the tomb.

The resentment of bitter grief had died out in my heart; sorrow had been purged of selfishness; I felt the calm presence of the dead at my elbow where'er I went. Strength and quiet came to me in voiceless communion.

When the southwest sun hung gilding the clover, over miles of upland I passed, as I had roamed with him, twisting the bronzing sweet fern from its woody stem, touching the silken milkweed to set free its floss, halting, breast-deep in crimsoning sumach, to mark the headlong, whirling covey drive through the thorns into the purple dusk.

Nor was I lonely at these times, for he walked with me

always over the land he had known, and his voice was in the soft, mild winds he loved so well.

With the memory of Silver Heels it was different. Every scented stem of sweet fern was redolent of her; every grass blade quivered for her; the winds called her all day long; the brooks whispered, "Where is Silver Heels?"

Through our old playgrounds, in the orchard, on the stairs, through the darkened schoolroom I followed, haunting the vanished footsteps—gay, light, flying feet of the child I had loved so long, unknowing.

Wistfulness, doubt, tenderness, and sadness came and went like sun spots on an April day. I waited with delicious dread for her return; I fretted, doubted, hoped, all in the same quick heartbeat.

When the golden month drew near its end, I awoke one sun-drenched morning to hear the drums and pipes skirling the march of "Tryon County Men."

"Officer o' the guard! Turn out the guard!" bawled the sentry under my window.

As I looked out the drums came crashing past, and behind them tramped the kilted Highlanders with claymore blades shining in the sun. It was the new regiment organized by Sir John, picked men all, and fierce partisans of the King. Behind them came the reorganized battalion of yeomanry, now stripped clean of rebel suspects, and rechristened "Johnson's Greens." I watched them swinging north into the purple hills for a month's training.

In a short time a knocking at my door brought a gillie with Colonel Guy Johnson's compliments, and would I dress in my uniform to receive Sir John, who was expected for breakfast.

My heart began to beat madly; could it be possible that Sir John had brought Silver Heels, after all?

I dressed in my red uniform, tied my silver gorget, hung my sword, and drew on my spurred boots. I twisted a strip of crape in my hilt, shook out the black badge on my sleeve, and went downstairs, very soberly, in the livery of the King I must one day desert. Perhaps I was now wearing it for the last time.

As I reached the porch Mr. Duncan came hurrying past.

"Sir John is in the village," he said, returning my salute, "and he has an escort of your regiment at his back."

"Where is Colonel Guy?" I asked; but at that moment he came out of the stable in full uniform, and Mr. Duncan and I joined him at salute. He barely noticed me, as usual, but gave his orders to Mr. Duncan and then looked across the fields toward the village.

"Is Felicity with Sir John?" I inquired.

"No," he answered, without turning.

My throat swelled. Where was she, then? What did all this mean?

"By the by," observed Colonel Guy, carelessly, "Sir John has chosen another aide-de-camp in your place. You, of course, will join your regiment at Albany."

I looked at him calmly, but he was again gazing out across the fields. So Sir John, who had never cared about me, had rid himself of me. This brought matters to a climax. Truly enough, I was now wearing my red uniform for the last time.

I looked across the yellowish fields where, on the highway,

a troop of horse were galloping toward the Hall. I watched them indifferently. Soon the horsemen came sweeping up past the ranks of presented firelocks and halted.

And now I saw Sir John, in his major-general's uniform, slowly dismount, while a gillie held his stirrup. Alas! alas! that he must be known by men as the son of his great father!—this cold, slow man, with distrustful eyes and a mouth which to see was to watch.

Sir John greeted Colonel Guy. Then, as I gave him the officers' salute, he rendered it and offered his hand, asking me how I did.

I reported myself quite recovered, and in turn inquired concerning his own health, the health of Aunt Molly, and of Silver Heels; to which he replied that Mistress Molly with Esk and Peter was in Quebec; that Felicity was well; that he himself suffered somewhat from indigestion, but was otherwise in possession of perfect health.

He then presented me to several officers of my own regiment, among them a very young cornet, who smiled at me in most friendly fashion. His name was Rodman Girdwood, and he swaggered when he walked; but so frankly did he ruffle it that I could not choose but like him and smile indulgence on his guileless self-satisfaction.

"They don't like me," he said, confidentially, as I took him to my own chamber so that he might remove the stains of travel. "They don't like me because I talk too much at mess. I say what I think, and I say it loud, sir."

"What do you say—loud?" I asked, smiling.

"Oh, everything. I say it's a shame to send British troops into Boston; I say it's a double shame to close the port and starve the poor; I say that Tommy Gage is in a dirty business and I, for one, hope the Boston people will hold on until the British Parliament find their senses. Oh, I don't care who hears me!" he said, throwing off his coat and sword and plunging into the water basin.

"I trust I have not shocked your loyalty, Mr. Cardigan," he said, using a towel vigorously.

"Oh no!" I laughed.

"I don't mean to be discourteous," he added, smoothing his ruffled lace, "but sometimes I feel as though I must stand up on a hill and shout across the ocean to Parliament, 'Don't make fools of yourselves!' "

I was laughing so heartily that he turned around in humorous surprise.

"I'm afraid you are one of those disrespectful patriots," he said. "I never heard a Tory laugh at anything I said. Come, sir, pray repeat 'God save the King!' "

"God save"—we began together, then ended—"our country!"

I looked at him gravely. He, too, had grown serious. Presently he held out his hand. I took it in silence.

"Well, well," he said, "I had little thought of finding a comrade in our new cornet."

"Nor I in the Border Horse," said I, quietly.

He turned to the mirror and began retying his queue ribbon. After a twist or two the smile came back to his lips and the jauntiness to his carriage.

"It's all in a lifetime," he said. "Lord! but I'm hungry, Cardigan!"

"Come on, then," I said. "We subalterns must not keep our superiors, you know."

"They wouldn't wait for us, anyway," he said, following me downstairs to the breakfast-room, into which already Sir John and his suite were crowding.

The breakfast was short and dreary. When it was ended, Colonel Guy Johnson conducted his guests to the porch, where they made ready for the inspection of our two stone blockhouses and the new artillery in the barracks.

Supposing I was to follow, as I no longer remained aide-de-camp to the major-general, I started off with Rodman Gird-wood, but was recalled by a soldier, who reported that Sir John awaited me in the library.

Sir John was sitting at the great oak table as I entered, and he motioned me to a seat opposite. He held in his hands a bundle of papers, which he slowly turned over and over.

He first informed me that he had selected another aide-de-camp, not because he expected to find me unsatisfactory, but because in these troublous times it was most desirable that young, inexperienced officers should join the colors as soon as possible. He expected me, he said, to return to Albany with the squadron that had served him as escort.

To which I made no reply.

He then spoke of the death of his father, of the responsibilities of his own position, and of his claim on me for obedience. He spoke of my mission to Cresap and the Cayugas as a mistake in policy; and I burned to hear him criticize Sir William's acts. He asked me for my report, and I gave it to him, relating every circumstance of my meeting with the Cayugas, my peril, my rescue, the fight at Cresap's fort, the treachery of Dunmore, Greathouse, Connolly, and the others.

He frowned, listening with lowered eyes.

I told him how narrowly Silver Heels had escaped from Dunmore. Then I related every circumstance in my relations with Walter Butler, from my first open quarrel with him here at the Hall on through his deadly attack on me, and finally how he had fallen under my fury in Dunmore's presence.

Sir John's face was expressionless. He deplored the matters mentioned, saying that loyal men must stand together. He pointed out that Dunmore was the royal Governor of Virginia; that offending him was most unwise. He regretted the quarrel between such a zealous loyalist as Walter Butler and myself, but coolly informed me that he had heard from Butler, and that he was recovering slowly from the breaking of an arm, collar bone, and many ribs.

This calm acknowledgment that Sir John and my deadly enemy were in such intimacy set my blood boiling. His amazing complacency toward these men, after the insults offered his own kin, took my breath.

It was, he said, my duty to lay aside all rancor against Lord Dunmore and Captain Butler. This was not the time to settle personal differences. Later, he could see no objection to my calling out Walter Butler or demanding reparation from Lord Dunmore, if I found it necessary.

I was slowly beginning to hate Sir John.

But I was contented to hear that Walter Butler lived; for, though no man on earth deserved death more than he, I had not wished to slay any man in such a manner. I could wait, for I never doubted that he must one day die by my hand.

Sir John now spoke of the will left by Sir William. He held a copy in his hand and opened it.

"You know," he said, "that my father has invested your small fortune most wisely. The income is ample for a young man, and on the decease of your uncle, Sir Terence, you will come into his title and estate in Ireland. This should make you wealthy. Sir William, however, saw fit to provide for you further."

He turned the pages of the document slowly, frowning.

"Where is my own money?" I asked.

Sir John passed me a letter, sealed, which he said would recommend me to Peter Weaver, the lawyer in Albany who administered my fortune until I became of legal age. Then he resumed his study of the will.

He searched out the first clause that referred to me and read it aloud in his cold, passionless voice:

"Item. To my dearly beloved kinsman and ward, Michael Cardigan, I give and bequeath the sum of three thousand pounds, York currency, to him or the survivor of him. Also my own horse Warlock."

Sir John turned several pages, found another clause, and read:

"To the aforesaid Michael Cardigan I devise and bequeath that lot of land which I purchased from Jelles Fonda, in the Kennyetto Patent; also two hundred acres of land adjoining thereto, to be laid out in a compact body between the sugar bush and the Kennyetto Creek; also four thousand acres in the Royal Grant, next to the Mohawk River, where is the best place for salmon fishing; also that strip of land from the falls or carrying-place to Lot No. 1, opposite to the hunting lodge of Colonel John Butler, where woodcocks, snipes, and wild ducks are accustomed to be shot by me, within the limits and including all the game land I bought from Peter Weaver."

Sir John folded the paper and handed it to me, saying, "It is strange that Sir William thought fit to bequeath you such a vast property."

"What provision was made for Felicity?" I asked, quietly.

"She might have had three thousand pounds and a thousand acres adjoining yours in the Kennyetto Patent," replied Sir John, coldly. "But under present circumstances—ahem—she receives nothing."

I thought a moment. In the hallway I heard the officers returning with Colonel Guy Johnson.

"Where is Felicity?" I asked, suddenly.

"She is near Boston," he said, frowning. "Her lawyer is Thomas Foxcroft in Queen Street."

"When will she return here?"

"She will not return."

"What!" I cried, springing to my feet.

Sir John eyed me sullenly.

"I beg you will conduct in moderation," he said.

"Then tell me what you have done with my cousin Felicity!"

"She is not your cousin, or any kin to you or to us," he said, coldly. "I have had some correspondence with Sir Peter Warren, which, I may say, does not concern you. Enough that Felicity is not his niece, nor any kin whatever to him, to us, or to you. Further than that I have nothing to say, except that the young woman is now with her own kin, and will remain there. Better for you," he added, grimly, "and better for us, if you had not meddled with what did not concern you and had allowed Lord Dunmore to wed her."

"Dunmore! Wed Felicity!" I burst out.

"Why not? Such as Felicity may feel highly honored by the regard of his lordship."

Sir John's contemptuous tone as he spoke Felicity's name, his utter disregard of all I had told him about Dunmore, set me trembling in every limb. I sprang up, furious.

"Dunmore is a scoundrel!" I stammered. "A black scoundrel! An infamous, treacherous murderer! How dare you ——"

"You will control your temper here at least," he said, pointing to the card-room, where Colonel Guy Johnson and the Border officers were staring at us through the open doors.

"No, I will not!" I cried. "I care not who hears me! And I say shame on you for your heartlessness! Shame on you for your callous, merciless judgment, you bloodless hypocrite!"

"Silence!" he said, turning livid. "You leave this house to-night for your regiment."

"I leave it in no service that tolerates such blackguards as Dunmore or such cold-blooded beasts as you!" I retorted, tearing my sword from my belt. Then I stepped forward and, looking him straight in the eyes, slammed my sheathed sword down on the table before him.

"You, your governors, and your King are too poor to buy the sword I would wear," I said, between my teeth.

"Are you mad?" he muttered, staring.

I laughed.

"Not I," I said gayly, "but the pack o' fools who curse my country with their folly, like that withered, half-witted Gov·

ernor of Virginia, like that pompous ass in Boston, like you yourself, sir, though Heaven knows it chokes to say it of your father's son!"

"Major Benning," cried Sir John, "you will place that lunatic under arrest!"

My major started, then took a step toward me.

"Try it!" said I, all the evil in me on fire. "Go to the devil, sir!—where your own business is doubtless stewing. Hands off, sir!—or I throw you through the window!"

"Good gad!" muttered Benning. "The lad's gone stark!"

"But I still shoot straight," I said, picking up Sir William's favorite rifle and handling it most carelessly.

"Mind what you are about!" cried Sir John, furiously. "That piece is charged!"

"I am happy to know it," I replied, dropping it into the hollow of my arm so he could look down the black muzzle.

And I walked out of the room and up the stairs to my own little chamber, there to remove from my body the livery of my King, never again to resume it.

I spent the day in packing together all articles that were rightly mine, bought with my own money or given me by Sir William. I made two bundles of my property, done neatly in blankets.

Then I hailed a gillie from the orchard, bidding him saddle Warlock with a dragoon's saddle, and place forage for three days in the saddlebags. After that I dressed me once more in new buckskins, this to save the wear of travel on my better clothing, of which I did take but one suit, that being my silver-gray velvet, cut with French elegance.

Now, as I looked from the windows, I could see Sir John,

Colonel Guy, and their guests mounting to ride to the village, doubtless in order that they should be shown Sir William's last resting-place. So I, being free of the house, wandered through it from cellar to attic, because it was to be my last hour in the only home I had ever known.

I strayed through the silent, sunny rooms, touching the walls with aching heart, and bidding each threshold adieu. Ghosts walked with me through the dimmed sunbeams; far in the house, faintest familiar sounds seemed to stir, half-heard whispers, the echo of laughter, a dear voice calling from above.

But I could not linger overlong listening to those murmurs of the past, for the gillie came to announce that Warlock waited. I bade him carry my two packets down, and followed myself with Sir William's long rifle, and otherwise completely equipped with hatchet, knife, powder and ball, flint and tinder, and a small stewpan.

With these Warlock was laden like a pack-horse, leaving room in the saddle for me. The gillie held my stirrup; I mounted and, with tears blinding me, turned my horse's head south on the Albany post road.

Mr. Duncan, standing near the stable, gazed at me in astonishment.

"Ho!" he called out. "More wood-running, Mr. Cardigan? Faith, the scalp trade must be paying in these humming days of peace!"

I tried to smile and gave him my hand.

"It's good-by forever," I said, choking. "I cannot use the same roof that shelters my kinsman, Sir John Johnson."

He looked at me very gravely, asking me where I meant to go.

"To Boston," I replied. "I have affairs with one Thomas Foxcroft."

There was a silence, he still holding my hand as though to draw me back.

"Why to Boston?" he repeated, gently.

"To wed Miss Warren," I replied, looking him in the eyes.

He stared, then caught my hand in both of his.

"God bless her!" he said. "I give you joy, lad! She's the sweetest of them all in County Tryon!"

"And in all the world beside!" I muttered, huskily.

And so rode on.

My journey to Albany was slow, easy, and uneventful. Once arrived there, I had no great difficulty in finding Peter Weaver. He informed me that my uncle, Sir Terence Cardigan, was dying o' drink in Ireland, and wished me to go to him. I politely declined, and told him why. He was a pleasant, kindly man, a gentleman in bearing and a courteous friend; I felt no reluctance in giving him confidential information about my private affairs.

While in Albany I bought a ring of plain gold to fit halfway on my little finger, judging Silver Heels's finger to be of that roundness.

I stayed but one day in the town. At dawn of the following morning Warlock and I took the Boston road; and how the dear fellow did gallop, though he carried but a buckskin dragoon without company or colors or commission to bear arms!

The first two days of my travel were almost without incident, lovely, calm October days through which sunlit clouds

MY JOURNEY TO ALBANY WAS SLOW, EASY, AND UNEVENTFUL

sailed out of the west, and the wild ducks drifted southward like floating banners in the sky.

On the third day Warlock cast both hind shoes, and I was obliged to lead him very carefully, mile after mile, until, toward sundown, I entered a little village, where in a smithy a forge reddened the fading daylight.

The smith, a gruff man, gave me news of Boston. He said that the Port Bill was starving the poor and driving all decent people toward open rebellion. As for himself, he declared that he meant to march at the first drumbeat.

At that, I held out my hand. He gave me a brawny, blackened fist to shake, and then I rode away in the dusk.

To make up for the delay in traveling afoot all day, I determined to keep on until midnight, Warlock being fit and ready without effort; so I munched a quarter of bread to stay my stomach and trotted on.

The moon came up, but was soon frosted by silvery shoals of clouds. Then a great black bank pushed up from the west, covering moon and stars in somber gloom, touched now and again by the dull flicker of lightning.

After a while, far away, the low muttering of thunder sounded. Soon the dark silence around turned into sound; a low, monotonous murmur filled my ears. It rained.

Hoping to find shelter, I urged Warlock forward toward two spots of light which might come from windows very far away, or from the lamps of a post chaise near at hand.

Reining in, I was beginning to wonder which it might be, when my horse reared violently, and at the same moment I knew that somebody had seized his bridle.

"Stand and deliver!" came a calm voice from the darkness.

I already had my rifle raised, but my thumb on the pan gave me warning that the priming was soaking wet.

"Dismount," came the voice, a trifle sharply.

I felt for the bridle, which had been jerked from my hands; it was gone. I gave one furious glance at the lights ahead, which I now saw came from a post chaise standing in the road close by. Could I summon help from that? Or had the chaise also been stopped as I was now? Certainly I had run on a nest of highwaymen.

"How many have you?" I asked, choking with indignation. "I'll give three of you merry gentlemen a chance at me if you will allow me one dry priming!"

CHAPTER TWENTY

THERE was a dead silence. The unseen hand that held my horse's head fell away, and the animal snorted and tossed his mane. I cautiously felt around until I found the bridle, and noiselessly began to work it back over Warlock's head.

"Now for it!" I thought, gathering to launch the horse like a battering-ram into the unknown ahead.

But just as I drew my light hatchet from my belt and lifted the bridle, I almost dropped from the saddle to hear a meek and pleading voice I knew call me by name.

"Jack Mount!" I exclaimed, incredulous even yet.

"The same, Mr. Cardigan, out at heels and elbows, lad, and trimming the highway for a purse-proud Tory. Are you offended?"

"Offended!" I repeated. "Oh no, of course not!" And I burst into a shout of uncontrollable laughter.

He did not join in.

"Oh, you can laugh," he said, in a hurt voice. "But I have accomplished a certain business yonder which has nigh frightened me to death, that's all."

"What business?" I asked, weak from laughter.

"Oh, you may well ask! Gad! I lay here for the fat bailiff

o' Grafton, who should travel to Hadley this night with Tory funds, and—I stopped a lady in that post chaise yonder, and she's fainted at sight o' me. That's all."

"Fainted?" I repeated. "Where are her postboys? Where's her footman? Where's her maid? Is she alone, Jack?"

"Aye," he responded, gloomily; "the men and the maid ran off. If I'd only had Cade with me ——"

"But—where's the Weasel?"

"I wish I knew," he said, earnestly. "He left me at Johnstown—sent away—vanished like a hermit bird. Oh, I am certainly an unhappy man, and a bungling one at that. I wish you would come over to that cursed post chaise and see what can be done for the lady. You know about ladies, don't you?"

"I don't know what to do when they faint," I replied.

"There's ways and ways," he responded. "Some say to shake them, but I can't bring myself to that. Do you think—if we could get her out o' the chaise—and let her be rained on ——"

"No, no," I said, controlling a violent desire to laugh. "I'll calm her, Jack. Perhaps she has recovered."

As we advanced in the dim radiance of the chaise lamps, I looked curiously at Mount, and he up at me.

"Lord!" he murmured, "how you have changed, lad!"

"You, too," I said, for he was haggard and dirty and truly enough in rags.

"Poor old Jack!" I said. "Why did you desert me after you had saved my life? I owe you so much that it were a charity to aid me discharge the debt."

"Ho!" he muttered. " 'Twas no debt, lad, and I'm but a pottle-pot, after all. Now, I care not what befalls me, for

Cade's gone—or dead—and I've the heart of a chipmunk left to face the devil."

"Soft," I whispered. "The lady's astir in her chaise. Wait you here, Jack!"

And, dismounting, I advanced to the chaise window, cap in hand.

"Madam," I began, very gently, "I perceive some accident has befallen your carriage. Pray, believe me humbly anxious to serve you if there be aught wherein I may ——"

"Michael Cardigan!" came a startled voice, and I froze dumb in astonishment. For there, hood thrown back, and earnest, pale face swiftly leaning into the lamp rays, I beheld Marie Hamilton. She thrust both hands toward me, laughing and crying at the same moment.

"Oh, the romance of life!" she cried. "I have had such a fright! A highwayman, Michael, *grand Dieu!*—here in the rain, pulling the horses up short, and it was, 'Ho! Stand and deliver!'—with pistol pushed in my face, and I to faint—not frightened, but vexed and all on the *qui vive* to hide my jewels. Then comes this great ragged, handsome rascal, aghast to see me fainted, a-muttering excuse that he meant no harm, but had been waiting for another chaise—and I lying *perdu*, still as a mouse.

"*Vrai Dieu,* but I did frighten him well, and now he's gone, and I in a plight with my cowardly postboys, maid, and footman fled, Heaven knows whither!"

The amazing rapidity of her chatter fair confounded me.

"Dear friend," she sighed, "dear, dear friend, what happiness to feel I owe my life to you!"

"But you don't," I blurted out. "There never was any danger."

"Lord save the boy!" she murmured. "There is no spark o' romance in him!" And fell a-laughing in that faint, low mockery that I remembered on that fatal night at Johnson Hall.

"You are mistaken," I said grimly. "Romance is the breath of my life, madam. And so I now plead freedom to present to your good graces my friend, Jack Mount, who lately stopped your coach upon the King's highway!"

And I caught the abashed giant by his ragged sleeve and dragged him to the chaise window, where he plucked off his coonskin cap and stared wildly at the astonished lady within.

But it was no easy matter to rout Marie Hamilton. True, she paled a little, and took one short breath; then, like sunlight breaking, her bright eyes softened and that sweet, fresh mouth parted in a smile which spite of me set my own pulse a quickstep marching.

"I am not angry, sir," she said, mockingly. "All cats are gray at midnight, and one post chaise resembles another, Captain Mount—for surely, by your exploits, you deserve at least that title."

Mount's fascinated eyes grew bigger. His consternation and the wild appeal in his eyes set me hard a-swallowing my laughter.

"Jack," said I, smothering my mirth. "do you get your legs astride the leader, there, and play at postboy to the nearest inn. Here, give me your rifle."

"And you, Michael," asked Mrs. Hamilton, "will you not share my carriage, for old time's sake?"

I told her I had my horse and would ride him at her chaise wheels, and so left her, somewhat coolly, for I liked not that trailing tail to her invitation—"for old time's sake."

"What the foul fiend have I to do with 'old time's sake'?" I muttered as I slung myself astride o' Warlock and motioned Jack Mount to move on. " 'Old time's sake!' Faith, it once cost me the bitterest day of my life, and might cost me the love of the sweetest girl in earth or heaven!"

Riding on through the fine rain, I thought much on the smallness of this our world, where a single hour on an unknown road had given me two companions whom I knew.

God grant the end of my journey would give me her for whose dear sake the journey had been made!

Thinking such thoughts, lost in a lover's reverie, I rode on and on, until I was roused to find the chaise turning into a tavern yard. Mount called. A yawning ostler came with a light, and at the same instant our little fat host in shirt and apron toddled out to bid us welcome. Mrs. Hamilton gave me her hand and jumped to the ground on tiptoe.

"Mad doings on the road, sir!" said our host, rubbing his hands. "Chaise and four stopped by the penny stile two hours since, sir. Ay, you may smile, my lady, but the postboys fought a dreadful battle with the highwaymen. You laugh, sir? But I have these same postboys here, and the footman, too, to prove it!"

"But, pray, where is the lady and the chaise and four?" asked Mrs. Hamilton, demurely.

"Heaven knows," said the innkeeper. "The villains carried it off with the poor lady inside. Mad work, my lady! Mad work!"

"Maddening work," said I, wrathfully. "Jack, borrow a post whip and warm the breeks of those same postboys, will you? Lay it on thick, Jack!"

Mount went away toward the stable, and I quieted the astonished landlord and sent him to prepare supper, while a servant lighted Mrs. Hamilton to her chamber. Then I went out to see that Warlock was well fed and bedded fresh; and I did hear sundry howls from the villain postboys in their quarters overhead, where Mount was nothing sparing of the leather.

Presently he came down the ladder, and laughed sheepishly when he saw me.

"They're well birched," he said. "It's a mercy if they sit their saddles in the morning." Then he took my hands and held them so hard that I winced.

"Gad, I'm that content to see you, lad!" he repeated again and again.

"And I you, Jack," I said. "It's time, too, else you'd be in some worse mischief than this night's folly. But I'll take care of you now," I added, laughing. "Faith, it's turn and turn about, you know. Come to supper."

"I—I hate to face that lady," he muttered. "No, lad, I'll sup with my own marrowbones for company."

"Nonsense!" I insisted, but could not budge him. "Well, have it as you wish then, Jack," I said. "But come into my chamber when you've supped. I'll be there. Lord! what millions of questions I have to ask!"

"To be sure, to be sure," he murmured; then walked away toward the kitchen, while I returned to the inn.

We supped together, Mrs. Hamilton and I, and found the cheer most comforting. But our talk over it was somewhat disconcerting.

She, of course, knew nothing of my journey to Pittsburg, nor of any events there that might have occurred after she had left. I told her nothing save that Felicity was in Boston and that I was journeying thither to see her.

"Is she not to wed the Earl of Dunmore?" asked Mrs. Hamilton.

"No," said I, quietly.

"La! the capricious beauty!" she murmured. "Sure she has not thrown over Dunmore for that foolish dragoon, Kent Bevan?"

"I hope not," said I, maliciously.

"Are you jealous?" she taunted me.

I smiled and shook my head.

"But you once were in love with your cousin," she persisted. "And jealousy then had fast hold on you! Or was it something else? Ah, do you remember how you played with me at that state dinner held in Johnson Hall? You rode me down roughshod, Michael, and used me shamefully there, under the stairs."

"I'll do the like again if you provoke me," I said, but had not meant to say it, either.

"The—the like—again? And what was that, pray?"

"You know," I said, sulkily.

"I think you—kissed me ——"

"I think I did," said I, "and left you all in tears."

It was brutal, but I meant to make an end.

"Did you believe that those were real tears?" she said, innocently.

"By Heaven, I know they were," said I, with satisfaction, "and small vengeance to repay the ill you did me, too."

"What ill?" she asked, opening her eyes in real surprise.

But I was silent and ashamed already. Truly, it had been no fault but my own that I had taken up the gage she flung at me that night so long ago.

"I do not understand you, Michael," she said, with a faint smile, ending in a sigh.

"Nor I you, bonnie Marie Hamilton," said I. "Suppose we both cry quits?"

"Not yet," she said. "I have a little score with you, unsettled. Mine be the right of challenge."

What the mischief did she mean? The game was running on too fast for me.

"Safely they defy who challenge, those in chains," I said, but my pulse was beating unreasonably fast. "I cry you mercy; you have won."

After a long silence she raised her eyes, dancing with mockery.

"I give you joy, Michael," she said, "if, as I take it, these same chains and fetters that you lately wear are riveted by Cupid."

But I answered nothing, attending her to the door, where she dropped me the lowest of curtsies.

So I to my own chamber in no amiable frame of mind, and still tingling with the strange charm of my encounter. Presently there came a timid scratching at the door. I opened it and Mount sidled in. He regarded me doubtfully, but sat down when bidden and began to complain:

"Now, if you are minded to chide me for taking the road, I'm going out again. I can't bear any more, lad, that I can't! —what with Cade gone and me in rags, and stopping Councilor Bullock near Johnstown with pockets bare of aught but a cursed sixpence—and now I must needs fright a lady into a faint ——"

"What on earth is the matter with you?" I broke in, peevishly. "I'm not finding fault, Jack. If you mean to spend your life in endeavors to impoverish every Tory magistrate in America, I can't help it, though you must know as well as I that there's a carpenter's tree and a rope at the end of your frolic."

"No, there isn't," he said, hastily. "I'm done with the highway. Lord, lad, I took to it not for the money, but for sport. And soon there'll be fighting enough to fill my stomach; mark me, the crocus that buds white this spring will wither red as blood!"

"War?" I asked, thrilling to hear him.

"Ay, surely, surely in the spring," he told me, and sat silent until I broke in upon his thoughts.

"Why did you desert me, Jack?" I asked.

"Faith, I hung about with Cade, doing no harm, sitting in the sun to wait for news from you. Mr. Duncan gave us news and made us welcome on the benches in front of the guard-house. And Mistress Warren would have us to eat with her —only I was ashamed. But Cade went and supped with her.

"Lad, Sir John Johnson is not a gentleman I should grow too fond of. His courtesy is a shallow spring, I'm thinking, and over-sour to suit my teeth."

"What did Sir John do?" I asked, growing red. "Surely he thanked you and Cade for saving his kinsman's life; surely he made you welcome at the Hall, Jack?"

"Surely he did nothing of the kind," grunted Mount. "Sir John sent word that we had best find quarters in Johnstown taverns and not set the hounds barking in his kennels."

It was like a blow in the face to me. Jack saw it and laughed.

"It's not your fault," he said. "If he's your kin, it's to be borne, lad, and that's all there is to it."

I set my teeth and swallowed my shame.

"So we went to Rideup's old camp," he continued, "and there I lay and—tippled, lad. I'll not deny it, no!

"Cade never drank. He is mad, lad, quite mad. He thought he saw his little daughter in Miss Warren, and he waited all day to see her come out to the guardhouse and give the news of your sick bed to your Lieutenant Duncan. So one day, when you were surely out of danger, comes Cade to the tavern and bids me good-by, talking wildly of his lost daughter, and I, Heaven help me, lay abed with my head like a top all humming for the ale I'd had, and thinking nothing of what he said save that his madness grew apace.

"And that night he went away while I slept in my cups. When he came not I hunted through the town for him. I was half crazy; I could not think he'd left me there of his own free will, and many a fight I had with the soldiers. Finally that fat councilor—Bullock, I mean—would have had me jailed for a matter of damaging his Tory constable. So I gave him a fright on the highway and left your Tryon County for a quieter one. That's all, lad."

What he had told me of Cade Renard troubled me. If Felicity had been strangely lost to her own family, and had been restored, doubtless she was now sweetly happy. I did not want such happiness disturbed by a mad forest runner and his luny fancies.

"Do you think Cade followed Miss Warren to Boston?" I asked.

"My journey is to find that out," he said. "Ah, lad, a noble mind was wrecked in Renard's head. I miss him, and I must look for him."

My candle was burning very low now. Mount rose, shook himself, and said good night.

"Good night," I said, and did not light another candle, but betook myself to bed.

UNDER IT A SENTRY MOVED

CHAPTER TWENTY-ONE

B Y NOON of the next day we were well on our way toward Boston, I riding beside Mrs. Hamilton's carriage
wheels, Jack Mount perched up on the box, very gay in a new
suit of buckskins which I had bought for him from a squaw
in the village.

At our start in the early morning I had handed Mrs. Hamilton to her chaise, and stood in attendance while she tied on
her velvet sun mask in silence, but watching me smilingly
through the eyeholes.

"Merci," she said, in a whisper, after I had disposed her foot-mantle around her ankles; and I closed the carriage and mounted Warlock nimbly, impatient to be gone.

"Michael," she said from the chaise window.

"Madam," I replied, politely.

"Let Captain Mount ride your horse, and do you come into the carriage. I have so much to tell you ——"

I made what excuse I could. She tossed her chin.

"I shall die of *ennui*," she said.

"Count the thraves in the stubble," said I, laughing.

"And talk to my five wits of the harvest? How amusing!" she retorted, indignantly.

"Repent the past, then," I suggested, smiling, and signaled the footman and postboys.

The chaise creaked off down the road, and I dropped behind, turning a quickly sober face to the rain-washed brightness of the world.

So we journeyed until noon. At Grafton we stayed our hunger; then on along the Charles River, with the scent o' the distant sea in every breath we drew.

On the highroad that afternoon, we passed scores of farmers' wains, piled with vegetables and fruit and sacks o' flour, all bound for Boston, where the poor were starving and the rich went hungering because the King of England had been angered to hear men prate of human rights.

Since the first day of June the Boston Port Bill had been in effect and the city was sealed to commerce. No food could come in over the waters of the bay. So the farmers of Massachusetts Bay brought their harvests by land to the famine-stricken city, and sister colonies sent generously of their best with the watchword: "Stand fast, Boston! A king's anger is a little thing, but human rights shall not perish until we perish, every one!"

It was sunset as we turned into the Roxbury road, with the salt wind blowing the marsh reeds and ruffling the shallow waters of the harbor to the north and east. Northeast the steeples of Boston rose, blood-red in the setting sun; distant windows flashed fire; weather vanes turned to jets of flame.

The red glow enveloped the road over which we traveled, now in company with scores of other vehicles, all moving slowly, as though the head of the column had been checked by something.

I rode on slowly, passing Mrs. Hamilton's chaise and riding along the stalled line of vehicles until, just ahead, I caught a glimpse of an earthwork flying the British flag. Under it a sentry moved, bayonet glittering as he turned, paced on, turned again.

I shall never forget that first coming to Boston, nor my first sight of the city's landward gate, closed by British earthworks, patroled by British bayonets, with the red standard flying in the setting sun.

The Providence coach was standing in the road to my left, the six horses stamping restlessly, while the red-nosed coachman muttered and complained and craned his short bull-neck to see what was blocking the highway ahead.

"It's them darned cannon," he grumbled. "They're a-haulin' some more twenty-four pounders into the right bastion. Ding it! My horses are ketchin' cold while we set here in a free land waitin' His Majesty's pleasure!"

But presently the line of vehicles ahead suddenly started, and those behind moved on.

The huge mail-coaches came swaying past me. As the Philadelphia coach rumbled up, I glanced idly at the window where a young girl leaned out, sucking a China orange. Our eyes met for a moment; the girl dropped the orange and stared at me; I also eyed her sharply, certain that I had seen her somewhere before. The coach passed. I sat on my horse, looking after it, cudgeling my wits to remember that red-cheeked buxom lass, who seemed to know me, too.

Then, just as our chaise rattled by, it came to me in a flash that the girl was the thief-taker's daughter from Fort Pitt.

I rode up beside Mount and told him in a low voice that Bully Bishop's lass was ahead in the Philadelphia coach, and that he had best watch out for Billy Bishop himself.

He shrugged his shoulders, not answering, but I noticed that his quick eyes roamed alertly as the chaise passed in between the British earthworks on Boston Neck.

We drove on through the city to Queen Street, where we drew up at a very elegant mansion. There, dismounting, I took Mrs. Hamilton from the carriage.

"If," she said, slowly, "I should bid you to supper at my house, would you hurt me with refusal, Michael?"

I explained politely that I cared not to leave Mount, and that also we must seek a tavern as soon as might be, for we had much business on the morrow which could not wait.

She listened, with a faintly mocking air, then thanked me for my escort, and finally curtsied, saying in a low voice: "Your charming Miss Warren is doubtless impatient. Pray believe me that I wish you joy of your conquest."

I thought she meant it, and it touched me. But when I stepped to her dooryard to conduct her, she turned on me like a flash, and I saw her eyes all wet and brilliant, and her teeth crushing her underlip.

"For a charming journey in my own company I thank you," she said. "For your conceit and your insufferable airs I will find a remedy—remember that! My humiliation under your own roof is not forgotten, Mr. Cardigan, and it shall not be forgotten until you pay me dearly!"

Astonished at her bitterness, I found not a word to answer. A manservant in purple livery opened the door. Mrs. Hamilton turned to me with perfect composure, returning my bow with the smile of an angel, and tripped lightly into her house.

I returned to the street, where Jack Mount was waiting for me, patting Warlock.

"Well, Jack?" I asked, wearily.

"The 'Wild Goose Tavern' is ours," he said—"good cheer and company to match it."

I walked out into the paved street, leading Warlock, and Mount swaggered along beside me, whistling lustily. We came at last to an ancient, discolored, rambling structure, from which hung a red signboard depicting a creature doubtless intended for a wild goose.

"Lord, Jack!" I said. "I'm minded to seek other quarters."

"Never trust to the looks o' things," he laughed. "Come on to the cleanest taproom in Boston town and forget that the shutters yonder need new hinges!"

I led Warlock into the mews to a clean, well-aired stable, and then Mount and I went into the tavern. A half-dozen sober citizens in string-wigs sat there, silently smoking clay pipes with stems full three feet long.

"Good evening, the company!" said Mount, pleasantly.

The men repeated his salutation, looking at us sleepily.

"God save our country, gentlemen," said Mount.

"His mercy shall endure," replied a young man, quietly removing the pipe from between his teeth. "What of the Thirteen Sisters?"

"They sow that we may reap," said Mount, slowly, and sat down, motioning me to take a chair in the circle.

The men looked at us curiously, but in silence, although their sleepy, guarded air had disappeared.

Presently the landlord came in and whispered to us that we might sup at our pleasure in the "Square Room" above. So, with a salute to the silent smokers, we rose.

In the so-called "Square Room" was a long table, with some three dozen covers spread for guests, and to this long, tenantless table our host most civilly conducted us. Then, after a word aside with Mount, he left the room to hasten preparations in the kitchen.

After he had gone, Mount told me that his name was Barclay Rolfe, and that he was brother to Jim Rolfe, of the "Virginia Arms" in Fort Pitt. In their brief aside he had told Mount of seeing Saul Shemuel in Boston on an errand for Cresap.

"A good lad, Shemmy," Mount said, thoughtfully, and then sat silent till our dinner was served.

After we had done justice to the toothsome boiled cod and the great wild goose, roasted brown, we withdrew to a small table in a corner, a servant bringing thither our nuts and hot bowls, and also some writing materials for me.

I seized the pen and set to work:

October 28, 1774.

THOS. FOXCROFT, ESQUIRE,
   Solicitor, Queen Street,
      Boston.

MY DEAR SIR—At what hour this evening will it prove convenient for you to receive the undersigned upon affairs of the utmost urgency concerning Miss Warren, whose interests I believe you represent?

The instant importance of the matter I trust may plead my excuse for this abrupt intrusion on your privacy.

Pray consider me, Sir,

Yr most obliged and obedient Servt
MICHAEL CARDIGAN.

At the Wild Goose
   near Wiltshire and Chambers Streets.

Sealing the letter, I bade the servant take it and wait for an answer.

Mount had taken a pipe from the stranger's rack, and was now peering out of the window and puffing away in vast contentment.

Northward, across the water, the lights of Charlestown glimmered through a thin fog. Nearer, in midstream, rose the black hull of a British warship, battle lanthorns set and lighted, stabbing the dark tide below with jagged shafts of yellow light.

As for Boston, or as much of it as we could see over the shadowy roofs and slanting housetops, it was deathly dark and still. Truly, we sat in a tomb—the sepulcher of all good men's hopes for justice from that distant England we had loved so well in kinder days.

Musing there by the window, we scarcely noticed that the room behind us was filling. Already at the long table a dozen guests were seated, some conversing, some playing absently with their glasses, some reading newspapers.

"Do you know any of these gentlemen, Jack?" I asked in a low voice.

He swung around in his chair and surveyed the table.

"Aye, all o' them," he said, returning their amused salutations. "They all belong to the club that meets here."

"Club? What club?" I asked.

"The Minute Men's. I meant to tell you that you're a member."

"I a member?" I repeated, in astonishment.

"Surely, lad, else you never could ha' passed these stairs. I am a member; I bring you, and now you're a member."

Mount watched the effect of his words on me and grinned.

"You didn't know that I am one of the Minute Club's messengers? That's why I went to Pitt. Did you think I went there for my health? Nenny, lad. I had a message for Cresap as well as you, and I gave it, too."

He laughed, and moistened his lips at the hot bowl.

"Paul Revere, the goldsmith, is another messenger, but not of the Minute Club. He is higher—goes breakneck to York for S. A., you know."

"What is S. A.?" I broke in. "You all talk of J. H. and S. A. and the Thirteen Sisters, and I don't understand."

"S. A. is Sam Adams," said Mount surprised. "J. H. is John

Hancock, a rich young man who is with us to the last gasp. The Thirteen Sisters mean the thirteen colonies."

"But what is this Minute Men's Club?" I asked, curiously.

"Headquarters for delegates from the Minute Men and all alarm companies in Massachusetts Bay—the companies where half of the men are ready to march at a minute's notice. One officer from every company is delegated to attend the Minute Club here, so that he can keep his company in touch with the march of events.

"Besides that, the club has a corps of runners, like me, to travel with orders when called on. I'm in for a rest now, unless something pressing occurs."

"And—what am I in this club?" I asked, smiling to see how well Jack Mount had kept his secrets since I first knew him.

"You? Oh, you are a recruit for Cresap's battalion," said Mount, much amused. "We recruit here for certain companies."

"Is Cresap coming here?" I asked, eagerly.

"He marches in the spring with his Maryland and Pennsylvania Rangers—to help turn this pack o' bloodybacks out of Boston, lad!"

I sat silent, pondering on the strange circumstances of these months that had brought me so swiftly, from my boyhood's isolation, into the thick of the tremendous struggle between King and colony.

That Mount had coolly recruited me without my consent disturbed me not at all, for had I been free to select, I should have chosen to serve under Cresap. I told Jack as much, and his face brightened with pleasure. He insisted on presenting me to the company—which was now fast filling the room—as one of Cresap's Rangers.

The gentlemen I met were most kind and polite. They were a sturdy, clean-limbed company, neatly but not fashionably attired.

A group of the young officers drew me into conversation, and I was surprised to find that they were fully informed about the part I had played in recent events.

"We hear all the news," one of them told me, with a friendly smile. "We have our agents everywhere, listening, watching. We know, for instance, that Walter Butler has traveled north in a litter. We know that Dunmore scarce dare show his hand in Virginia for the shame you put upon him and the growing hatred of the people he governs. We know that Sir John Johnson is fortifying Johnson Hall and gathering hordes of savages and Tories in Tryon County. Aye, Mr. Cardigan, we know, too, that the son of your father will fight to the death for the cause which his honor demands that he embrace."

"My father died for his King," I said, slowly.

"And mine, too," said the young officer, "but were he not with God today, I know where he would be found."

Others began to join our group. Mount, who had been conversing with a handsome, fashionably dressed young man, approached our table with his companion, and presented me to him. Thus I had the privilege of a few minutes' personal talk with young John Hancock, whose wealth did not prevent him from risking all for a principle.

Though I was inclined at first to undervalue Mr. Hancock —to think him an egotistical young fop—before the evening was over I knew him for a true leader. His short speech before the assembled Minute Men that evening was no orator's effort; yet in its very simplicity it was a masterpiece certain to move men to action. As I listened, I realized afresh that war must surely come.

For me, despite my burning desire to see Silver Heels as soon as might be, that evening was one of intense interest.

It was late when the servant returned from Mr. Foxcroft, with a curt note from that gentleman, promising to receive me at one o'clock in the afternoon of the day following.

As I stood twisting the letter in my restless fingers, Jack Mount came up, his eyes bleak with misery.

"Cade has never returned to this tavern," he said. "No one here has either seen or heard of him since he and I left last April for Cresap's camp. Lad! lad! He's dead and buried these long weeks. I know it! I shall never see him more except in my dreams."

I could not comfort him. I could only keep him company till sleep came creeping on us both.

CHAPTER TWENTY-TWO

WHEN I woke the next morning the sun was swinging like a red lamp above the smoky east, its round, inflamed lens peering through a smother of fog.

Jack Mount came in presently, with a silent nod of greeting.

A servant brought us a bowl of stirabout and some rusks and salted codfish, and we breakfasted there in my chamber, scarcely speaking. I should have been exulting at my nearness to Silver Heels, but a foreboding had weighed on me since first I unclosed my eyes. I could scarcely swallow any food. Presently I pushed away my plate, drew paper and ink before me, and fell to composing a letter. From the taproom below a boy came to bring us our morning cups, and we washed the salty tang from our throats. Mount lighted his yard of clay and lay back, puffing smoke at the fog-dimmed window-panes. I wrote slowly, drinking at intervals.

The morning draught refreshed us; and when at length sunshine broke out over the bay, something of our dormant spirits stirred to greet it.

"How silent is the world outside!" said I, listening to the sea birds' mewing, and mending my quill with my hunting-knife.

"Misery breeds silence," Mount replied.

"Are men starving here around us?" I asked, trying to realize what I had heard.

"Aye, and dying of it. The sun yonder no longer signals breakfast for Boston. Better finish your fish while you may."

He fell silent again, pulling slowly at his pipe as I wrote on, completing my letter.

When it was finished, I re-read it:

BOSTON, October 29, 1774.

TO MISTRESS FELICITY WARREN:

DEAR, DEAR SILVER HEELS,—Being cured of my hurts and having done with Johnson Hall and my dishonorable kinsman, Sir John Johnson, I now take my pen in hand to acquaint you that I know all, how that through the mercy of Providence you have been reunited with your honored parents, long supposed to have been with God. I did think to receive a letter from you ere I left the Hall; yet none came. So I insulted Sir John and took Warlock, who is mine of a right, and I am come to Boston to pay my respects to your honored parents and to acquaint them that I mean to wed you, as I love you, my honored cozzen, but feel no happiness inasmuch as a deathly fear hath possessed me that all may not be well with you.

I further acquaint you that my solicitor hath news that my uncle, Sir Terence Cardigan, Bart., is at a low ebb of life, being close to his Maker through much wine and excesses, and hath sent for me, but I would not stir a peg till I have found you, dear Silver Heels, to ask you if you do still love that foolish lad who will soon be Sir Michael Cardigan to the world but ever the same Micky to you, though if war comes to us I doubt not that my title and estate will be confiscated inasmuch as I shall embrace the cause of the colonies.

My sweet Silver Heels, this letter is to be delivered to your solicitor, Mr. Thomas Foxcroft, and by him instantly into your own hands.

Dear maid, if your honorable parents will permit, I shall this day venture to present myself and formally demand your hand in that sweet alliance which even death cannot end.

Your faithful and obedient
servant and devoted lover
MICHAEL CARDIGAN.

The writing of this letter had comforted me. I directed it and, summoning a servant, charged him to bear it instantly to Mr. Foxcroft.

"You will go with me when I get my answer, Jack?" I asked as the messenger vanished.

Mount turned his massive head toward me like a somber-eyed mastiff.

"Daylight is no friend o' mine," he said, slowly. "In Boston here they peddle ballads about me and the Weasel, and some puling quill-mender has writ a book about me, the same bearing a gallows on the cover."

"Then you had best stay here," I said. "I can manage alone, Jack."

"Nay, lad, I'll go with you," he insisted. "I'll not be shut up by fear of a foolish thief-taker." And he buried his nose in a pot of beer.

An hour passed in silence, save for the continual trotting to and fro of the boy from the taproom, bearing deep, frothing tankards for Mount.

"Have a care," I said at length. "If you drink like that you'll be out and abroad and into every foolish mischief. Be a man, Jack!"

"I'm all salty inside like a split herring," he said, and reached for a fresh pewter.

Two hours had dragged by before my lank messenger returned breathless with a letter for me that I saw at once was from Silver Heels herself.

Mount gaped at me; then a delicate instinct moved him to withdraw. I heard him leave the room, but did not heed his going, for I was already deep in the letter:

DEAR LAD, MY OLD COMRADE,—Mr. Foxcroft did summon me to consider your letter of last evening, how it were best to inform you of what you should know.

Now comes your letter of this morning by your messenger, and leaves me atremble to breathe its perfume of the love which I had, days since, resigned.

For I did write you constantly to Johnstown in care of Sir John, and no answer came save one from Sir John saying you cared not to answer me my letters. This cruel insult from Sir John could not have been the truth in light of the letter now folded in my bosom.

But it is plain to me, dear heart, that you as yet know nothing of what great change has come to me. And so, I must, for honor's sake, reveal to you what manner of maid you would now court; not that I doubt you, Michael, dear soul of chivalry and tender truth!

Know then, my friend, that I am hopelessly poor in the world's goods; know, too, that the new name I bear is a name now marked for pity or contempt. It is the death of my pride to say this. Yet I say it.

My father is old and broken. His faculties have failed. His property is gone; he does not know it. He sees around him the shadows of the past; he talks with the dead as though they sat at his elbow.

It is all so pitiful, so strange, so hopeless that it seems still an untrue dream from which I am too weary and stunned to rouse.

Long ago, in a distant year of sunlight, I remember a child called Silver Heels, whose mad desire for rank and power crammed her silly head till, of a sweet May day, love came to her. Love drove her to folly; love reclaimed her; love lies still in her heart, watching for you with tireless eyes.

Dear heart, would you take me? Even after all you now know? Do you still want me, Michael?

I once most wickedly said that if I had been humbly born, I would not for my pride's sake wed with you. It is not true, Michael; I will wed with you. But if after what you have learned, you care no longer to wed me, do not write me; do not come to give me reasons.

Mr. Foxcroft attends me. We will await you at his house, at noon, and if you come—as, God help me, I believe you will—then I shall teach you what a maid's love can mean.

FELICITY.

"Mount!" I cried, all of atremble. "I shall wed this noon! Get me a parson, man!" And I began tearing off my buckskins and flinging them right and left, shouting for Jack the while, and dressing in my finest linen and my silver-gray velvet.

The tapboy heard my shouts and came to say that Mount had gone out. So I bade the boy hasten forth and buy me a large nosegay with streamers, and fetch it to me instantly; and then returned to my toilet with a feverish haste that defeated its own purpose.

At last, however, I hung my sword, dusted the hair powder from frill and ruffle, buckled shoon and knees, and shook out the long soft lace over my cuffs. Then I found the ring I had bought in Albany, and placed it in my silver-webbed waistcoat.

The inn clocks chimed for ten as the lad brought me a huge nosegay all fluttering with white silken streamers.

"Where is my companion?" I asked, red as a poppy under his grins.

"Below, sir," replied the lad, hesitating.

"Drunk?" I demanded, angrily.

"Tolerable," said the lad.

With that I seized my nosegay, set my small French hat on my head, and went down the side stairway to the street.

Mount, swaggering on the taproom porch, spied me and rubbed his startled eyes. But I seized him by the painted cape of his fox-trimmed hunting-shirt, and jerked him to and fro savagely.

"Idiot! Tippler! Pottle-pot!" I cried, in a rage. "I'm to be married—d'ye hear? Married! Married! Get me a parson! Take my nosegay! So! Now walk behind me as if you knew what decent folk are accustomed to do at a sudden wedding!"

"How can I get you a parson if I'm to march here behind you, bearing this nosegay?" he remonstrated, sidling away toward the tavern again.

"You stay where you are!" I said; then I called a servant and bade him find a parson to go instantly to the house of Thomas Foxcroft in Queen Street, and there await my coming.

Mount, almost sobered through sheer astonishment, regarded me wildly.

"Jack, old friend," I said in a burst of happiness, "I've found her, and she will be my wife by noon! Give me joy. Jack!— and mind that nosegay, idiot! Hold it aloft, else the streamers will trail in the dust! Now, then! Follow me! Gingerly, idiot, gingerly!"

And away I marched, scarce knowing what I did in my excitement, but turning now and again to see that Mount followed, bearing the nosegay with proper care.

"If you are to be wedded at noon," he said, timidly, as we were hurrying through Cambridge Street, "what are we going to do until then—walk the streets like this? Lord! what a fool I feel!"

I stopped short. It was quite true that I was not expected at Mr. Foxcroft's before noon, and it was now but ten o'clock.

"I can't sit still in that tavern," I said. "Let us walk, Jack. Two hours are quickly past. Come step beside me—and mind those ribbons! Jack! I am mad with happiness!"

"Then let us drink to it," suggested Mount, but I jerked him to my side and started on, with the vague idea of circling the city in a triumphal march.

On and on we tramped through those Boston streets, coming out finally on the Common.

There I looked restlessly at my watch; it was eleven o'clock. An hour yet till noon—till I should see Silver Heels!

I composed myself, and Mount and I leaned back against the railing of the south burying-ground, watching the busy life of the camp on the Common. I had never before seen so many soldiers together, nor such a brilliant variety of uniforms. Small wonder that the townspeople, too, lingered to watch them.

Presently Mount lighted his pipe and sat down under a tall elm, still carefully clutching my nosegay.

I sat down beside him and we watched the marines drilling. But before long I sprang to my feet impatiently, adjusted my sword, and dusted the skirts of my coat.

"It's not half past eleven yet," observed Mount.

"I don't care," I muttered. "I shall go to Queen Street now. Come, Jack! I cannot endure this delay, I tell you."

He did not answer.

"Come, Jack," I repeated, turning around to summon him. "What are you staring at, man?"

As I spoke a roughly clad man pushed in between me and Mount, swinging a knobbed stick; another man followed, then another. Mount had leaped to his feet and backed up to my side.

"It's Billy Bishop's gang!" he said, thickly. "Leave me, lad, or they'll take us both!"

Before I could comprehend what was on foot, a half-dozen men were surrounding Mount.

"Go!" muttered Mount, fiercely, pushing me violently from him.

"No, you don't!" said a cool voice at my elbow. "We want the Weasel, too, for all his fine clothes!"

The next instant a man in a red neckcloth had seized my hands in a grip of iron, and clapped the gyves on one of my wrists. With a cry of rage I tore at my manacled hand and sprang at the fellow. He struck me a fierce blow with his cudgel, and ran around the edge of the swaying knot of human figures that was slowly bearing Mount to the ground.

Then Mount rose, hurling the pack from him, and striking right and left, I saw the nosegay fly into a shower of blossoms, and the silken ribbons flutter down under the trampling feet.

Swinging the steel manacle locked on my right wrist, I beat my way to Mount's side, and faced the thief-taker and his bailiffs.

They rushed us against the fence of the burying-ground, bruising us with their heavy cudgels. I had my sword out, but could not use it, the manacles on my wrist clogging the guard. I heard cries of: "Death to the highwaymen!" "Kill the rogues!" A vast crowd was surging up on all sides; soldiers drew their hangers and pushéd their way to the side of the baffled bailiffs.

"Give up, Jack Mount!" cried the stout man with the red neckcloth. "Give up, in the King's name! It's all over with you now!"

"If you'll let this gentleman go, I'll give up," said Mount, sullenly. "Answer me, Billy Bishop!"

"Come, come," said Bishop, in a bantering voice, "we know all about this gentleman, Jack. Don't you worry; we'll take care he has a view of the Roxbury Crossroad as well as you!"

The taunt of the crossroads gallows transformed Mount into a demon. He hurled his huge bulk at the solid mass of people; I followed, making what play I could with my small-sword, but in a moment I was down in the dust, blood pouring from my face, groping blindly for the enemies who were already clapping the irons on my other wrist.

Through the roar and tumult I was dragged into a stony street and crushed into the pit of a crowd, which hurried me on resistlessly. Far ahead in the throng I saw the head and shoulders of Jack Mount overtopping them all.

The mob halted at a cross street to allow a cavalcade of horsemen to pass. Then a coach, escorted by dragoons, passed very close to us; a gentleman looked out to seek the reason of the uproar. It was Walter Butler!

"A thief, sir," cried a bailiff, "taken by Bishop on the Mall! Would your lordship be pleased to see his comrade, the notorious Jack Mount?"

"Drive on," said Butler, impassively.

The crowd began to hoot and jeer as the bailiffs pushed me

forward once more through the dust of Cornhill up Queen Street.

And so, crushed by the awful disgrace, writhing, resisting, disheveled, I was forced into the courthouse on Queen Street, across the yard, and into the gates of the prison, which crashed shut behind me.

CHAPTER TWENTY·THREE

I WAS taken, in company with Jack Mount, on Monday morning, the 29th of October, 1774, without the faintest justification or excuse, save that I had been seen conversing with Mount on the Mall. From the 29th of October until the 15th day of December I lay in chains in that vile iron cage known as the "Pirates' Chapel," in company with Mount and eight sullen, cursing ruffians, taken in piracy off the Virginia capes.

During those six weeks not an hour dragged by but I believed it must be the hour for my delivery from this hideous injustice. Yet I was not blind. Calmly I faced the terrible dilemma; I fully understood that while Walter Butler held Governor Gage's ear, and while the Governor held the civil power at his own pleasure, and used it as whim or caprice moved him, I could neither hope for a hearing before a magistrate nor dare expect a trial by my countrymen.

As for communication with the outside world, there was no possible chance. Our steel cage was set in the center of a stone chamber, the barred windows of which opened on a bare stony parade.

Our cage was bedded with straw like a kennel; our food was brought us three times a day, in earthen bowls. A wooden spoon went with each bowl; otherwise the feed differed nothing from the feed of dogs.

Mount, in the beginning, had conducted like a madman. All that first night he had stalked the cage, and deep in his blue eyes had burned a terrible light.

At first the eight ruffians caged with us, among whom there was but a single Englishman, watched him in dogged silence. But as the night wore on and his pacing never ceased, they growled sullen protest. Then he slowly turned on them, baring his white teeth.

From that moment they gave him room and he ruled the cage as a silent, powerful beast rules, scarcely conscious of the cringing creatures who huddle around his legs.

In the daytime, the light in the stone chamber was gray. Night brought thick, troubled shadows creeping around the single candle that dripped from an iron socket riveted to the wall. Then the shades of the jailers fell across the floor as the large lanthorn was set outside in the corridor, and all night long the shuffling tread of the sentry marked the dead march of time.

So went six weeks.

One day toward the middle of December as I lay on my belly, grimly musing, I saw distinctly a woman's face peer through the thick grating that separated the corridor from our stone chamber.

After a while the face disappeared; I lay still a moment, then touched Mount's arm.

He turned his haggard face to me.

"Bishop's daughter is in the corridor," I whispered.

"Where?" asked Mount, vacantly.

"Out there, behind the grating. She might do something for —for you."

"Yes," he said, "she might."

That night Mount lay awake, watching the grating.

At dawn I awoke to watch. The day passed in horrible monotony. But toward evening we heard the noise of hammers overhead, and terror seized on all in the cage, for we believed that workmen had come to build gibbets. The next morning, when our jailer arrived to fetch us water, I questioned him, though I scarcely expected a reply. But he hesitated, glanced up at me, and finally informed me that the hammering was made by carpenters who were reconstructing the upper tiers of the prison for the new warden and his family.

I continued my questioning, but he soon silenced me with a shake of his head.

"I know nothing about your case," he said.

"Or about the others here?" I asked.

He paid no attention.

Mount, whose morbid curiosity had been aroused by the sight of some workmen digging holes in the prison yard, stood up to watch them. The other prisoners also huddled to the south side of the cage. The jailer glanced at them significantly, then at me, and passed his withered fingers over his corded throat.

I stared at him, numbed with horror. He shrugged his shoulders and shuffled away.

That night I sat close to Jack Mount, my hand on his broad shoulder, crushing back the lump in my throat. I wondered how soon he was to die.

At dawn I stood up to gaze fearfully out into the prison yard. Snow had fallen; workmen were digging at the holes with pick and crow.

When the jailer brought breakfast to us, he laid two bundles of sailcloth under the windows beyond our cage. Later he returned and carefully nailed each strip of cloth over the windows, hiding our view of the prison yard.

Mount asked him why he did that, and the other prisoners became restless and suspicious, calling out to the jailer in Spanish and Portuguese.

The Englishman laughed scornfully: "They're planting trees in the yard outside. We'll all climb them soon, won't we, jailer?"

"By Heaven!" muttered Mount. "They are planting gallows!"

When he had shrouded the windows, the jailer scrambled briskly to the floor and hastened out through the wicket, unheeding the shrill cries of the ruffians, who had rushed to the other side of the cage. When the wicket slammed, a dead silence followed; then one of the Spaniards uttered a piercing scream and fell down, tearing and biting at his chains.

"Die like a man! Die like a man!" said the Englishman, contemptuously; but terror had seized another ruffian, and he began shrieking out prayer on prayer.

Mount, pale and composed, lay in our corner, watching the wicket, a straw between his white teeth. I sat beside him, my heart hammering under my torn shirt, resolutely crushing back the terror that was feeling my throat with icy fingers.

"Do you believe they are setting the gibbets?" I asked.

"Yes," he said.

After a moment he added: "Why did you not leave me, lad? This is foul company for a gentleman to die in."

Terror choked me. I sank face downward in the straw, and lay there shaking till the candle was lighted at night.

Black, whirling thoughts swarmed through my brain; again and again I fought the battle for courage, only to lose it and again find myself faint with horror, tearing silently at my chains.

"Now that I know I am to die," said Mount, calmly, "I shall die easily enough. It was hope that hurt. I shall die easily."

"I shall die hard," I stammered. "No one will know it, but I shall die hard out there in the snow."

"I will stand next to you if I can," said Mount. "If you feel weak, reach out and touch me. I shall jest with the hangman. It is easy; you will see how easy it can be."

I raised my head to look at him.

"You care nothing," I said, fiercely. "You will see Cade Renard, and you care nothing! But I am leaving *her*!"

"God will right all that," said Mount, gravely.

"As for death," I blurted out, pronouncing the word with an effort, "I can die as coolly as you. But—but a gentleman's son—on the gibbet—hanging in chains between thieves—the disgrace ——"

Shame strangled the voice in my throat, my head reeled.

"Our Lord so died," said Mount, slowly.

I sat still as a stone. Mount gathered his knees in his hands and chewed his straw peacefully, blue eyes fixed on vacancy. Presently I plucked his sleeve.

"Yes, lad," he said, without turning.

"You are not afraid that I will not know how to meet—it?"
I asked.

"No."

"I am—am not afraid," I whispered. "I mean to bear myself without fear. I shall speak to you when—we are ready.
You shall see I am not afraid. Will they pray, Jack?"

"When? Now?"

"No, tomorrow."

"They will say a prayer on the gallows, lad."

"Will they take off our chains?"

"No."

"How—how long shall we hang?"

"A long time, lad."

"Could anybody know our features?"

"The weather will change them. Have you never seen a
crossroads gibbet?"

"No. Have you?"

"Yes, lad."

After a silence I said, "I hope no one will know me."

He did not reply. The candle-flame in the dripping socket
swayed in icy draughts from the wicket; the Spaniards muttered and moaned and cried like sick children; the Englishman stood in silence, staring at the windows through which
he could not see.

Presently he came over to our corner. We had never before
spoken to him, nor he to us, but now Mount looked up with
a ghost of a smile and nodded.

"It's all behind that window," said the Englishman, jerking his thumb over his shoulder. "We'll know all about it this
time tomorrow. Is the young one with you afraid?"

"Not he," said Mount.

The Englishman sat down on his haunches.

"What do you suppose it is?" he asked.

"What? Death?"

"Aye."

"I don't know," said Mount.

"Nor I," said the Englishman, with an oath, "and I have dealt it freely enough, too. Have you?"

"Yes," said Mount.

"And he?" glancing at me.

"Once," I replied hoarsely.

"I've watched men die many times," continued the Englishman, "and I'm not a whit the wiser. What makes the dead look so small? Have you ever killed your enemy? Is there satisfaction in it? No, by Heaven! for the second you stop his breath he's gone—escaped. And all you've got is a thing at your feet with clothes too large for it."

He looked at me musingly. "You're six feet," he said. "You'll shrink to five foot six. They all do. I'll wager you are afraid, young man!"

"You lie!" I said.

"Spoken well!" he nodded. "You'll die smiling, yet."

At that moment a faint metallic sound broke on our ears. We listened; the Spaniards ceased moaning and sat up. The sound came again—silence—then the measured cadence of footfalls.

Mount had risen; I also stood up. The Spaniards burrowed into the straw, squealing like rats. Tramp, tramp, tramp, came the heavy footfalls along the corridor.

"Halt! Ground arms!"

Lights blinded our dazzled eyes; bayonets glittered.

An officer stepped to the lanthorn, unrolled a parchment, and began to read very rapidly. I could not distinguish a word of it for the cries of the Spaniards, but I saw the jailer unlocking our cage, and presently two soldiers stepped in and drove out a Spaniard at the point of their bayonets.

Shrieking, sobbing, supplicating, the Spaniards were thrust out into the corridor; the Englishman went last, with a contemptuous nod at Mount and me, and a cool gesture to the soldiers to stand aside.

Mount followed. But as he stepped from the cage, a soldier pushed him back, shaking his head.

"Not yet?" asked Mount, quietly.

"Not yet," said the soldier, locking the cage and flinging the iron key to the jailer.

CHAPTER TWENTY·FOUR

WE WERE condemned to death without a hearing by a military court sitting at Fort Hill, before which we appeared in chains. The 19th of April was set for our execution; we were then taken back to Queen Street.

This time, however, we were conducted to the upper tier of the prison, recently finished. Our cells were clean and not very cold, and our food was better. Moreover, they finally unlocked our irons, leaving us without manacles, in order that our sores might heal.

It was now the 1st of January, 1775. The New Year brought an important change for us, the appointment of Billy Bishop as warden of our tier. He and his family occupied the apartment at the west end of our corridor; and on the day they moved in, I hoped that at last our fighting chance for life had come.

All day long I watched the famous thief-taker installing his family in their new dwelling-place. Mrs. Bishop, a blowsy slattern with a sickly baby, sat on a bundle of bedding and directed her buxom daughter.

The wench had lost her bright color, and something, too, in flesh. That she knew Mount was here under sentence of death was certain; I could see the sorrowful glances she stole at the grating of his cell when she passed it.

As the early winter night fell, the corridor grew quiet. But presently I heard soft footfalls. I stepped forward and pressed my face to the grating. Dulcima Bishop stood within two feet of my cell.

"Will you speak to me?" I called, cautiously.

"La! Is it you, sir?" she stammered, all atremble.

"Yes. Come quickly, child! There, stand with your back to my cell. Are you listening?"

"Yes, sir," she faltered.

"Do you still love Jack Mount?" I asked.

Her neck under her hair crimsoned.

"Will you help him?" I demanded, under my breath.

"Oh yes, yes!" she whispered, turning swiftly toward my grating. "Tell me what to do, sir! I knew he was here. I ——"

"Turn your back," I cut in. "Don't look at my grating again. Now listen! This is the 1st of January. We are to die at dawn on the 19th of April. Do you understand?"

"Yes, sir."

"You are to get us out, do you understand, child?"

"Yes—oh yes, yes! How, Mr. Cardigan? Tell me and I'll do it!"

"Then go to Jack's cell and let him talk to you. And have a care they do not catch you gossiping with prisoners!"

The girl glanced up and down the corridor, then stole timidly down to Mount's cell.

I laid my ear to the grating and listened; they were whispering, and I could not hear what they said.

"Jack," I called out after a time in a low voice, "tell her to find Shemuel if she can."

"Quiet, lad," he answered. "I know what is to be done."

Before I could speak again, a distant sound warned the girl to her room once more. I waited a while, but she evidently dared not come back. So I lay down on my iron cot and tried to think.

A young moon hung over King's Chapel, shedding a tremulous light on the snowy parade. Very dimly I could make out the tall shapes of eight gibbets, stark and black against the starry sky. From them hung eight bundles that had once been men.

But I watched the stars peacefully, thinking of the stars that lighted our misty hills in Johnstown; I thought of Silver Heels and my love for her, and how, by this time, she must deem me the most dishonorable and craven among men. I thought of this calmly; long since I had weathered the storms of grief and impotent rage that had torn me as I lay in chains in the "Chapel."

No, all would yet be well; some day I should hold her in my arms. All would be well; some day I should hold the life of Walter Butler on my sword's point and send his red soul howling! Yes, all would be well ——

A ray of light fell on my face; I turned and sat up as the key in the cell door gritted.

Full under the flare of a lanthorn stood a man in a military uniform of scarlet and green. Behind him appeared Warden Bishop, holding the lanthorn.

"This is the Weasel, sir," he said. "At least he goes by that name, although the Weasel I have chased these ten years was a different cut of a rogue. But it's all one, Captain; he was took with Jack Mount, and he'll dance a rope-jig the 19th of April next."

"Why not sooner?" asked the officer.

I started violently.

"Why not hang him sooner?" inquired Walter Butler again, moving back a step into the corridor. He limped as he walked and leaned on a cane. My mark was still upon him.

"Well, sir," said Bishop, scratching his ears, "we hung eight coast-scrapers in November, and two sheep thieves in December. We've got three pickpockets to swing this month, then Symonds, the wharf robber, is to go in February. There's no room in March, either, because the Santa Cruz gang goes up the 13th—seven o' them in chains—and the gallows yonder ain't dropped last year's fruit yet, and the people hereabouts complains o' the stench of a hot day and a south wind ——"

"Can't he change places with some other rogue?" interrupted Butler, impatiently.

"Lord, no!" cried Bishop, horrified. "They don't do no such things in Boston, sir."

"They do in Tryon County," observed Butler, eyeing me coolly. Presently a ghastly smile stretched his pallid face.

"Well, well," he said, "so you are to sail to glory at a rope's end, eh? You wouldn't burn, you know. But the flames will come later, I fancy. Eh, Mr.—er—Mr. Weasel?"

"Are your broken bones mended?" I asked, quietly.

"Quite mended, thank you."

"Because," I said, "you will need them some day ——"

"I need them now," he said, cheerfully. "I am to wed a bride ere long. Give me joy, Weasel! I am to know the day this very night."

I could not utter a sound for the horror that froze my tongue. He saw it, fastened his eyes on my face, and watched me, silent as a snake with its fangs in its paralyzed prey.

"Would you care to see the famous Jack Mount, Captain?" asked Bishop, swelling with pride. "I took him myself, sir. All the papers had it—I have the cuttings in my room; I can fetch them, sir ——"

Butler did not appear to hear him.

"Yes," he continued, thoughtfully. "I ride this night to Lexington. She's a sweet little thing. I think you have seen her—perhaps picked her pocket. When we are wed we shall come to Boston—on the 19th of April next."

I sprang at him, stone-blind with rage. But the steel door crashed in my face; the locks rattled.

All that night I lay on the stone floor of my cell, by turns inert, stupid, frantic.

When Bishop came in the morning he thought me ill and summoned the prison apothecary; but ere that individual appeared, I was quiet and self-possessed, ready to convince him

I needed no nostrums. All that day I watched for Dulcima; twice I saw her go to Mount's cell, but could hear nothing of what they whispered.

Now as I was standing, looking out of the grating, I chanced to glance down, and saw that the apothecary had left his case of herbs and drugs on a bench just outside my cell door.

Idly I read the labels on the bottles and boxes: "Senna, Jalap, Brimstone, Es. Cammomile, Saffron Pills, Tinc. Opium ——"

Opium? An easy death.

I gazed at the dark flask, scarcely a foot below me, but maddeningly out of reach beyond the grating. Presently I turned around, caught up the coarse towel beside my wash-bowl, drew from it some threads, twisted them, tied on more threads, and made a running noose at the end.

There was nobody in the corridor. I heard voices in Bishop's room, whither the apothecary had gone to examine the baby at Mrs. Bishop's summons. Very carefully I let down my thread, fishing for the bottle's neck with my slip-noose; but the neck was so placed that I could not snare it; and I drew up another bottle instead, bearing a badly blurred label.

What the bottle contained I could not decipher, but hid the tiny flask in a depression under a loose fragment of stone in my flooring where a black beetle had his abode. Then I returned to fish for my opium flask, but could not snare it. Finally I drew in my string just as the apothecary came out. He picked up his case, closed it, and took himself off.

That night I asked for a jug of water. After all was still, I got my tiny flask, poured a single drop of its contents into my basin, filled it up with water, and then returned the flask to its hiding-place.

"We shall see," I muttered, "whether there be any virtue of poison in my purloined bottle's contents," and I caught the poor little black beetle who had come out to enjoy the lamp-light.

Now as the drop from the flask had been diluted many hundreds of times by the water in my bowl, I argued that if this solution dealt death to the beetle, a few drops, pure, would put Jack Mount and me beyond the hangman's hands.

Poor little beetle! how he struggled! I was loath to sacrifice him, but at last I dropped him into the bowl.

He did not swim; I watched him for a moment, and finally touched him. The little thing was stone dead.

That I had a terrible and swift poison in my possession I now felt sure, and I feared that the apothecary might return next day and institute a frantic search. But the careless pill-roller apparently did not miss that one tiny flask, or at least raised no hue and cry.

When opportunity offered, I called to Dulcima and bade her tell Jack Mount that I had the poison and would use it on us both if we could not find other means to escape the gallows.

The poor child took the message, and presently returned, wiping her tears, to say that Jack had every hope of liberty; that I must not despair, and that she, Dulcima, had already communicated with Shemuel.

She handed me a steel awl, telling me to pick at the mortar that held the stones on my window ledge, and to fill these holes with water every night, so that the water might freeze and crack the stones around the base of the steel bars.

I had never thought of such a thing!

Eagerly and cautiously I set to work making holes. But it was heartbreaking labor, and so slow that at the end of a week I had not loosened a single bar.

At the end of the next week Dulcima let me know that Jack had loosened one bar of his window. So I worked like a madman at my own still unyielding bars, for Jack refused to stir a peg unless I could escape, too.

It was now the middle of March; a month only remained to us in which to accomplish our liberty.

If only the freezing weather continued! But to my despair, a warm thaw set in. In vain I worked at the bars. It rained, rained, rained, day after day.

Weeks before, Mount had sent the girl to seek out Mr. Foxcroft and tell him of my plight. I also had sent by her a note to Silver Heels.

The girl returned to report that Mr. Foxcroft had sailed for England early in November, and that nobody there had ever heard of a Miss Warren in Queen Street.

Then Butler's boast came to me, and I sent word to Shemuel, bidding him search Lexington for Miss Warren. I had not yet heard from him.

Meanwhile Mount communicated, through Dulcima, with the Minute Men's Club, and already a delegation headed by Mr. Revere had waited on Governor Gage to demand my release on grounds of mistaken identity.

The Governor laughed at them, asserting that I was notorious; but as the days passed, so serious became the demands from Mr. Revere, Mr. Hancock, and Mr. Otis, that the Governor sent Walter Butler to assure these gentlemen that he knew Mr. Cardigan well, and that the rogue in prison who pretended to that name was, in fact, a notorious felon named the Weasel.

At this, Shemuel came forward to swear that Mr. Butler and I were deadly enemies and that Butler lied, but he was treated with scant ceremony, and barely escaped a ducking in the mill pond by the soldiers.

Meanwhile Mr. Hancock had sent a message to Sir John at Ononcaga, urging him to come to Boston and identify me.

No reply ever came. Possibly Sir John never received the message. I prefer to think so.

Matters were at this pass when I finally gave up all hope of loosening my window bars, and sent word to Jack Mount that he must escape that very night. But the frightened girl returned with an angry message of refusal from the chivalrous blockhead.

The next day it was too late; Bishop's suspicions somehow had been aroused, and he soon discovered the loosened bars in Jack Mount's cell.

How the brute did laugh! He searched Mount's cell, discovered the awl and a file, shouted with laughter again, summoned masons to make repairs and, still laughing, came to visit me.

I did not dare to leave my poison flask under the stone. As I heard Bishop coming, I drove the glass stopper firmly into the flask and then placed it in my mouth, together with the small gold ring I had bought in Albany, and had so far managed to conceal.

It was a desperate move; I undressed myself as Bishop bade me, and sat on my bed, faint with suspense, while he rummaged. He found the depression where I had hidden the flask. The awl lay there, and he pouched it with a chuckle.

When Bishop had gone, I drew the deadly little flask from my mouth, trembling, and chilled with sweat. Then I placed it again in its hiding-place, hid the ring in my shoe, and slowly dressed. Bishop did not search my cell again.

And now the days began to run very swiftly. On the 18th of April, toward five o'clock in the evening, a turnkey, passing my cell, told me that General Gage was in the prison with a party of ladies, and that he would doubtless visit my cell. He added grimly that the death watch was to be set over us in an hour or two and that, thereafter, I could expect no more visitors from outside until I held my public reception on the gallows.

Laughing heartily at his own wit, the turnkey passed on, and I went to the grating to listen and look out into the twilight of the corridor. No one was around.

"Jack," I called hoarsely, "the death watch begins tonight."

CHAPTER TWENTY-FIVE

I LISTENED a moment, then called again, the words half strangling in my throat.

"Jack, the death watch begins tonight!"

Quite cheerfully then he answered me. On the first night of our imprisonment, he had conducted like a madman, but on this night, decreed to be our last on earth, his calmness strengthened me.

"Pooh!" he said. "Wait a bit. There's time to cheat a dozen gibbets 'twixt this and dawn."

"Yes," said I, bitterly, "we can cheat the hangman with what I have in this little flask."

"You must give it to the girl," he said. "She will flavor our last draught with it if worse comes to worst."

At that instant I caught sight of Dulcima Bishop passing quickly along the corridor, and I called her and gave her my flask, glad to have it safe from the search the death watch was certain to make.

The child turned pale when I bade her promise to serve us with a more honorable death than the one planned for us on the morrow.

"I promise, sir," she said, faintly, and added, "I have a knife for—for Jack—and a file."

"It is too late for such things," I answered. "If you cannot get the keys from your father, there is no hope for us."

Her face, which had become terribly pinched and thin, quivered. "If—if I could get the keys ——" she began.

"Unless you do so there is no hope, child."

There was a silence; then she cried, chokingly: "I can get them! I will get the keys! Oh, do you think he can go free if I open the cell?"

"He has a knife," I said, grimly. "I have my two hands. Open the cells and we will show you."

She covered her eyes with her hands. Jack called to her; she started violently, turned and went to him.

They stood whispering a long time together. I paced my cell, with hope battering at my heart. If she could only open that door!

"Are you listening?" whispered Dulcima at my grating again.

"Yes," I answered.

"Be ready at seven tonight!" she said. "I will open your door."

"I am ready," I answered.

At that moment the sound of voices filled the corridor, and the girl fled. First came a dozen turnkeys, then the chief warden, and then came a gentleman dressed in a long dark cloak with a scarlet-and-gold uniform gleaming below. Was that the Governor?

He passed my cell, halted, glanced around, then retraced his steps. After a moment I heard his voice down the corridor; he was saying:

"The highwaymen are here, Mrs. Hamilton, if you would care to see them."

I began to tremble. Far down the corridor I heard a woman laughing. I knew that laugh.

"But," persisted the Governor, "you should really see the highwaymen, madam. You never beheld such a giant as this rogue, Jack Mount."

The voices seemed to be receding. I sprang to my grating; Mrs. Hamilton's saucy laughter rang faintly and more faintly.

Half a dozen keepers were lounging near my cell. I summoned one sharply.

"Tell General Gage that Mrs. Hamilton knows me!" I said. "A guinea for you when she comes!"

The lout stared, grinned, and finally shambled away.

I waited in an agony of suspense; after a long time I knew that the keeper had not delivered my message. Then I called out fiercely for Bishop to come to me; I called unceasingly, striking at the bars until my hands were bathed in blood.

At length Bishop arrived, in a rage, demanding to know why I was creating such an uproar.

In vain I insisted that he take my message to Governor Gage; he laughed an ugly laugh and refused. Mrs. Bishop, whose infant was now very sick, came out, wrapped in her shawl, carrying the baby to the prison hospital for treatment, and a wrangle about supper began between her and Bishop.

My words were ignored; Bishop demanded his supper at once, and his wife insisted that she must take the child to the hospital without delay. Finally Bishop yielded, cursing.

"Then draw me a measure o' buttry ale. D'ye hear?" he growled at his wife. "If I'm to eat no supper till you get back, I'll want a bellyful o' malt to stay me!"

But Mrs. Bishop waddled off contemptuously, declaring that he could die o' thirst for aught she cared.

Dulcima stood watching the scene stolidly. Bishop turned on her with an oath, and ordered her to draw his evening cup; she unhooked the tankard that hung under the lanthorn, hesitated, and looked straight at her father. He gave her a brutal shove, demanding to know why she dawdled while he thirsted, and the girl moved off sullenly, with flaming cheeks.

When she returned from the buttry with the frothing tankard, the warden drained the measure to the dregs. He handed the empty tankard to his daughter and then smacked his lips with a wry face.

"Ugh!" he muttered. "The ale's spoiled! Why didn't you taste it, you baggage?" he demanded. "Stir yourself now and draw me a cider cup to wash this cursed brew out o' me!"

There was a crash. The girl had dropped the tankard.

Quick as a flash Bishop raised his hand and dealt his daughter a blow on the neck that sent her to her knees.

"Break another pot and I'll break your head, you gaby!" he roared. "Get up or I'll ——"

He choked, gasped, lifted his shaking hand to his mouth, and wiped it.

"Curse that ale!" he stammered. "It's sickened me to the bones!"

He turned and pushed open his door, lurching forward across the threshold. A moment later Dulcima passed my cell, her face averted.

I went to my cot and lay down, face buried, teeth set in my lip. I had not been able to get help from Governor Gage. I had little faith that Dulcima could help us. A numbness seemed to settle like chains on every limb. Dully I waited for the strokes of the iron bell sounding the seventh hour. All hope was slowly dying.

A few moments later a strange movement inside my cell aroused me, and I opened my hot eyes.

Peering through the dusk, I saw a man seated beside my cot, his eyes fixed steadily on me. I sat up and asked him what he desired.

He did not answer. A ray of candlelight fell on the bright barrel of a pistol that lay across his knees.

"What do you wish?" I repeated. "Can you not watch me from the corridor?"

There was no reply.

Then at last I understood that this gray shape brooding there at my bedside was a guard of the death watch, pledged never to take his eyes from me for an instant.

Ding-dong! Ding-dong! The prison bell was at last striking the seventh hour. At the last jangle I rose and began to pace my narrow cell.

The lanthorn above Bishop's doorway burned brightly; the

corridor was quiet. No sound came from Mount's cell. I could hear rain drumming on a roof somewhere; that was all.

Presently it occurred to me that I had not seen Bishop since six o'clock when he had gone into his room, cursing the ale his daughter had fetched him. This was unusual; he had never before failed to sit there on his threshold after supper, smoking his long clay pipe.

Minute after minute passed.

Suddenly, as I stood at my grating, I saw Dulcima Bishop step from the warden's door, close it behind her, and noiselessly lock it. She stood there a moment, swaying; then she made a signal towards Mount's cell. The next instant I saw Jack Mount bound noiselessly into the corridor. He caught sight of me, held up a reddened knife, pointed to my cell door, and displayed a key.

Instantly I turned around and sauntered toward my bed. The deathwatch kept his eyes on me.

How was I to get at him?

Pretending to be occupied in rearranging my tumbled bedding, I strove to get partly behind him, but the fellow turned his head as I moved and watched me steadily.

To spring on him meant to draw his fire, and a shot would be our undoing.

As I hesitated there, holding the blanket in my hands, the lamp in the corridor suddenly went out, plunging my cell in darkness.

The guard sprang to his feet; I fairly flung my body at him, hurling him to the stone floor.

Instantly, light flooded my cell again; I heard my iron door opening; I crouched in fury on the struggling man under me, whose head and arms I held crushed under the thick blanket. Then came a long, silent struggle, but at last I tore the heavy pistol from his clutch and beat him on the head with the steel butt of it until his straining limbs relaxed.

Pistol in hand, I rose from the quiet heap on the floor and turned to find my cell door swinging wide and Dulcima Bishop watching me with dilated eyes.

"Is he dead?" she asked, and broke out in an odd laugh that stretched her lips tight over her teeth. "Best end him now if he still lives," she added, in a half whisper.

I hoped the man was not dead—but I thought he was. At any rate, I felt sure he was harmless.

She lifted the lanthorn from the floor and motioned me to follow. At the end of the corridor Mount stood waiting.

"The trail's clear," he whispered, gayly. "Now, lass, where is the scullions' stairway? Blow out that light, Cardigan! Quiet, now. Give me your hand, lass—and t'other to the lad."

The girl blew out the light and drew me into the darkness. Groping forward, I almost fell down a steep flight of stone steps. Down, down, then through a passage, Mount leading, the girl fairly dragging me off my feet in her excitement, and presently a door creaked open and a deluge of icy water dashed over me.

It was rain; I was standing outside the prison, ankle deep in mud, the free wind blowing, the sleet driving full in my eyes.

"Oh, this is good, this is good!" muttered Mount, in ecstasy. "Smell the air, lad! Do you smell it? Lord! How sweet is this wind in my throat!"

The girl shivered; her damp, disheveled hair blew in her

face. She laid one shaking hand on Mount's wet sleeve, then the other, and bowed her head on them, sobbing convulsively.

Mount bent and kissed her.

"I swear I will be kind to you, child," he said, soberly. "Come lass, gay! gay! What care we for a brace o' dead turn-keys? Lord! how the world will laugh at Bully Bishop when they hear I stole his girl along with the prison keys! Laugh with me, lass! Soon we will be wedded and happy!"

"Happy, Jack—happy?" she stammered, raising her white face to his.

He swore roundly that he would make her happy, that he would end his days in serving her on his marrowbones for gratitude.

But suddenly she laughed, turned her bright, feverish eyes on us with a reckless toss of her head, and drew the poison-flask from her bosom.

"You think," she said, "that we no longer need this little friend to sorrow? You are wrong!"

And ere Mount or I could move, she raised the tiny flask and dropped the dark scarlet contents between her teeth.

"I drink to your freedom, Jack," she said, blindly, reeling into Mount's arms. "Your—freedom—Jack," she gasped, smiling. "My father drank to it—in ale. He lies dead on the floor of it. All this—for—for your freedom, Jack!"

Mount was kneeling in the mud; she lay in his arms, the sleet pattering on her upturned face.

"For your freedom," she murmured, drowsily—"I would burn forever. But, oh, the torment—the fire in me, Jack!"

Her body writhed and twisted; her great bright eyes never left his. Presently she lay still, lifeless. A moment later the prison bell broke out wildly through the storm, and a gunshot rang from the north guardhouse.

We placed her under a tree in the new grass, and covered her face with willow branches, all silky with the young buds of April. Then, bending almost double, we ran south along the prison wall, turning west as the wall turned, and presently came to the wooden fence of King's Chapel.

Mount gained the top of the fence from my shoulders, and drew me up. Then we dropped.

There were lights moving in Governor's Alley and the mews. The prison bell rang frantically behind us.

"It's the alarm, Jack!" I whispered.

He gave me a dull look, then shivered in his wet buckskins.

"She can't lie out there in the sleet," he muttered, bloodshot eyes roving restlessly in the darkness. "I'm going back!"

"No, Jack, no—don't do that!" I begged; but he cursed me and brushed me aside.

Back over the wall he dropped. I started to follow, but he shoved me roughly and bade me mind my own concerns.

I leaned against the foot of the wall; the sleet belted me; I bared my throat to it. After a while I heard Mount's laboring breath on the other side of the wall, and I climbed up to aid him.

He held her in his arms. I took the body from him; he climbed over, and received it again, cradling it gently in his great arms.

"Go you and find a pick and spade in the mews, yonder," he said. There was a fixed stare in his eyes that alarmed me. "Go!" he repeated. "It is the least we can do!"

"Jack," I said, "we cannot stay here to be taken again! You

cannot bury her now; the ground is frosted; people will hear us!"

He glared at me, then swung his heavy head right and left. The next moment he started running through the storm, still cradling his burden. I followed, not knowing what he meant to do.

At the King's Chapel gate he turned in along a dim gravel path, hedged with dripping box. Around us lay the head-stones of the dead, with here and there a heavy tomb loom-ing up.

For a moment he halted, peering about him. A square white sepulcher surmounted a mound on his right; he laid his pitiful burden in my arms and stepped forward, grasping the slab. Then, with a heave of his powerful back, he lifted the huge stone, laying open the shadowy sepulcher below.

"Give her to me," he muttered.

He wiped the raindrops from her face and laid her in the sepulcher. Together we replaced the slab; it taxed all my strength to lift one end of it. The bell of the prison clanged frantically.

Mount stood back, breathing heavily, hands hanging. I waited in silence.

"What a little thing she was!" he muttered. "What a child —to—do—that! Do you think she will lie easy there?"

"Yes," I said.

At the sound of my voice Mount roused and turned sharply to me.

"The thief and the thief-taker's daughter!" he whispered, with a ghastly laugh. "They'll make a book of it—I warrant you!—and hawk it for a penny in Boston town!"

He touched the slab, all glistening with sleet, gripped the edge of the sepulcher, turned, and shook his fist at the prison. Then, quietly passing his arm through mine, he led the way out of the Chapel yard, guiding me between the soaking hedges to the iron gate, and so out into the black alley.

Almost immediately a man shouted: "Stop thief! Turn out the guard!" and a soldier, in the shadow of the wall, fired at us.

Mount glared at him stupidly, hands dangling; the soldier ran up to him and presented his bayonet, calling on us to give up.

The sound of his voice roused Mount. He seized the musket, wrenched it from the soldier, and beat him into the mud. Then swinging the weapon by the barrel, he knocked down two bailiffs who were closing in on us, and we took to our heels.

Through reeking lanes, foul alleys, and muddy mews we ran, or lurked to listen.

The town appeared to be alive with British soldiery; mounted pickets roved through the streets; parties of officers passed continually; squad after squad of marines crossed our path.

"But all this pother is never made on our account," muttered Mount, presently, as we hid in Belcher's Lane to avoid a party of dragoons. "There's something else in the wind. There's deviltry a-brewing, lad. We had best start for the 'Wild Goose.' "

Through the mud, we crept on and on, along back roads and shiny lanes, skulking at long last into Green Lane, and so came in sight of the "Wild Goose Tavern." Then, as we

THROUGH REEKING LANES, FOUL ALLEYS AND MUDDY MEWS, WE
RAN, OR LURKED TO LISTEN

crossed Chambers Street, a man standing in the shadow of a tree started forward as we came up.

Mount halted and drew his knife, snarling like a jaded wolf.

"Mount! Cardigan!" cried the man.

"Paul!" exclaimed Mount, eagerly.

The goldsmith wrung our hands.

"It is the beginning of the end," he said. "The Grenadiers are to march. I've a horse on the Charlestown shore. Gage has closed the gates on the Neck."

"What do the Grenadiers want?" asked Mount.

"They want the cannon and stores at Concord," replied Revere, in a low, eager voice. "I'm waiting for Clay Rolfe. If the Grenadiers march by land, Rolfe hangs a lamp in the steeple of the Old North; if they take boats, he hangs two lamps. I guess they mean to cross the bay. I've got a good horse across the water; I'll have the country folk out by daylight if the troops stir an inch tonight. Wait—there's Rolfe now!"

A dark cloaked figure came swiftly out of the mews, swinging two unlighted lanthorns. It was Clay Rolfe, our landlord at the "Wild Goose," and he grasped our hands warmly, laughing in his excitement.

"Your boatman is ready under Hunt's Wharf, Paul," he said. "You had best row across the bay while the rain lasts."

"Yes," said Revere, "I've no mind to run the fleet yonder under a full moon." He gripped our hands again and turned.

"Don't forget, Rolfe," he said—"one if by land; two if by sea!"

Rolfe turned to us.

"Gage has officers watching every road outside of Boston;

but Paul will teach them how fast news can travel." He glanced at the sky; rain fell heavily. "It won't last," he muttered. "There'll be a moon tonight. Come, Paul."

They saluted us and walked rapidly down Green Lane.

"If Shemuel is at the 'Wild Goose,' " I said, "perhaps he has news for me."

We entered the inn and found it deserted by all save a servant, who recognized us and bade us welcome.

"The Grenadiers are out tonight, sir," he said to me. "All our company has gone to join the Alarm Men at Lexington and Concord."

"Where is Shemuel?" I asked.

"He is watching the Province House, sir; General Gage entertains tonight. It is all a ruse to quiet suspicion, sir. But we know what is on foot, Mr. Cardigan!"

Gossiping away, the lad served us with bread, cheese, pickled beef, and a noggin of punch, and we listened, tearing at our food, and gulping it like famished beasts.

He brought me my clothes of buckskin, and I tore my rotten prison rags from me—alas! the shreds of that same silver-velvet suit which I had put on six months since, to wed with Silver Heels.

We stripped to the buff; the lad soused us well with steaming water and again with water like ice.

Mount encased his huge frame in his spare buckskins, and I once more dressed in my forest dress. Then when the lad had brought us our arms, I asked:

"Where is my horse? Have you looked to him, lad? By heaven, if aught of mischance has come to him ——"

"The great black horse, Warlock, sir?" cried the lad. "He is stabled in the mews, sir. Mr. Rolfe has had him cared for like a baby; the head groom takes him out every day, Mr. Cardigan, and the horse is all satin and steel springs, sir."

"Where is he? Get a lanthorn," I said, huskily.

A moment later, in the mews, I heard a shrill whinny, and the tattoo of shod hoofs dancing.

"Warlock!" I cried.

The next instant my arms were around his neck.

CHAPTER TWENTY-SIX

IT WAS nearly ten o'clock; a freezing rain still swept the black Boston streets.

In the dark mews behind the "Wild Goose Tavern" had gathered a shadowy company of horsemen, a half-score of unfortunate patriots who had not been quick enough to leave the city before the troops shut its landward gates. They had met at the "Wild Goose" to consult how best they might get away and join their comrades at Lexington and Concord.

Some were for riding to the Neck and making a dash across the causeway; some wanted boats, among the latter, Jack Mount, who naturally desired to leave the town speedily.

"What think you, Mr. Cardigan?" demanded an officer of Sudbury militia.

"I know only that I shall ride this night to Lexington," I said, impatiently, "and I am at your service, gentlemen, by land or sea. Pray you, decide quickly while the rain favors us."

"Is there a man among us dare demand a pass of the Governor?" asked the Sudbury officer, abruptly. "By Heaven! gentlemen, it is death by land or by sea if we make to force the lines this night!"

"And it is death to me if I stay here cackling," muttered Mount as we caught the distant gallop of dragoons.

We sat moodily in our saddles, huddled together in the darkness and rain.

"If John Hancock were here he could perhaps get us a pass through Mrs. Hamilton," remarked an officer. "The fair lady has great influence over Governor Gage."

"Perhaps *you* could persuade her to get us a pass," Mount muttered to me.

But I shook my head. In the prison, in those last hours, I had thought in my extremity to beg help from Mrs. Hamilton. Now, however, I remembered that though she might not have known that I was there behind those iron bars, waiting for death, she had known that Jack Mount was there. And she had known that Mount was my valued friend. Yet she had not turned over a finger to bring him comfort in what all believed his last moments; had gone lightly away, laughing in gay indifference.

All that I now remembered; and I remembered, too, almost the exact words Marie Hamilton had last spoken to me, bitter words bred of deeply wounded pride. "For your conceit and your insufferable airs I will find a remedy," she had said. . . . "My humiliation shall not be forgotten until you pay me dearly."

No, I would not chance asking Mrs. Hamilton to help us get a pass.

Perhaps I did her a grave injustice. But I dared not trust to our old friendship. She herself had practically declared it at an end. I would acquiesce. Regretfully but firmly. Now and for all time.

Mount did not press his suggestion. For a brief time the

handful of us sat there, crouching on our rain-drenched horses, drearily debating our course.

Suddenly somebody clutched my elbow, and I swung around instantly, one hand on my hunting-knife. A lanthorn, appearing for a moment, was swung up toward my face. I caught a glimpse of Saul Shemuel clawing at my sleeve. Then all was dark again. I learned later that the lad from the "Wild Goose" who had guided Shemuel had thrust the lanthorn back under his coat and returned to the inn as silently as the two had come out.

With a word to the nearest officer, saying that a messenger had brought me urgent personal tidings, I touched Jack Mount and together we backed our horses out of the huddle, with Shemuel scurrying beside us.

Some little distance away, we stopped and Mount leaned down to give Shemmy a mighty embrace.

"I haf brought Foxcroft," Shemuel panted at me. "Mr. Foxcroft he hass come today on dot *Pomona* frigate. It wass printed in dot *Efening Gazette*, all apout Foxcroft how he iss come from Sir Peter Warren to make some troubles for Sir John Johnson mit dot money he took from Miss Warren, sir!"

"Foxcroft! Here?" I stammered.

"Yess, sir; I run fast to Queen Street, and I told him how you wass in dot prison come, und he run fast to Province House, but too late, for we hear dot bell ring und dose guns shooting. Und I said, 'I bet you Jack Mount he hass run avay!' Und some dragoon soldiers come into Cornhill, calling out, 'Dose highwaymen is gone!' So I vatch outside, and Mr. Foxcroft he goss into Province House, sir, to make some troubles mit Governor Gage apout Sir John Johnson und dot money of Miss Warren! Und aftervards I pring Mr. Foxcroft here to find you, and now he vaits in Mr. Rolfe's tavern."

. THE WEASEL

Leaving Shemuel to hold Warlock, I reëntered the inn and found a stout, florid gentleman, swathed in a riding-cloak, whose eyes snapped as he cried:

"Are *you* Michael Cardigan? Well, where the devil have you been, sir?"

"I've been in prison, under sentence of death," I replied.

"Where have *you* been, sir, to leave your client, Miss Warren, at the mercy of Walter Butler?"

"I've been in England, sir, that's where I've been!" he cried, hotly. "I've been there to find out why your blackguard of a kinsman, Sir John Johnson, should rob my client of her property. And I've found out that your blackguard Sir John has not only robbed her of her means, but of her rightful name! That's what I've done, sir. Now I am going straightway to notify my client in Lexington. And if it does not please you, you may go to the devil!"

His impudence and oaths I scarcely noted, such a fierce happiness was surging through me. I could have hugged the choleric barrister; I beamed upon him when he bade me go to the devil, and I seized his fat hands and thanked him so gratefully that he stared at me open-mouthed.

"My dear sir, my dear, dear friend," I cried, "let us go together to Lexington to find my cousin, Miss Warren."

"Have you a pass, sir?" he demanded.

"No," I answered, grimly.

"Nor I!" he fumed. "And they tell me no one may leave the city this night without a pass. By order of that meddlesome ass, Governor Gage! But I take it we are free agents, sir, free agents. I, for one, shall go! They shall not stop me."

"Nor me," I returned. "Nothing under heaven can keep me from going to Lexington! Have you a horse stabled here? No? Can you hire one? Then hire him, and get into your saddle!"

It was Shemuel, however, who undertook to hire horses, one for Mr. Foxcroft and one for himself. Though it did not take him long, the rain had ceased and the moon hung over the bay by the time we were all in the saddle and ready to ride, passes or no passes.

Of the half-score of officers whom we had left sitting their rain-drenched horses, none remained. They had chosen to risk crossing the bay under the guns of the *Somerset* rather than attempt to force the Neck.

"God go with them!" said I. "We'll ride to the shore and see what can be done."

So we rode down through the darkness toward the bay.

While we were slowly approaching the shore, I heard sounds in the darkness, and as we came out through a fringe of trees a stirring sight lay before us. Below in the moonlight, the shore swarmed with soldiers, teamsters, and boatmen. Companies of Grenadiers were marching toward the wharf at the end of Hollis Street; companies of light infantry and marines were embarking in boats that lay rocking along the shore; a scow freighted with horses was being pushed out into the bay.

"Suppose," whispered Mount, "we lead our horses aboard that other scow yonder!"

In another moment I had dismounted and was leading Warlock toward a cove where a half-dozen boatmen were standing in a scow, resting on their long sea poles.

"If they ask questions, knock them into the water!" said Mount, calmly, and repeated his instructions to Foxcroft and Shemuel.

It was a desperate attempt. Yet its very audacity was in our favor; the boatmen, when they saw us coming, hastily lowered a plank bridge from their heavy scow, and Mount coolly waded out into the water, guiding his horse aboard.

I followed with Warlock. Shemuel's horse swung round in the water, slinging the little Jew on his face in the mud, and then, with a vicious squeal, flung up his heels and cantered off.

Draggled and dripping, Shemuel stood watching the flight of his horse until I bade him come aboard without delay.

Mr. Foxcroft, meanwhile, had dragged his horse aboard, and Mount ordered the boatmen to push off. As the men took up their sea poles, I heard them whispering to each other that Mount and I must be scouts sent ahead to spy for the soldiers.

The wind whipped our cheeks as we swung clear of the land; the boatmen presently took to their muffled oars. Far to our left the line of troop boats floated, now undulating across the bay; the beacon in Boston flared out red as we rounded Fox Hill.

Presently Mount touched my arm and pointed. High up in the dark haze above the city two bright lights hung. So we knew that Rolfe was watching from the belfry of the Old North Meetinghouse, and that Paul had read the twin lamps' message and was now galloping west through the Middlesex farms.

We did not dare ask where we were to be landed. But presently one of the rowers gave us our cue.

"You land at Phipps' Farm, sir?" inquired a sweating boatman of Mount, resting his oar.

Mount shook his head mysteriously.

"We are on special service, lads," he said. "Ask no questions, but put us ashore at Willis Creek, and tell the colonel to give you a guinea apiece for me."

At this impudent remark the boatmen began to row with

renewed vigor, and as the distance slowly increased between us and the troop boats, I began to breathe more freely.

Slowly the dark shore took shape before us. Presently the boatmen changed to their poles once more. The tall reeds rustled as our scow drove its square nose into the shallows and grounded with a grating jar.

"There's a road swings northwest through the marshes," said Mount, wading out to lead his horse up through the rushes. "Follow me, lad."

Foxcroft had mounted; Jack climbed stiffly into his saddle; I was preparing to set foot to stirrup when Shemuel seized my arm convulsively. A patrol of British light-horse were picking their way down the shore in the moonlight. I slung my legs across Warlock, just as they hailed us.

"Get up behind! Quick!" I whispered to Shemuel, and in an instant he was up behind me.

Up the shore we all crashed through the rushes, driving straight out into a marsh, our horses floundering, and the light-horsemen firing their pistols at us from the firmer ground above.

A ball grazed Warlock; his neck was wet with blood.

"They'll murder us all here!" cried Foxcroft. "Charge them, in Heaven's name!"

Mount heard him and bore to the left; I followed; knee to knee we lifted our crazed horses out of the marsh and hurled them into the little patrol of light-horse.

Their sabers flashed before our eyes. Then we were on them, among them, plunging through them, miraculously unharmed, and pounding away northward over a hard gravel road.

They discharged their pistols, a few of them followed us, but all pursuit ceased below Prospect Hill. We galloped, unmolested, into the old Charlestown and West Cambridge Road, and flew onward through the night.

As we rode, from behind us the sound of bells came quavering across dim meadows; out of the blue night, bells answered; we heard the reports of guns, the distant clamor of a horn blowing persistently from some hidden hamlet.

"The alarm!" panted Foxcroft at my elbow as we pounded on. "Hurrah! Hurrah! The country lives!"

"Jack!" I called, through the rushing wind, "the whole land is awaking behind us! Do you hear? Our country lives!"

"Ay, lad, at last she lives!" cried Mount, passionately, and swept on through the night.

"Ring! Ring out your bells!" we shouted, as we tore through a sleeping village; and behind us we could see candle-light break out from the dark houses, and hear the clangor of the meetinghouse bell as it began swinging, warning the distant farms that the splendid hour had come.

But we dared not ride through the dark town of Lexington, not knowing but that it might be swarming with dragoons. We decided to let down fence rails and cut across the fields to gain the Bedford Road.

Mr. Foxcroft piloted us. As I rode by his side I could scarce believe that, yonder, close at hand in the darkness, Silver Heels slept. My heart began a-drumming.

"You are sure she is there?" I asked, plucking Foxcroft's sleeve.

"Unless Captain Butler has prevailed," he said, grimly.

I choked, and trembled in my saddle.

"Do you—do you believe she would listen to him?" I muttered.

"Do you?" he asked, turning on me.

"No!" I answered, and rode on with set teeth.

We crossed a stony pasture and came finally to a narrow lane, lined with hazel. We turned into it, single file, leading our horses. The lane conducted us to an orchard, and through the trees I saw the moon shining on the portico of a white mansion.

"Is that the house?" I whispered.

Foxcroft nodded.

We led our horses through a weedy garden up to the neglected portico. There was a light in the house. We tied our hard-blown horses to the fluted wooden pillars of the portico and, stepping to the door, rapped heavily. The hard beating of my heart echoed the rapping. Intense silence followed.

After a long time, pattering, uncertain steps sounded inside the hallway. The door opened to its full width. In the flaring candle-light stood a little old man; his huge shadow wavered beside him on the wall.

It was the Weasel!

On his wasted face a senile smile flickered; he laid his withered hand on his breast and bowed to us, advancing hospitably to the threshold.

"Cade!" whispered Mount. "Cade, old friend! How came you here?"

The Weasel's eyes turned on Mount with no light of recognition in them.

"You are welcome, sir," said Cade Renard, in the ghost of his old voice. "I pray you enter, gentlemen; we keep open house, ah yes!—you are welcome to Cambridge Hall; believe me, most welcome."

He raised his childish voice and called out the names of servants, doubtless long dead. The hollow house replied in echoes.

"My servants must be in their hall," he said, without embarrassment. "But pray, gentlemen, follow me. The grooms will take your horses to the stables."

Leading us into a great room, bare save for a few chairs, he begged us to be seated, then seated himself, and fell a-babbling of ancient days and of people long since in their graves. Nor could we check him.

And all the while Jack Mount sat staring with tear-smeared eyes, great fists clasped convulsively; and Saul Shemuel huddled close to me; and Foxcroft leaned, elbow on knee, keen eyes watching the little madman who sat serenely babbling of a household and a wife and a life that existed only in his stricken brain.

"What in Heaven's name is he doing here?" I whispered to Foxcroft.

"Quiet," motioned Foxcroft, turning his head to listen. I, too, had caught the sound of a light footfall on the stair. Instinctively we all rose; the Weasel, muttering and smiling, ambled to the dark entry.

Then out of the wavering shadows, into the candle-light, stepped a young girl. Her face was deadly white; her fingers rested in the Weasel's withered palm; she saluted us with a slow, deep reverence, then raised her steady eyes to mine.

"Silver Heels! Silver Heels!" I whispered.

Her eyes closed for a moment.

"My daughter, gentlemen," said the Weasel, tenderly.

Her gray eyes never left mine; I stepped forward; she gave a little gasp as I took her hand.

"Who is this young man?" said the Weasel, mildly. "He is not Captain Butler, dear?"

"No, father."

In the silence I heard my heart beat heavily. A minute passed.

"Silver Heels! Silver Heels!" I cried, with a sob.

"Do you want me—now?" she whispered.

I caught her fiercely in my arms; she clung to me with closed eyes.

And, as we stood there, I heard the measured gallop of a horse on the highway, coming nearer, nearer, turning now close outside the house, and now thundering up to the porch.

Instantly Jack Mount and Shemuel glided from the room; Foxcroft silently drew his pistol; I reached for my rifle and turned smiling to Silver Heels.

"Do you know who is coming?" I asked.

"Yes."

I stepped to the center of the room. The door opened gently, and there in the moonlight stood Walter Butler.

CHAPTER TWENTY-SEVEN

HE HESITATED on the threshold, dazzled by the candle; then, like lightning, his sword glittered in his hand, but Mount, behind him, tore the blade from his grip and flung it ringing at my feet. Butler stood there confronting us, his blank eyes traveling from one to another, his thin lips twitching in an ever-deepening sneer.

"Something is dreadfully wrong, gentlemen," quavered poor Cade Renard. "This is Captain Butler, my daughter's affianced. I pray you follow no ancient quarrel under my roof, gentlemen. I cannot permit this difference between gentlemen in my daughter's presence ——"

Mount quietly drew the little man to the door and led him out, saying, tenderly: "All is well, old friend. You have forgotten much in these long days. You will remember soon. Go, dream in the moonlight, Cade. She was ever a friend to us, the moon."

Suddenly Butler turned on Silver Heels, his face distorted.

"You have played the game well!" he whispered, between his teeth.

"What game?" I asked, with deadly calmness. "Pray say what you have to say at once, Mr. Butler."

Again his gaze shifted from face to face, seeking vainly for mercy.

"That she-devil swore to wed me!" he broke out, hoarsely, pointing a shaking finger full at Silver Heels. "She—swore it!" His voice sank to a hiss.

"To save my father from a highwayman's death!" said Silver Heels, deathly white.

A cold fury blinded me so I could scarcely see Butler. I cocked my rifle and drew my hand across my eyes to clear them.

"This is not your quarrel!" he said, desperately. "This woman is the daughter of Cade Renard, a notorious highwayman known as the Weasel. I doubt that you, Sir Michael Cardigan—for your uncle is dead, whether you know it or not!—would care to claim kinship in this house! Would you wed with the Weasel's child?"

"If she were the child of Tom o' Bedlam she is still betrothed to me! I know not," I said, "whether you be human or demon, and so perhaps you may not burn in hell, but I shall send you thither very soon."

And I laid my hand on his arm, and asked him if he

were minded to die quietly in the garden, while Mount grimly pushed him toward the door.

"Do you mean it?" he burst out, shuddering. "Am I not to have a chance for life? This is murder, Mr. Cardigan!"

"So dealt you by me at the Cayuga stake," I said.

"Yet—it is murder you do. If my hands are not clean, would you foul your own?"

"So dealt you by me in Queen Street prison," I said, slowly.

"Yet, nevertheless, it is murder. And you know it. This is no court of law, to sit in judgment. Are the Cardigans the public hangmen?"

"Give him his sword," I cried, passionately. "I cannot breathe while he draws breath! Give him his sword or I will slay him with naked hands!"

"No!" roared Foxcroft, hurling me back.

Then he stooped, seized the hilt of Butler's sword and snapped the blade in two, casting the fragments from him in contempt.

"The sword of a scoundrel!" he said. "The sword of a petty malefactor—a pitiful forger ——"

"Liar!" shrieked Butler, springing at him.

Mount flung the maddened man into a chair, where he lay, white and panting, staring at Foxcroft, who now stood by the table, coolly examining a packet of documents he had drawn from an inner pocket.

"It is all here," he said—"the story of two cheap dabblers in petty crime—Sir John Johnson and Mr. Walter Butler— how they did conspire to steal from Miss Warren her wealth, her fair fame, and the very name God gave her."

"Liar!" muttered Butler again, between ashen lips.

Foxcroft turned fiercely to me.

"Mr. Cardigan, your honorable kinsman, Sir William John-son, left Miss Warren property in his will. Sir John found, in the same box that held the will, a packet of documents and letters addressed to Sir William, apparently proving that Miss Warren was the child of a certain lady who had left her husband to follow the fortunes of Captain Warren—her child by her own husband, Cade Renard, a gentleman of Cambridge."

"The Weasel!" burst out Jack Mount.

"But she is not his child, sir!" cried Foxcroft, turning on Mount. "She is Captain Warren's own child; I journeyed to England and proved it; I have papers here to prove it! The letters supposed to have been written to Sir William by Sir Peter Warren were forged; the documents supposed to have been unearthed from the flooring in the captain's cabin of His Majesty's ship *Leda* were forged. I can prove it! I can prove that Walter Butler was the forger! I can prove that Sir John Johnson knew it! And Sir John and Captain Butler conspired to make Miss Warren believe herself the child of a half-crazed forest runner who had been vowing that she was his own child!"

He glared at Butler, and then continued:

"In my presence these three men broke the news to her. And, by Heaven, sir, I had never suspected villainy had not that contemptible fool, Sir John, attempted to bribe me to silence should anything ever occur to cast doubt on the relationship betwixt this fellow Renard and Miss Warren!"

The lawyer paused, grinding his teeth in rage.

"I accepted the bribe—to quiet suspicion! But I set out to follow the matter to the bitter end, and I have done it! It's a falsehood from A to Zed! I shall have the pleasure of flinging Sir John's bribe into his face!"

He laid his hand on my arm, speaking very gently.

"Mr. Cardigan, Miss Warren is the truest, bravest, sweetest woman I have ever known. When it was made clear to her that this lunatic Renard was her father, that she must now give up all thought of the family on which she had so long imposed—and give up all pretensions to *you*, sir—she acquiesced with a truly noble dignity. Not a whimper, sir, not a reproach, not a tear. Her first thought was of pity for her father—this little, withered lunatic, who sat there devouring her with his eyes of a sick hound. She went to him before us all; she took his hand—his hard, little claw—and kissed it. By Heaven! gentlemen, I almost wept!"

There was a moment of hushed silence before Foxcroft spoke again.

"Then came Butler, the forger," resumed Foxcroft, pointing at him. "And when he found that, after all, Miss Warren honored herself too highly to seek a rehabilitation through his name, he came here and threatened this poor old man's life— threatened to denounce him as a thief and have him hung at a crossroads, unless she wedded him! Then—then she consented."

Butler was sitting forward in his chair, his eyes on vacancy. He did not seem to hear the words that branded him; he did not appear to see us as we drew closer around him.

"In the orchard," muttered Mount; "we can hang him with his own bridle."

We paused for an instant, gazing silently at the doomed man. Then Mount touched him on the shoulder.

At the voiceless summons he looked up at us as though stunned.

"You must hang," said Mount, gravely.

"Not that! No!" I stammered. "I can't do it! Give him a sword—give him something to fight with! Jack—I can't do it! I am not made that way!"

There was a touch on my arm; Silver Heels stood beside me.

"Let them deal with him," she murmured. "You cannot fight with him; there is no honor in him."

"No!—no honor in him!" I repeated.

He had risen, and now stood, staring vacantly at me.

"By the mighty!" cried Mount. "You can't let him loose on the world again!"

"I cannot slay him," I said.

"But a rope can!" said Mount.

"Do you then draw it," I replied, "and never rail more at the hangman!"

After a moment I opened the door. As in a trance, Butler passed out into the moonlight; Mount stole close behind him, and I saw his broad hunting-knife glimmer.

"Let him go," I cried, wearily. "I choke with all this foul intrigue. Is there no work to do, Jack, save the sheriff's? Faugh! Let him go!"

Butler slowly set foot to stirrup; Mount snatched the pistol from the saddle holster with a savage sneer.

"No, no," he said. "Trust a scoundrel if you will, lad, but draw his fangs first. Oh, Lord! but I hate to let him go! Shall I? I'll give him a hundred yards before I fire! And I'll not aim at that! Shall I?"

If Butler heard him he made no sign. He turned in his saddle and looked at Silver Heels.

Should I let him loose on the world once more?

Should I, who had him in my power and could now forever render the demon in him powerless—should I let him go free? Should I?

War was at hand. War would come at dawn when the Grenadiers marched into Concord town. To slay him, then, would be no murder. But now?

Mount, watching me steadily, raised his rifle.

"No," I said.

What was I to do? There was no prison to hale him to; the jails o' Boston lodged no Tories. Justice? There was no justice save that mockery at Province House. Law? Gage was the law—Gage, the friend of this man. What was I to do? Once again Mount raised his rifle.

"No," I said.

So passed Walter Butler from among us, riding slowly out into the shadowy world, under the calm moon. Heaven witness that I conducted as my honor urged, not as my hot blood desired.

So rode forth mine enemy, Walter Butler, unpunished for the woe that he had wrought.

Again Mount raised his rifle.

"No," I said.

A little breeze began stirring in the moonlit orchard; our horses tossed their heads and stamped; then silence fell.

After a long while the voice of Mount recalled me to myself; he had drawn poor Renard to a seat on the rotting steps of the porch.

"Now do you know me, Cade?" asked Mount, again and again, his great arm about the Weasel's stooping shoulders.

The Weasel's solemn eyes met his in silence.

Mount forced a cheerful laugh.

"What! Forget the highway, Cade? The King's highway, old friend? The moon at the crossroads? Eh? You remember? Say you remember, Cade."

The blank eyes of the Weasel were fixed on Mount.

"The forest? Eh, Cade? Ho!—lad! The rank smell o' the moss, and the stench of rotting logs? The quiet in the woods, the hermit bird piping in the pines? Say you remember, old friend!" he begged. "Tell me you remember! Ho! lad, have you forgot the tune the war-arrow sings?"

And he made a long-drawn, whispering whimper with his lips.

In pantomime he crouched and pointed; the Weasel's mild eyes turned.

"The Iroquois!" whispered Mount, anxiously. "You have fought them, Cade; you remember? Say that you remember!"

"I—I have fought the Iroquois," murmured the Weasel, "but it was years ago—years ago ——"

"No, no!" cried Mount, "it was but yesterday, old friend— yesterday! And who went with you on the burnt trail, Cade? Who went with you by night and by day, eating when you ate, starving when you starved? It was I, Cade!" cried Mount eagerly. "I!"

"It was Tah-hoon-to-whe, the night hawk," murmured the little man.

"It was I, Jack Mount!" repeated the forest runner, in a loud voice. "Hark! The Iroquois war drums! The game's afoot, Cade! Rouse up, old friend!"

But the Weasel only stared at him with his solemn, aged eyes.

Mount stood still for a long while. Then, with a gulping sob, he sank down beside his ancient comrade and hid his head in his huge hands.

The Weasel looked at him sorrowfully; then rose and came slowly towards Silver Heels.

"They say you are not my daughter," he said, taking Silver Heels' hands from mine. "But—we know better, my child. We will smile at their idle talk, in the long summer evenings, will we not, my child?"

"Yes," said Silver Heels, faintly.

"There is much, sir, that I forget in these days," he said, turning gravely toward me—"much that I cannot recall. I cannot always remember the name of a new and welcome guest—believe me, most welcome. I think your name is Captain Butler?"

"Sir Michael Cardigan," whispered Silver Heels.

"And welcome, always welcome to us here in Cambridge Hall," murmured the old man.

Foxcroft, who had gone to the shabby barn, came back and whispered that there were no horses there, and no vehicle of any description; but that, nevertheless, we had best start for Albany immediately.

I left it to him and to the others to persuade poor Renard that a journey was necessary that very night; and to them also I left the care of providing for us as best they might.

When Mount had drawn poor Cade away, and when Fox-croft and Shemuel began rummaging the great house for what necessaries and provisions it might contain, I went into the shadowy room where Silver Heels waited by a window, her face upraised in the moonlight.

"Silver Heels! Silver Heels!" I murmured, holding her by the hands and never moving my eyes from her tender eyes. And we looked and looked, nor gazed our fill.

"All these piteous days!" she said, slowly.

"Aye—all of them! And each hour a year, and each night-fall a closing century. Silver Heels! Silver Heels! You are un-changed, dear heart!"

"Thin to my bones, and very, very old—like you, Michael."

"We have young souls."

"Yes, Michael. We are young in all save sorrow."

"And you are so tall, Silver Heels ——"

"Span my waist!"

"My hand would span it. Ah! Your head comes not above my chin for all your willow growth!"

"Your hands are rough, Sir Michael."

"Your hands are satin, sweet."

"Yet I wash my kerchief and my shifts in suds."

How the moon glowed and glowed on her.

"You grow in beauty, Silver Heels," I said.

"When you are with me I do truly feel beauty growing in me, Michael."

Far in the night a cock crowed in the false dawn.

She raised her face; her mouth touched mine; then all my soul grew dim and warm and faint, with her arms around my neck and her face like a blossom crushed to mine.

"Ah, what happiness, what happiness!" she whispered.

Presently, in the stillness that followed, a voice broke out from somewhere beyond the porch:

"Ready, Cardigan! The horses wait at the barn!"

Soon we were off, Foxcroft on his horse in the van, then the Weasel on Jack Mount's with Mount afoot, leading the horse, then Silver Heels on Warlock, with one hand on my shoulder as I walked at her side, and finally Shemuel bringing up the rear.

On we went through the night, and we fully intended to circle Lexington. But we missed our way and before we realized it, we had come in full view of the Lexington Meeting-house, with the Concord Road running into our road on the left and "Buckman's Tavern" on the right, all ablaze with candle-light.

"It is past three o'clock," said Foxcroft. "The British should have been here ere this if they were coming."

Mount tossed his horse's bridle to Foxcroft and walked toward "Buckman's Tavern," where a throng of men were standing. I heard him greet them with a hearty "God save our country"; then he disappeared in the crowd.

Presently he came striding back, followed by an hostler.

"The militia have been yonder under arms since midnight," he said. "A messenger rode in ten minutes since with news that the road was clear and no British coming. We can get a post chaise here"—he nodded toward the hostler.

"I guess the redcoats ain't a-coming, gentlemen," said the man, with a grin.

"Then we had best bait at the tavern," said Foxcroft, quickly; and he led the way.

As we threaded our path through the crowd of men and boys I noticed that all were armed with rifles or old-time firelocks. They appeared to be mostly honest yokels, clad in plain homespun.

The simple repast that was set before us refreshed us greatly. Mount, sitting close beside the Weasel, urged the old man to eat, and he did, mechanically, with dazed eyes fixed on space.

One thing I began to notice—he no longer watched Silver Heels; he scarcely appeared to be aware of her presence. Once only he spoke, asking what had become of his rifle.

Presently Foxcroft and Shemuel went to the stables to see that our post chaise was well provisioned, and Mount led Renard away to watch the feed-bags filled. Silver Heels and I walked together to the tavern porch.

The road from Boston divides in front of the Meeting-house, forming two sides of a grassy triangle. Near this village green a few armed men still lingered, and a score of men sat around us on the damp tavern steps, listlessly balancing their rifles between their knees.

Suddenly there came a far cry through the misty chill of dawn: "The British are coming! The British are coming!"

The next instant a drum was banging, and the men around us had stumbled to their feet, rifles in hand.

At that same moment our post chaise came lumbering around the corner of the tavern yard, Mount acting as post-boy, and Foxcroft, the Weasel, and Shemuel riding together in the rear.

I placed Silver Heels in the chaise, with my eyes still fixed on the foggy Boston Road.

"Isn't it a false alarm?" inquired Foxcroft, anxiously, as an officer of the militia came running past.

But the officer called back that it was doubtless true.

"Which way?" cried Foxcroft.

No answer. More of the militia and Minute Men ran by us, to join the line that was slowly, raggedly, forming on the green, while the old Louisburg drum rolled, vibrating sonorously, and a fife's shrill treble pierced the air.

"Cardigan, which way are they coming?" cried Foxcroft, standing up in his stirrups. "They say there are redcoats behind us and more in front."

"Turn your horses, Jack!" I said. "Turn back toward Concord!"

"There's redcoats on the Concord Road!" cried a woman, running out of a house close by with a sack of home-molded bullets.

I flung myself astride Warlock and ranged up alongside Mount.

"Can we not take the Bedford Road?" I asked, anxiously.

"They say the British are betwixt us and the west," replied Mount.

"Then we should make for the Boston Road!" I said, impatiently; "we can't stay here ——"

"Look yonder!" broke in Foxcroft, excitedly.

Out into the Boston Road, in the gray haze of dawn, trotted a British officer, superbly mounted, and straight on his heels marched the British infantry, moving walls of scarlet topped with shining steel.

"Halt!" cried a far voice; the red ranks stood as one man. An officer galloped alongside of the motionless lines and, leaning forward in his saddle, shouted to the disordered group on the green, "Stop that drum!"

"Fall in! Fall in!" roared the captain of the militia; the old Louisburg drum thundered louder yet.

"Prime! Load!" cried the British officers, and the steady call was sent back from company to company.

With the utmost difficulty, because of the press of gathering spectators, I backed our post chaise into the stable-yard. We had scarcely reached a corner of the yard where the chaise was safe from bullets, when a British major came galloping into the green, with drawn sword.

"Disperse! Disperse!" he called out, angrily.

"Stand your ground!" roared the militia captain. "Don't fire unless fired upon! But if they mean to have a war, let it begin here!"

"Disperse!" shouted the British major. "Lay down your arms! Lay down your arms and ——"

A shot cut him short; his horse reared in agony.

"Good Lord! they've shot his horse!" cried Foxcroft.

" 'Tis his own men, then," broke in Mount. "I marked the smoke."

"Disperse!" bellowed the maddened officer, dragging his horse to a standstill—"disperse, ye rebels!"

Behind a stone wall a farmer rose and presented his fire-lock, but the piece flashed in the pan. A shot rang out, but I could not see who fired.

Then a British officer fired his pistol and, on the instant a bright sheet of flame girdled the British front, and the deafening roar of musketry shook the earth.

Through the billows of smoke, I saw the British major rise

in his stirrups, and, reversing his sword, drive it downward as signal to cease firing. Other officers rode up through the smoke, shouting orders that were lost in the dropping shots from the militia, now retreating on a run past us up the Bedford Road.

"Halt!" shouted the British major, plunging about on his wounded horse through the smoke. "Stop that firing! D'ye hear what I say? Stop it! Stop it!"

No one heeded. Then a volley from the British Tenth Foot drowned his voice, and the red-coated soldiers came bursting through the smoke on a double-quick. Behind them the Grenadiers rushed forward, cheering.

Shots came quicker and quicker.

I galloped to the chaise and jerked the horses back, then wheeled them westward towards Bedford, where the remnants of the militia were sullenly falling back, firing across at the British, now marching on past the Meetinghouse up the Concord Road.

"No! No!" cried Foxcroft, "we cannot risk it! Stay where you are!"

"We cannot risk being butchered here!" I replied.

Silver Heels was standing straight up in the chaise. Her face had grown very white.

"They've killed a poor young man behind that barn!" she whispered as I leaned from my saddle and motioned her to crouch low. "They shot him twice."

I glanced hastily toward the barn and saw a dark heap lying in the grass behind it.

"Look at the Weasel!" muttered Mount, clutching my arm. The Weasel was hastily climbing out of his saddle, rifle in hand. His face had grown flushed and eager, his eyes snapped with intelligence, and his movements were quick as a forest cat's.

"Cade!" quavered Mount. "Cade, old friend, what are you doing?"

"Come!" cried the Weasel, briskly. "Can't you see the redskins?"

"Redcoats! Redcoats!" cried Mount, anxiously. "Where are you going, Cade? Come back! Come back! They can't hit us here! Redcoats, Cade, not redskins!"

"They be all one to me!" replied the Weasel, briskly, scuttling away to cover under a tuft of hazel.

"Don't shoot, Cade!" bawled Mount. "Wait till we can gather our people! Wait! Don't fire!"

But "bang!" went the Weasel's long brown rifle.

"Hold those horses!" said Mount, desperately. I seized the leaders; Mount slipped from his saddle and ran out to the Weasel's bit of cover. He caught the Weasel by the arm and tried to drag him back by sheer force.

As the two struggled, I saw the entire British column marching swiftly up the Concord Road. From the Bedford Road our militia fired slowly across at the fast vanishing troops. A small flanking party returned our fire, but the main column pressed on in silence.

The Weasel at last yielded to Mount and returned with him to us.

A restless, silent crowd had gathered at "Buckman's Tavern," where two dead Minute Men lay on the porch, stiffening in their blood.

Back along the muddy Bedford Road trudged the remnants of the scattered Lexington company of militia. The old Louisburg drum was sounding the assembly. Men seemed to spring from the soil; they came hurrying across the distant fields singly, in twos and threes, in scores. Far away in the vague dawn bells rang out in distant villages.

The women and children of Lexington were gathering around our chaise. Silver Heels sprang out as she realized their need. Women were thrusting their children into the vehicle, imploring us to save them from the British.

"Michael," said Silver Heels, looking up with cool gray eyes, "we must get the children away."

"And you?" I asked, sharply. She lifted a barefooted urchin into the chaise without answering.

A yoke of dusty, anxious oxen, drawing a hay-cart, came clattering up, while their driver followed on a trot beside them.

"The children here!" called Silver Heels.

In a moment the hay-cart was full of old women and frantic children; but already other vehicles were rattling up.

Then there came a heavy pounding of horses' hoofs, a rush, a cry, and a hatless, coatless, haggard-faced rider drew up.

"More troops coming from Boston!" he shouted. "Lord Percy is at Roxbury with three regiments, marines, and can non! Paul Revere was taken at one o'clock this morning!" And away he galloped again.

Silver Heels laid her hand on my arm.

"If the British are at Roxbury," she said, "we are quite cut off, are we not?"

I did not answer.

At that moment the Lexington company came marching into

the Bedford Road, Indian file, Captain Parker leading. Into "Buckman's Tavern" they filed and fell to slamming and bolting the wooden shutters, and piercing the doors and walls for rifle-fire.

"You must go with the convoy, Silver Heels," I said.

Her gray eyes met mine gravely.

"We must stay," she said.

"They are bringing cannon. Can you not understand?" I repeated, harshly.

"I will not go," she said. "Every rifle is required here. I cannot take you from these men in their dire need. Dear heart, can you not understand me?"

"Am I to sacrifice you?" I asked, angrily. "No!" I cried. "We have suffered enough ——"

Tears sprang to her eyes; she laid her hand on my rifle.

"Other women have sent their dearest ones. Look at those dead men on the tavern steps! Look at our people's blood on the grass yonder! Would you wed with a pink-and-white thing whose veins run water? Do you forget I am a soldier's child?"

A loud voice bellowing from the tavern: "Women here for the bullet-molds! Get your women to the tavern!"

She caught my hand. "You see a maid may not stand idle in Lexington!" she said, with a breathless smile.

MINUTE MAN

CHAPTER TWENTY-EIGHT

SILVER HEELS stood in the taproom of "Buckman's Tavern," casting bullets; a barefoot drummer boy watched the white-hot crucible and baled out the glittering molten metal.

Near the window sat some Woburn Minute Men, cross-legged on the worn floor, rolling cartridges. From time to time the parson of Woburn, who had come to pray and shoot, took away the pile of empty powder-horns and brought back others to be emptied.

The tavern was dim and damp; through freshly bored loopholes in the shutters sunlight fell, illuminating the dark interior.

In their shirts, bare-armed and bare of throat to the breast-bone, a score of Lexington Minute Men stood along the line of loopholes, their long rifles thrust out.

Jack Mount and the Weasel lay, curled up like giant cats, at the door, blinking peacefully out through the cracks into the early sunshine. I could hear their low-voiced conversation from where I stood at my post, close to Silver Heels:

"Redcoats, Cade, not redskins," corrected Mount. "British lobster-backs—eh, Cade? You remember how we drubbed them there in Pittsburg, belt and buckle and ramrod—eh, Cade?"

"That was long ago, friend."

"Call me Jack, Cade!" urged Mount. "You know me now, don't you, Cade?"

"Aye, but I forget much. Do you know how I came here?"

"From Johnstown, Cade—from Johnstown, lad!"

"I cannot remember Johnstown."

Presently the Weasel peered around at Silver Heels.

"Who is that young lady?" he asked, mildly.

Silver Heels heard and smiled at the old man. The faintest quiver curved her mouth; there was a shadow of pain in her eyes.

The fire from the crucible tinted her cheeks; she raised both bared arms to push back her clustering hair. Hazel gray, her brave eyes met mine across the witch-vapor curling from the melting-pot.

"Do you recall how the ferret, Vix, did bite Peter's tight breeches, Michael?"

"Aye," said I, striving to smile.

"And—and the jackknife made by Barlow?"

"Aye."

She flushed to the temples and looked at my left hand. The scar was there. I raised my hand and kissed the blessed mark.

"Dear, dear Michael," she whispered, "truly you were ever the dearest and noblest and best of all!"

"Unfit to kiss thy shoon's latchet, sweet ——"

"Yet hast untied the latchets of my heart."

A stillness fell on the old tavern.

Then a voice called down from the pigeon-loft above, "Is there a woman below to sew bandages?"

"Truly there is, sir," called back Silver Heels.

She started toward the stairway, then turned to look at me.

"My post is wherever you are," I said, stepping to her side. As we went up the stairs I stooped to kiss her little hand.

"There is a long war before us ere we find a home," I said.

"I know," she said, faintly.

"A long, long war; separation, sadness. Will you wed me before I go to join with Cresap's men?"

"Aye," she said.

"There is a parson below, Silver Heels."

Her face went scarlet.

"Let it be now," I whispered, with my arm around her.

She looked up into my eyes. I leaned over the landing rail and called out, "Send a man for the parson of Woburn!"

Presently the good man came, in rusty black, shouldering a fowling-piece, his pockets bulging with a Bible and Book of Common Prayer.

"Is there sickness here—or wounds?" he asked, anxiously, peering up the stairs.

"Heart-sickness, sir," I said. "We be dying for the heart's ease you may bring us through your holy office."

At length he understood—Silver Heels striving to keep her sweet eyes lifted when he spoke to her, and I quiet and determined, asking that he lose no time, for no man knew how long we few here in the tavern had to live. In the same breath I summoned a soldier from the south loophole in the garret, and asked him to witness for me; and he took off his hat and stood sheepishly twirling it, rifle in hand.

And so we were wedded, there in the ancient garret, the pigeons coo-cooing overhead, the blue wasps buzzing up and down the window glass, and our hands joined before the aged parson of Woburn town. I had the plain gold ring I had bought in Albany for this purpose, nor dreamed to wed my sweetheart with it thus!—and, oh, the sweetness in her lips and eyes when I drew it from the cord around my neck and placed it on her smooth finger at the word!

Little else I remember, save that the old parson kissed her, and went away down the creaking stairs with his fowling-piece over his shoulder, leaving us standing mute together under the canopy of swinging herbs.

There was a pile of cotton cloth on the floor; presently Silver Heels sank down beside it and began to tear it into strips for bandages.

I looked from the window, seeing nothing.

Soon the Minute Man at the south loop spoke:

"A man riding this way—there!—on the Concord Road!"

Silver Heels on the floor worked steadily, ripping the snowy cotton.

"There is smoke yonder on the Concord Road," said the Minute Man.

I roused and rubbed my eyes.

"Do you hear firing," he asked, "far away in the west?"

"Yes."

"Concord lies northwest."

The firing became audible in the room. Silver Heels raised her head with a grave glance at me. I went and knelt beside her.

"It is coming at last, little sweetheart," I said. "Will you go now? Foxcroft will take you across the fields to some safe farm."

"You know Sir William would not have endured to see me leave at such a time," she said.

"Yes, dear heart, but you cannot carry a rifle."

"But I can make bullets and bandages. I will not go."

"I command."

"No." She bent her fair, childish head and the tears fell on the cloth in her lap.

"Look! Look at the redcoats!" called out the Minute Man at the attic window.

As I rose I heard plainly the long, resounding crash of musket firing, and the rattle of rifles followed like a hundred echoes.

"Look yonder!" he cried.

Suddenly the Concord Road was choked with scarlet-clad soldiers. Mapped out below us the country stretched, and over it, like a blood-red monster worm, wound the British column.

And now we could see feathery puffs of smoke from the roadside bushes, from distant hills, from thickets, from ploughed fields, from the long, undulating stone walls. Faster and faster came the musket volleys, but faster yet rang out the shots from our yeomanry, gathering thicker and thicker along the British route.

The old tavern was ringing with voices now—with commands and with calls. The young officer in charge shouted for silence and attention, and ordered us not to fire unless fired upon, as our position would be hopeless if cannon were brought against us.

"To your posts!" he roared then, drawing his sword and coming up the stairs two at a jump. He stopped short when he saw Silver Heels and glanced blankly at me; but there was no time now for her to take to flight, for as he stepped to the window beside me, pell-mell into the village green rushed the British light infantry, dusty, exhausted, enraged, with staggering groups bearing dead or wounded comrades.

Close on their heels tramped the Grenadiers. Soldier after soldier staggered and fell from the ranks, utterly exhausted, unable to rise from the grass.

The lull in the firing was broken by a loud discharge of musketry from Fiske's Hill, and presently more redcoats came rushing into the village, while at their very heels the Bedford Alarm Men shot at them. From every direction, our militia came swarming—from Sudbury, Westford, Lincoln, Acton; Minute Men from Medford, Stowe, Beverly, and Lynn.

Below me in the street I saw the British officers striving

madly to reform their men, desperately urging them into line, while thicker and thicker pelted the bullets from the Minute Men and militia.

They were brave men, these British officers; I saw a young ensign of the Tenth Foot fall with a ball through his stomach, yet rise and face the storm until shot to death by a dozen Alarm Men on the Bedford Road.

TERRIBLE WAS THE VENGEANCE THAT FOLLOWED IT

It was dreadful; it was doubly dreadful when a company of grenadiers suddenly faced about and poured a volley into our tavern, for then the tavern fairly vomited flame into the square, and the British went down in heaps. Then through the smoke I saw the massed infantry reel off through the village, out across the land, firing frenziedly right and left, pouring volleys into farmhouses, where women ran screaming out into the barns, and frantic watch-dogs barked, tugging at their chains.

It was not a retreat, not a flight; it was a riot, a horrible saturnalia of smoke and fire and awful sound as the British column burst south across the land, crazed with wounds, blood-mad, dealing death and ruin to all that lay before it.

Terrible was the vengeance that followed it, hovered on its gasping flangs, scourged its dwindling ranks, which withered under the searching fire from every tuft of bushes, every rock, every tree trunk.

Already the ghastly pageant had rushed past us, leaving a crimson trail; already the old tavern door was flung wide and our Minute Men were running down the Boston Road and along the ridges on either side, firing as they came on.

I, with Mount and Shemuel and the Weasel, hung to the left flank of the British till two o'clock, when, about a half-mile from Lexington Meetinghouse, we heard cannon, and understood that the relief troops from Boston had come up.

Then, knowing that there were guns enough and to spare without ours, we shouldered our hot rifles and trudged back to "Buckman's Tavern," through the dust.

So we reëntered Lexington; and on the tavern steps Silver Heels stood, her tired, colorless face lighted up, her out-stretched hands groping for my shoulders; and I to take her in my arms, for she had fallen a-weeping.

In the south the thunder of the British cannon muttered, distant and more distant; the storm had passed—for a time.

And now came Jack Mount, riding postilion on the horses which drew the post chaise; behind him trotted the Weasel, leading out Warlock; and after him plodded Shemuel. Silver Heels saw them and smiled through her tears.

"Truly we stayed and did our duty, did we not, dear heart?"

"With your help, sweet."

"NORTHWARD WE JOURNEY, LITTLE SWEETHEART"

"And deserted not our own!"

"Yours the praise, dear soul."

"And did face our enemies like true people all. Is it not so, Michael?"

"It is so."

"Then let us go. Let us say farewell to Mr. Foxcroft and thank him once again for all his kindness, and then be on our way. I am sick for my own land and for the happiness to come."

"Northward we journey, little sweetheart."

"To the blue hills of Tryon and the scented brake?"

"Aye, home."

And so, guarded by our faithful three, we started for the north, out of the bloody village where our liberty was born at the first rifle-shot, out of the sound of the British Cannon, out of the land of the salt sea, back to the inland winds and waters and the incense of our own dear forests.

CHAPTER TWENTY-NINE

BACK to the blue hills of Tryon. Hills unploughed, un-harrowed, save by the galloping deer; hills, sweet islands in a dark pine ocean; hills of the morning—Silver Heels' and mine.

After a long delay at Albany and weary days on the trail, we came one sunrise to those beloved blue hills, and by nightfall we were in Johnstown. Not in Johnson Hall; never while Sir John lived could we enter its dear familiar portals. But Sir John could not rob us of our memories, and we were content to light our first hearth fire in the great stone house I had leased from Peter Weaver, a house that stood close to the church where Sir William lay.

In Albany I had refused to agree when Mr. Weaver urged that the law deal with Sir John for attempted fraud. I could not drag Sir William's son forth to cringe before the rabble. But I had been glad to learn that, what with my inheritance from Sir Terence and our legacies from Sir William, Silver Heels and I should have plenty. We planned that when the war was over we would build us a home midway 'twixt Johnstown and Fonda's Bush, where our lands joined.

Meanwhile we could be content in the great stone house. And through the sweet Maytide, while Shemmy roamed on secret errands, Jack Mount and Cade Renard sunned them-selves under the trees in our garden, dozing and dreaming. Yet we all knew that out in the dark world God was shaping the destiny of a people; and with the gentle winds of June there came to us ever-thickening rumors of the times that were to try men's souls.

It was on a primrose morning that I awoke to find Silver Heels, already arrayed for the day, leaning from the case-ment, calling to me in a strange, frightened voice: "Michael! Michael! They are coming over the hills—over the hills, dear heart, to take you with them!"

Swiftly I dressed me in my leather. Then at the window, there in the fresh dawn, I listened with her. But I heard noth-ing, and I would have drawn her gently away, when from below came up a roar from Mount:

"Sir Michael! Cresap is on the hills with five hundred men of Maryland!"

"You must go!" said Silver Heels. Her face was marble, glorified.

Scarce knowing what I did, I threw my long rifle on my shoulder and ran out swiftly through the garden.

Suddenly the street was filled with riflemen, marching silently and swiftly, with moccasined feet, their raccoon caps pushed back. On their hunting-shirts, lettered in white across each breast, I read, *Liberty or Death.*

Jack Mount and the Weasel came up, rifles shouldered, coonskin caps swinging in their hands.

"We will watch over your husband, my lady," murmured Cade Renard.

"Aye, we will bring him back, Lady Cardigan," muttered Jack.

Silver Heels, holding them each by the hand, strove to speak. But words would not come. Yet she smiled, with trembling lips. Then the smile dimmed. She caught my hands and kissed them.

"For our honor—go!" she gasped. "Michael! Michael! Come back to me ——"

"Truly, dear heart—truly! truly!"

"Ho! Cardigan!" rang out a voice like a pistol-shot from the passing ranks.

Through my tear-dimmed eyes I saw Cresap, sword shining in his hand.

"We come!" cried Mount, shaking his rifle toward the rising sun. "Give us liberty or give us death!"

High above his head flashed Cresap's shining sword.

Half a thousand rifles shook high; half a thousand deep voices roared thunderously through the stony street:

"Liberty! Liberty or Death!"

And when, as all men know, that liberty at last was won, we returned—even as we had promised—Jack Mount, Cade Renard, and I. Returned to long mellow years in the blue hills of Tryon.

Content, I sit at dusk with her I love, tying my soft feather-flies just as I tied them for Sir William in the golden time. The trout have nothing changed, nor have I.

"Listen, Micky," murmurs Silver Heels, and again I listen with her.

From above comes the babble of the children old Betty is tucking into bed, and from near by comes the ripple of sweet water flowing on under the clustered stars.

THE END